"I keep telling myself that she just can't get much better, but with every book she amazes and surprises me!" —*The Best Reviews*

Praise for the futuristic fantasy of
Robin D. Owens

Heart Search

"Will have readers on the edge of their seats . . . Another terrific tale from the brilliant mind of Robin D. Owens. Don't miss it."
—*Romance Reviews Today*

"A taut mixture of suspense and action . . . that leaves you stunned."
—*Smexy Books*

"Thank you, Ms. Owens, for this wonderful series."
—*Night Owl Reviews*

Heart Journey

"Sexy, emotionally intense, and laced with humor . . . Draws readers into one of the more imaginative otherworldly cultures."
—*Library Journal*

"[A] skillfully crafted read for any lover of futuristic or light paranormal romance."
—*Fresh Fiction*

"It is no secret that I love Ms. Owens's Heart series . . . [A] wonderful piece of fantasy, science fiction, romance, and a dash of mystery. *Heart Journey* is no different, a delight to read."
—*Night Owl Reviews*

Heart Change

"The story accelerates as new dangers to Avellana crop up, and the relationship between Signet and Cratag develops, making for a satisfying read."
—*Booklist*

continued . . .

"Each story is as fresh and new as the first one was. I am always delighted when a new Heart book is published!" —*Fresh Fiction*

"A satisfying return to an intriguing world. Cratag and Signet will leave you wanting more." —*The Romance Reader*

Heart Fate

"A true delight to read, and it should garner new fans for this unique and enjoyable series." —*Booklist*

"[This] emotionally rich tale blends paranormal abilities, family dynamics, and politics; adds a serious dash of violence; and dusts it all with humor and whimsy." —*Library Journal*

"A wonderfully delightful story . . . The author's creativity shines." —*Darque Reviews*

Heart Dance

"[A] superior series." —*The Best Reviews*

"I look forward to my yearly holiday in Celta, always a dangerous and fascinating trip." —*Fresh Fiction*

"Sensual, riveting, and filled with the wonderful cast of characters from previous books, as well as some new ones, *Heart Dance* is exquisite in its presentation." —*Romance Reviews Today*

Heart Choice

"The romance is passionate, the characters engaging, and the society and setting exquisitely crafted." —*Booklist*

"Maintaining the 'world building' for science fiction and character-driven plot for romance is near impossible. Owens does it brilliantly." —*The Romance Readers Connection*

"Well-written, humor-laced, intellectually and emotionally involving story, which explores the true meaning of family and love." —*Library Journal*

Heart Duel

"[A] sexy story . . . Readers will enjoy revisiting this fantasy-like world filled with paranormal talents."
　　　　　　　　　　　　　　　　　　　　　　—*Booklist*

Heart Thief

"I loved *Heart Thief*! This is what futuristic romance is all about. Robin D. Owens writes the kind of futuristic romance we've all been waiting to read; certainly the kind that I've been waiting for. She provides a wonderful, gripping mix of passion, exotic futuristic settings, and edgy suspense. If you've been waiting for someone to do futuristic romance right, you're in luck, Robin D. Owens is the author for you."
　　　　　　　　　　—Jayne Castle, author of *The Lost Night*

HeartMate

Winner of the 2002 RITA Award
for Best Paranormal Romance
by the Romance Writers of America

"Engaging characters, effortless world building, and a sizzling romance make this a novel that's almost impossible to put down."
　　　　　　　　　　　　　　　　—*The Romance Reader*

"Fantasy romance with a touch of mystery . . . Readers from the different genres will want Ms. Owens to return to Celta for more tales of HeartMates."
　　　　　　　　　　　　　　　　—*Midwest Book Review*

"*HeartMate* is a dazzling debut novel. Robin D. Owens paints a world filled with characters who sweep readers into an unforgettable adventure with every delicious word, every breath, every beat of their hearts. Brava!"
　　　　　　—Deb Stover, award-winning author of *The Gift*

"A gem of a story . . . Sure to tickle your fancy."
　　　　　　　　　　—Anne Avery, author of *A Distant Star*

Heart Fortune

Robin D. Owens

BERKLEY SENSATION, NEW YORK

THE BERKLEY PUBLISHING GROUP
Published by the Penguin Group
Penguin Group (USA) Inc.
375 Hudson Street, New York, New York 10014, USA

USA I Canada I UK I Ireland I Australia I New Zealand I India I South Africa I China

Penguin Books Ltd., Registered Offices: 80 Strand, London WC2R 0RL, England
For more information about the Penguin Group, visit penguin.com.

This book is an original publication of The Berkley Publishing Group.

Berkley Sensation Books are published by The Berkley Publishing Group.
BERKLEY SENSATION® is a registered trademark of Penguin Group (USA) Inc.
The "B" design is a trademark of Penguin Group (USA) Inc.

Library of Congress Cataloging-in-Publication Data

Owens, Robin D.
Heart fortune / Robin D. Owens.—Berkley Sensation trade paperback edition.
pages cm
ISBN 978-0-425-26393-8
I. Title.
PS3615.W478H447 2013
813'.6—dc23
2013014511

PUBLISHING HISTORY
Berkley Sensation trade paperback edition / August 2013

PRINTED IN THE UNITED STATES OF AMERICA

10 9 8 7 6 5 4 3 2 1

Cover art by Tony Mauro. Cover hand lettering by Ron Zinn.
Cover design by George Long.
Interior text design by Kristin del Rosario.

To my long-term beta readers Fred and Kay.
You always help.

Characters

Jace Bayrum: Adventurer, leather worker, hero.

Zem: Jace's animal Familiar companion.

Glyssa Licorice: SecondLevel PublicLibrarian, GrandMistrys.

Lepid: Glyssa's animal Familiar companion.

In Druida City:

GreatLord Laev T'Hawthorn: Entrepreneur. (*Heart Search*)

GreatLady Camellia Darjeeling D'Hawthorn: One of Glyssa's best friends, HeartMate to Laev, teashop/restaurant owner. (*Heart Search*)

The Licorice Family:

FirstLevel PublicLibrarian, GrandLady D'Licorice: Rhiza Licorice, Glyssa's mother.

FirstLevel PublicLibrarian, GrandLord T'Licorice: Fasic Almond Licorice, Glyssa's father.

FirstLevel PublicLibrarian, GrandMistrys: Enata Licorice, Glyssa's older sister.

Short Appearances:

T'Ash (*HeartMate*)

Danith D'Ash (*HeartMate*)

Zanth: Premier CatFam of Celta. (*HeartMate*)

Tiana Mugwort: SecondLevel Priestess, one of Glyssa's best friends.

Artemisia Primross: Healer. (*Heart Secret*)

Garrett Primross: Private investigator. (*Heart Secret*)

At the Excavation of the Starship, Lugh's Spear:

Andic Sanicle: Adventurer, frenemy to Jace.

Funa Twinevine: Adventuress, current lover of Andic, former lover of Jace.

Trago: Healer.

Symphyta: Healer.

Myrtus Stopper: Primary cook.

GrandLady Helena (Del) Elecampane: Owner of the project, cartographer. (*Heart Journey*)

Shunuk: GrandLady Helena's FamFox. (*Heart Journey*)

GrandLord Raz Cherry Elecampane: Owner of the project, actor. (*Heart Journey*)

Rosemary: GrandLord Raz's FamCat. (*Heart Journey*)

Maxima Elecampane: Helena and Raz's daughter.

Carolinia: Maxima's FamCat.

One

EXCAVATION OF *Lugh's Spear,* THE LOST STARSHIP,
421 Years After Colonization,
End of Summer

*A*dventure *beckoned in the form of a girder angling down into the* brown earth. The whole excavation of the ruin of the starship *Lugh's Spear* was a challenge, an adventure. And Jace Bayrum was always up for one.

This project had it all, physical challenges: Yeah, he'd dug, and operated machinery to uncover that girder, along with the rest of the camp. There were intriguing mysteries: One of the three starships that had brought the colonists from Earth to Celta lay under his feet. The ground had collapsed under it only days after landing. Who knew what treasures were inside—knowledge, that data bank of the colonists' genetic psi traits—but ancient artifacts, too. And he got a cut. The pay was acceptable, if not great.

Good people to work with, though sometimes, like now, when ten different people checked out that very intriguing beam angling down into the rough man-sized hole, they seemed too damn slow for him. They all wanted to get into the ship. He wanted to be first. He'd volunteered and won the right.

Everyone in the camp was standing around, staring at the cleared and dusty area, talking. Sweating lightly, like he was, in the hot and humid summer air, under the bright blue sky.

This job came with the spice of danger that got a man's blood pumping.

And it came with a whiff of fame. Fame—though he wasn't too interested in fame, at least not the go-down-in-the-history-book kind. The past didn't matter—well, only the past he was digging up right now, the project, the adventure. The future didn't matter much as long as he had enough gilt to take care of himself. The now, and what was happening, and enjoying himself, that was more important than all the rest. Though he did like the buy-you-a-drink-at-the-bar kind of fame.

As they opened more of the hole, he *itched* to walk along that wide girder, go down into the bowels of the midsection of the starship. He shifted his feet, wanting to go already, explore. See things no one had for centuries, that was a rush. Aces high. He wanted to *do*, not hang around with the rest of the expedition everlastingly talking.

He'd objected to the physical harness, not wanting the chance of getting tangled in something down there, but was now layered with enough spellshields that his entire body itched at the feel of them, including his eyes.

"Go!" said the owner.

Jace stepped onto the piece of metal two-thirds of a meter wide, felt the settling as it took his weight. Light-footed, he headed toward the opening.

The beam moved under his feet, threw him off balance, and he fell. Shouts from watchers. The earth giving way beneath him. Dust. Rocks pounding him. Plummeting down.

He thumped hard enough that his breath went from his body. He fought passing out and remained conscious by the skin of his teeth. He'd fallen under the beam, and rock crowded around him but didn't crush him. Hard to tell how big the pocket of air he was in was . . . maybe enough that he wouldn't die, even without the spellshields.

It was colder down here, and he shivered. The whole thing made him recall the first time he cheated death. Shudders racked him at the memory.

He and his father and mother had gone over to the nearest city to purchase some fancy worked metal box his mother had insisted on having—one both he and his father had worked hard to give her the gilt for. Not that his father had cared about that; he blindly adored his wife.

Jace had been almost seventeen, close to becoming an adult and not so blind to his mother's greed.

Evening was turning into night when they reached the river. The box had cost enough that they didn't have gilt for the return ferry, but there was a free rope across the river and a raft to pull along. His and his father's massive muscles should be enough to get them across with help from his mother's small Flair.

They'd been in the middle of the river when the guide rope had broken.

His mother had screamed, turned white-faced, and clutched her box to her. Her gaze went to Jace's father, skimmed across Jace, looked to the opposite shore. "I can do it!" she cried. "I can teleport there if you bond with me and give me your energy. I can see the bank well enough, but it has to be quick. If you love me, link with me! Save me!"

"Of course, Marian." Jace's father set his one hand on her shoulder, held out the other to Jace. "We will save you." His voice, deep, calm, as he confronted his and Jace's own danger in heading down the rapid river on an old raft.

"I—" Mind frantically scrambling, Jace took his father's hand.

"One, two, *three*!" his mother screamed and Jace's strength, his energy, got yanked out of him to fund her teleportation.

His father fell to his knees, toppled sideways, breaking Jace's hold. More sucking of . . . Flair? . . . from Jace, ripping from him.

And the raft . . . the Flair keeping the raft together fell apart, siphoned by his mother.

The shock of the cold and tumbling water took Jace's breath. He strove to stay close to his papa.

His father's head turned. "She. Made. It." He sighed out, looking gray, wasted.

Jace grabbed his father's great hand, panic and wild grief and fury crashing through him in great swaths of emotion. He tried to swim, swallowed water. Reached for a better grip on the man, ripped his thin, worn shirt.

"Papa!"

Slowly, slowly his father's lips moved. "Take. Care. Of. Your. Mother."

His eyes glazed, his whole body released, and his last words were, "Marian, love." He let go of Jace's hand and rolled facedown into the water, swept away.

Great emotions can trigger a dreamquest Passage, releasing inner psi power, Flair. That happened, though Jace didn't figure that out until later. A huge burst of fever-heat flashed through him, *lifted and threw* him to the riverbank his mother had landed on.

He didn't see her. She and her box were already away and not looking back.

So he didn't either. He huddled under tall bushes that night and in the morning walked away to find work on a caravan heading for the northern continent a few days later.

He'd heard she'd remarried.

So much for love.

Now Jace shuddered so hard his body banged against rock. He couldn't breathe. Darkness threatened, and with each shallow breath he struggled for better memories. Hell if he was going out recalling the worst day of his life.

The face of a woman flashed before him.

He'd had the best sex with her . . .

Everything went dark.

DRUIDA CITY

Her HeartMate was in danger! The vicious jerk on the minuscule bond between them blew it wide open. Yanking on Glyssa's strength, demanding she pour energy into him—into shields surrounding him—to save him. She did, crumpling where she stood, watching in horror as time seemed to slow and the crate of ancient glass recordspheres—priceless books and journals—fell to the unforgiving marble floor of the PublicLibrary. Twenty-four original colonist tales to be shattered and she couldn't lift a finger to help.

The cost for her HeartMate's life.

Instant tears blurred her vision as she panted a prayer to the Lady and Lord to save the spheres. In the slowness of fear, caught between microseconds, she saw the spheres hit a small, thick rug that Glyssa had completely forgotten was there, bequeathed by a former patron. Sheer luck.

Except for one ball that hit and exploded into shards.

She huddled, gasping, all the exposed surfaces of her skin tingling, unable to move. Shock tears dribbled down her face. Good thing no one was on this study floor except her.

Her HeartMate was safe . . . and coming out of the darkness of unconscious. And as his feelings, his first instinctive fear at being trapped, filtered through her, she understood, stunned, that the adventurous man she'd had a fling with and couldn't find later was now at the excavation of *Lugh's Spear* in the center of the continent.

Gently, gently she sent a whisper of caring, of comfort, to him along their bond and felt him settle, thought she heard the same shouts of help he did.

Even as her own Family and friends began to react to her collapse.

"Glyssa! What's wrong? I felt the pull on our bond!" Camellia Darjeeling D'Hawthorn, one of Glyssa's best friends, ran from the teleportation pad to Glyssa, helping her to her feet.

What's wrong? Glyssa's father demanded mentally, *You drew on our Family connection.*

Stick to the truth, sort of. *I felt a little queasy. I'm all right now.*

You may be getting the virus going around. Glyssa's mother's voice in her mind was cool. *Leave work now. We don't want you infecting any patrons.*

Part of working with the public. Good thing none of the rest of us have it, Glyssa's sister, Enata, snipped, disgruntled even in her telepathic speaking.

I think I can stave it off if I take a little of my sick time, Glyssa replied weakly, mind-to-mind with her Family, the FirstLevel Librarians of Druida City. Glyssa hadn't finished her master program to become FirstLevel yet. Still needed a "field" trip and formal paper.

I'll check on you after work, her mother said absently, her mind already veering off into something more interesting. The attention of Glyssa's father and sister, the pressure of their Flair, their psi power, dropped from Glyssa, too.

Meanwhile, Camellia had helped Glyssa to a reading chair, gathered the twenty-three recordspheres and put them back in the crate, and said a spell to reassemble the shattered one. Hopeless.

With a sigh and a flick of the fingers, Camellia gathered all the shards and dust and disposed of it. Lifting the crate from the floor, Camellia also smoothed out the chips in the wood, then placed it on the table next to Glyssa's chair and tapped it. "Tell me that breaking these would not be a career-ending move."

"I can't."

"Your Family's standards are too high," Camellia said.

"We keep all the knowledge of Celta," Glyssa defended. "These are irreplaceable." She stroked the nearest orb with trembling fingers.

"And they've all been copied, and more than once," Camellia said.

"Nothing like hearing the original colonists' voice, or seeing their writing, or experiencing the impressions of their memories," Glyssa said.

"Huh," Camellia said. "What's wrong?"

Glyssa wet her lips, still feeling pale. No doubt her freckles were standing out against white skin, and her paleness made her red hair look all the more carroty. "My HeartMate needed my Flair and energy. To save his life."

"Wow," Camellia said, absently polishing each of the recordspheres with a softleaf she'd pulled from her tunic pocket. She must have been in one of her teahouses. "Did he demand it?"

"No. I just felt the need through our link and gave what I could. He asked for nothing. He never has." Glyssa could tell her friend the whole truth. "This isn't the first time he's been in danger. Now and then I could feel a tug on our connection, but not quite enough to find him through our link." She wasn't going to let that connection go this time, would strengthen it. Right now the link was just physical attraction showing up in sexy dreams, a shared past of a wild weekend affair, and the potential for a lifelong love.

She tilted her head as she traced the golden bond.

"Now you can find him?" Camellia asked.

"Yes. Now I know where he is." Determination fired within Glyssa, giving her the energy to sit tall. Determination and extreme curiosity. Her vision sharpened. "Camellia, my HeartMate, Jace, is at the excavation of the starship *Lugh's Spear*."

Camellia grimaced. "Your HeartMate is there, and my husband and HeartMate wants someone to be there on my behalf."

"And your Laev is right," Glyssa said. "You are a descendant of the Captain of that starship, by law you are entitled to a third of the artifacts, or the proceeds from the sale of the artifacts."

Camellia's mouth turned down. "That doesn't matter to me as much as him being remembered and honored for the hero that he was." They stared at each other for a minute.

"You're going to your guy, aren't you?"

"Yes. And I've been wanting to visit *Lugh's Spear*, too. I can make it the field trip needed as part of my final process to become a FirstLevel Librarian." She nearly wiggled in her seat—such an adventure for herself, too! A project of awesome discovery.

"Your parents aren't going to like this."

"No." She'd work around that somehow.

Camellia tapped the empty hole where the shattered sphere had been. "And how much trouble is this going to be for you?"

Glyssa let out a puff of sigh. "It was the index of the other recordings kept in this crate. Lucky. I can say that a patron of the library wanted to see it and dropped it, and then make a new one."

Smiling, Camellia said, "Not a lie. You are a patron of the library."

"Yes, I am."

"Well if you're going to the excavation, you can be the source of information Laev and the rest of the FirstFamilies council have on that project. I'll have him contact you. You can go on our behalf if your Family nixes your field trip and paper on the expedition."

A chill slipped through Glyssa at the thought of not making FirstLevel Librarian, failing in the career she'd started at ten years old. She swallowed hard.

Camellia picked up one of the spheres, read the title and made a face. "Another boring history." She stared at Glyssa, then perked up. "You could write a paper on my ancestor Captain Netra Sunaya Hoku." Camellia's eyes brightened as she put the ball back into its cushioned nest. "Better, you could write something more popular than a paper. A . . . a novel or a play, or something." She nodded decisively. "Yes, that's what I want. I want regular people to read about my ancestor, understand how he saved so many lives." She grabbed Glyssa's hands. "Say you will."

"I don—"

Glyssa, what happened! chimed in her other friend, Tiana Mugwort, mentally. *I was attending a lecture by the high priest and couldn't respond before now, but felt your need.*

So Glyssa and Camellia shared their thoughts with her.

"Incoming scry from GreatLord T'Ash, at T'Ash Residence, for SecondLevel Librarian Glyssa Licorice," said the voice of the PublicLibrary.

Camellia looked at her. Glyssa shrugged. She didn't know why the lord would call her. She'd never met the man. "I'll accept it," she said.

The nearby wall scry screen cleared, then showed a large and scowling T'Ash holding a fox kit by the scruff of his neck. Off screen came the hisses of a very angry cat.

"Glyssa Licorice?" T'Ash snapped.

"That's me," she said.

"My HeartMate informs me that this one." He gave the young fox a tiny shake. "Is your Fam Companion. Come get him. Now." The scry went black.

Camellia laughed. "Sounds like GreatLady Danith D'Ash has given you a Fam."

Two

Glyssa rubbed her temples. *"This isn't the right time to get a Familiar.* I can't take a young thing out to an excavation."

"You shouldn't," Camellia agreed. "But do you want a Fam or not?"

"Oh, I do!" Energy surged through Glyssa. Need for a companion, since she'd be leaving her two best friends, her Family . . . all that she knew.

"You should buy one of those automatic teleportation collars that will send him to D'Ash if he gets hurt," Camellia said.

"It can't teleport him thousands of kilometers!"

"They must have a Healing clinic," Camellia said. "You can set the collar for that."

Glyssa's mind whirled. "I must leave as soon as possible."

"Well," Camellia pointed out, "T'Ash did say *now*."

Glyssa had meant for the excavation.

"My Family expects me to be at home . . . sick." Though a Fam *would* perk anyone up.

"T'Ash is not a man you want to cross," Camellia pointed out.

"All right. I'll 'port to our garage and take the glider."

Camellia hugged her. "Laev will be scrying you about being our rep at *Lugh's Spear*." She kissed Glyssa on the cheek. "I'll see you later." She went to the teleportation pad and left.

Glyssa put away the recordspheres—with a new index—and headed out.

A few minutes later the glider pulled up to Danith D'Ash's offices. She was the animal healer and person who usually assigned Fams and was awaiting Glyssa's arrival, holding and petting the little fox.

From what Glyssa could see, the young Fam didn't need soothing. His tongue lolled out of his slightly open muzzle and his eyes gleamed with wild glee.

The glider stopped and the door lifted. Glyssa began to slide out when Danith D'Ash hustled up and the foxling jumped from her arms onto the seat. Glyssa winced at the little claw holes in the upholstery.

You are my FamWoman! The excited telepathic voice was accompanied with a few small barks from the red and white fox. His red fur was about the color of Glyssa's hair.

Then he was in her lap, putting his paws on her shoulders, licking her face with a rough tongue and sending fox breath her way. He felt . . . simply wondrous, small and lithe and trembling with excitement.

In an instant he'd dropped to her lap and curled up, draping a fluffy tail over his nose.

"I need a programmable collar," Glyssa said, dazed.

Danith D'Ash handed her one.

The fox lifted its head. *I do not like that.*

"It will break away if you're caught on anything," Glyssa said.

He snapped his teeth at D'Ash, so she floated it into the glider and to Glyssa. "The collar will return your Fam here . . . I'll give you the exact coordinates for my son's office." The lady's cheerful smile held an edge of strain.

"I'm actually leaving for the excavation of *Lugh's Spear* for my field trip to obtain my FirstLevel librarianship," Glyssa said, petting the young fox. "I suppose I shouldn't take him." She didn't want to give him up.

D'Ash's brows came down. "No, you shouldn't—"

But D'Ash's husband and HeartMate exited her offices and joined her, towering over her and laying a huge hand on her shoulder. "The kit will be fine." T'Ash lifted his chin. "We've had troublesome animals here before, but *that* one. He'll be fine. Good to meet you, GrandMistrys Licorice. Merry meet and merry part and merry meet again." With a wave of his hand, the glider door snicked shut and they were off.

"Home, please," Glyssa said to the Flair-powered vehicle. It picked up speed and exited through the T'Ash spellshields and gates in seconds. The gates clanged behind them.

Her fox turned and sat on her lap, looking up at her. *Adventure!*

She couldn't deny the glee in his eyes that matched a surge in her heart. "Yes. And now to name you."

You are a Licorice of the PublicLibrary Licorices, he said. *I asked the T'Ash ResidenceLibrary for Licorice names*—He'd done research! Glyssa was thrilled.

—and the Residence gave me some and I chose Lepid.

"Oh, clever fox!"

He licked her on her chin. *I am. I am a CLEVER fox. More clever than any old cat, more clever than—*

"Let's not get into that. And my Family lives in a house across from the library. We don't have any Fams—"

I am the FIRST Licorice Fam!

"Yes, but the PublicLibrary itself has two cats. You must be nice to them." She looked at the wriggling fox, figured that would tax the kit. "At least until we leave the city. There's plenty of exploring to be done in our house and the library. Avoid the cats."

Of course! Lepid said.

Glyssa figured that was a promise easily broken by her new, young Fam. "If you get seriously scratched by the cats, I'm not sure you'll be able to go with me."

Not go!

"That's right. You'll have to stay here until you are well. But I will have to go, because my trip arrangements will be made by another GreatLord, Laev T'Hawthorn, whom I can't deny." She hoped. But Laev had been wanting to poke his nose into the expedition, and was a wealthy entrepreneur, a gambler. Surely he'd be all right with her plans.

Lepid grumbled a little in acknowledgment, then hopped from her lap to look out the window at the city as they left the rich noble estates. *I think I like running better than sitting in this glider.*

Glyssa didn't tell him that the trip across the continent would have him cooped up in an airship for septhours. It would be fast as opposed to stridebeast—there weren't any roads—but confining. Her perscry—personal scry pebble—played the chord she'd assigned to Laev T'Hawthorn, and she slid a thumb across it. "Here," she said.

He grinned at her, and yes, the man was rubbing his hands. "Camellia told me of your offer, Glyssa. I'm also working on a satellite communications system from the starship here to the *Lugh's Spear* encampment. You'll be taking out some equipment. Everything is ready. I'll send you the documents—all the financial information regarding your salary and duties, a couple of other people are interested in your reports—Camellia will send you more copies of her ancestor's journals and maps, and I'll keep you up to date on my consortium for putting up a communications satellite. You'll be traveling with equipment," Laev said in satisfaction, "and will be leaving in two days."

"Thanks," Glyssa said faintly. Two days! No time to procrastinate telling her parents.

They'd turned onto the broad city street that the main PublicLibrary fronted.

"Merry meet," Laev said.

"And merry part," Glyssa gave the formal response.

"And merry meet again." The lord's smile was quick and charming. "I'll see you tomorrow evening at GreatCircle Temple for a blessing ritual."

"Right," Glyssa said. The scry pebble darkened as Laev ended the call. She drew in a large breath as the glider pulled into the drive before her house.

Now all she had to do was tell her parents she was leaving.

Excavation of *Lugh's Spear,*
The Next Morning

The camp was abuzz with the news that an unscheduled single-zoom airship had arrived and the pilot had headed straight to headquarters.

It only took seconds for rumors to bound through the encampment. Jace wasn't close enough to the owners to casually stroll into their pavilion and ask what was going on, and his bump of curiosity wasn't such that he panted to know. Unlike his friendly rival, Andic Sanicle, who lingered near the main tent.

Jace headed out to look at the excavation.

A couple of years ago, an expedition had been put together by the Elecampanes and they'd legally claimed a great amount of uninhabited land. No one had believed they'd find the lost starship, but after some effort, the location of *Lugh's Spear* had been determined. Now the project, also run by the Elecampanes, showed the huge outline of the starship.

The landing on Celta had been hard, the ship had broken with some lives lost, then, a few days later, the ground beneath the massive vehicle had given way and it had fallen and been covered with rockfall.

The colonists had tried to make a community, some had stayed and died out in a few generations—Celta remained hard on her new people—but most had trekked to the city of Druida, where the intelligent starship *Nuada's Sword* had landed.

Jace had seen the plays depicting the discovery of Celta and the ensuing journey. Hard not to when GrandLord T'Elecampane was the noted actor Raz Cherry. The man did theater productions even in camp.

A shiver twitched between his shoulder blades as he scented water in the air from Fish Story Lake and the Deep Blue Sea. No, this time he thought that Celtans not Earthans, would stay. The location was great . . . one of the reasons that the Captain had decided to land here. He'd been right about that.

Unfortunately, from what Jace understood, he'd also been right to worry about that landing.

Jace shook off the past and the future and walked toward the hole in the ground where the beam was, stared at it. When he'd fallen, the spellshields had protected him. It had taken a couple of septhours to dig him out, and he'd felt the strain of the lack of air, though he'd fallen into a small air pocket and the spellshields provided minimal air for three septhours.

He'd landed on an actual metal floor, and though he'd been trapped—and one of his hates was being constrained—he'd had time to check out the hole's dimensions. Beyond a not-too-deep rock slide to his left should be a stretch of corridor. His mind had danced with notions of what might be there.

But though the owners of the project, the Elecampanes, had listened to him, since the accident no one had gone back down. Instead they'd been, once again, scouting out the entrances of the ship, to dig near there.

Frustrating. He *yearned* to see what wonders the Earthans had left. When the ship had landed so hard and broken, the colonists had only been allowed one large sack of personal items, and that had included the Captain, the immediate former Captain, and his wife. Not many had been permitted back into the ship. Those who had, had brought out things to set up the community.

A lot had been lost when the ship had gone down. All sorts of treasures inside.

"Greetyou," said a soft voice, and an equally soft arm slipped between his side and his chest, since he had his hands jammed in his trous pockets. Forcing an easy smile on his face, he looked down at Funa Twinevine. He'd stopped having sex with her casually when he'd understood that she was also sleeping with his rival, Andic Sanicle. She was a hard worker, but she also had her eye on the treasures and was a shade more greedy and less honorable than Jace was comfortable with.

Three

Jace had known a lot of adventurers, one of his favorite types of women to play with. Funa was certainly easy on his eyes with a heart-shaped face, wide, lush mouth, and large, dark-brown eyes. She'd been inventive and flexible in bed, something he also enjoyed.

"Greetyou," he said.

She frowned, pursing those lovely lips that he had no intention of ever kissing again—at least not until after she stopped sexing with Andic—and leaned against him. His body remembered being atop a bedsponge with her, but his mind and emotions remained cool. He kept the smile, though.

Funa stroked his arm. "You haven't been friendly, lately."

He grunted and shook his head. "I don't like sharing a woman. Just irrational that way."

"You can't tell me what to do." She stepped back, fitted her hands on her hips.

"No. And I won't. Do as you please."

Tossing her sleek, long hair over her shoulders, she said, "You didn't ask for exclusivity."

He hadn't even thought about that. Truth was, he hadn't cared enough about her to think of that, but he knew she wouldn't want to hear that, who would? "My mistake." He made it regretful.

"Hmph." Her shoulders wiggled. "I don't want to give up Andic as a lover."

Jace winced. "Ouch."

And she let go a full-bodied laugh, punched him lightly in the shoulder, then sent him one of those under-the-eyelash sexy looks. "Not yet, anyway."

Andic had discovered the last cache of artifacts near the camp, had gotten his cut for them up front.

Jace had empty pockets but hopeful dreams. He turned back to eye the beckoning but dark and narrow hole in the ground. He'd bet he could still fit, and in a couple more meters, if there was a passage, it would be wide.

Now Funa sighed. "That opening is so tempting, isn't it?" She looked out at the crew heading with two heavy-duty earth-moving machines to where the Elecampanes thought the midship main door was.

"Yeah," Jace said. Too tempting. He'd only get in trouble if he went down. And though he didn't mind trouble, exploring on his own might get him thrown off the project. Not worth that.

So he turned back toward the camp some meters distant, saw Andic wave at Funa. She hurried from Jace's side, and as a twitch hit between his shoulder blades, he knew he'd been right to refuse her. Just logical.

Didn't have anything to do with recent dimly remembered erotic dreams. Or that very strong tug on his emotions he'd felt the day before. Or the incredible four-day sex weekend he'd had with that redhead, Glyssa Licorice, he'd visualized as he'd fallen down the damn hole. Really.

Years ago he'd had to force himself to forget Glyssa's name, and now he recalled it again.

He scuffed back to his battered tent—large enough for two, to give him the personal space he needed—realized he kicked up dust on the dry land, and picked up his feet and hit the easy stride he liked the best. Too much thinking hampered a guy.

Druida City

Glyssa stood in front of the review panel that would approve her field trip and a paper, pursuant to the procedure to become a First-Level Librarian of Celta. This was supposed to be a formality, but she knew it wouldn't be. "I intend for my field trip to be to the excavation site of the recently located starship, *Lugh's Spear*. And for my research to be on the last Captain of that ship."

Her mother's lips flattened, and Glyssa kept her flinch inside. Her father's disappointed expression was worse. Her older sister hefted a long-suffering sigh.

As always, her mother spoke first. "We were under the impression that your final research studies would be on HouseHearts—one of the reasons we allowed you so much time in the PublicLibrary HouseHeart. And we believed that your field sabbatical would be around the city, and perhaps to a few of the budding sentient Residences outside of Druida and in Gael City."

"GreatLord T'Hawthorn requested I write a biography of the Captain of the starship *Lugh's Spear*. How Netra Sunaya Hoku commanded the ship as it landed, his leadership of the colonists on the journey to Druida City, and, perhaps, research his later life after he gave up fame and status as one of the FirstFamily GrandLords." That topic would appeal to her supposedly egalitarian Family, though bringing up Laev T'Hawthorn's name contrasted with that. Even her Family, who disdained the appearance of wealth and status, was aware of the highest social strata of the planet . . . and that Glyssa had connections there, since one of her best friends had married into that level.

Glyssa continued, "Laev has wanted a representative at the excavation for a while. His HeartMate, Camellia, not only is invested emotionally in the excavation, but under our laws, has a financial interest in the salvage of the ship."

"He's a sharp entrepreneur," Glyssa's father said with a hint of admiration.

"Will he be funding your trip?" Glyssa's sister asked, acid in her tone, more from envy, Glyssa thought, than from worry that Glyssa's research might be less than impartial.

Glyssa drew a sheaf of papyrus from the long, rectangular pocket of her formal gown, walked the pace to the desk the FirstLevel Librarians sat behind, and gave them the copy of the files Laev had sent to her.

Her father grunted, her mother looked up sharply. "This includes facsimiles of Captain Hoku's journals!" *Now* she was excited. Camellia had been dilatory in giving that to the PublicLibrary though all of them had nagged her about it.

"I will have full cooperation from Camellia and Laev, and a letter of introduction to the Elecampanes who own and run the project, and who may bring me on as a secretary of the project."

"A *secretary*," her sister sneered.

Glyssa met her mother's eyes, then her father's. "Apparently they have no official secretary or historian for the site."

Her Family gasped as one.

"Inconceivable," said her sister.

"This must not be allowed." Her father stood. He had a strain of restlessness and during times of great emotion, couldn't keep still. Glyssa was beginning to feel like she might have inherited that from him. Deep inside, part of her sang at the thought of adventure.

Her mother clicked her tongue and her father resumed his seat. D'Licorice adjusted her sleeves on the table and intoned. "Is there anything else the applicant wishes to say about her field studies?"

Glyssa gritted her teeth briefly, but bowed her head. She'd decided to reveal all about the project, but not about her HeartMate. "Great-Lady Camellia D'Hawthorn wishes not only a monograph on her ancestor, the last pilot and Captain of the starship *Lugh's Spear*, she wishes a more popular story written for the general public." The two plays based on the discovery of Celta were immensely popular. Glyssa shivered at the thought of providing a story for a third.

"Camellia would want something more easy to read," Glyssa's sister said nastily.

"Camellia is a successful businesswoman, not a scholar," Glyssa shot back.

"Such comments are not pertinent to this review panel," Glyssa's mother snapped.

Glyssa straightened her spine, tried to keep her expression remote, as was expected. "I have agreed to the challenge." Again she slid her gaze across her Family's faces. They'd lapsed into scholarly impassivity also.

Her sister leaned forward. "What will you do if we do not approve of this field trip?"

Glyssa had hoped no one would ask that question. She lifted her chin. "I believe the excavation of the lost starship, *Lugh's Spear*, a ship different than our own *Nuada's Sword* here in Druida, a ship whose culture during the long trip from Earth to Celta was radically different than that of *Nuada's Sword*, is of great importance. And, as we all know, *Lugh's Spear* carried knowledge about the colonists' genetic psi power that *Nuada's Sword* doesn't have. *Lugh's Spear* is not only vital to us in illuminating our past, but for future generations." That was the definition of a discipline of study, and she backed the truth of her words with Flair, psi power. "If this panel does not find official merit for my work, I will proceed without its blessing."

"I am concerned that you will be so far away . . . and the excavation is dangerous," her mother said.

Glyssa figured that was one reason her HeartMate had been drawn there. "I believe GreatLord T'Hawthorn is working with Commander Dani Eve Elder and the starship *Nuada's Sword* in the implementation of a new long-distance communications system."

They all looked fascinated at this, too. Her sister's mouth dropped open.

"You have been busy," her father said.

Glyssa nodded.

Her mother said, "I approve the field study. But I expect more than reports or notes as proof of progress. I wish monograph pages . . ." she paused, "and pages and chapters of a 'popular work' with every weekly communication sent from the camp."

Swallowing, Glyssa nodded. Sounded rough to her, a setup for failure. She was a slow writer and everyone knew it. She'd have to make the most of every moment she had at the excavation.

"I agree," her father said.

Her sister pursed her lips, let the moment hang. The decision had to be unanimous. All Glyssa's muscles tensed.

"I suppose I agree, too." She made her sigh low and drawn out and Glyssa nearly flinched. She'd always hated that sigh, which her sister knew.

"The student's final research paper and the field trip for that research is approved," Glyssa's mother said.

"But she is not a FirstLevel Librarian until she turns in her paper," Glyssa's sister said, smiling widely. Leaning back on her chair, she lifted a hand and studied her nails. "And since the student is abandoning her initial project of HouseHearts, I will pursue that."

Glyssa stopped protest from escaping her mouth. Then recalled she'd spent years cultivating people who might talk, in general, about the HouseHearts in their intelligent Residences. Good luck to her sister in trying to pick up that.

"I don't think so," their mother said. "We will put that project in abeyance at this time."

Glyssa's sister scowled, but Glyssa's stomach sank as she realized she was right. Her mother was setting her up for failure.

"Yip! Yip, yip, yip, yiiippp!" Lepid zoomed through the cat door, followed by the two library cats. He leapt onto the wide desk, scattered all the organized papyrus, then ran around the room and finally bounded into Glyssa's arms, continuing to yip and taunt the cats.

"What is that?" Glyssa's sister asked.

"A fox!" Glyssa's father exclaimed, walked over, and scratched Lepid's head, grinning at Glyssa. "You got a FoxFam!"

"Yes."

We do not want him here, said the calico cat.

The PublicLibrary is OURS, said the long-haired brown cat. *OURS only. Two Cats is enough.* Glyssa thought the large building could accommodate five, and the annex one.

"I presume D'Ash gave him to you because he caused trouble," Glyssa's mother said.

Glyssa's parents were very smart.

"He's the same color as your hair," Glyssa's sister said, patting her deep auburn chignon.

"Calm down, everyone," her mother said. "He won't be staying here in the library."

Hisses turned to cat mutters with a lot of whisker twitching. Tails high, the cats stalked to the Fam door and through it.

Lepid rubbed Glyssa's father's hand with his head. "He's a charmer," her father said.

Glyssa's mother came around the desk. A small furrow showed between her brows. "Do you plan on taking such a young Fam to the excavation?"

"Yes," Glyssa said. She touched the black collar around Lepid's neck. "I can program this for the excavation's clinic." She'd checked that the camp had a medical facility.

"Very well," her mother said in a smooth tone that had everyone looking at her. "We will deal with any further logistics when you and Lepid return." She enveloped Glyssa in a warm embrace—as if that would ease the sting of being managed.

Her mother definitely didn't approve of the trip. Glyssa set her chin. Too bad. Lepid wriggled out of her grip, jumping onto the floor.

"Tiana Mugwort is conducting a ritual at GreatCircle Temple for the success of my endeavors this evening at NightBell. You all will come, won't you?" Glyssa asked.

Her sister sent her another look, eyes glinting with envy.

"Of course," her father said. He put an arm around her mother's waist, rolled his shoulders under his formal robe. "Glad this is over."

Bending, he kissed Glyssa's cheek. "You can do this, pumpkin." Then he kissed his HeartMate. "Last appointment of the day. Let's go home and list items we want Glyssa to look into when she's at the site."

They all teleported away, though Glyssa was sure that her mother and father were heading for the bedroom as opposed to their study. Her sister left without a word.

Adventure! Lepid said.

There was that. Glyssa grinned, did a little dance step.

"And finding my HeartMate," Glyssa murmured, picking up the small fox again. She hadn't mentioned her HeartMate to her Family. They would strongly disapprove of her previous fling, and would be irritated that she was mixing the personal with the professional—as if they didn't do that all the time. But though her parents were HeartMates, fortune hadn't granted her sister a fated mate. Enata had not found a man she wished to have as her husband yet. So Glyssa rarely spoke of her own HeartMate.

Are there foxes where we are going? Lepid asked.

A brief wave of dizziness at the relief of being given what she wanted—the last step in the ladder of her career—washed through Glyssa, made her limp. Mixed with that was the nervy excitement of facing a completely unfamiliar experience. "I don't know." She was beginning to think she didn't know far too much.

No. Don't think of that. Despite everything, she would not fail. She'd claim her love, and write her thesis and a popular work for Camellia, and take that last step for her career.

Nothing would stop her, not even her mother's maneuvering.

As they walked to GreatCircle Temple that evening, her parents were cheerful and Glyssa's sister had gotten over her snit. A summer breeze cooled off the heat of the day and the sky was a soft blue with pink streamers.

The number of people who'd gathered inside the Temple to take place in the ceremony, to wish Glyssa well on her journey, surprised her. She'd expected her best friends to be there, Camellia D'Hawthorn

and Tiana Mugwort, who was officiating the ritual. And she'd
thought Laev, Camellia's HeartMate would be there, too, but some
of the other librarians of the main PublicLibrary and its branches
attended, as well as a sprinkling of the greatest nobles in the land—
the FirstFamilies. Those people descended from the colonists who
funded the original space voyage.

That nearly made Glyssa giddy. Moving in such a social strata as
an unequal could be dangerous. But a few of them had ties to the
owners of the excavation project—the Elecampanes.

People lined up in twos, mostly married couples and HeartMates.
Since Tiana stood as priestess and Lady in the center of the circle
and Camellia and Laev were together, Glyssa was stuck with her
thin-mouthed, damp-palmed sister.

But once the circle was joined and the energy cycled around, the
pure delight of linking with others buoyed her spirits. Even her sister
smiled.

And the ritual went well, the Flair and blessings sent out into the
world in general, some to the PublicLibrary, most to the excavation—
some draped around Glyssa, went sparkling into her blood, and
transferred to her Family.

By the time of the last prayer and opening of the circle, joyful
conversation and hope for more information about the starship,
about *themselves*, filled the room.

Camellia had donated much of the refreshments, and the good
food pumped up the atmosphere even more.

When people left, Glyssa and Camellia and Tiana stayed talking
among themselves in close-friend-speak about men. Camellia was
gloriously happy with Laev, Tiana remained disappointed that her
HeartMate didn't look for her, no doubt put off by the terrible scan-
dal in her life. They both gave Glyssa personal blessings and tokens
for her HeartMate search and claiming, and ordered her to link with
them telepathically at least once a week to stay in touch. The three
of them practiced their mental conversation until Laev came in and
wanted to talk about the technical and business portion of the
project—reminding Glyssa that she'd be leaving the very next

morning . . . which had Lepid shooting around the room again, barking happy fox yips.

Finally they all teleported home and despite the lovely energy, Glyssa fell into bed and into sleep . . . and she rolled over and touched her lover—drawn once more into the hot bond with her HeartMate.

Four

Yes, his skin was damp from the summer heat under her palms and he groaned in the way that made her catch her breath as she slipped her hands down his chest. Yes, she *needed* to touch him, feel the lean but strong lines of his muscles, *know* that he was whole . . . and though this was telepathic, his body would reflect the truth.

He slept and she knelt next to him, stroking up his sides, sliding her hands over his shoulders, tracing the line of his jaw with her thumbs, feathering over his cheeks. Beautiful man. She leaned closer, attracted by his spicy smell, touched her tongue to his collarbone to taste him.

Healthy man.

Very healthy, as he caught her in his arms and rolled them over, yanked the diaphanous gown she wore open, put his hands on her breasts.

Her turn to gasp and groan. She liked the feel of him on her, the slight hair-roughness of his skin as he moved against her, tantalizing, tempting. Seducing.

Just being with him seduced her. More exciting than any man, the scent and taste and the feel of him. How his rhythm of loving matched hers.

He murmured nonsense words and she put her mouth on his and he opened his lips and rubbed his tongue against hers. His hands clamped around her butt and she welcomed the squeeze, the familiarity of him mingling with the innate knowledge that they belonged together. She yearned, and even her body understood that soon they would join in more than dreams. Yes.

Their tongues tangled, stroked and the flavor of him—*his* energy—mixing, matching, mingling with hers until desire held a scent and a promise of fulfillment.

He thrust into her, filled her, and she clamped her arms around him, arched with him, to the beat of the fast sex. Yes. Yes. Yes!

*J*ace awoke near dawn. He'd had another sex dream, and while it had been great, he had to use some energy to cleanse himself and his bedding, which was getting tedious. He sniffed deeply, but his tent didn't smell bad . . . in fact, his nostrils strained to capture Glyssa's remembered fragrance, even though his mind knew she hadn't truly been present. In the dreams he could smell her, the perfume she used, lilac, he thought, and woman. And womanly lust. That was the best.

He grabbed a robe and headed toward the showers. Spell cleansing was all well and good, but he liked the feel of cool water sluicing down his body. Plenty of water in the area. Plenty humidity . . . from the huge inland Deep Blue Sea and the nearby Fish Story lake.

As he passed by Andic's tent, Funa emerged, stretching. Her silkeen robe was a lot thinner than his own sturdy thick cotton. She sent him a sleepy and sexually satisfied smile that yet had a come-hither look, and he forced himself to curve his mouth and gave her a casual wave. Would have been good to have had a real woman in his arms last night, though even the in-person sex with Funa hadn't been as good as what he'd had with Glyssa Licorice.

Despite himself, and the nature of flings, he'd remembered more than her name. GrandMistrys Glyssa Licorice, second daughter of

GrandLord and GrandLady Licorice, of the PublicLibrary Licorices, an ancestral heritage of duty, obligation, and being trapped in a Family . . . this one not the little-f bad family like his, but a *Family,* with big expectations.

Since Glyssa had gone wild in Jace's arms, he figured that most of her life being a slave to Family tradition and duty and whatever had made her repress her passions. He'd liked the effect in bed, but didn't think they'd have much in common otherwise.

A tiny wisp of an idea snuck into his mind about Heart-Mates. Could Glyssa—*No!* Stop now. He *wouldn't* think of HeartMates.

He wasn't ready for a HeartMate, didn't think he'd ever be ready for those ties. Didn't really believe in HeartMates, anyway, just legend . . . despite seeing the lovey-dovey Elecampanes.

Husband-wife love really didn't exist and families were traps.

Raz Cherry Elecampane was an actor and had acted himself into believing in HeartMates, and had worn down his more hardheaded wife.

And, yeah, Jace had felt those bonding dreams during the dreamquests that freed his Flair-psi-magic. He'd even made a HeartMate token, but still didn't believe in real love between couples.

Lady and Lord knew he hadn't seen loving between his own parents . . . his father's adoration of a selfish woman who gave and withheld affection and sex wasn't love.

Nope, he wasn't going down that road. No permanent woman who would make him beg. Or do the opposite, cling to him. Not happening.

He stepped into the shower tent, dropped his robe, and let the cool water pound the stupid idea of HeartMates back into a tiny part of his brain . . . or sense into his emotions. He didn't care where he'd stashed the notion before, but he wanted it *gone.*

Along with the tiny bud of yearning for loving and being loved. Another legend. People used each other in marriage. Loving was just a damn lie.

Druida City,
The Same Morning

After TransitionBell and before dawn, Laev and Camellia Hawthorn picked Glyssa up at the Licorice house.

Laev's sleek new glider held three easily and sped through the night to Southern Airpark. Lepid slept in a basket over Glyssa's arm. He'd worn himself out running around the library "looking at secrets before we go." Hopefully not chasing the cats. Though if he had, Glyssa wouldn't hear about it because her Family had retired before she and the fox had gone to bed. Not that she'd slept well.

They exited the glider into the night and walked to the waiting airship that had a cockpit for two and a long fuselage for storage. It looked fast. Faster than the fat, ungainly ships she and her Family occasionally took to check out the Gael City Libraries under their direction.

Glyssa's steps lagged as she headed toward the open cockpit door, glass wrapped around the whole front of the airship. She swallowed, steadied her nerves. She didn't like heights, but she *would* do this.

Her friends hugged her before Laev helped her with the long step up and into the zoom-ship. She shivered and told herself she was chilled, though the night was warm.

Laev patted the side of the portal. "This baby will get you to the excavation in half a day. Fast and serviceable." He looked at the pilot. "All the equipment on board?"

She lifted a brow at him. "A non-Flaired transport came from *Nuada's Sword* with a lot of items. Everything is fine and stowed safely." The pilot glanced at Glyssa in her traveling clothes, short tunic and narrow-legged trous. No extra material. "Also a giant duffle gear bag from Outside Outfitters."

Taking Glyssa's hand to kiss it, Laev said, "The very latest in camping gear for you."

"What?" Glyssa knew her eyes rounded.

"He had a great time choosing and buying everything," Camellia said. "There's also furniture, the new miniaturized sort that becomes full-sized when activated by a Flair spellword." Camellia sounded disapproving. But then all three of the friends liked beautifully worked furnishings. "So the chairs and tables, cabinets, et cetera, aren't very sturdy." She stepped into the airship to hug Glyssa tightly. "Be safe, and—" Camellia switched to mindspeech. *Let me know when you are there and all is fine.*

Glyssa hugged her friend back. Doubts spun through her mind and she squashed them. Concentrate on the adventure of it all!

I will, she replied telepathically. Thank the Lady and Lord that mental bonds had no distance limits . . . at least on Celta.

Camellia fixed the harness over Glyssa and the basket holding her new Fam, then placed a huge hamper of food and drink "for the trip" in the spacious area around Glyssa's feet. As Camellia hopped back down, she narrowed a look at her husband. "You did keep the idea of safety uppermost in your mind, didn't you, for Glyssa's tent? Didn't just choose what was the latest and looked the best?"

He put on an offended expression. "Of course I chose the most secure option."

"Time to go," said the pilot.

"Keep in touch!" the Hawthorns said in unison, then grinned at each other in delight, leaned in to kiss, Glyssa's last sight of them as the airship door thunked shut and the airship rose.

It reassured her that she was doing the absolutely right thing in going after her HeartMate—finding adventure herself.

Septhours later, they landed without a bump at a cleared area the pilot said was designated for airships.

Glyssa and the pilot off-loaded her supplies while most of the people milled around the back end of the airship and storage area, moving the equipment from *Nuada's Sword* with great care under the gazes of the Elecampanes.

Suddenly, a shriek came to her ears. "No! Catch that FoxFam!"

Glyssa whirled, her chest constricting, as she saw Lepid heading for a hole in the ground. "Lepid!" she yelled. He didn't listen.

*J*ace *had been sauntering to the airship like the others in camp when the* woman stepped out of the cockpit. He stared, stunned. Rumor had it that this ship brought brand-new tech for communications over a long distance developed by the sentient starship *Nuada's Sword*, in Druida City. And an Important Personage.

He stopped, tucked his thumbs in his belt, and stared as he recognized Glyssa Licorice. The librarian he'd been having sex dreams about. A person who he'd never thought would be caught in the wilds of Celta.

A small animal dashed by him, then a scream came from behind him and he spun in time to see a fluffy foxtail wave as it started down the beam. A young FamFox. Great.

"Lepid!" Glyssa shouted.

Swearing and chanting the best damn spellshields to protect himself that he knew, he bounded toward the girder, running fast enough that he felt his hair lift and the sweat on his scalp dry. He got to the beam angling into the ground just in time to see the small fox stop and look over its back, mouth open and tongue loose in a smile.

"Wait!" Jace yelled.

Five

♥

The fox flipped his tail. Catch me if you can! I looove hiding places, and this smells WONDERFUL. Smells all through the camp!

Which might be why the Elecampane Fams—two cats and a fox—had taken one sniff and never returned. Obviously "wonderful" was in the nose of the sniffer.

Another twitch of the tail and the fox disappeared into the hole. Jace struggled with temptation for a few seconds. Drew up memory to visualize what he'd seen down there the last time. A small clear area with a metal wall in front, a loose rockslide to his left. Solid wall of rock and debris to his right and behind him, though the top of another wall could be seen. At the end, when they'd opened it up and pulled him out, he'd seen sky.

With a last prayer to the Lady and Lord and a final test to his personal spellshields—he didn't think the fox had any—Jace walked down the beam. No trembling under his weight, a good sign.

When he reached the hole, he sat and scooted downward. "I'm coming." He kept his voice low, not wanting anything to trigger another landslide.

He was answered by a series of high, excited yips from the fox below. People shouted, words and maybe his name, but nothing he heard clearly. He slid into the hole, the leather of his trous caused him to pick up speed and he nearly lost his balance. "Coming down!" he said just before he tipped off the beam.

He landed with bent knees in the gloom at the bottom of the hole. Blinking as his eyes adjusted to the dimness, he saw no sign of the fox.

Scrabbling sounded to his left. "Are you there . . . Lepid?" That was the name Glyssa had screamed.

Rock fell from above, striking him on his left shoulder. He jumped to the side, coughed, put his arms over his face, caught a glimpse of a fox butt wriggling through a hole at the top of the rock.

"Whee!" The fox's noise accompanied rock sliding on the other side of the left pile. Jace eyed the top where a rectangle of black showed. He could squeeze through it . . . if sufficiently foolhardy.

I see. I SEE, man!

Wiping his arm across his mouth even though he'd try telepathy, Jace pushed a mental comment to the fox. *What do you see?* He heard scratching and clicking that made him think of dancing paws, then a dash away. . . .

I see storage boxes, I see a hallway. I see more rocks. I see HOLES.

Envy whipped through Jace. "Come back here at once!" He scrambled for a threat. "Or I'll ensure you have no treats for a month, a *long* time."

He sensed the fox pausing, ears cocked. *Treats? I will get treats?*

Did that mean he hadn't? Uh-oh.

Jace's shoulders tensed. *I promise. Come back now so you can tell all that you have seen to everyone!*

So I can tell all that I have seen to everyone! The fox gave a cheerful chirrup.

Paw sounds running back. Leaps on the other side of the rockpile.

Rockslide! Yelps of pain!

Jace plunged forward into the scree, taking bruising hits against his body, muscling through, snatching the fox just before a big chunk of metal hit red fur. Jace hunched over, turning his head for breath, while the sound of the fall echoed.

The small, young fox shivered in his arms. *You are fast!*

"Thanks." He coughed at the renewed dust in the air, straightened and pivoted back to see the pile was now no more than three-quarters of a meter high. The rest of the rockfall had spread out into a room that held several round-cornered storage boxlike objects. A shelf with several smaller boxes had netting pulled over it and sealed against the wall. He wanted to run and open a box or two and see what was inside.

Not his place, and man, he wished it were. Wished he had enough gilt to convince the Elecampanes to take him on as a partner. Then he'd . . . Stupid. *Stup!* He didn't have the means, he was just a worker.

When the dust diminished he noted a corridor leading off the room, a tilted and crumpled sheet of metal bisecting it, some boulders, but also dark space.

He gritted his teeth. People were shouting down at him.

"I'm fine," he yelled up. "We're both fine!"

It took fortitude he didn't know he had to turn away from the beckoning adventure, back to the girder going up. The clear area around his feet was less, since rock had fallen there, too. He scuffed a foot to send some pebbles back toward the piles, making the spot less treacherous for the next feet coming down.

He didn't know who'd be the next down, but . . .

"Are you sure you're all right?" boomed Raz Cherry T'Elecampane.

"Yes. Coming up!"

The fox whined low in his throat, then wriggled and looked up at Jace.

I found a secret way! I am a hero!

Jace smiled. He understood that bright and shiny feeling.

The hole above was bigger now, he could easily see the deep blue sky and high, scarflike white clouds. He kicked at the beam which had fallen to a lower angle, but it seemed to rest solidly against rock. The girder didn't move. Steadying his grasp on the fox, he began walking up. His work boots gripped the metal through the dust, didn't slip or slide. He kept a good hold on the wriggling fox.

This has been very fun! Lepid said.

As people began to see them, they cheered. He strode faster, grinning. He'd beaten the odds again. He'd cheated death again.

He was a hero again.

Just the way he liked it.

"Thank you so much!" a woman gushed—Glyssa. Her voice tweaked his nerve endings as she broke away from Raz T'Elecampane holding her back in the circle of people watching. Jace didn't like seeing the man's hands on her.

No mistaking her carroty hair tightly controlled in a braid around her head. He *would not* remember the springy abundance of that hair slipping across his body.

She flushed when she saw him, glanced aside, brushed at the severely cut tunic and trous suit of dust brown.

The fox licked Jace under his chin. He enjoyed it, the weight of the animal, too.

I like you, too, Lepid said.

All right, the FoxFamiliar could read his mind or sense his emotions. He tightened his inner shields.

Lepid whined in disappointment. *I can't hear you as much, now.*

"You don't need to."

And Glyssa was there, pale again and breathing hard with fear, followed by Funa Twinevine who eyed him narrowly.

"Thank you so much." Glyssa looked up into his eyes and he knew she hadn't forgotten their sex fling, either. She glanced aside. "GentleSir."

His muscles relaxed slightly, glad she was playing this cool. He wasn't ready to acknowledge their past small affair. If she was here for a while, they'd have to relate out of bed.

The FoxFam hopped back into her arms and licked her. Jace's gaze fixed on her moist skin, remembered the taste of that. More than her skin.

"You're welcome, GentleLady," he said.

She stuck out her hand as the young fox climbed up her chest and settled around her shoulders. "Glyssa Licorice," she said, "and my Fam is Lepid."

He took her fingers . . . cool and smooth, and he accepted the sizzle of desire that went straight to his groin as he kept his face stuck in a casual smile. He found himself bowing over her hand, something he hadn't done since he'd met GrandLady Del D'Elecampane. Some women's presence simply demanded that. The innate elegance of Glyssa had always called to him.

A snort came from Funa. Andic walked up to stand next to Jace. He released Glyssa's fingers as he straightened and let Andic shoulder him aside.

"Andic Sanicle," the man said, taking her hand and also bowing. "And surely you belong to the PublicLibrary Licorices, the GrandHouse?"

She smiled at Andic. "Surely I do. I'm here to help with the recording of these historic events."

Another huff from Funa at the statement and Glyssa withdrew her hand from Andic, pivoted to Funa. "And here for my field trip and research to qualify for my FirstLevel Librarianship status."

"Huh." Funa crossed her arms.

"Hey, Glyssa," shouted the pilot from long meters away. "Come get your stuff."

"Excuse me, please." Glyssa nodded to them and turned, hurrying back toward the airship and a new, huge two-meter-long duffle bag of licorice red that would take Flair to move. With the coat of arms of the PublicLibrary.

Jace watched the sway of her body as she walked, supple, energetic, just like she'd been in bed.

The fox on her shoulders looked back at him, barked, and loosened his jaw in a smile, tongue out to taste the air.

"As for you . . ." She lifted the fox and as her path angled away Jace saw her making a grumpy face at the kit. "You be more careful, and can you *please* mind what I say?"

Lepid gave a sharp bark, though Jace couldn't think the FoxFam had agreed.

"Interesting woman," Andic said. "I heard she's connected to the FirstFamilies somehow. Friendship, I think."

Jace jerked. That hadn't been true when he'd first met Glyssa at the middle-class social club, he was sure. Someone would have mentioned it. He didn't care for nobles much, and like anyone with a bit of sense, would definitely avoid the highest of that lot.

"Worth cultivating," Andic said.

"Hmm." Now Funa sounded thoughtful.

And Jace became all too aware of the quickened throb of his pulse, the sweet tang of desire on the back of his tongue that he wanted to satisfy by kissing Glyssa, running his mouth over her body.

Unlike the other two, he didn't want to get mixed up with Glyssa. At least that's what his brain thought. His body was another matter. He let a sigh sift quietly out his nostrils. The odds of him being able to keep his hands off Glyssa Licorice were damn low. He wasn't much on resisting temptation.

Glyssa could feel Jace's—and others'—gaze on her as she walked to the items stacked in a neat pile: the picnic hamper, Lepid's basket, her large pursenal, and a giant duffle bag. The last was provided by Laev, her Family wouldn't have had the coat of arms put on the thing. She wasn't sure what all was in the bag. She touched the coat of arms, activating the anti-grav Flair spell. The duffle rose waist high.

Lepid jumped from her shoulder to the bag. It didn't even rock under his weight. She ran her finger under his collar. "This didn't catch on anything when you were underground?"

No. I found a secret way into the ship. I am a HERO.

She tapped his nose. "You scared me. And we must sync your collar synced to the medical clinic here. Especially if you can't be trusted to stay with me."

One of the owners of the project, Raz Cherry T'Elecampane, joined them, aiming a charming smile at them. "He'll be fine." Raz's smile widened. "Especially since my lady has a FoxFam, Shunuck, who will help you keep an eye on him."

Lepid's eyes rounded. *Another FoxFam!*

"That's right." Raz rubbed Lepid's head, tweaked his large ears. "My daughter and I have cat Fams. I assure you that they will also keep Lepid in line." He met Glyssa's eyes. "We've cleared an area near our pavilion to set up your own."

A pavilion! Did she have a pavilion? "Thank you." How close was it to Jace's? She still had to control her breath from the first sight of him, how he'd appeared more vivid than anyone else. Her heart still beat fast. Everything in her *yearned* for him . . . just to be in his company. But his eyes had been wary when they'd rested on her and she'd kept a mask on.

Raz T'Elecampane stared at her, raised a brow. She yanked her attention back to him.

He waved at the ship where his HeartMate stood with the pilot and some workers, uncrating the communications equipment.

"You have any ideas how that stuff goes together or works?"

"Oh!" Glyssa flushed. She bent down to her large pursenal and drew out a portfolio of papyrus along with a pack of recording spheres. "I'm sorry. Here are the specifications and the instructions."

Raz Elecampane gingerly took the objects, smiled her apology away. "I won't be handling this. I'm the people person."

She believed that, the man's charisma was palpable. He'd been a leading actor in Druida and at his own theater outside the city for years. She and her friends had taken turns with infatuations with him after seeing him perform when they were younger.

"Del!" he called. "I have the data!"

His HeartMate and wife looked up, strolled over with a long-legged stride that showed she'd walked the world. She nodded her curly and bright blond head to Glyssa, stuck out a hardened hand that Glyssa shook. "Greetyou, GrandMistrys Licorice. Good to have you here." She cocked a brow at Raz. "My HeartMate has been agitating for a better detailed record of the project." Del shrugged strong shoulders. "But I prefer to hire and pay excavators."

"Laev T'Hawthorn and Camellia D'Hawthorn are handling my salary," Glyssa said.

Del's mouth tightened. Raz frowned.

Del said, "We've tried to keep the FirstFamilies out of the project." She arrowed a look at Glyssa. "Especially Laev T'Hawthorn, that one is a pistol."

Raz took his HeartMate's arm. "We prefer to control the excavation of the ship," Raz said smoothly. They began walking from the landing field to the tent city organized into rows with one large red and yellow pavilion.

Glyssa nodded. "I can understand being wary of Laev. My best friend, Camellia Darjeeling, was sucked into his orbit a few months ago and suddenly here I am."

They laughed at that.

"Not that I don't have a burning curiosity." She glanced at the huge outline on the ground, under which they believed *Lugh's Spear* rested.

"I've heard your curiosity is as hot as your hair," Raz teased.

He was one to talk, his own hair was auburn.

I am red, too, Lepid said, looking at them. *And I am a hero. I opened up a new room and a hallway.*

They all stared at him.

"'Fools rush in,'" Raz murmured as if quoting, though Glyssa didn't recognize the words or the source.

"What did you see down there, fox?" asked Del.

BOXES! And a room! And a hallway!

"Boxes," Glyssa breathed, sharing a glance with Raz and Del.

Del took work gloves from her belt and slapped them on her thigh. "I'd better order some security around the hole. And we'll move the work there?" she asked her HeartMate.

"Absolutely," Raz said.

Lepid gave one more yip, danced the few steps along the duffle, then curled up and dropped into sleep.

"Young ones," Del said indulgently. She aimed her gaze at the hole. "You said you're friends with Camellia Darjeeling?" she asked Glyssa.

"Since grovestudy days."

"Huh. Camellia Darjeeling, who's now D'Hawthorn, helped us with the general blueprints," Del said.

"More." Glyssa angled her pursenal. "Camellia has finally parted with copies of the last Captain's, Netra Sunaya Hoku's, journals."

Raz and Del came to a stop, both staring at Glyssa. "You have them in there?" Del asked.

"Yes."

Del eyed her. "You might be worthwhile after all."

Raz bumped his HeartMate with his hip. "Helena D'Elecampane!"

"Thank you," Glyssa said. "I am humbled by your opinion. I will endeavor to live up to it." She dug into her bag and handed over copies of the original journals for the Elecampanes. She had a set of her own.

"Not much here," Del grumbled.

"The last Captain was awakened from the cryonics tubes to pilot the ship down. The journals provide great insights into the last days of the journey, the ship life—rather militaristic—and the previous Captain." Glyssa cleared her throat. "And as your own ancestor, the original D'Cherry, stated in her own diaries, Hoku was fond of maps."

Del stared at the papyrus, then glanced back toward the communications equipment. Sighing, she gestured to Raz to take the journals. "You look through the journals. Get Maxima, our daughter," she explained to Glyssa, gesturing to a small band of people in the distance, "in on it, too." She scanned Glyssa. "Hmmm. How'd you like an assistant? Maxima is interested in history and stuff."

"Sounds good," Glyssa lied.

After a sharp nod, Del walked back to the airship.

"We hadn't anticipated that the communications equipment would be so large. Larger than the space we'd dedicated for it." Raz shrugged. "Del will handle it."

"I'm sure," Glyssa said, falling into the easy pace he set as they moved toward the largest personal pavilion—not quite as large as what she reasoned was the mess tent farther down the large main pathway. "Del seems eminently efficient."

"Yes, and she's taken over the technical side of things, though she does love her maps."

"Her maps and charts are prized by the librarians," Glyssa offered.

"She'll never give up her cartographic career, though it is not as important to her—to us—as this project right now." Raz lit with an inner fire that Glyssa thought was all sincerity, no actor's show. "Imagine, uncovering the last starship! The wonders within, the knowledge we will discover about Earth and our ancestors." He pulled his mind from whatever visions spun in that creative head of his and gave himself a shake, aimed another charismatic smile at her. "And most of our team believe as we do, are as fascinated by the project as we are. One of the factors we considered when hiring, for instance, Jace Bayrum." Raz's eyes twinkled. He was an observant people person, all right.

They'd reached the Elecampane's pavilion and Raz moved toward an open area a couple of meters away. "This is your spot. We'll talk later," he said with a quick grin that was even more charming because it seemed more sincere. "About Captain Hoku, your duties, the excavation, the communications equipment. Everything."

"Thank you for this opportunity," Glyssa said. Weariness from her restless night before, the trip, the dazzling first sight of Jace, and the scare by Lepid began to weigh down on her.

"You're welcome," Raz said. "I think we will all work well together." He took her hand and bowed over it with the most grace she'd ever experienced, including Laev who'd been drilled in First-Families etiquette. When Raz straightened, he said, "Jace Bayrum is one of us, a believer in our quest." Raz paused. "However, I do not think Andic Sanicle or Funa Twinevine have that in common with us."

A delicate warning. Glyssa nodded. "Thank you."

"Midafternoon tea will be served in a few minutes, feel free to join us in the dining tent." With a last wave, he loped to his pavilion and disappeared, leaving Glyssa staring at a large area of cleared ground.

She stiffened her spine, not letting herself droop. The sun beat down on her, hot and affirming that she and her loved ones were alive—but also adding sticky sweat to her weariness. There weren't as many trees as she'd expected . . . cleared for the excavation, a wide meadow turned into a camp, surrounded by green and cool forests. She'd seen that as they landed, the width of the wide land between Fish Story Lake and the Deep Blue Sea.

With a touch on her duffle, she lowered it to the ground. Then she bent over and lifted Lepid, moving him to some cushy-looking ground cover she couldn't identify. Not many Earthan-Celtan hybrids here, she didn't think. Her own FamFox wriggled around a little, releasing a pleasant herbal tang into the air from his bedding, snuffled, but didn't wake. Good.

Eyeing the duffle, she figured out the opening mechanism was a simple slip-tab spell and ran her finger down the seam, saying a soft spellword. The bag yawned wide and showed a lot of unfamiliar items. Taking up a third of the area was a small no-time food storage unit. Glyssa stared. Her own personal no-time. She'd bet the last silver sliver of her salary that it was fully stocked. Amazing.

She took out the top object, four round sticks about the length of her hand with a wrapping of gossamer material. Heavy Flair spells clung to the thing, but she had no idea what it was or what to do with it.

More than the sun made her hot. She knew people were watching and the flush of embarrassment and irritation rose to her skin. Her cheeks must be red. She fought back tired, cranky, feeling-*stupid* tears.

Her HeartMate wanted to pretend they were strangers.

Six

Jace accepted claps on his shoulder and congratulations at saving the fox—and intense looks of envy that he'd been down again into the ship. Then Del Elecampane crisply asked for volunteers and people left him for the new communications equipment or for their own business.

His gaze went to Glyssa again and he saw Raz T'Elecampane walk away from her.

Jace was torn. He wanted to see—and put his hands on—the new equipment. But he also wanted to spend a little time with—and put his hands on, a lot—Glyssa Licorice.

And, yeah, he'd like to see what was in that duffle from Outside Outfitters, probably the latest in camping equipment. With his usual curiosity, he wondered what that looked like. Maybe he needed to know—a good rationalization.

Emotions churned inside him, aided by the dump of adrenaline in chasing the fox down to the corridor of *Lugh's Spear*, the discovery of the rooms, the near loss of the fox and the triumphant return. Maybe that's why his pulse surged when he'd seen her.

He wasn't quite sure *what* he felt about her being here. Resentment that she'd shown up as if she were following him? Couldn't be.

She hadn't appeared last year. Though he—they?—had been having those sex dreams.

Eh, he didn't want to think of his emotions, he'd figure them out later. His gaze was drawn to her, probably something that would happen often since her hair shone red and coppery in the sun.

When she stared flushed and furious at the small package she held, shaking the compacted pavilion in her hands, he sauntered over. She sure did smell good.

"Can I help?" he asked.

She scowled at him, her prettily arched cinnamon brows wrenched down. Her lips flattened—they looked so much nicer when she smiled—before she said primly, "Yes, please." She angled her head as if she suspected he was laughing at her.

He kept his smug smile from showing and held out his hand.

He must not have been as expressionless as he'd thought since she smacked the sticks and the thin gauze into his palm.

"Not done much outside living?" he asked, unrolling the gauze from the Flaired set-up sticks. Such compact equipment. Nice.

"No," she said.

"This is your pavilion." He bent down and tapped one stick into the hard ground with an anchor spell.

"That!"

She sounded so disbelieving he glanced up at her with a smile. "You need to get out of your library more often, Red."

She sniffed, tapped her foot, then crouched down beside him. "Tell me how to help, and how it works."

"We've got curiosity in common," he said, rising and unrolling the line of gauze to the next stick. A lot of gauze, a huge pavilion.

"Yes." She followed him, and smiled. The tension line between her brows released. Maybe she liked looking at him as much as he liked looking at her.

"This is a Flaired pavilion, built mostly of magic."

"Hmmm."

"You noticed how much Flair it contained?"

"Oh, yes, my hands tingled."

"I'd say the spell is funded for at least a year."

"A year!"

He cocked a brow at her. "Someone wanted to make sure it didn't fail. Good security spells, too, so you'll be safe. Someone imbued it with a lot of power." He took the next stick from her and tapped it down.

"That would be GreatLord Laev T'Hawthorn," she said. Jace scowled at the idea of another man doing so much for her—until he saw her staring at his backside.

"GreatLord T'Hawthorn?" Jace prompted. This had to be her FirstFamily noble connection, and what a connection—with one of the richest men on the planet.

"Um," she said, then smiled shyly at him, palm out for the third stick. "Can I unroll it?"

"Sure. You call him Laev?" Jace couldn't let the mention of another man stand as it was.

She began to unroll the gauze on the ground, stopped every few steps to make sure it was perfectly straight. Looked like the pavilion was a boring rectangle to Jace. He'd have gone for an octagon or something.

"Laev is one of my best friend's husband and HeartMate," she said. She bent down to move a rock out of the way of the gauze. "Camellia Darjeeling." Again Glyssa smiled. "More like a sister to me."

He finally recognized the name in connection with Glyssa. When he and Glyssa had spent that long weekend together, they hadn't talked much. But she had mentioned her friends, like now. He'd forgotten their names.

He recalled that he and Glyssa had just had sex and ate and slept a little and had sex again. No. Don't think of that. Don't think of this nice large pavilion that must include a private bedroom, or what kind of bedsponge she might have.

She was taking twice the time to run the line of gauze than he had. Usually he'd get impatient, and was a bit surprised that he wasn't. He enjoyed her company, just being with her, not quite soothing, but she didn't irritate him with excessive energy, either. They seemed to match.

She stopped. "Did we put the door on the south? I don't like a south-facing door. I prefer an east-facing door. I like morning sunlight."

Jace grit his teeth as he stared at the lines they'd run. He knew enough about Flaired gauze to understand it had to be handled carefully. Even top-of-the-pyramid stuff, like this.

"If you set the door to the east, you'll face the Elecampane's tent and not the main path through the camp," he said.

Her chin set stubbornly.

He gestured to the gauze. "And working with that stuff, winding and unwinding, can get messy. One of the reasons the Elecampanes went with old-fashioned Flaired-canvas."

She pouted. "Oh." But she didn't go on unrolling the line, just looked at what they'd laid out.

Jace suppressed the urge to walk away and let her deal with the setup on her own. "I don't know about the latest in these sorts of pavilions, but I heard that the best have an option to determine windows as needed."

"Oh!" She brightened, sighed a little, then shook her head. "Laev bought all the gear. We Licorices do not believe in spending such gilt on our persons."

Her Family had been nobles since the second generation of colonists, they must have money, and they didn't use it to make their lives more comfortable? Jace's brows rose but he kept his mouth shut.

Glyssa looked toward her duffle that must contain wonderful stuff. "There should be instructions in there on how to make windows."

"I can help you with that," Jace said.

She nodded and began her slow, picky, progress again. He heard shouts of satisfaction from the area set aside for the new communications instruments—what looked like a series of small, thin wire grids. "Rumors have it that we will be testing a new communications system."

"Oh, yes," Glyssa said. "Laev is working with *Nuada's Sword* and Dani Eve Elder, a commander of that Ship, to put an artificial satellite into orbit around Celta, based on ancient Earthan data, since our Celtan science is not like the old tech."

Jace stopped. "Put equipment into space!"

"Yes." Glyssa stopped frowning at the straight line of gauze and looked up at him with a smile. "Curious?"

"Oh, yeah!"

She sighed. "I'm sure that *Nuada's Sword* will viz the launch of the satellite for all of the city of Druida, and maybe the closer towns, to see."

"We'll miss it," Jace said, disappointed.

"Yes, we will." She handed him the next peg and he set it in the ground, repeated the spell aloud for her so she could do the last one on her own.

Glyssa stared at the outline of *Lugh's Spear.* "This ship wasn't sentient like *Nuada's Sword.*"

"No, a pity," Jace said.

"You think?" She shook her head. "I don't. How horrible it would have been for the ship to have known it was dying . . . that no one could save it. None of the colonists had the means to rescue it."

Jace shuddered. "Hadn't thought of it that way. Trapped and unable to be saved. Terrible, all right."

She'd stopped when he'd kept going and his step brought him close to her. Closer than any but lovers should be. He took a pace away, didn't like how his heart leapt when his body had brushed hers. He thought he saw disappointment in her face.

Glyssa *was* disappointed. Reluctantly she placed the last small spike, pointed end down, checked twice to make sure it was in line with all the other corners, and murmured the raising spell. The gauze stretched to two-meter-high walls, took on a purple tint—Laev T'Hawthorn's color—as they became opaque. There was even a pointed top to the pavilion and what appeared to be vents. Occasional markings showed and as she studied them, she saw that they looked like spaces for windows.

Even as she turned to Jace, he'd walked to the eastern side, narrowed his gaze, and dragged his finger in a rectangle high in the tent wall where the sun would angle as it rose.

Lepid jumped to his feet, shook himself out and yipped, running straight into the door opening.

Our space! Ours! It is a big tent!

"A pavilion," Glyssa corrected automatically. She went to the door, gestured for Jace.

He tucked his fingers into his belt, rocked back on his heels and shook his head.

Her smile faded and her jaw clenched, but she pushed through the light shield of the door—had Laev tuned it for her and Lepid? Amazing Flair—to see her FamFox prancing around.

It is big for the camp, he said, *but not as big as our house or our library.*

He leapt up and she caught him in her arms, snuggling with him, and took him on the very short tour. The pavilion was nothing short of impressive. It actually had *three* rooms. An outer room like a sitting room, complete with space for the no-time food storage unit, a bedroom only slightly smaller, and her very own tiny toilet and waterfall room. What luxury. When Laev T'Hawthorn bought something, it was the most lavish item possible.

She went back out to exclaim her pleasure to Jace, and see what other furnishings might be in the huge bag, but he was gone. Dammit!

And she barely saw him the rest of the day. She ate in the Elecampanes' tent, discussing the new communications instrumentation and her duties, the new communications system and Maxima helping her, *Nuada's Sword* launching the communications satellite, and the excavation.

By the time they were done hashing out the security for the new hole down to *Lugh's Spear*, and the revised plan for earth removal from the site, night had fallen and she'd dragged herself and a snoozing Lepid into their pavilion . . . where she'd increased the size of the furniture and set it up, along with lovely rugs for the sitting room, and the latest in thick, portable bedsponges, big enough for the two of them, though her FoxFam headed for his own basket.

As a finishing touch, she hung the mobile containing a thousand colorful cranes she'd made a while back using her creative Flair for origami.

With the last spurt of Flair energy she had, she contacted Camellia telepathically. *I am here and doing well.*

Lovely to hear! Her friend sounded cheery, lively . . . well, it was a couple of hours earlier in Druida City. So strange, this time difference, something Glyssa had never had to consider or take into account before.

Is he as gorgeous as you remember? asked Camellia.

More. Older, more muscles. Glyssa laughed. She recalled her first glimpse of him that had dazzled her. He looked like a poet or a dreamer, narrow face with dark brown hair and deep auburn highlights . . . but, of course his bold and wild silver gray eyes gave him away.

He wasn't a dreamer, more like a swashbuckler.

A wonderful word, ancient and Earthan. Glyssa rolled it in her mouth. Swashbuckler. She just wished it didn't apply to her Heart-Mate. She didn't think swashbucklers were all that stable as lovers. Well, she'd already found that out, hadn't she?

Is he kind? demanded Camellia.

More like dangerous, but Glyssa wouldn't tell her friend that. Dangerously exciting. Camellia prized kindness in men. *He helped me set up the pavilion.*

Oh, good! Camellia said.

Glyssa yawned. Her weariness must have been transmitted along the sister-friendship-bond because Camellia said, *You've had a very long day. Thank you for letting me know all is well.*

Welcome, Glyssa said. *Merry meet and merry part.*

And merry meet again, love you.

I love you, too. 'Night.

Her FoxFam gave a fake snore even as she petted him.

"Good night, Lepid," she muttered as she changed into her nightgown and fell onto the bed, pulling up the thin and bespelled covering that wouldn't keep her too warm or too cold.

Good night, FamWoman.

The last thing she said was, "I worry about you, please stay in the tent."

*H*elp! *Help! Something pawed at Jace. He opened his eyes to too-close* predator muzzle and bad FoxFam breath, sat up so the fox tumbled from his lap, felt the slightest dig of sharp claws in his groin and woke fast.

Help! the fox yipped again.

Jace scanned the animal in the gloom of his tent. Looked okay to him. "What?" he grumbled.

There is a hurt Fam. Come!

Grunting, Jace threw off the bespelled and padded cover and rolled off the bedsponge. For an instant he envied Glyssa her wonderful tent that she could stand up in instead of hunch. A hurt Fam. The crew had a few, he thought, though they kept close to their people and tents. Fams were still rare and prized.

The most adventuresome were, of course, those companioned with the owners: Shunuk the FoxFam, Rosemary and Carolinia the cat Fams. Shunuk had more experience than Jace, so he figured the wounded Fam wasn't him. In any case, saving any Fam would be a heroic thing to do.

Which was why Lepid was here, he was sure. Nipping at Jace's ankle as he drew on a shirt.

Come, come! Lepid sunk his teeth into the bottom of the old, soft trous Jace wore to bed and pulled, ripping.

"Stop that. I'm coming as fast as I can."

HURT.

Okay, that was a cause for concern. He tugged on half boots, hoping he wouldn't have to travel far, wished he could dress a little more in protective clothing. "Why aren't you bothering Glyssa?" Jace grumbled.

She would scold. She told me to stay in the tent. Place is too little.

Yeah, right. No doubt she was sleeping right now on a bedsponge big enough for two. Where he'd like to be.

And you and I shared an adventure, already! Lepid dashed out of the tent and danced impatiently. Most of the local animals had been scared away from the encampment area and there were wards against the dangerous ones. Still, Jace strapped on his old blazer that could only stun and hoped it would be sufficient. A wounded animal—Fam or not—would bring predators.

With another grunt, Jace exited. Lepid took off running, as fast as his young and small legs could take him. Jace started out at a trot, feeling older this morning just from watching the Fam. They headed south, in the direction of the Deep Blue Sea.

Oh, yeah, Glyssa would like that her FamFox had left the camp entirely.

The morning light spilled over the horizon in long shoots of sunlight. Another beautiful summer day.

Frantic FamFox barks sounded and Jace put on speed, stretching his muscles. Felt good. He saw Lepid scaring birds, as big as he was and with wicked beaks, away from a dark lump on the ground. FamFox didn't have much sense. Glyssa would not approve of this adventure, either.

Jace lengthened his stride, his breathing a little rapid, but not too bad. Still in good shape. Could run for another couple of kilometers.

He is here! Lepid had turned in Jace's direction and bounced up and down on his paws. *Hurry!*

"Who does he belong to?" asked Jace. Something odd about the fallen animal.

I . . . be . . . long . . . to . . . my . . . self. Large . . . man. The voice in Jace's head came high, with sighing air-notes.

"Who's his companion?"

Seven

The FoxFam just shook his head, and as Jace took the last few meters, the lump became a bird. A large, predatory bird. Jace slowed his run. He didn't know of any BirdFams. Not in the camp, not at all.

He stopped and squatted by the bird, a Celtan bird called a hawkcel, as long as his forearm. He didn't look good. Blood on his chest and one wing was broken. Beautiful bird with rust-colored, black and white feathers, a touch of yellow around the glazed eye. Made Jace's chest hurt. "How are you doing?"

With . . . care . . . I . . . will . . . live, he said.

Jace wasn't too sure. He seemed to be breathing too fast. Who knew?

Take him to camp! Lepid insisted.

"Of course," Jace said, a little too heartily. He sucked in a breath through his nose. "I'm going to lift you now."

The bird's eye closed.

Jace slid his hands under the bird, lifted, trying to ignore the wicked beak that could rip his arm open.

Thank . . . man. The bird went limp, and Jace tensed. He cradled him against his chest and ran fast back to the camp, that had begun to stir. The Healers—two—who manned the medtent got up early.

52

People liked to walk at dawn and look at the pretty scenery and sometimes came back injured from the wilds.

He got to the clinic and found the flap tied back, a small wavering spellshield against dust and bugs showing in the opening. Hunching his body over the bird, he pushed through.

"What's wrong?" asked the Healer, standing behind a high table with a bedsponge.

"Bird," Jace said.

"A *bird!* We don't treat birds here." The Healer stepped back, a disgusted expression on his face.

"He's a Fam," Jace said.

Lepid hopped onto a stool, mouth open and tongue lolling. *We will take him to D'Ash! She is a wonderful Fam Healer!*

Jace spared Lepid a glance. "D'Ash is a long way away."

"There are no BirdFams in camp," the Healer said decidedly.

"He's sentient," Jace insisted. "Can you please look at him? Maybe splint his wing?"

"Birds are dirty and carry disease," the Healer said.

"Lepid, go wake the other Healer. They share the green tent, the one that—"

Smells like Healers. I know that one! I saw it last night when I explored. I go! He hopped down and ran out the door.

"Wait," the Healer protested. "She didn't get much sleep last night."

"Wonder why," Jace grumbled. *They'd* had sex and he hadn't. He felt deprived. "I'm putting the bird down."

Carefully, he set the FamBird on the bedsponge table on its uninjured side. "Bird, can I wipe down your chest with a wet cloth—water?"

The bird struggled a little. Jace stroked his head with his finger. "Steady, you're safe. I won't let anything happen to you."

Breast . . . does . . . not . . . need . . . outside . . . care. I . . . can . . . Heal . . . myself. Jace hadn't known that FamBirds could lie so well. Obviously the hawkcel was too much of a predator to allow himself to show weakness. Then he moved slightly, turning his head and Jace saw the gleam in his eye—as if just being away from outside gave the Fam hope. He trusted people for some reason, and for a hawkcel in this area, that was puzzling.

Wing . . . hurts. Perhaps not as alpha as Jace thought.

"I heard that, I think," said the female Healer, bustling in with a cheerful smile. She glanced at her colleague and snorted. "Your scared-of-animals thing slow you down?"

"Look at that beak and those claws!" the man protested.

Lepid followed and hopped back up on the stool, yipped. *HE IS NOT AN ANIMAL! HE IS A BIRD.*

The Healers winced. "And I definitely heard that, FoxFam. Don't project so loudly," the woman said, then cooed over the bird, stroking the feathers around the puncture in his breast. "We'll take care of you." She touched the wound and Jace sensed her sending Healing Flair into the bird, mending tissues. The avian Fam relaxed a bit more.

"How did you get hurt?" Jace asked.

The hawkcel rolled his eye. *Fighting two others for a wounded groundruck. They are tasty. I lost.*

"How come you're intelligent?"

We have been intelligent for generations. We have watched the camp and the people. Most humans have good energy.

"Good morning, Symphyta, Trago, Jace." Glyssa walked in. She stared at Lepid. "Where have you been? I thought I asked you to stay in the pavilion."

Lepid turned his head to Jace. *We went on a walk. We found a wounded BIRDFAM!*

So FoxFams could lie, too. But were damn clever. As Lepid no doubt expected, Glyssa's attention focused on the hawkcel on the table. "Oh, poor thing." She used almost the same coo as the female Healer, Symphyta, had.

The man stalked from behind the table. "Too crowded in this one-table, backwoods, forsaken clinic. I'm getting breakfast, maybe hear some more about those boxes you discovered." He nodded to Jace. "Much more interesting and lucrative than treating some stupid hawkcel."

"I'll join you," Jace said, turning for the door opening.

A screech came from the bird. *NO! My FamMan stays!*

Catching his breath, Jace pivoted back. "FamMan, bird?"

He clicked his beak. *Yes. I like you. You have nice hands. You are my FamMan.* Another small click. *I need a human to help me.*

Warmth settled around Jace's heart. Fams were still uncommon and prized and went to nobles first. Usually. He inclined his torso a little. "Honored."

The male Healer, Trago, snorted and left.

"BirdFam, Jace will grasp your wing and hold it out so I can look at the bones that need setting, then place them correctly. You will not bite or claw me," Symphyta said, gesturing to Jace for him to take the two steps to the table. Glyssa faded back near the stool where her own Fam sat and rubbed his head. Lepid blinked slyly at Jace. Yeah, they'd gotten around the sexy librarian.

Tentatively, Jace found the bones at the end of his *new Fam's wing*, gently stretched it out as the female Healer moved the hawkcel onto its back.

My name is Zem, the bird said, fixing his eyes on Jace.

"Thank you," Jace said.

Humming tunelessly and working quickly the Healer examined the wing Jace held. He didn't break his gaze with his Fam . . . a connection was spinning between them and he realized the bird gained strength and calm from him. So he lowered into his balance and concentrated on keeping steady.

The bird flinched. Both women murmured soothing words louder. Lepid hummed nasally. Jace sent calm and energy to Zem.

A few minutes later, the female Healer said, "Done. The bones are set and I gave them a little Healing boost." Her smile curved her lips and faded fast. "I'm not an animal Healer."

"Thank you," Jace said. "How much do I owe—"

"I'm not an animal Healer," she said as if affronted, but her eyes were kind. "No charge."

Zem hopped to his feet, looking much better, and walked over to Jace. Keeping an eye on sharp talons, Jace folded his left arm across his body for a perch, then lifted his Fam, who settled against him with a tiny exhalation. *FamMan.*

"Yes," Jace said, petting the bird's head. Such soft feathers. He thought that was why the women cooed. Despite beak and claws, the bird's body looked soft.

Symphyta briskly cleansed the table with a spell couplet, looking in the direction of the dining tent where the other Healer was. "I think I need to acquire a personal tent of my own, and my judgment in men is not as good as I'd believed. Being a Healer doesn't automatically mean you're a good person." She sounded as if she scolded herself, then glanced at Glyssa, who had an arm around Lepid. The FoxFam leaned against her.

"I'm here for the adventure like most of us, sure," Symphyta said. "But I'm a Healer, first and always, not a treasure hunter." She switched her gaze to study Jace. "You're not still sleeping with Funa, are you?"

Glyssa jolted.

Jace kept a smile on his face. "No." He didn't look at Glyssa, and unlike the other males in the room, didn't want to lie. "But I'm not available." He wasn't sure of his feelings, especially for Glyssa. She seemed to want to get closer, but the remote camp wasn't like an anonymous social club in Druida City you could just walk away from. Sexing with someone always sent ripples through the community. He didn't want that.

Symphyta said, "Pity you're unavailable. I heard you're a better lover than Healer Trago."

Why did women talk about these things?

"Well, when they get the communications thing going, I'll order a tent from Druida and have the pilot bring it the next time a flight comes."

"I wish you well," Jace said.

She offered a hand and a smile. "We haven't spoken much or gotten to know each other, yet. Friends?"

He clasped her fingers, released them. "Friends."

Symphyta turned to Glyssa and Lepid. "Welcome to the camp, GrandMistrys Licorice."

"Call me Glyssa." She offered her own hand and it looked as if she squeezed warmly. Her smile was genuine, too. "This is Lepid." She stroked the FoxFam, her eyes warm and tender with a gaze Jace wouldn't mind seeing aimed at him.

"Lepid, eh?" Symphyta said.

Yes.

"You went down in the hole to *Lugh's Spear* yesterday and discovered the boxes," the Healer said.

Lepid's small chest expanded. *Yes!*

"With Jace. And walked with Jace this morning and found Zem."

Yes!

"And are a young fox." Symphyta met Glyssa's gaze. "I'm not an animal Healer but I do my best to help as a Healer for the camp Fams."

"Thank you," Glyssa said, then added firmly, "And we need to key Lepid's collar retrieval spell to this clinic." Glyssa frowned. "Though I'm not sure I trust Trago."

The Healer shrugged. "Maybe when I order that tent, I'll put out the word that the camp could use another Healer, see if we pick up anyone."

"That sounds good," Glyssa said. She dug into her trous pocket and pulled out a piece of gilt. "Will that cover the fee?"

"For sure. C'mere, fox." Symphyta patted the table.

Lepid whined.

Not sure I like a wimpy foxkit in my territory, said a loud telepathic voice.

Jace and Glyssa turned toward the scruffy FoxFam sitting on the threshold of the door. He was Del D'Elecampane's Fam, who'd traveled continents with her one step at a time as she mapped Celta.

Lepid snapped his teeth. *I am a HERO!*

"Lepid!" Glyssa scolded, sounding horrified. Jace settled back on his heels, stroking Zem and suppressing a smile. The interaction between the reckless foxkit and strict Glyssa would be entertaining.

I am Shunuk, this is my FamWoman's camp, the other fox asserted. *So far you have fallen down a hole and dragged back a sick bird.*

"Hey!" Jace protested, recalled who he spoke to, and moderated his tones. "Most excellent FoxFam Shunuk, may I introduce you to my new HawkcelFam, Zem?"

Zem clicked his beak once. *FoxFam,* he said. His mental voice sounded deep, manly, though Jace wouldn't say that aloud. Better than any of the other Fams in camp.

Shunuk rumbled. *May I sniff?*

"I don't know," Jace answered. "Are you going to hurt my Fam?"

Of course not! But I have not seen a BirdFam before. Does it smell different?

"I don't know." Jace kept a smile on his face. "Zem?"

He may sniff, Zem said in a quiet mental voice that Jace knew only he could hear. The notion of a private telepathic channel with his Fam warmed him with affection, too.

Lowering into a crouch, Jace watched keenly as Shunuk sniffed Zem.

He is an acceptable Fam, Shunuk said, then whirled and snapped at Lepid, who leapt to the bedsponge and was restrained by the Healer.

Shunuk chortled. *You are only provisionally accepted, foxkit.* The older fox swaggered out, tail gently waving.

"Stay still, Lepid," the Healer said. "The sooner you stop this wriggling, the sooner I can set the retrieval spell."

Lepid caught Jace's eye and glared.

Was promised a treat. YESTERDAY! Have not gotten a treat.

This time Jace reached into his pocket, drew out a bit of fur-rabeast jerky, snapped a bite off and tossed it to Lepid who snagged it with his teeth and gobbled it down.

Zem's head tilted and his bright black gaze fixed on Jace. *I would like some of that, too. But not for treat, for food.*

Jace gave him a small bite. "We'll go get you food at the breakfast tent. And show you around. Later, ladies."

Later, ladies, projected Zem.

They left Lepid whining.

* * *

$\mathcal{M}$idmorning, *Glyssa stood with most of the camp, watching the hole* with the girder being widened with manual labor, spellcasting, and Flaired machines working together.

Lepid sat a half meter away from her, still peeved at her for keying his collar to the Healing clinic. He'd informed her with wide tail lashes that the BirdFam, Zem, needed him to capture live and newly dead prey for food. Lepid would spend several septhours a day doing that until Zem had healed enough to hunt his own food.

Zem particularly liked fish, but Lepid was unsure of his hunting skills in that area.

The images that rose to her mind when informed of this gave Glyssa the queasies, but she just agreed through a tight throat. She stated her expectations, too, that Lepid go slowly and not fish by himself, and that she wished he would remain in the tent at night with her.

He'd just sniffed.

Jace sauntered to her, Zem perched on his newly padded shoulder. *Greetyou, Glyssa,* said Zem.

"Greetyou, Zem." Glyssa gave a little curtsey to the bird. Her curiosity about him had been roused earlier, and she was pleased that she now had something more in common with Jace—a Fam. She knew from experience that a FamPerson could talk about their companion for hours.

She glanced at Jace, knowing she didn't dare push him. Too many other unattached female arms she could drive him into. He was also the kind of man who liked to initiate most sexual moves. Didn't stop her body from tingling in his vicinity.

So she kept a blandly pleasant expression on her face and said, "And thank you, GentleSir Bayrum, for walking with Lepid this morning."

Jace ducked his head, a slight flush came to his tanned cheeks. "We aren't formal here. Please call me Jace . . . Glyssa."

"Thank you," she said simply.

A huge grinding noise came and they both focused their attention on the hole—it appeared a portion of the starship had been found and peeled back!

"Oh!" She grinned, knew her eyes sparkled, and shared a look with Jace.

He smiled back at her. "Looks like after two years we are finally making progress."

She shifted from foot to foot. "I'm so pleased to be here during this momentous time."

"Yeah." He tilted his head. "And record it?"

"Yes." Did she dare refer to their past fling? She didn't think so.

The next septhour showed excruciatingly slow progress on the hole—they hadn't wanted to harm the outer shell of the spaceship. But standing with Jace, listening to his comments, being in his company, was luxurious. Even though something low and needy throbbed inside her.

At the end, the Elecampanes called a halt after the descent and tunnel was opened and cleared, then set a guard by the hole.

Most people wandered away and Glyssa knew Jace would follow if she didn't detain him. Clearing her throat, not quite looking at him, she said, "I spent much of yesterday setting up my tent."

He looked down at her with a mild expression in his eyes, but one quirked eyebrow. "It's a pavilion."

She felt heat on her cheeks, cleared her throat *again* reflexively, why did she *do* that, and continued, "I spent yesterday setting up and arranging the pavilion I was given. Would you show me around the camp?" That was about as far as she'd push right now.

He hesitated too long, but her ego was saved when Lepid raced back to her and jumped around her feet. *I will show you the camp! I know all the tents! I know all who live in the tents!* He sniffed lustily as if demonstrating the power of his nose. *I know where everything is!*

"Thank you." She crouched down and ran her fingers through the soft fur of her dusty pet. "I'd like to see Fish Story Lake and the Deep Blue Sea, also."

They are not near flights, Zem said.

Jace added, "Both are some kilometers away. In that, Captain Hoku chose his spot well, to land the starship *Lugh's Spear* midway between them. We don't have personal vehicles here, and only the few who have been here through previous seasons can chance teleporting. There *is* a stable, as a few hardy souls rode here across the continent. A dozen stridebeasts. But most of us must walk when we have the time and inclination to do so."

Stretching her mouth in a too-bright smile, she looked up at him—he was scowling—and said, "I understand."

He jerked a nod, tilted his head in the direction of the communications equipment that the Elecampanes had moved on to rearrange. "Later, Glyssa."

Good afternoon, Glyssa, Zem said.

"Yes, later. Good afternoon, Zem," she replied faintly, covering the huge well of disappointment inside her.

Jace strode away from her and she spent the day with her Fox-Fam, forcing herself to banish the letdown and enjoy the simple pleasure of Lepid's company as she bonded more deeply with him.

The camp was set up in orderly rows, comprised of all sorts of tents—and two living pavilions—hers and the Elecampanes'. The large mess tent was in the middle of the camp, the four cleansing tents and four latrine tents at the edge, and a storage and workshop near the middle. The stable was toward the south, closer to the Deep Blue Sea side of the encampment.

She was impressed by the organization that provided both closeness and privacy if a person wanted such.

As the sun set and twilight deepened the sky, stars appeared. Many more stars than she could see in Druida, thick spangles.

She sat in one of the two camp chairs she'd placed before her pavilion. Lepid curled on her lap, ready to talk to every curious passerby and be petted in between visits.

Jace didn't stop by. At first that irritated her—then she just *knew* that they'd be dreaming together tonight. The bonds between them had arisen and twined, thick sensuality layering and cycling back and forth.

They'd enjoy dream sex that she hoped to turn into more than sex, true loving. Become more than occasional lovers—friends. HeartMates.

She just had to figure out how to make that happen.

Glyssa shared some talk with Funa Twinevine and Andic Sanicle, definitely adventurers with an eye on her because of her connection with Camellia and Laev—whom she'd admitted knowing. She thought Lepid had been indiscreet in that matter, chattering about his noble friends.

He liked his glory, her FamFox.

Symphyta, the Healer, whom Lepid studiously ignored, also dropped by. The woman good-naturedly answered Glyssa's questions regarding the staff's and the camp's history. Enough so that Glyssa knew she could really dig more data from the Healer, especially if she served good food and drink. The camp food was simple and filling, but the Healer appreciated the last delicacies packed in the trip basket.

Finally, reluctantly, the Healer rose from her chair with a sigh and a grimace, saying she was sharing a tent with Funa Twinevine— not that Funa would be there most nights. The woman liked her lovers.

The stream of people coming to visit with Glyssa dwindled. She saw the other Healer, Trago, start down her aisle, then he spotted Lepid and turned back. No loss there.

But the serenity of the night, the lovely weight of her Fam on her lap, and the gentle camaraderie had worked on her, soothing her from the slight rebuff Jace had given her in the morning, and his lack of company this evening.

So she let the quietude of the extraordinary place, the different atmosphere showcasing the soft velvet of the sky and diamond brightness of the twinmoonslight and starshine, encompass her. She leaned back and *felt* the link between her and her lover, her Heart-Mate, hum with anticipation.

Soon they would love.

Eight

Glyssa waited until no one walked the hard earth of the camp pathways before she went to the cleansing tent. The waterfall in her pavilion took more water than she was comfortable hogging.

She didn't like the camp showers—they were antique and stingy showers, not the lush waterfalls that most city residents were accustomed to. The recycled water here had a distinct odor. The only good thing she could say about them was that they were better than any cleansing spell and they relieved the heat of the late summer days.

After her shower, she felt less sticky and just plain better, as if her body was finally adjusting to the local day/night cycle. Lepid, who'd kept her cheerful company both coming and going on her walk, hadn't seemed to have had any trouble whatsoever with the change in time . . . perhaps hadn't even noticed it.

As she returned, she saw a few spellglobes in tents, but quiet enveloped the camp. Lepid pushed his basket to the sitting room, before a low window she'd made just for him to look out, and curled up without complaint. She decided that the day of exploration and activity had tired him—and that his behavior was suspiciously docile. He might be hoping to slip out of the tent as he had done that morning.

She toyed with the notion of invoking a spellshield to keep him in, but that showed little trust for her Fam, and all relationships were built on trust. Her FamFox now had a collar that would teleport him to the Healing clinic, and most of the staff had seen him and knew him . . . and gossip certainly traveled fast in the camp. She'd know almost immediately if he got into trouble again.

Glyssa smiled as she heard too-loud-fake-snoring from her Fam, but said nothing. Tonight she intended to have another dream sexual encounter with her HeartMate and it was just as well that Lepid was at the far front corner of the tent from her bed. That would be good when, hopefully, she and Jace made love in reality. She'd already slipped a silence spell on the bedroom walls—they'd be able to hear sounds, but no one, not even Lepid, would hear her or her lover.

She dressed in a thin, white linen nightgown that was barely opaque, deliberately purchased for Jace. She'd discovered during that wild weekend that he became more aroused when she was in a few clothes rather than totally naked. She thought the nightgown would tantalize him, too.

"Good night, Lepid. I love you," she called from the opening of her bedroom.

Good night, FamWoman. I love you, he replied.

Then she waved her hand and the flap between the sitting room and bedroom rolled down. She held her breath, but her Fam didn't object . . . in fact, he went back to his fake snoring.

Settling onto the cushy and comfortable bedsponge, large enough for two, she set the intention in her mind to visit her HeartMate in her dreams. Dream sex, then true rest for the remainder of the night sounded excellent.

Sleep and lucid dreaming came quickly. She stood over the man who lay on a mattress supported by a cot. Close by, *his* FamBird sat on a perch, head bowed, beak tucked into his front feathers, sleeping. She smiled, then glanced at Jace again, seeing the glitter of his gaze as he stared at her face—no doubt pale, though blood flooded her cheeks as his scrutiny went to her breasts until her nipples tightened, then he scanned down to the shadow between her thighs.

Her blood pounded and she knew she flushed more, including her breasts. Her knees weakened and breath came quick and her insides quivered with desire as her body readied for him—his touch, his sex inside her.

Even as her mind spun, and she swallowed, she understood that this night needed to be more than physical intimacy. She needed to move their fling into the past, ensure that sex moved more into loving. How, she wasn't sure, but could only follow her instinct . . . and her heart.

So she smiled with all the tenderness, all the joy she felt at seeing him again, finally being with him. Everything she could show him, and that he would accept here in dreams, that he might shun in the public light of day in the camp.

"Jace," she whispered, and thought *beloved*. Again she swallowed, held out a hand. "I want you." Her hand trembled. "Do you want me? Here? Now?"

He flung off a thin blanket and stood, naked, ready for sex. In the dream there was twinmoonslight that limned the fine bones of his face, touched the glitter of his eyes with silver. And tonight she saw him better, their bond not so stretched over a long distance.

She touched his chest, muscles more defined than they'd been, wider, and with a few scars. Smiling, she trailed fingers to his hips, then back up, rubbing his tiny nipples. He shuddered and a pulse of pleasure surged through her that she could please him, that they would rise to ecstasy together, explode into release together.

She wet her lips and he groaned, bent his head, kissed her, then his hands settled on her hips, brought her close so that she felt his passion. Her lust spiked, she wanted to be naked, too, reached down and yanked up handfuls of cloth.

His mouth brushing against hers, tantalizing, lifted and curved in a wicked smile. "Shhh," he said. "Let me." His eyes were half-closed and she knew she'd judged him right. He liked her partially clothed best.

He let loose of her hips, then took the gown, pulled it back with a fist on the curve of her bottom until the little excess material was tight against her, binding around her breasts and hips. He stepped back, looked at her, and even in the dim light she could see that his cheeks and lips darkened with his own sexual flush.

"Jace," she panted. Her nipples felt too tight, and the cloth chafed them slightly, pinging sizzles of desire through her. She took a step forward, pressed against him again, *rubbed* against him, his sex thick and hard against her abdomen, her breasts against his chest.

"Lord and Lady, woman!" He picked her up and tossed her onto the cot and bedsponge. Surprisingly comfortable . . . he lifted her hips, pulled her gown up to her waist, then lowered himself on her. His left hand turned her head; she must have looked startled because he chuckled. His right hand was busy sliding down the front opening tab on the yoke of her nightgown, slipping inside and palming her breast, thumb flicking over her nipple, making her twist, needing more, needing him.

"Jace."

In a low voice, he said, "I like how you say my name, especially breathless like that." His smile turned wicked. "I like you breathless and writhing." His lips were hard on hers now and she groaned and opened her mouth and let his tongue plunge into her, sucked on his—that simply tasted of Jace, a flavor she'd never forgotten. She yearned to taste him for real, not this shadow taste of memory. Soon. Soon. She hoped. She prayed.

His hand skimmed from her breast lower, stopped as he reached the end of the yoke opening.

Any other man would have ripped the gown from her. Not Jace. He took his hand from inside her gown, shifted.

And in that few seconds of reprieve from his tormenting touch, she understood what she needed to do . . . simple and instinctive. Give. Give herself to him, give him all the tenderness, all the loving, all the respect she felt for him. Hold nothing back.

So when he touched her damp folds between her thighs, stroked and drove her mad with need for him, she surrendered.

He was repeating something, but her mind had hazed so much, the yearning spiraling so high within her that she couldn't understand him. Her hands clenched over his shoulders, distantly she heard her own whimpers. He was so much larger that she couldn't move, especially not in desperate need.

But she could tilt her hips, rotate them, tease *him*. Set her hands on his shoulders, dig her fingernails into his skin.

Which had him groaning, swearing, and lunging into her.

The rhythm, the connection between them perfected. Almost, almost, she could see the golden HeartBond. But he would have to accept, and he'd be shocked with it, and . . . thought was gone, desire ruled, the rising to ecstasy, the feel of her lover's body against hers, the thin cloth caught between them, maddening and exquisite all at once.

His groan and emptying that pushed her into fabulous pleasure.

Her arms fell from him, limp, and he collapsed on her, and the bedsponge on the cot cradled them both.

When she could lift a shaky hand, she funneled her fingers through his hair, bit her tongue to keep the comment about how much longer it was, how the sun had burnished it until she could see deep auburn notes. A pity for their children, that, to have both parents with red in their hair. Someday.

She was ready to claim him, to give him her HeartGift and let the law force him to wed her. And that was simply wrong. Coercing him would lose him.

Though his heart, his emotions, might want more than sex, want the loving and affection and respect she'd given him tonight, she didn't think he'd acknowledge that even to himself. If she let her eyes close she could see the thick and brilliant bond between them.

He rolled and they settled on their sides, facing each other. With thought trickling in, she hoped she looked all right.

Jace touched her cheek. "Glyssa."

She snuggled closer. "Mmm."

"I'm glad you're here."

Sighing, she said, "Nice." Wasn't foolish enough to comment further. She believed he'd regret any vulnerability on his part in the morning.

His voice roughened and he curved his hand over her bottom, kneaded. Her eyes opened to see him grinning again.

"I really like this nightgown."

She shrugged. He didn't know her well enough to realize she liked big, sloppy, flannel gowns, nothing at all like what she wore.

He raised her leg and placed it on his hip, rubbed his sex against her. He was reviving fast, and she felt her own smile. Again she stopped a comment behind her lips—it had been a long time since she'd had sex. Do *not* get into that conversation.

With a hand stroking him hard and another wiggle, they were joined again, and it was wonderful, him inside her, where she'd wanted him since the night he'd left after their fling.

They stared into each other's eyes. Hers had to be wide.

She could see no trace of color in his irises, and wanted light as part of their loving. Not now. Not yet. Maybe soon. That might become a mantra.

"Glyssa," he said, and it echoed in her ears and whispered in her mind and sizzled in her blood.

One stroke.

She moaned, saw a bead of sweat appear on his temple, slide slowly down his face, out of reach of her tongue. She leaned up and nibbled along his jaw. His turn to moan, to plunge again and again, then stop, driving her to move under him more.

He kept her still by anchoring her to the bed with the weight and angle of his hips. "No," he said. Bent and brushed a kiss on her lips. His every movement sent waves of pleasure through her so she craved him.

"No," he panted. "So good. Need to make it last."

She tried to relax, to savor him inside her. He was here and hers for now, for this exquisite moment. Savor. Bind him to her with the physicality of sex, as she'd been bound to him for years. No other would do—not for her. She'd prove to him that no other would do for him, either.

His face, so dear already. The clean lines of his bone structure, a rectangular face, beautiful to her. A face that matched his long, lean body.

He grunted, moved again and again, slow, measured thrusts that had her gasping, arching, sharing each iota of pleasure, the fullness of him within her stimulating her desire, stoking her passion, enthralling her mind until only the drive to release mattered.

The scent of him, bay rum like his name, spicy and masculine, mixed with perspiration, mixed with the heady perfume she'd worn. All so real.

Soon. Soon.

Her body throbbed with pleasure, burst asunder. She cried out at her climax, heard his low moan and he collapsed on top of her, fitting *right*. Wrapping her arms and legs around him, she claimed him this way.

"Glyssa." Once more, his saying her name caused rippling thrills—this time the tenderness in his tone went straight to her heart. He mumbled unintelligibly then his body loosened as he fell asleep.

Yes, he was heavy, and the cot wasn't wide . . . she could have formed a pretty dreamscape for them, but she'd wanted the hint of reality. Having him close was all she'd desired for a long, long time. That he felt comfortable enough to fall asleep with her had tears of joy creeping from under her own lashes.

With Flair, she moved them slightly until they curled together, as always after sex—making love? She thought so, this time, at least on her part. Even in dreamtime they stayed together, resting, touching, petting.

She fought sleep as long as she could, knowing that once she fell deep into that state, she'd move away from him, leave him. She could hold on to him until then.

And, sometimes, when she fell asleep first, she sensed he held on to *her* until he succumbed. That was the best feeling, and gave her hope.

But not tonight. The emptiness waiting in her luxurious tent claimed her.

* * *

Come quick, come quick! Bad people saying bad things about FamMan. They got him!

"Huh?" Glyssa batted away Lepid's scratchy claws on her shoulder.

He screeched in her ear, had her jolting up.

Hopping around her, he shouted mentally. *BIG BAD THING HAPPENED. THEY THINK FAMMAN DID IT.*

Glyssa shook her head, but excited and noisy voices came from outside her pavilion. She grabbed underwear and slipped into it, frowning that she smelled like her own dream sex, and yanked the first folded clothing from the top of the stack inside her trunk. A licorice red ankle-long tunic with several pockets, including long, square, sleeve pockets. Not really appropriate for running through a camp, but good enough.

Running to the commotion made her more out of breath than she liked. She needed more exercise. Besides dream sex. Besides regular sex, even.

Near the hole to the ship, two rumpled and angry men held Jace, who appeared livid—pale under his tanned skin.

"I did not do this," Jace stated.

The Elecampanes showed up. "We were told we had a break in security and a theft?" Del asked.

"That's right. Someone took us out," said one of the big guys holding Jace.

"Took you out?" Del frowned.

An angry shrug. "Drugged us or something. We don't sleep on the job!"

"Yeah, we don't. But we did," said the other man.

"You checked the hole and the contents when you woke up?"

"Yeah. One of the smaller boxes is gone," said the man. "We found evidence that this guy—this Jace Bayrum—was there."

Nine

♥

*H*e *dropped stuff at the bottom of the girder."* One meaty hand offered a hawkcel's feather, a small specialized-looking knife, some leather scraps, and a partially tooled leather pouch.

Glyssa's breath caught. She had a finely tooled and engraved wallet that Jace had made with his creative Flair.

"I didn't drug or hurt either of these two. I didn't steal any box. I didn't do it. I'm *innocent*," Jace snapped as he straightened tall. "I left the pouch and scraps in the workshop tent. Someone is deliberately implicating me."

"These are serious charges," Del said.

Her husband nodded. "That they are. Andic Sanicle, you went down with Jace yesterday to survey that first room with a viz recorder. Will you do so again, now?"

Andic cocked a brow at Jace, more in doubt at his protestation of innocence than backing him up, Glyssa thought. Without a word Andic took out another recording sphere from his pocket, clambered down the angle of the girder into the ship, stayed only a couple of minutes, and returned. He handed the new sphere to Del Elecampane, shaking his head. "Someone's been down there, all right. Smears of footprints. And at least one smaller box is missing."

"It wasn't me," Jace insisted.

Glyssa stared at him and when he met her eyes, she raised her brows. He shook his head. Even under these circumstances he didn't want to acknowledge their relationship. She opened her mouth to say he'd been with her—and he had, in dreams, connecting even in sleep now and then throughout the night, but he scowled. She backed off. For now. She would have to say something, despite Jace, but not in public.

I can solve this mystery, Shunuk, Del D'Elecampane's FoxFam said, projecting telepathy loudly enough that those with pretty good Flair could hear him. *I know all here. I will use my superior nose to identify the culprit.* He pointed that nose at Lepid and lifted the skin of his upper muzzle to show teeth in a sneer.

Lepid yipped beside her, sitting but wiggling his butt. *MY NOSE IS BETTER THAN YOURS.* From the gasps of people around her, more could hear Lepid than Shunuk. Glyssa had been told that with each younger generation of Fams, their telepathy and Flair got better. Just as humans.

Del D'Elecampane's fox sneered at Lepid. *Can't be.*

Lepid growled, his expression angry. *I could not smell the intruders. You won't be able to, either.*

We will see. The older fox trotted the short distance to the hole, sniffed lustily, yipped and hopped away so fast he turned top over tail in a somersault.

"What is it?" Del demanded.

Sitting paws over nose, Shunuk broadcast loudly. *Someone or someones put nasty, hurt-nose-smell around the hole! Can't smell! Bad!*

"Huh." Del walked over to where her Fam had sniffed, crouched down and sifted some of the soft dirt into her hands, frowning. "Looks like some kind of chili pepper to me."

"That would frustrate Fam noses," said the female Healer.

Del stood, hands on hips. "I don't want to stop our project." Her face hardened as she scanned the camp, eyes flinty. "Nor do I want to call in an expert such as the tracker Straif T'Blackthorn or one of his sons."

A few people gasped. Glyssa wondered if the perpetrator was one of them. The initial shock was dissipating, Glyssa's temper went on a slow simmer. Her HeartMate had been falsely accused!

"I—" she started.

Zem screeched. People shifted, Jace struggled in the grip of his captors. Glyssa looked around, saw the fluttering BirdFam on the ground where he'd fallen from Jace's shoulder.

"Watch out!" she ordered, moving over and picking him up, going close enough to Jace that she could smell the scent of him. Still unsmiling, jaw flexing, he nodded to her as she set Zem back on his shoulder.

Another teetery balance and flapping wings and the hawkcel settled, turned his colorful head to stare at the Elecampanes. *I was with my FamMan all night.* Zem snicked his beak. *He was restless.*

A flush tinged Jace's cheeks.

Del looked down at her fox, Shunuk. "Fams have been known to lie."

I do not lie. Zem extended his wings and cawed.

"Nor do—" Glyssa started, caught Jace's furious gaze. She frowned back at him, compressing her lips.

Raz Cherry Elecampane picked up his own FamCat, set her on his shoulder and petted her. "I am willing to reserve my opinion at this moment since I recall seeing the craft items on one of the workshop tent's tables."

"Not the knife," Del said. "He doesn't leave his tools there. Nobody smart does."

"Are we sure it's his knife?" Raz stroked his FamCat.

"I keep my tools in my tent." An ironic smile twitched on and off Jace's face. His shoulders had stiffened and he avoided looking at Glyssa. "But I have a simple security spell on the tent, like most of us."

The Elecampanes linked hands, and when they spoke, it was in unison and pumping enough Flair into the atmosphere around them that brilliant auras surrounded them. "We will not tolerate theft during this excavation. When we find the culprit who removed the box, we will file charges and ship him back to Druida City to stand trial."

Del D'Elecampane stated, "I've already sent a mental notice to Straif T'Blackthorn alerting the FirstFamilies of this theft." Her lips curled, then she added, "Those nobles will ensure all of Druida City knows that any 'found' colonist antiques must be scrutinized and the origin proven beyond any doubt."

Her stare swept the tense crew, fixed on Jace. "I repeat, whoever stole from us—from all of us, since we all have a stake in this venture—will certainly pay. Let Jace loose. GentleSir Bayrum, please bring your tool kit to our pavilion." The Elecampane couple turned and strode away, Shunuk FoxFam trotted beside them, sneezing and whining.

Glyssa knew she shouldn't approach Jace, but couldn't help herself, especially since the rest of the staff scattered, no one coming near him.

She kept pace with his angry stride, reached out to touch his arm, let her hand drop when he snarled at her. "Keep out of my business, Glyssa. Let me handle this. I can take care of myself."

She stopped, gulped. Anger for him transformed into anger at him and she flushed with heat, fisted her hands. He yet ignored her.

Too bad.

She turned on her heel and caught up with the Elecampanes. The owners were also being given a wide berth by everyone else. Lepid followed her, though at a greater distance, watching the waving tail of the older fox.

"This is not going to help morale," Raz Cherry T'Elecampane said.

"We should have anticipated this more than we did," Del D'Elecampane said.

"We have plans," Raz soothed. "We found an entrance to the ship sooner than we'd expected. Time to implement higher security."

Glyssa heard Del's teeth grind. "At considerable cost."

"We are on budget. But perhaps it is time to offer shares to our crew."

Del grunted. "Get them more invested in the project." Her nostrils widened. "Turn everyone into a spy on everyone else. I *hate* that."

"We'll figure something out. Maybe it's time to present another tension-releasing concert or play."

Del laughed shortly, elbowed her mate in the ribs.

"That's your first response to bad morale." Her mouth thinned. "But I want justice."

A good opening, Glyssa picked up speed, joined the two, just as Del stopped to sweep an arm across the opening of the owners' pavilion. "I want justice, too. And I can vouch for Jace's whereabouts last night."

Snorting a laugh and shaking her head, Del said, "That's fast work. Come on in and tell us."

Lepid sent Glyssa mentally, *I am going to the stables to talk to my stridebeast friend, Alaba.*

She'd have liked him with her, but Del's FoxFam, Shunuk, sat just inside the tent, glaring at Lepid, and Glyssa didn't think it an appropriate time to talk about clashing Fams. *Have a good time.*

I will! Alaba is going with the cook for mushrooms and other foods in the forest. Maybe I will go, too. He ran off.

Ah, food was involved, Lepid's interest explained.

I think the cook is dishing out breakfast now. Maybe you can wait at the breakfast tent for me. Glyssa almost *felt* Lepid skid to a stop.

I will go there after seeing my friend.

Fine.

The Elecampanes settled onto a twoseat. "You can confirm Bayrum's whereabouts last night?" Del prompted.

"It's not exactly what you think," she said.

Raz raised a brow.

Glyssa flushed again, knowing the blood in her face clashed with her hair. She straightened her shoulders. She would never be as expressive with her body as the actor, hardly anyone would be. She wouldn't let that undermine her self-confidence.

Clearing her throat, she said, cheeks flaming *again*, "We, ah, experienced sex dreams." A big breath. "Legally, I can tell you *in confidence* that we're HeartMates."

Now she received sincere surprise from them both.

"That's why you're here!" Del's brows lowered.

"Sexy dreams, eh?" Raz Cherry Elecampane patted his lady's knee and winked at Glyssa. "We know about sexy dreams."

But Glyssa hadn't known that Del Elecampane could blush so. "Ah," Glyssa said, directing her gaze to Del. "I'm also here for the exact reasons I told you yesterday. I *have* contracted with the Hawthorns to do a paper—a story—on Captain Hoku, and I will submit that story as my field paper, as part of my work for my FirstLevel Librarianship.

"Hmm," said Raz, inclining his head. "We continue to accept you and your duties and activities as we agreed yesterday, then." Another raised brow and smug look. "No wonder Zem called Jace restless."

The Elecampanes laughed.

"Yes," Glyssa said.

After a short pause, Del said, "So, about this dream sex." She didn't look at her husband or Glyssa. "In our experience—" she stopped, cleared her own throat. "You said you could vouch for him all night."

"We have a bond," Glyssa responded stiffly. "And this is the first time I've seen him in years."

"You knew him before?" Raz asked.

Glyssa *hated* revealing all this. "Yes."

"Hmm," Raz muttered.

"I went to bed late, early this morning, and we spent much of the time together or linked. I would have known if he'd left his tent, been excited by descending into the ship by himself, taking a box. I'd have felt such an . . . adventure."

"Would you have?" Del questioned.

"Yes."

"Truly?" Del pressed.

"Yes! I am very sensitive to him at the moment."

"I deduce that Jace Bayrum doesn't know that he's your Heart-Mate?" Raz asked.

"No."

"Nothing wrong with a woman going after her love," Del D'Elecampane gritted out.

"No, indeed," Raz said, picking up his wife's hands and kissing her fingers, then he grinned at Glyssa. "Especially if it includes dream sex."

"Here," Jace called out from the threshold.

Glyssa jolted and turned, seeing his shadow on the canvas. Her pulse thumped hard. How much had Jace heard?

"Come in." Del pulled her hands from her HeartMate's, flicked her fingers, banishing the security spellshield and the tent flap opened.

Jace strode in without Zem, stopped and glared at Glyssa. "You! Didn't I ask you not to interfere in my business?"

"GrandMistrys Licorice had information she thought she should tell us."

"Dream sex." Del's lips curved.

Raz shrugged, all casual. "Dream sex isn't so unusual between couples who've had a fling."

Glyssa didn't know how he'd figured out she and Jace had only had a brief affair, but she knew Raz Elecampane was trying to minimize the connection between Glyssa and Jace, helping her keep the secret that they were HeartMates.

Raz bent a stern look on Jace. "You aren't the only one affected by the theft."

"No, just the one affected most." Jace held out a worn leather roll. "My small trim knife is missing."

Del took the case, opened it. One of the slips was empty. She stroked her fingers over the soft, butterscotch-colored leather. "I don't feel any spellshields on this."

"It only had the minimal, easily broken," Jace said.

"Like your tent shield," Raz said.

"That's right."

"I see," Del said.

Raz stared at them thoughtfully. "Perhaps it would be best if we decided, despite all your protestations of innocence, the statement by GrandMistrys Licorice, and your Fam's 'evidence,' to keep you, Jace Bayrum, aboveground and away from the action for the moment."

Jace flinched.

All the blood drained from Glyssa's head. She'd made things worse, not better for Jace.

Raz continued smoothly, "And though we'll privately keep an eye out for GrandMistrys Licorice, we'll show the utmost confidence in her and let her roam as she will."

A noise strangled in Glyssa's throat. This was so bad!

"This should help us flush out the wrongdoer or wrongdoers." Another hard and direct look from the actor. "What is between you two is none of our business. Our business here is this project which we have funded and which we run. Our primary goal remains the same, to excavate this last starship for history and for profit." Raz stood and Del rose with him.

"I understand," Jace said. Fury emanated from him, snapped down his connection with Glyssa. Sweat beaded on her neck and slithered down her spine. She didn't look at him, he was so angry.

Jace jerked a bow to the owners. "Until later." He audibly inhaled, stared at them. "I did not go into the ship last night and steal a box. I am as committed to this venture as you—"

"Not really," Del said. "We have a fortune invested in this excavation."

"I *have* spent two years of my life here. Not only because I've found you to be good employers, but because I'm interested in more than the money. I'm interested in the ship and our ancestors themselves."

"You think your ancestor arrived on *Lugh's Spear*?" Del asked, real curiosity in her voice.

Jace stood tall. "I don't know. My family didn't keep track of our line." Another sucked-in breath. "But I know the ship is very important to the history of Celta, and I liked working on the project, being a part of this."

Raz's brows lifted. "Past tense? Do you leave us on the next shuttle, then?"

Ten

Do you let whoever framed you win?" Glyssa put in. *She was stuck here, couldn't follow Jace if he left on the next airship, even though she wanted to.*

Jace didn't look at her. "This conversation isn't productive."

"It's a matter of pride, isn't it?" Raz asked softly, sympathetically, and Glyssa was struck that he used his voice, his manner, to get the results he wanted all the time. She couldn't truly gauge how sincere he might be.

"The accusation of theft smears a man," Jace said. "I leave now and the problems continue on the site, and you'll know it isn't me."

"Yes, theft smears," Del snapped. "You leave now and rumors will follow you wherever you go."

Raz put a hand on his HeartMate's shoulder. "Neither of us have ever been incriminated of wrongdoing. We don't know what Jace might be feeling."

"You're an actor, you can imagine," Jace said. "I'll consider my options until the next airship."

Glyssa wet her lips, said softly, "You also must consider your BirdFam, your companion who has only known this area."

"Later," Jace said, pivoted on his heel and walked out of the tent.

As he stalked away, she contacted him mentally, *Jace!*

Glyssa, I don't want to be beholden to you, dependent on you. Taking and not giving is bad.

We're . . . lovers.

We WERE lovers.

We should support each other, depend on each other.

You tried to manipulate me.

The situation, not you!

Tried to manipulate the Elecampanes, then. That is not a quality I admire. One I don't believe belongs between even acquaintances.

Acid coated her throat. She'd never been a victim of injustice and she'd taken her own status and her place in the world for granted. And now everything had come tumbling down.

She didn't know a lot about Jace's background, but *did* know from occasional comments that he'd never had the advantage of a deep bond with a loving family. She'd guessed that his parents hadn't been strong emotionally, hadn't supported him well.

Now Jace was charged with being a dishonorable man.

And her bumbling had made things worse.

The Elecampanes were staring at her. She wanted to press them for assurance that they believed her, believed in Jace like she did, and knew she couldn't.

Their faces were inscrutable. She couldn't tell whether they thought she and Jace were conspiring against them or not.

Maybe they even believed that Laev T'Hawthorn had hired her to undermine the project. Or that Camellia D'Hawthorn, whose share of the ship's treasures would be large, wanted Glyssa to spy for her, let Camellia know when the excavation reached the Captain's Quarters.

Glyssa had been so naive, so sure that just being a Licorice would proclaim her honesty, that telling them she was HeartMates with Jace would show them that he was honorable, too.

She wasn't in Druida City anymore with the backing of her Family and friends.

Her lips thinned and she lifted her chin. This is what she wanted, this chance to be somewhere new, do something different, even if it dented her pride and sense of self.

She'd grow. Hurt made a person grow.

But she didn't have to like these particular circumstances.

She dipped a curtsey, ready to leave without saying anything else, since her throat had dried and she wouldn't force words. Her mind spun with all the threads of conniving that might blanket the camp.

She knew she was innocent. She knew Jace was innocent. But now his name was smeared and the Elecampanes would do nothing to wipe that away—and the camp would probably follow their example. Whoever had set up Jace had achieved his purpose.

Meanwhile the Elecampanes would outwardly show they were pleased with her, though they'd privately made it clear she was under suspicion.

Terrible outcome of all *she* had planned.

After one furious jab of anger at her, Jace had closed down their link to a width smaller than a fox's whisker.

Less than two days here, and she'd made a mess of everything. A bigger mistake than any other in her life. So much for her self-image of calm, collected efficiency. That was in a shambles, too.

After a few breaths, she cleared her throat with croaking sounds. "I need my breakfast and to supervise Lepid's. I'll see you later." Considering her schedule, she said, "I am due to meet with your daughter, Maxima, and go over Captain Hoku's journals, the map he made of the ship." Glyssa gave them a cool look. "I would prefer to work in my pavilion instead of here or the workshop."

Raz inclined his head. "Workshop doesn't sound safe to me."

"Parents!" a girl's voice called before the Elecampane's sole child, teenaged Maxima, strolled into the tent, carrying a long-barreled blazer. Her chubby cat rode on her thin shoulder.

Glyssa blinked. Maxima had struck her as a serious student who wouldn't be out of place as a public librarian—that the girl carried a weapon and seemed competent with it, surprised her.

"We took a walk to where the wounded hawkcel was found," Maxima said, moving with her father's grace as she put the gun away in a locked and spellshielded cabinet set in the far corner of the room. "There was little to be seen, nothing that might have caused harm to the bird."

"It's been a full day since the attack," Del said. "Things happen quickly in the wild."

Maxima said, "I heard that someone knocked out the guards and broke into the ship last night, stole a box. That evidence was found that Jace Bayrum did it and that Glyssa the librarian"—the girl's gaze flicked to Glyssa—"got an immediate crush on him and came here to intervene for him."

Glyssa's face flamed. She'd never been the target of salacious gossip before, either. So much for her professional standing in the camp, no doubt tarnished forever as a love-starved woman. "That is untrue," she stated coolly. She wasn't about to tell the girl of a sexual fling, or talk to her about HeartMates.

"I think all of it is untrue," Maxima said. "I don't think Jace did it."

The older Elecampanes shared a glance that Glyssa couldn't read, perhaps speaking to each other telepathically. Probably had been doing so all the time she'd been in their pavilion.

"What we intend to do about the matter is our business," Del said, but in a mild tone belying the reprimand.

Maxima's cat leapt from her shoulder, sniffed. *I like Jace.*

"Because he sneaks you food," Maxima said.

"We will be proceeding with the excavation as we decided last night, theft or no theft," Raz said.

Maxima glanced at Glyssa. "We'll be studying the journals?"

"Yes. Scan a couple of your copies and choose the one you believe will be the most useful." Glyssa didn't wear a timer on her wrist to check. "I haven't had my breakfast, and I have requested that we work in my pavilion, starting at NineBells."

Maxima's eyes lit. "Oh, in a top-of-the-pyramid new pavilion! Most excellent." Her brows wiggled. "I hear you have a little no-time filled with good food and drink."

"I do, but I'll be eating in the mess tent." She'd have to nerve herself to do that, face everyone gossiping about her. And she'd have to dress well. Her stomach rumbled. "Please, excuse me." She left, head high, and kept a serene face and straight posture the few paces to her own tent next door, not that she saw much. For some *stupid* reason, her eyes had filled with tears.

At being judged so quickly? At being thought lovestruck—had she let her feelings for Jace show so openly? At the whole humiliation of not being believed . . . She didn't know, and though she'd like to hide in her pavilion, it wouldn't be wise.

The absolute best thing she could do was to eat among the others and poke fun at herself and her situation, and that idea had her writhing. The *worst* thing she could do was to act stuck-up and professional . . . but that was her default manner.

This was not the library. Not a place her Family had ruled for generations.

This was a brand-new place, and she'd have to work in a different way to relate with people as never before.

This part of the adventure wasn't fun . . . but it *was* challenging.

*J*ace *found the two guys who guarded the ship the night before, looked* them in the eyes and repeated that he hadn't hurt them. Since they grunted in response, he didn't think they believed him. Chin jutting, he strode through the camp back to his tent to cache his tools. People avoided him.

"Hey, Jace!" called Symphyta, the Healer.

He turned, tried to wipe the scowl from his face as he saw the curvy, wholesome blonde jogging to him, her full breasts bouncing. What was it about him that he had no inclination to bed her? That he still itched to get his hands on a thin redhead with modest attributes? A pushy redhead who couldn't keep her mouth closed. It had been obvious she'd *shared* the fact that they'd connected in sexy dreams . . . had a brief affair a while back . . . with the owners of the project. Like Jace wanted everyone—anyone—to know that.

The camp was full of women he hadn't rolled around on a bed-sponge with yet and might want to.

"You still speaking to me?" he asked, when she reached him.

Several people had already looked away from him, moved from out of his path as he'd walked to the new communications center.

She stopped and jerked her chin up, her pale blue eyes irritated. "Of course I am. I happen to believe your bird. Who is in the mess tent, waiting for you. You left him with the cook."

"Damn." He'd completely forgotten his new friend. A friend who'd stood by him. Turning on his heel, he strode fast toward the tent.

Symphyta kept pace with him. "And I think that you'll find you have plenty of friends in camp."

"I'm a friendly guy," he said sourly.

"Yes, I'm sure several people resent your popularity."

That had him sending her a surprised look. "You think that's part of it? I thought it was just because I'm damn poor." Too poor to have enough gilt on hand to pay for a return to Druida on the shuttle without a previous withdrawal from his bank. Should have kept more gilt on hand . . . though he had a tendency to gamble it away in boredom. Well, he hadn't been bored since the redhead and her fox . . . who now sat outside the mess tent looking at him . . . had arrived.

Symphyta snorted. "Like we aren't all poor here. I couldn't quite make it in a first-class HealingHall and wouldn't settle for a city clinic. So here I am. The frontier."

"But you believe in what they—we—are doing."

She shrugged. "Enough. The Elecampanes are interesting, influential, and wealthy people. They single-handedly built a community in Verde Valley. A community that will be establishing a small HealingHall soon."

He stared at her. "Huh."

Another shrug, this one irritable. "That's what that jerk Trago told me to get me out here." They were at the mess tent and she stopped. "I've eaten." She glanced around the camp and he followed her gaze, once more noting the neat and orderly layout of the tents—

most of them as shabby as his, with the exceptions of the Elecampane's pavilion and Glyssa Licorice's shimmering new Flaired one.

"And I'm needed at this camp. I like the energy of this place. I like the verdant landscape, the forest and the grasses and the two large bodies of water in the distance." Again she moved her shoulders. "I think this place would suit me more than the mountains where the Elecampanes live." Symphyta patted his shoulder, gave him a compassionate look like a sister or a friend. "You're popular and personable and lucky enough here with the treasures you've found to arouse jealousy and resentment. That's what it is. Later."

She turned and walked away and Jace was left to face the reproachful look of the young fox alone.

Lepid belched. *I am full because MY FamWoman fed me. Zem is empty.*

Jace flinched. "I'm here to remedy that." Ignoring the small fox, he entered the canvas tent. Good smells hovered in the air, and he realized that he'd burned off the couple of bites of the dry travel bar he'd eaten as he walked in the dawn with Zem. Jace had been grabbed and hauled to the ship before the fox had caught the first mouse for Zem.

Guilt wrapped around him, especially since he saw Zem perched on the top rung of a high-backed wooden folding chair. The hawkcel's gaze fixed on Jace. He'd been ignoring the fat cook who held out a plate of raw ground furrabeast bites.

Striding up to the cook, Jace took the plate gently from the shorter man, clapped him on the shoulder. "Thanks so much, Myrtus. I'm sorry Zem's so persnickety. He doesn't know much about people." Jace reached out and gently stroked Zem's head. The tension in the bird—stress Jace realized he'd *felt* through their bond—eased. "Zem, this is Myrtus Stopper, a very good cook. Myrtus, this is my FamBird, Zem."

Zem cocked his head. *GREETYOU, MYRTUS,* he projected loudly.

Myrtus nodded, smiling. "Greetyou, Zem, you are a very beautiful bird."

Zem said, along their private bond, *I cannot tell if the meat is good. It IS dead.*

Yeah, and Jace had no doubt Zem would rather crunch live mice or shrews or whatever.

"Lepid?" he called. A sharp movement caught his glance— Glyssa sitting at the far table in the corner with a bunch of others. Even as he watched, her color came up, but she didn't look his way.

The fox trotted in. *You called me?*

Jace lowered the plate. "Have a bite of meat." *Sniff and tell me if it is good. I think Zem's having trouble with his nose, uh, beak.*

One fast dart of a fox tongue and a slurp later, Lepid made a humming noise in his throat and grinned ingratiatingly at the cook. *THIS IS VERY GOOD.*

Myrtus's lip curled. "Sly fox."

Lepid tried huge eyes and an innocent look. They didn't work on the cook.

"Thank you for all the trouble you went to, Myrtus." Jace held up one of the damp spheres of ground meat for Zem. The bird's beak opened and he took it delicately from Jace's fingers. A surge of affectionate possessiveness and pride swamped Jace.

Thank you, Myrtus, said Zem.

"You're welcome, hawkcel BirdFam."

I am Zem, Myrtus.

"You're welcome, Zem." Then the cook said, "Bayrum," expressionlessly and walked away. Jace got the idea that he'd been put in the same "sly" category as Lepid. He rolled a shoulder, shrugging it off, feeding Zem more food.

His scan of the hall caught on Glyssa again. He tested the bond between them, exceedingly narrow, good.

He shouldn't be irritated that she ignored him, that something in her manner told him that she'd continue to avoid him. That circumstance was exactly what he'd wanted.

But it did annoy him.

Eleven

A couple of septhours later, Glyssa was in her pavilion, arranging the table she'd set up for them in the outer room.

"Here, GrandMistrys Licorice!" Maxima called from the door.

"Come on in, it's open, the only spellshield is against insects," she said, staring at the strawberry-blonde's dissatisfied expression as the girl trudged in, carrying the fancy box holding the copies of Captain Hoku's journals. "What's wrong?"

Maxima sniffed. Placed the box carefully, though Glyssa sensed she wanted to plunk it down. Yes, a *good* girl, pretty much like Glyssa was. Had been. Would continue to be? She wanted to put her "good girl" mentality in the past.

Huffing a breath, Maxima slipped into the chair in front of the table, picked up the teapot, and poured a stream of amber liquid, fragrant with a hint of jasmine. A smile finally tugged at her lips as she eyed the flatsweets.

"I can't read the journals. They are in Old Earthan. My father's mother, FatherDam, taught me but I still can't read them! My ancestress, the first D'Cherry, doesn't write like Captain Hoku."

"Oh." Glyssa blinked. "I believe that Captain Hoku was of the Geek Class. He was, after all, a trained starship pilot." She went into her bedroom and to the chest that held her personal reference materials and dug out a large book—a scholarly dictionary of Old Earthan. She balanced a tray holding several recordspheres on the top. "These might help," she said.

Now Maxima's eyes gleamed as she took the tray. The girl's mouth showed flatsweet crumbs.

"I hadn't realized that the different classes of Ancient Earth had a different language."

"Languages," Glyssa corrected absently, putting the book on the table and pouring her own tea, noticing that Maxima had already eaten all of her share of the flatsweets. "The Ancient Earthans had several languages, not only of different classes, but of different locations—ah, different continents. Our ancestors endeavored to develop a single language for Celta, even on the three starships. That mostly worked, but language does transform, you know. I believe that those in Chinju have a significantly different accent from us of Druida, and vice versa, of course."

"Of course." Maxima sat with Glyssa and watched, perky, as Glyssa found the section labeled "Geek Class." She glanced over at the girl and smiled. "One of the spheres is a copy of your ancestress' diaries."

"Excellent!" Maxima beamed.

"Many of the colonists who came here on *Nuada's Sword* were of Geek Class and preserved their personal journals and records for us, as well as writing this." She tapped the reference volume.

Maxima wriggled in her seat. "Nothing like a good library."

"No." Glyssa grinned back at her.

"And good librarians are rare," Jace said from the doorway, his voice laden with innuendo. Zem rode on his shoulder and Lepid panted a little beside him.

"What are you doing here?" Glyssa asked sharply.

He lifted his brows. "I am not allowed to work at either the communications center or at the site of the entry into the ship."

"That's so wrong!" Maxima exploded.

Jace strolled in and patted her shoulder, bent and scooped up a couple of flatsweets. "Thank you for your support."

I could eat a cocoa flatsweet, Lepid said, sitting by Glyssa's chair, fluffing up his tail because he knew she thought it was beautiful.

She eyed him dubiously. "Isn't cocoa bad for animals?"

A toothy smile. *Not for foxes.*

"He lies," Jace said with a smile at Lepid that included her. "Though I have heard oats are good for Fams, and there are such things as oat flatsweets."

Glyssa had stilled, only her eyes moving. Why was he acting as if he was easy in her company, hadn't been furious with her only a couple of septhours ago?

"How do you know?" asked Maxima, smiling at him and running her fingers through her hair. Glyssa suppressed a wince. The teen obviously had an infatuation with Jace. Trouble ahead.

Jace turned his easy smile on her, and Glyssa sensed Maxima was the reason he'd come to the tent. The owners' daughter, someone definitely on his side and who hadn't embarrassed him. He'd put up with Glyssa if Maxima was here, a person who would be easy in his company. And his manner toward Glyssa held an edge that Maxima might not notice. Not to mention that he could probably feel the anger Glyssa felt toward *him.* No, they wouldn't connect, not even in dreams, anytime soon.

"I know about fox food because I had a traveling companion with a FoxFam," Jace said.

Glyssa wondered if the companion had been female.

"A traveling companion," Maxima repeated, no doubt also considering the gender of that person.

Jace walked to the side of the pavilion and brought back another chair, put it at the end of the rectangular table that would seat six closely, next to Maxima who had her back to the door and opposite Glyssa.

"How can I help?" Another deliberately charming smile showing a dimple in his cheek that Glyssa didn't trust.

Maxima pinkened, swept a wide gesture—"Here"—and knocked over the recordspheres tray. They went rolling. Red now, Maxima lunged for one, missed. Jace caught two near him and Glyssa snatched one in midair, stuck it in the tray. Her fingers brushed Jace's as he returned the two he held. She *felt* her brows lowering, twisting as her expression turned to a frown, even as her heart beat a little harder at his nearness, the currently unwanted attraction between them.

Their stares met, held, his gray eyes cool, her own hot. Yes, her cheeks were hot and she could almost feel her hair crackling with annoyance.

She withdrew her hand, fast, nearly tipped over the tray again, then bent below the table and helped a flustered Maxima with a sphere that had rolled far under the table. "No harm done," Glyssa said—knowing that wouldn't ease the girl's mortification at her clumsiness. A girl didn't like to look stupid and clumsy in front of an older man she crushed on.

Neither did an adult woman. The difference was that Glyssa had experienced infatuations before and lived through them.

Lepid took advantage of the situation to get two licks in on Glyssa's cheeks that cheered her as she sat again.

Flatsweet, pleeease?

She looked at her Fam. "No flatsweets for you."

He sniffed, slid his eyes toward her. *I will go hunt, then.*

Since Maxima and Jace watched Lepid, Glyssa believed they heard him, too.

"Stay within a quarter kilometer of camp. I'm sure the camp itself has enough vermin to give you a good hunt."

Lepid chuffed. *There is another FamFox here and at least two FamCats.*

Glyssa smiled at him. "That's right, why don't you speak with Del Elecampane's FamFox?"

A small growl rumbled from Lepid's throat. *I do not like him.*

Glyssa was sure it was the other way around. The older fox didn't like Lepid.

He stood, glanced around, eyes bright over his pointed muzzle. *Bo-ring here with you all just looking at papyrus.*

"I'm sure it is," she said.

Her Fam looked up at Zem. *If I find a good treat for you, a mouse or a rat, I will call, like this.* He yipped loudly three times.

"Don't you have a telepathic connection with the hawkcel?" asked Glyssa.

Zem clicked his beak and projected mentally, *The fox is young and proud of his kills.*

Glyssa winced. "Uh-huh." She waved her fingers at Lepid. "Go."

His lower jaw dropped in a foxy smile and she wondered if she was doing the right thing, letting him roam the camp freely. But there were enough complications in the tent with regard to tangled relationships to distract her. She didn't need an antsy Fam, too.

After one last lick of her hand, Lepid bolted from the tent, ears up, tail flying. *I will search the stables first.*

Jace said to Maxima, "I'm happy to help."

"That's wonderful," the girl enthused.

She flipped open the box and Glyssa saw a couple of additional journals and some loose papyrus inside. "There's a detailed map of the ship . . . Hoku called them 'specs' or 'blueprints,'" Maxima said.

Stiffening, Jace said, "Yeah?"

Glyssa recalled when her friend Camellia D'Hawthorn had sent a copy of the blueprints to the Elecampanes. Another set was in the PublicLibrary, and the originals stayed in the T'Hawthorn Residence vault. Evidently the Elecampanes had kept the blueprints secret from the crew.

"I'm not sure that your parents want that information disseminated," she said. Both Maxima and Jace scowled at her.

"Are you questioning my honor, too?" Jace snapped.

She rubbed her forehead. "Of course not."

Maxima stuck out her chin in a gesture that Glyssa, as a younger sister, had used herself. Dammit, she needed to be more sensitive.

"I think I know who can keep a secret and who can't," Maxima said.

Which, of course, made Glyssa wonder what secrets Jace might be keeping that Maxima might know. Glyssa's nose twitched. She did have a *tiny* problem with curiosity.

"Jace won't tell anyone about the blueprints, and that's what we're supposed to be working on today, right?"

"Checking the maps against entries in the journals, yes." Glyssa took the teapot and the flatsweet plate off the main table and put it on a smaller one, moved the two cups to one corner, and spread out the specs. Each sheet showed one level and there were three, probably those Hoku was most familiar with.

"I'm honored at your confidence," Jace said, his expression smoothing as he gave a little bow to Maxima.

She glowed, swept a look at him from under her eyelids before glancing at Glyssa. "You don't mind if Jace stays and works with us, do you?"

Now she asked.

If it had been anyone but Jace, Glyssa would have bundled the blueprints and journals up and taken them next door to the Elecampane's tent.

But the need to spend time with her HeartMate throbbed inside her, even if he was annoyed and angry with her.

Glyssa told the truth. "No."

"I promise to be helpful." A charming smile from the man that Glyssa didn't trust—he remained irritated with her. He lifted Zem off his shoulder and set him on the back of her best chair.

Glyssa eyed the BirdFam dubiously. "Maybe I should put some papyrus down for Zem."

The hawkcel cast a beady glare at her. *I am a clean bird.* Another snick of his beak. *I am also a tired bird.* He closed his eyes.

"We took care of our personal needs before we came in," Jace said easily. He smoothed the maps, frowned. "Hmm." Staring at the papyrus, he angled the plans a little, and Glyssa saw that he'd set the ship to match the angle of the ship's outline that had been delineated on the ground outside.

Glyssa looked at the map. Unlike the intelligent starship in Druida City, *Nuada's Sword*, which was one massive cylinder, *Lugh's Spear* had graceful, modified wings, angled back like the ancient Earthans' air machines. More interesting in Glyssa's point of view, but she wouldn't be telling *Nuada's Sword* that.

She wasn't the only one who focused on Jace's long and elegant finger as he traced the outside line of the ship to behind the right wing.

They worked together well, though watching Maxima attempt to flirt with Jace was painful in more ways than one. As the minutes passed, Glyssa realized Jace was clueless about the girl's puppy love since he treated Maxima like a younger sister. She wondered at that—he struck her as an observant man—but she figured he just had man blindness about this.

She'd have liked to have warned him, but he wouldn't listen to her.

Midmorning the alarm of the camp pulsed in the pattern of "interesting information." Maxima's face lit with a grin. "I wonder what's going on!"

She headed out of the tent at a jog, leaving Glyssa alone with Jace. "Where do we gather?" She already knew, but asking such a basic question would keep her from commenting on Maxima's crush on him and alienating him. No man liked to be given advice he didn't ask for. All right, no *person* cared for unsolicited advice in general.

He lifted his brows. "There's a cleared circle a couple of rows in."

"Ah. I'm sorry I embarrassed you this morning," she said.

He grimaced.

"I was just trying to help." She knew the instant the words dropped from her lips that it was the wrong thing to say.

His head came up, his expression turned stormy. "I don't need your help. Like I said, I don't like being dependent on anyone. Or anyone being dependent on me," he said, but Glyssa sensed more. He didn't like to be dependent on lovers.

But his words hurt.

She bit her lip. "Sorry." Back stiff with tension, she walked to the pavilion's threshold. "I will endeavor not to try to help you again, even if you *do* need it." She walked out of the tent, nearly blindly and bumped into someone who was hurrying toward the open area. "Pardon," she muttered. Then she sent a loud and private mental call, *Lepid!*

Coming!

Back in the tent, Zem lifted his wings. *You were not nice.*

Jace scowled. "Maybe not, but I don't want to get tangled up with Glyssa Licorice here in camp. One or two nights of sex are fine, but after that people think there's a relationship and relationships are difficult here." Gossip got hideous. He'd been careful to keep all his dealings with lovers light. And though his body yearned for her, he'd known quickly she wouldn't want only a couple of nights of sex. She was different than the other women in the camp. Higher status, more serious. More of a woman who'd want forever from him, everything from him, until he lost himself in pleasing her. Like his father had his mother.

"We can't just fly out of here, like you. There's nothing outside of camp but thousands of kilometers of wilderness. You live here within your community. I have to live within mine."

The bird made a noise that Jace understood to be like a human snicker. He moved his shoulders, relaxing them from a high line of tension, before lifting his Fam to perch on his shoulder.

By the time they reached the circle, everyone was there, but Maxima found him and led him to where she stood with Glyssa—who ignored him.

"Your attention, please," Raz T'Elecampane said, easily sending his voice through the space, quieting the crowd.

Twelve

Expectation seethed through the crowd, Glyssa felt it, too.

Raz T'Elecampane's mobile face creased into a broad smile. "This afternoon the starship in Druida City, *Nuada's Sword*, will be launching the communications satellite that will link with the array it sent us. By tomorrow we should be able to have active communication with the city!"

Someone near her gasped harshly, and she tried to turn but the crew roared and jostled in exuberant approval.

Raz raised his palms, said calmly, "Those of you with relatives in Druida City who are tired of telepathic communication can sign up on a schedule to make scrys."

"*Is* there viz capability?" asked an eager woman.

"Yes," Raz said. "However, our day here is earlier by three septhours than Druida City."

"Huh?" someone said.

"It's a big planet," Del D'Elecampane raised her voice. "It rotates. The sun reaches us, dawning and setting, before it reaches Druida City on the western edge of the continent."

"You remember how long it took us to get here, big stup," a woman to Glyssa's left joshed, elbowing a large man.

"Yeah, yeah." He bent down and smacked a kiss on her lips.

What did this mean for the whole civilization of Celta? Would they be able to speak with those on the Chinju continent soon? Glyssa shivered with anticipation.

"That takes care of our announcement for today—" Raz began, but Del interrupted, sending a look at Glyssa. "Most of you know already that we have retrieved a large storage container from *Lugh's Spear*. GrandMistrys Licorice, we would appreciate your expertise in reading the letters on the side." Del's gaze scanned the group. "Landolt, your Flair for sensing things within objects would also come in handy. We would request that you be assigned to the main team exploring the ship, please."

The man next to Glyssa jolted, then flushed and muttered, "Claustrophobia," as people stared at him.

Funa Twinevine—whom Glyssa hadn't noted being so close—snorted. "You came to an *excavation* of a starship when you know you have claustrophobia?"

Landolt, tall and thin with sandy hair, sent her a fulminating look. "Pays fliggering well."

"That's enough," Raz said. He gave a slight bow. "Thank you for attending the announcement."

"Always do," Funa muttered. "Gotta know what's going on, more'n just gossip."

The crowd began to break up and Glyssa walked forward, as did Maxima. Jace did not. The girl glanced back at him, said, "Come on!"

A mixture of emotions spurted to Glyssa from Jace along their bond: renewed anger, hope, curiosity.

She suppressed a smile at the last, *wonderful* to know he was a curious man . . . that he almost matched her in that.

"Come *on*." Maxima twined her arm within his, tugged. "The parents don't want you to go down into the ship. I can't imagine that they could object to you being around while Glyssa examines the box." The girl jutted her chin again.

Glyssa didn't think Maxima's parents were aware of her

infatuation with Jace, but the way the girl was acting, it wouldn't take long for them to discover. And because stupid jealousy niggled at her, Glyssa took Jace's other arm.

He frowned, but she ignored that, chuckling and glancing up at him with a smile. "And you've been with us all morning, struggling with ancient Earthan languages."

"Yes." Maxima nodded. "You belong with us."

"At least this morning," Glyssa said.

"Honored," Jace said, but his smile was for Maxima.

Really stupid jealousy. Glyssa squashed it with the fact that *she* was Jace's HeartMate. But her hurting heart didn't listen.

A minute later she had to withdraw her arm from Jace's. She stepped forward to the cleared circle around the large storage box, an olive green with black broken-looking letters traced on it.

Many of the people who'd listened to the announcement had moved toward the single box pulled from *Lugh's Spear* to watch.

She squatted down and tilted her head to read the thing, *STX* was the abbreviation, along with a rounded rectangle with a black half circle pointing inward at one end. She sounded the first syllables out *Sub sis something*, the letters seemed frayed, *STIX*. Humming a little, she puzzled on it. This looked like . . . but she'd have to check. Snapping her fingers she *whisked* the big dictionary she'd left on the table in her pavilion into her outstretched hands.

For an instant the gasps around her impinged on her concentration, then she dismissed them. Flipping to the page she wanted, she studied it, then put the big book on the ground and again held out her hand, this time cupped, and translocated a recordsphere. This one was from the starship in Druida City that included its logs of the last months of the journey.

She swiped her hand over the sphere and a mechanical voice echoed . . . *"and two tons of subsistence sticks were dropped from our emergency stores to be transferred to Lugh's Spear, commanded by Captain Umar Clague, authorized by Kelse Bountry, Captain of this ship."*

Glyssa picked up the book, straightened, and snapped it closed, smiling with triumph at Raz and Del. "This is a 250 kilogram crate of subsistence stick food, originally from *Nuada's Sword*. One of the crates that *Nuada's Sword* sent to *Lugh's Spear*, described in your ancestress' diary!"

"A historic box of terrible tasting food, great." Funa sneered.

Glyssa ignored her and walked around the box. "It appears unopened."

"Landolt?" asked Del.

The tall man loped up to the box, placed his hands on the top and frowned in concentration. His fingers tensed as he used his Flair. "Yes. I sense, um, individual objects, a lot of them." A moment passed as his frown deepened into a scowl and sweat rolled down his face. "Each . . . is . . . wrapped? . . . in something not . . . not . . . I don't know what." He lifted his hands and his palms appeared red with effort and wet with perspiration. Huffing breaths, he stepped away. His knees folded and Jace caught him, grunted, and slipped the man over the shoulder not occupied by his FamBird. "I'll take Landolt to his tent." He walked off, and Glyssa turned in a casual manner to watch him.

Del D'Elecampane's mouth turned down and she flicked a hand. "I think one of our first messages will be to request that someone with Flair comparable to Landolt's come here." She glanced at her husband. "We should give Landolt a raise, and we'll have to figure out additional incentives."

Raz nodded.

A small cough came and everyone turned to Symphyta. "We also need another Healer. Or two." She met the Elecampanes' gazes and flushed. "And, perhaps," she whispered, "a subsidy." Her jaw worked as she stared beyond them. "We could ask the HealingHalls or . . . someone else . . . ." Symphyta's gaze slid toward Glyssa and she knew the Healer was thinking of T'Hawthorn. "To pay a Healer."

Del D'Elecampane grimaced. "We'll take care of it. Come talk to me later."

Raz smiled at Symphyta. "And I think you might want a tent of your own."

"She's fine staying with me," Funa asserted loudly.

Inclining his head, Raz said, "I'm sure she appreciates your offer." Again he looked at Symphyta. "Please, we'd like to discuss this with you some more."

"I'll be glad to talk to you," Symphyta agreed.

"A lot of talking," Del D'Elecampane grumbled.

Raz slipped his arm around his HeartMate's waist, kissed her temple. "That's management for you, darling."

"I s'pose," Del said, then went up to the box and circled it, glanced at Glyssa. "Thanks for helping us. I don't think that we'll open this just now." She shrugged. "Not if it's only subsistence sticks, I've heard enough about those from my husband's ancestress' diary to know they were nasty. And they'd be expired by now, too. If it had been the grain or seeds we found . . . that would be different."

"Yes," Raz agreed. "Several of the boxes discovered and vized by our people when they went into the ship are this color. Probably all the same."

Glyssa's turn to shrug. "Probably."

"You really aren't going to open it up?" asked Maxima, nearly hopping with impatience.

"Not right now," her mother said. "Perhaps you should return to your work with GrandMistrys Licorice. The bell announcing the first lunch seating will ring soon."

Maxima sniffed as if she was uninterested in food. But all three of them had nibbled most of the morning.

Raz nodded to the staff. "I would prefer only the newly formed Squad One that is authorized to descend into the ship remain. We will discuss our next steps."

Reluctantly, other people began to drift away. Del frowned at her daughter and Glyssa handed Maxima the recordsphere and began to walk to her tent. The girl followed.

"Have you watched and listened to all these yet?" Glyssa asked.

Maxima made a face. "Bo-ring."

Glyssa's lips twitched. "Yes. But there are some good nuggets in there."

"I don't know how you recall all that."

"Training." And Maxima Elecampane might not be pure librarian material after all. Though there *was* a lot of boring work that later might pay off in a librarian's life. Or could never pay off.

But here Glyssa was in an exciting venue, full of people who weren't like anyone she'd ever met. Adventurers, risk takers. Like her.

She grinned again.

Maxima studied the glass sphere as they walked back to Glyssa's pavilion. "This isn't like regular recordspheres."

The difference was barely noticeable. Glyssa was impressed. "No, they are archival quality, made with a lot of space for excellent quality vizes and audios." She nodded toward the glass ball. "The public librarians were allowed by *Nuada's Sword* to copy its logs of the journey only once. That is one of the secondary copies. We don't want to return to *Nuada's Sword* and beg for another—for which it would charge us a monstrous amount. It is not known for its generosity."

"Huh," Maxima said, rolling the ball in her hand, her fingers seeming to test the material, her brows drawn down as she focused. "I might . . ."

"Yes?"

"I might be able to make these spheres even better." She slid a sideways glance to Glyssa, pinkened. "I'm good with glass . . . and, ah, other stuff. Part of my Flair."

"What other stuff?"

The girl's shoulders lifted nearly to her ears. "Communications, mostly."

Glyssa narrowed her eyes, wondered exactly what that meant, but they'd reached her pavilion and Maxima darted inside.

"Show me how you figured out the words from the dictionary," the teen said as Glyssa entered, distracting her.

Zem *fluttered to the crosspole of* Landolt's *large tent as* Jace *took the* man inside and laid him on his meter-thick bedsponge. Landolt shared his tent with his two male lovers. One had accompanied Jace to fuss at him and watch Landolt. Neither a groggy Landolt nor the other guy thanked him, which rankled a little.

Stepping from the tent, Jace drew in a breath and smelled the camp—humans—a trace of the sweet scent of the plains, the forest and water in the distance. Zem cackled in warning before he stepped back onto Jace's quilted shirt shoulder. He'd added the pad that morning before their early walk to find food for his bird . . . pretty much a futile walk since Zem couldn't fly, Jace was too noisy, big, and clumsy to catch small mammals like mice, and he'd been found and detained before Lepid had found prey for the hawkcel.

Just before the announcement claxon had rung and broken up the little study group in Glyssa's pavilion, Jace had forgotten the charges against him and been satisfied with himself.

He'd felt lighter in spirit and satisfied with a job well done. He *had* helped with the map. Now he smiled with the inner knowledge that he'd *seen* the layout of the ship, the plans. So much easier to visualize in three dimensions when you see something in two.

Glyssa trusted him. She was pushy, but he sensed she had no doubt of his innocence.

The kid was nice. Staunch. A good thing in a friend, and he thought he had her as a friend.

Another breath and he jolted a little as the first lunch bell sounded and he headed toward the mess tent.

His mood soured as he walked. No one approached, and the personal space around him seemed to have tripled.

Just as he passed Sanicle's tent, the man made to step out, hesitated. Jace stopped and sent him a sardonic smile.

Sanicle grimaced, raised his hands. "No offense."

Funa Twinevine came up behind the man, wrapped her arm around his waist, smirked at Jace.

"No offense, what?" Jace pressed.

The man angled his body in a defensive fencing position . . . as if he and Jace had ever crossed swords. One hunched shoulder. "No offense, but I don't want to be seen with you. Your luck's turned bad."

"The worst," Funa said.

"A lot of bad luck going around the camp," Jace said tightly. "And most of it man-made bad luck aimed at me."

"Well, we don't want it smeared on us!" Funa sniffed.

Jace's jaw hurt from his gritted teeth.

Sanicle lifted and dropped his shoulders. "Even though you spent time in the tent with the sexy librarian who has FirstFamily friends and the owners' kid, that doesn't count for much." Sanicle's gaze went past Jace. "And there the new pretty lady is." He gave a hum of approval. "All that prissy manner bottled up under a redhead. Gotta be interesting."

A quick spear of jealousy stabbed through Jace. He knew for a fact that when Glyssa dropped the prissy manner in bed, she was all fire.

"Think I might try *my* luck with her," Sanicle said.

Funa dropped her arm from the man's waist and bumped him off balance with her hip. "I'm right here."

He glanced at her. "We don't have an exclusive arrangement."

Anger came to Funa's eyes and she simmered in it.

"Move, Bayrum," Sanicle said. "Leaving now."

Funa glared at him, then slanted a glare at Jace. "He's right about the luck thing. I don't want your bad luck rubbing onto me."

Jace just lifted a brow. Then he nodded and crossed into the middle of the main lane between tents. People continued to ignore him and Sanicle strode past him trying to catch up with Glyssa who walked toward the mess tent.

Face pouty, Funa took to the road, swinging her hips and gathering other male gazes. Another guy joined her and she broke into animated conversation.

Jace's mood dimmed by the continuing stickiness of "bad luck" and the accusation of theft, he reached the dining tent.

Unlike all the days before, no one called to him. No one even met his eyes.

Talk stopped when he came in, and after he got his clucker and greens, whispers hissed through the tent.

He ate in stoic silence, *not* looking to where people gathered around Glyssa to ask about her dictionary and the recordsphere and the box. *Not* listening for her laughter.

Too many people, Zem grumbled from the top rung of a wooden chair. His mental voice sounded thin. Jace studied him, didn't see that the bird appeared much different, but he was still learning what a healthy bird might look like. Jace reached out with his forefinger and stroked the bird's good wing. "Easy, now."

Feathers rustling, Zem tipped his head and stared at him, blinked. *That feels good.* His wing lifted a bit, went back to his side. *Bring me more food, please.*

"I'll do that."

Zem gave a mental sigh. *It will be dead but filling.*

"We'll get you well. I won't let anything happen to you," Jace vowed. He already loved the bird fiercely.

Thank you, FamMan.

Just that had him forgetting that people avoided him. He, Jace Bayrum, had a *Fam!* A wonderful, beautiful *Bird*Fam unlike any other telepathic companion Jace had ever heard of.

Head high and with a steady step, Jace walked past all the tables, ignoring more whispers and over to the cook again. Trago the Healer jerked his elbow into Jace's path but with a fancy bit of footwork, he dodged. Trago cursed at him anyway.

Without actually looking Jace in the eye, the cook scraped some raw ground clucker and furrabeast onto Zem's plate and Jace returned to the end of the table where he and Zem sat alone.

So what if the others thought he was bad luck? Even resented him enough that they preferred to think him a thief? He had Zem, and Maxima believed in him. That should be enough.

He'd accept it as enough.

Raz Cherry T'Elecampane stepped into the tent and walked straight to Jace. Though the actor's face wore a mild expression, sparks of ire danced in his eyes.

"What's wrong?" Jace asked.

"I don't know how the rumor started and how it passed around so quickly, but your 'bad luck' has tainted my, *our*, project."

Thirteen

What happened?" Jace asked.

Raz T'Elecampane scowled down at him. "Gossip has already circulated the camp that it would be dangerous to open the box because it might have deadly Earth spores in it. A terrible virus from Earth that will kill Celtans . . . or something."

Jace choked on a bite of clucker. "What!"

Raz nodded. "Who knows what we might open and release? Stories of cursed camps and expeditions are making the rounds, too. I take it you did not start this rumor?"

Jace stood, kept his expression mild because others were watching. He spoke in a low tone, "No."

"Gossip also stated that you instigated that notion."

Jace shrugged, trying to appear less angry than he was. "Someone has a hate on for me . . . and I didn't have much time to start such a rumor. I took Landolt to his tent, neither he nor one of his partners talked to me. I didn't talk to them."

He raised his voice so it echoed throughout the tent. "On my way here I talked with Andic Sanicle and Funa Twinevine, both of whom are here. They are the only ones I spoke with. They know what I know."

"You fligger!" Funa yelled, then rose from her place, dumped her metal plate and utensils into the cleanser with a clatter and stormed out.

Jace nodded at Funa. "She thinks I'm bad luck, so does Sanicle. I wouldn't put it past either one of them to talk me down, and Zem and I reached here after they did. Did the gossip come from this direction?"

Raz shrugged. "Who knows? Everyone here has enough Flair to be telepathic with good friends or lovers." His smile sharpened with teeth. "You've had several lovers here."

"Yes," Jace said. "I'm friendly with a lot of people. Doesn't mean that someone didn't set me up for theft and isn't smearing my name. Someone wants my rep blackened."

Raz rocked back on his heels, also seemingly casual. "Perhaps." His blue stare met Jace's. Cold, considering. "Once a project gets a reputation as being unlucky, it's hard to keep it going, keep staff."

"And any little thing that goes wrong is blamed on bad luck . . . or me," Jace said. Since his appetite for the rest of his meal—overcooked greens—had been spoiled, Jace picked up his metal plate, took it over to the garbage, scraped off the leftovers, and slipped his plate in a track of the cleansing bin. When he turned back toward his place, Raz was gone.

Jace felt the gazes of everyone else in the tent. Bending down, he offered his arm to Zem and left.

Not wanting to gather with the others to watch the communications set up—he knew no one in Druida and had on a good brood—he spent time using a shovel. He dug with others at the place where the Elecampanes believed the main entrance to the starship to be . . . who knew how many levels down? They only had two big earthmovers that anyone with a little Flair could power. Jace wasn't given the option to use those, either.

*A*fter lunch, *Glyssa strolled with most of the camp to the new* communications center, which still didn't look like much to her. Lepid coursed ahead of her and ran back. *Everyone is coming. All the peoples.*

He barked in excitement. About two-thirds of the folk looked on indulgently, but the rest scowled at his behavior. Nothing she could do to curb him right now, but she got the idea that they should take walks—all right, she'd walk and Lepid would run—a couple of times a day. The exercise would do her good and she'd explore more of the camp, maybe even walk along the outline of the ship that was within sight of the tents.

Soon she headed back to work, stretching her legs as she sauntered in the open air, enjoying the sunlight. In Druida City, she spent most of her time in the PublicLibrary and teleported home to her Residence, hardly ever getting outside . . . and forgetting about time as it passed.

She already knew that here in the camp she'd be very aware of the time. Unlike in the city, nature affected people's lives greatly here. Breakfast began near or at dawn, lunch at midday and dinner just before dark. A couple of septhours after dark and campfire stories everyone retired. Meals, sunrise, and sunset were the main time distinctions of the day.

She smiled, knowing she'd fall into that mind-set, too.

After dinner, Lepid deserted Glyssa again, saying that Zem needed more food, hadn't been eating enough. Since her small fox appeared unaccustomedly serious, she thought he told the truth. So she agreed he needed to hunt more for his "good friend."

She had no illusion why Lepid liked Zem so much. Her FoxFam had saved the bird and loved being the hero. Something she sensed was true of her HeartMate, too.

Not something she had ever considered important, like knowledge, or learning a new skill.

Had to be an aspect of self-identity. She didn't need to be a hero, didn't much—*hadn't* much—cared what others thought of her before today. When she thought of how the gossip had spread that she'd fallen into immediate lust with Jace . . . *that* had been humiliating. She'd formed and implemented a plan to poke gentle fun at her newness to the camp, her naïveté in living here, added a tiny touch of bumbling scholar. People had thawed toward her.

But if she had to divide them into groups she believed there were three: one bunch liked her for herself, was amused by Lepid, liked animals. Such as the Healer Symphyta.

One group thought she was snobbish, too fussy, and believed she embodied a number of other negative characteristics, or these folk simply *didn't* like animals. Trago, the Healer.

A calculating third portion thought she could be useful to them, maybe manipulated by them—a scholar who understood esoteric, uninteresting matters, but with little innate cleverness. Funa Twinevine.

She found herself building a persona to shield herself, not being completely open, for the first time in her life—outside her Family. *Glyssa at* "Lugh's Spear" as opposed to *Glyssa the SecondLevel PublicLibrarian* that most of her friends knew. Or *SecondDaughter*, in her Family.

Even after hours, duty called. Today she'd started work and it was time to set down her first day in a log.

With a few moves, Glyssa changed the large table into a smaller desk, no Flair needed, all excellent workmanship by one of the top luxury furniture providers, Clover Fine Furniture.

It felt odd to sit in the middle of the room at a little desk, but her desk in the PublicLibrary was larger than this pavilion room, with plenty of space to move around. Rolling her shoulders, she admitted a new discovery. She liked a lot of space around her as she worked, and preferred that to a huge desk. Trade-offs, something she should have anticipated she'd have to make, compromises with regard to her living space, but she hadn't because she hadn't correctly envisioned her space.

She'd have to keep this desk and her files—both papyrus and recordspheres—ruthlessly organized.

She'd known she'd have to compromise with Jace. She hadn't handled that well, either.

Early days.

She glanced out at the to-ing and fro-ing of the camp at sunset. This was one of the weeknights that a huge bonfire was lit in the circle and people gathered around it.

Though she wanted to be there, she was also tired of so many people being around her all the time and the lack of privacy. *That* she'd foreseen, but hadn't anticipated how naturally solitary she was and how much she stayed within her own little social circles. Though she had decided she wanted to change that. She wanted to experience the frontier and all the sorts of people drawn to a project such as the excavation of *Lugh's Spear*.

And she *would* be more extroverted. Tomorrow.

She set a stack of papyrus to her left and pulled out a writestick. Those tools were traditional and her Family, that is, the *First Level PublicLibrarians* insisted on such a written record so that old ways were not lost.

There came a wild, gleeful shriek in her mind, Lepid with feelings following closely: *I have it! I have the mocyn! Kill! Yum! Food for Zem, too!*

She withdrew fast, but knew her wonderful Fam had dealt bloody death. And was feasting on mocyn—the Celtan equivalent of Earthan rabbit.

Rubbing her face to block any images, she tried sinking her mind into a meditative state.

But anxious vibrations came to her from the Elecampanes' tent. Should she go over there or not?

Her nose twitched. They could always refuse to talk to her.

She headed to their canvas pavilion, stopped outside the threshold guarded on one side by two cats and the other, the older FoxFam, Shunuk. The cats eyed her and twitched their tails, said nothing.

Greetyou, GrandMistrys Licorice, Shunuk said. He peered around as if searching for Lepid.

"He's out hunting," she said. Lifted her chin. "He just caught a mocyn."

Shunuk lifted his upper muzzle in a sneer.

Ignoring him, she called, "Here!"

"Come in," Raz said.

He and his HeartMate sat on the inflatable twoseat. Maxima wasn't with them. The couple held hands, their expressions were smooth—rather like the expressions on Glyssa's parents' faces when an emergency came up at the PublicLibrary.

"What's wrong?" she asked, then winced.

The Elecampanes shared a look, then Del D'Elecampane got up to pace the short length of the sitting room and back, letting herself frown. "The rumors about a damn cursed project aren't dying. More like spreading like wildfire."

"Negative ideas are always easier to entertain than positive thoughts," Glyssa said.

Del laughed shortly, aimed a forefinger at Glyssa. "That's damn true."

Raz said, "And it can get boring here. We are, after all, essentially an isolated small town. We had all the crew we needed, so we haven't signed on very many this year." He smiled at her. "You're the newest face we've seen in months. The airship pilots don't tend to stay."

"Ah."

"Yeah, yeah," Del said. "But I don't like how some of the crew are spooked. Some people might have left already except that they'd have to walk out across the plains. Not much between here and Verde Valley, our place, which is the closest real civilization." She ran a hand over her HeartMate's head. "Because of you."

"Because of us." He reached out and snagged Del's hand, kissed it.

Thousands of kilometers, and they'd walked . . . or ridden it themselves with Maxima.

"I don't doubt some are considering heading back to Druida when the next ship comes in," Raz said.

"The cowardly ones," Del agreed. She stopped her pacing to sit next to her husband.

Raz chuckled and a not-quite-nice gleam came to his eyes. "Most of our staff are adventurers, mercenaries, those who don't fit well in cities and like the risk of the frontier."

Like Jace.

"Usually they live from paycheck to paycheck, and to get them out here, we offered a deal."

"Oh?"

"We'd fly them in. But if they wanted to leave, they had to find

their way back. We offered to take the cost of their return trip out
of their first paycheck."

That sounded a little bit mean to Glyssa. "Clever."

"Very. Only about twenty-five percent accepted that."

"So now some of them are stuck." D'Elecampane glanced at Glyssa.
"Including Jace Bayrum. Until they get their next check and make an
appointment with the airship company to pay for their return flight."

Raz cleared his throat. "Cherry Shipping and Transport, my
Family's company, is leery of taking I.O.U.s from our staff."

"Understandable." But sneaky. Glyssa ached for Jace. Trapped.
He wouldn't like that. She didn't dare offer him gilt.

"Of course, a lot of barter for goods and services goes on," Del
said. Again her light green eyes met Glyssa's. "Jace Bayrum does
quality leatherwork."

"Beautiful," Raz said. "I've purchased a few of his items myself
recently."

"Have you?" Del perked up.

Raz winced. "For holiday gifts. Don't tell Maxima."

"Of course not."

Glyssa thought of the wallet she had tucked away in her most
private no-time storage unit. How often she'd taken it out to look at
it, tried to sense the vibrations of the man who'd made it. "I have an
item of his work," she murmured.

"So do we," Raz said. He shared a significant look with his wife.
Hesitated, then gazed back at Glyssa. "We have his HeartGift."

Glyssa stopped breathing. "What?"

Del swept a hand around them. "When you travel a lot like Jace,
bunk down in camps like this, or merchant caravans, or whatever,
you keep what's important to you with you. We offer a very secure
vault for our staff. He put the HeartGift in there."

Raz said, "Naturally, since neither of us could see it well, and it
radiated intense Flair beneath the excellent spellshield, we knew
what it was when we stowed it."

"The HeartGift he made for me," Glyssa breathed. It was here.
At the camp. Where Jace could offer it to her and she could accept it

and they could be legally and formally mated. For a moment she was dizzy with the possibilities. Then her dreams crashed. He was barely speaking to her. If she thought hard, she'd still be irritated at him.

"Did you bring yours?" asked Raz softly, trying to draw the information from her.

Relationships were built on trust. She wanted them to trust her, so she had to give a little. "No. It's . . . fragile."

Del nodded. Shrugged. "All well and good, and this was a nice visit. But it didn't help us much." She stood again. "We still have problems, and if the majority of the crew get angry with us, we'll be in a bad fix."

"Final option is that we will have to subsidize their leaving," Raz agreed.

They both looked at Glyssa. "We don't want to shut this project down. Once we do, who knows how long it will take to get started up again?"

Del grunted. "Or Laev T'Hawthorn and Straif T'Blackthorn and the other FirstFamilies will swoop in and make it their own."

Now *that* was a possibility Glyssa could see. "I don't want that. This project is *yours*," she said before she thought.

"Thanks," Raz said drily.

Glyssa shrugged tightness from her shoulders. "Camellia deserves her share from Captain Hoku pursuant to Celtan salvage rights."

"We agree," Del said. "We've always agreed, even before her line of descent was proven in JudgementGrove. We are honorable."

Glyssa nodded politely.

"This venture has cost us a lot in gilt, energy, Flair, time," Raz said. "On a project like this, investigating the past, doing something never done before, superstition runs rampant." He spread his hands. "We are isolated from Druida City and the other smaller cities and towns established on the west coast. Below us is an ancient relic that could hold *anything*. Great, unimaginable treasures of the past. Knowledge of our ancestors and ourselves beyond anything we have now." His voice dropped. "Or terrible curses—bad air, sicknesses that still live on from the colonists, or have mutated from Earthan viri to a plague that could kill us all."

Del snorted and broke the spell that had enveloped Glyssa at the actor's words. "And we'll have to deal with danger, and greed. That greed has escalated since we opened the hole down into the interior of the ship." She squeezed her husband's shoulder. "Which we haven't yet planned for."

"We'll need dedicated guards. Men and women who actually hire out as those. We had that slated for next year. Time to move it up."

Sighing, Del subsided back into the twoseat. "So we need to offer shares in the project." She stared at Glyssa. "Current crew only. Deducted from their pay if they want. We'll offer that soon."

"Staff includes you, GrandMistrys Licorice. We did a little checking on you with *our* friends. You could make a bona fide gesture. Are you in or not?" Raz asked.

Her life wasn't here. This was only her third day here. Her Family, and their investments, were always conservative, and her gilt was mixed with theirs.

The way the rumors were running around the area, the dissatisfaction of some of the staff could bring down the whole venture. She'd be foolish to put gilt into this. To tie herself and her funds to the Elecampanes instead of Laev T'Hawthorn.

But the thrill of adventure, curiosity, and the yearning for a fascinating project had her saying, "Count me in."

Raz sprang to his feet, laughed, and hugged her tightly. He was a strong, charismatic man, no matter that he was older than she. A man she'd once had a tiny infatuation for, like most other girls in Druida City. She felt nothing but a low wash of affection for him . . . and excitement at the gamble she was taking.

Del stood, cocked her head, narrowed her eyes. "How much are we talking about from you?"

Since Glyssa had studied her finances before leaving, she named a fairly high figure, and gasped at Raz's renewed hug.

Del's eyes glinted as she grinned. "That should buy you some percentage points of the venture." She tucked her thumbs in her trous pockets. "We'll figure out what kind of bonus we can give you, too, in a choice of items recovered."

Glyssa's eyes went wide. Imagine having something from the starship *Lugh's Spear*!

"I'd bet good gilt that Jace Bayrum will be one of the staff who'll buy into the excavation," Del said.

Glyssa believed so, too. Maybe she was more like her HeartMate than she thought.

She could imagine his scowl at being tied to a venture financially, the same venture as she.

He wouldn't like it.

Too bad. She did. And she *loved* the excitement coursing through her. The dazzling hope of future discoveries.

"I can . . . I can write out a letter to transfer the funds to be taken to my bank by the next airship."

"We'll have a contract for you by then, one copy for us, one to be filed with the All Councils Clerk, one for you," Raz said.

The practical specifics jolted her back a little. No way to keep this from her parents, her sister. They would strongly disapprove and look more askance at her field study than ever.

Laev T'Hawthorn would be disappointed. So would Camellia.

She'd have to explain herself to all of them and she didn't know how.

Meanwhile Del D'Elecampane had grasped her arm in a show of unity, a bond of business, squeezed. Glyssa returned the pressure, but her airy thoughts had coalesced into a solid, heavy lump in her stomach.

What had she really done? How much trouble was she in now? With her Family since her money would be separated from theirs. With her friends, Laev and Camellia, who'd believed she was on their side if any struggle for control of the project manifested. With the expectations of the Elecampanes for the support she'd be expected to give them, subtly and openly.

With Jace who, if he subscribed to the project like she thought he might, wouldn't want to be linked with her through business for as long as the excavation went on.

Trouble, for sure. How much, she didn't know.

Fourteen

A little stunned, a little nauseous at the huge commitment she'd just made, Glyssa trudged back to her pavilion. Once the threshold air turned opaque and hardened behind her into a door, she settled herself. After a minute she slipped into the chair behind her desk and took up her writestick, focused on *work*. *That* she could control.

As she wrote, she marshaled her thoughts to record them on a sphere.

Glyssa finished her description of the day, being professionally cool with regard to the accusations against Jace—just relaying the facts. She spent a great amount of time on the description of the box retrieved from *Lugh's Spear*. This included an exact tracing of the letters on the carton, and her conclusions, then finished her account.

Satisfied with her report, both written and viz, she decided to use the same procedure for Camellia's project, a *story*, of her ancestor, the last Captain of *Lugh's Spear* and the pilot who'd landed the ship. The only starship that had had casualties when landing, though all experts at the time had agreed it had been a miracle that no more than seven had been lost.

She researched and thought. Crafted a word, a phrase. Outlined the story.

Time passed and the twinmoons rose. Their half-full, silvery light painted the empty path between the tents. She heard the murmur of voices, then singing. She could barely keep her eyes from closing.

Lepid! she mind-called her FoxFam.

A distant yap came. *I am by the fire. You should come, too. It is very pleasant.* A pause. *Though some people do not sing very well. I sing better than they.*

She laughed, then stood and stretched, set the page of her story atop the many sheets of papyrus she'd used to detail her report of the camp, the Elecampanes, the progress of her studies, as well as the investigations of others and the progress of the excavation. Put the longer outline for her story atop that.

I am going to bed now, she sent to Lepid.

I will come in when people go away, and I check my caches and munch a little snack. Wariness came through their link.

What is wrong?

I will find out if those cats or that other fox have found my caches and are eating from them.

Possessiveness and territoriality. She should have considered that. Other staff had Fams. *I will always provide food for you. You will never go hungry with me.*

You are a good FamWoman, Lepid said.

I hope so. And if your caches are not as you left them, please do not confront the cats or Shunuk fox. Let me handle that for you, too. She tried to sound sweetly reasonable.

All right. That seemed reluctant, but good enough for her as she slipped into her covers. *See you soon.*

*J*ace *tossed and turned. Glyssa didn't visit him that night in dreams,* either erotic or platonic. The irritation between them would keep her subconscious mind from drifting toward him for dream sex.

He hadn't really expected her to come to him.

Had he?

But he didn't sleep much, remembering the awful events of the day, his mind cataloguing them as if *he* was the librarian, not his phantom lover.

The morning had started out all right, with that walk with Zem and Lepid in the cool breaking dawn when most of the camp slept and the scents of nature ladened the air and he knew he strode through wilderness being tamed.

Then all his peace had been shattered as men had grabbed him and 'ported with him back to the opening of the ship. Accused him of theft! Of hurting the guards! Of being so greedy he needed something small and precious from the ship *now* and battered men to get it instead of waiting and sharing.

The day had deteriorated from there, the mortification of having Glyssa make excuses for him, his being banned from the communications and the excavation teams, being ignored at lunch.

And just before he'd joined Zem in the tent to sleep, he'd gone to the large circle around the central campfire . . . and been stuck on the outside of the circle instead of the first row. No one had smiled at him, invited him to scoot next to them. No woman had gestured for him to sit behind her and be her prop. No one had even met his eyes. That had all hurt.

His status in the camp had plummeted and, in fact, he couldn't gauge it, didn't know where he stood with the crew. He didn't like that at all.

People he thought were friends apparently weren't. Friendly rivals, like Andic, had turned sour toward him.

Tomorrow would be a tougher day as he adjusted his relationship with every single person in the camp. As he watched while others got to descend into *Lugh's Spear* and recover the boxes, others work around the communications equipment.

He did know one thing. There wasn't a curse on the camp, or a curse on him, but someone definitely wanted him framed.

He looked over at Zem who he'd set on a simple stand he'd made in the workshop, then Jace rolled over again on the too-thin bed-sponge, feeling battered in mind and heart. In the dark, he tested the tiny link between him and Glyssa. Still there. His body ached for a woman. Ached for Glyssa. No!

But in the black heat of the tent with sweat beading on his aroused body, he admitted the truth. He ached for one woman only.

Terrible thing. If he gave in to his lust, she could lead him around by the balls, like his mother had done with his father.

He listened as people drifted back to their tents, mostly in couples, talking, a small laugh here and there but not the usual loud cheerful chatter . . . this "bad luck" business affected others, too.

He hadn't felt so lonely in a long time.

Glyssa didn't sleep well. She'd gotten used to visiting Jace in her dreams. So she moved restlessly, waking throughout the night. Weather blew in with gusts of wind, and she enjoyed feeling safe in her pavilion, hearing the sounds of the camp in a spattering rain so much that it took her mind off the disasters of the day . . . so she didn't say the short rhyme that would soundproof her walls.

When Lepid zoomed through the door, deep in the night, after his nocturnal rambles, and hopped onto her bedsponge yipping a *FamWoman, good to see you! Good that you are up*, she welcomed him. She didn't even mind when he shook himself off and scattered wet on her and the covers.

"Want to cuddle?" Before she'd finished the sentence, Lepid had crawled near her hip and curled up, fluffing his tail. He shivered. *Cold and wet out there.*

Her hand went to his thick, coarse fur. "You are warm and safe here with me." But it was a reminder that the official end of summer would come within a month and the camp would close for the winter in no more than two months. What would the Elecampanes do then?

Surely Glyssa's story for Camellia would be done, as well as her field report. Her report was on schedule. Attracting Jace's attention and getting him to be her lover wasn't proving as easy as she'd anticipated.

She'd made a HeartGift for her HeartMate, of course, during her second Passage dreamquest at seventeen to free her Flair. And, by law, if she gave him his HeartGift and he kept it for a full eightday, she could claim him as her husband, bound to her alone for the rest of their lives.

She hadn't thought she'd need to do that, and her HeartGift was so precious to her, and her pride so full that she'd win Jace without it, she hadn't brought it with her. The origami hawkcel remained protected in her home bedroom safe. Foolish.

Lepid licked her hand, his tongue rough and damp, but love infusing his bond with her. *You are WISE FamWoman!*

Glyssa snorted, she only wished that were true.

Wiggling into a more comfortable fox-circle, Lepid said, *And we have the BEST pavilion. No wind in here. No rain.*

Which had Glyssa's thoughts winging toward Jace again. She sniffed. If *he'd* been less foolish, he could be here with her, sleeping or making fabulous love. She hoped he froze his ass off.

Fifteen

*J*ace tapped the opening tab near the top of his long, bespelled weather bag atop his bedsponge. The side gaped, letting in chill air. Grunting, he got out, drew on his heavier spring/fall clothes, muttering the heat activation Word on them.

He touched the bag and the thing rolled up into a round sausage. Maybe he wouldn't need it tonight, but he was glad he'd purchased the bag before the season began. He glanced over at Zem, who stood on his perch, feathers slightly puffed, his head drooping and his beak in his chest, asleep.

That had Jace sighing in relief. He'd crafted a large spherical weathershield atop Zem's perch in the middle of the night, a Flair spell he didn't often do himself since it was tricky. Usually he bought bespelled items like clothing and hats. To his surprise, the spellwork had gone unexpectedly well, as if he'd grown in Flair or matured in technique during the last few years.

He must admit that he preferred to apply hands and back and intelligence to problems rather than to rely on psi Flair magic. He supposed that was because his selfish mother had used her Flair to browbeat his slow thinking but physically impressive father.

Jace's mind skittered away from his father's death. Long past, never forgotten. Nor were the lessons he'd learned from it.

He'd heard his mother had died a while back and wasn't sorry. She hadn't been a good person. Thinking of her—that he might ever be as manipulative as she was—made him flush hot.

You're up, be quiet, said a grumpy Zem in his mind.

Jace glanced toward him. He looked the same.

Lost sleep because you were too restless last night. Better that you had mating dreams like other nights, Zem said. *Easier to ignore.*

Heat washed through Jace. He'd hoped Zem hadn't noticed.

A huffed breath from Zem, a click of his beak. *You should have listened to the wind and the rain, fallen into that rhythm.*

Jace blinked and stared. "I thought owls were supposed to be the wise birds."

Now Zem snorted, raised his head and opened his eyes to stare and blink at Jace. *Owls are arrogant. Hawkcels are best.*

"I'm sure." He stepped forward. Into a puddle, something he'd been ignoring. His tent wouldn't make it another season. Maybe not another storm.

Anxiety made his mind race. More expense, and digging dirt didn't pay as well as exploring the ship.

"Don't you want to eat?"

Later. Sleep more, Zem said. *Go visit your lady.*

"No. Nothing has gone right since that woman has shown up."

Zem looked up. *Not her fault. Not your fault. YOU go eat and feel better.*

Jace shrugged dismissively and headed out of his leaking tent into a pretty morning that failed to satisfy. He'd go over to the workshop tent.

A few people were around. No one greeted him.

*O*ver the following few days, Jace kept his usual manner, even if behind an outer smile and gritted teeth. He wasn't a thief and he didn't harm people. He hoped by staying the same, the crew would recognize this.

Every morning after the fox and Zem munched live or newly

dead small rodents, Jace took his Fam to the clinic where Symphyta checked the hawkcel out . . . and sent some generalized Healing energy through the bird.

She and Glyssa and Maxima were the only ones who treated him the same—no, Symphyta's interactions held a tinge of pity that really made his jaw ache, Maxima was fiercely defensive of him which clued him in that she saw him in a romantic light, and Glyssa treated him the same.

Jace watched with fisted hands stuck in his trous pockets as Sanicle and another couple of men brought up from the interior of the ship another one of the large boxes.

He spent time with Glyssa and Maxima in the tent working, but stayed outside of Glyssa's gathering personal circle. And, for some reason, that radiated a low-level ache around his heart.

Not to mention the ache in his lower body since they hadn't connected in sexy dreams for a while.

He couldn't convince himself that he needed to move on to another woman in the camp for *real* sex. He throbbed for Glyssa alone, which would worry him if he let it.

To no one's surprise except Glyssa's, the novelty of the communications center and talking to those in Druida wore off in a couple of days. Jace could have told her that most of the people here had few, if any, relatives, especially in the cities.

Most were like him.

But he didn't really care for study, and it wasn't his strong point. *Action* was.

So he shoveled never-ending dirt away from a large area where the main entrance was. He figured that was pretty useless. The top of the ship was at least three stories down, and from what he'd seen of the plans, the ship's main doors were levels lower than that.

Even with the two earthmovers, they weren't making much progress. But folk noticed his hard, simple work.

And though at first the rumors of a curse still circled, and his rep was still smudged, eventually people began to relax around him again.

Until the night when another storm rolled in.

* * *

$\mathcal{M}$idnight and lightning sizzled around the camp, painting the trembling windblown tents in searing silver.

Glyssa stood in a thick robe at one of the windows of her pavilion, holding a shivering Lepid. She'd set aside Hoku's journal and her too slowly progressing story to watch the show. Only the thin coating of Flaired gauze kept the storm from her—exciting.

For a moment she yearned to share the excitement with Jace, rolling around on his bedsponge. Or hers.

He'd been treating her like an acquaintance.

She could find him in a dream, make love to him there. He might even welcome her . . . she'd noticed the increased sexual frustration through their bond, though neither of them had mentioned it in their polite conversations.

Not that it would be appropriate to talk about that with Maxima around, and Jace was only near during the day when Maxima was with Glyssa. She wouldn't chase after him, tried to give him time.

As she watched, two terrible explosions shot fire into the sky and sound roaring through the camp.

Lepid yowled. *That was not the storm!*

Glyssa feared he was right. "Weathershield!" She gestured at herself and Lepid, coating them with Flair, then thinned the door and ran through. Mud stuck to her feet, slowing her, irritating her.

Lepid followed, barking his lungs out.

As she zoomed toward the closest fire, she heard the Elecampanes behind her.

People popped from their tents, most in rain gear, yelling and shouting.

Lepid shot ahead of her. *FamMan!* he called mentally.

Glyssa's throat closed. Surely he couldn't be hurt! She checked their bond. No. He was fine, a little sluggish from sleep. She narrowed the bond again before he caught her peeking and thought she was pushy.

Smoke and burnt canvas smell came to her nose and she stopped at an area of destruction.

Jace came up to her, but didn't speak.

The Elecampanes halted near.

Two people ran toward them from opposite directions, a dripping Funa Twinevine, half-clothed and wet so her lush body was on display, and a man who preferred guard duty.

"My tent," shrieked Funa Twinevine, swiping her wet hair from her face along with—tears? rain?

"The box!" the guy panted as he skidded to a stop in front of the Elecampanes. "Boxes. Both. Blown up."

Funa bent and picked up something, said a Word to cool it, swore, and then her face twisted into an ugly scowl. She stalked to Jace, flung a tough piece of tanned furrabeast leather at his face hard enough to cut his cheek. "This is your work. Just because I wouldn't sleep with you anymore you *do* this? You filthy fligger!"

Gasps came, everyone faded back from Jace. Glyssa wanted to hold out her hand to him, knew it would make fools of them both.

"I left that piece in the workshop tent," Jace said.

Didn't sound wise to Glyssa and she kept her mouth shut. Whatever little goodwill he'd managed to retrieve these past days had abruptly vanished with Funa's accusation.

A wan Symphyta jogged to them, a strangled whimper coming from her. "I was taking my usual late shower." She blinked wide eyes, staring at the debris. "I've lost everything."

Glyssa put her arm around the woman. "Let me know how I can help." She scanned the crowd, face set. "We will all help." Her eyes narrowed at Trago. "Did Symphyta leave anything in your tent?"

He shifted, but answered, his expression pitying as he shook his head. "It's been a while. I don't think so, but I'll look." Glancing down, he whispered, "You can sleep with me, you know."

"I have room," Glyssa said. "You didn't have insurance?" She aimed the question at Symphyta, then sent her gaze to Funa.

The crowd made disbelieving noises. Symphyta hugged Glyssa, then stepped away from her as if needing to stand on her own.

Glyssa flushed at the crew's reaction, lifted her chin. "Well, we can make a pool. Perhaps we can use the new communications system to set up a pool for gilt or provisions in Druida City, have the pilot bring things out with the next trip."

"That's an excellent idea for the use of our new system," Del D'Elecampane said. Her face hardened and she put her hands on her hips. "We will not tolerate these *human-made* incidents of vandalism and terrorism. When we find the culprit, we will prosecute him to the fullest extent of the law . . . when we get back to Druida City." Her smile wrinkled the lines at the corners of her eyes, showed teeth. Everyone understood her unstated threat. The Elecampanes were the law here in camp, on the frontier, as it had always been in human society.

A slow and stately Myrtus Stopper proceeded to them. He shook his head. "This was the second explosion, then?"

"Yes, my tent!" Funa snapped.

Myrtus held a bunch of oblong items in his hands.

"What are those?" Glyssa asked.

Another shake of his head. "As the guard said, the other explosion destroyed the crates we got from *Lugh's Spear*—"

"The curse!" a woman yelled.

"Damn bad luck," shouted a man at the same time. "Project is turning rotten."

"It's a human villain," Jace replied loudly. "Just one bad guy. Not a curse. Not bad luck. Not a project turning rotten."

But grumbles from people drowned him out more than the quieting rain and distant thunder.

"What are you holding?" Glyssa asked Stopper again, hoping the question would distract people from Jace.

"Some of the subsistence sticks from the crates." His gaze slid to the Elecampanes. "I tried one. Terrible, terrible. And in my expert opinion, if they once had nutritional value, they don't anymore. My Flair tells me so." He looked around the gathering. "I found these, I'm sure there are others. If you all bring them to me, I will take care of them."

"Sounds good," said Raz T'Elecampane. He raised his actor's

voice. "I suggest we all disperse now to our tents and leave further discussion for the morning."

Trago stepped forward. "You can stay with me, Symphyta. As a friend. Your own bedsponge." His voice was almost monotone.

"I have room," Glyssa repeated.

"And we have some spare tents and equipment for emergencies like this," Del Elecampane said. She smiled at Symphyta. "Take your pick."

With a trembling smile to Glyssa and a nod to Trago, Symphyta turned to Del D'Elecampane. "Thanks, I'd like that."

Raz T'Elecampane moved to put an arm around Symphyta's shoulder, and his weathershield enveloped her and would slowly dry her slicker, hat, and rain boots. "We can give you a pop-up tent for one. A little small . . ." He began to walk with her toward the Elecampanes' pavilion, the staff gave way before them.

Symphyta smiled up at him. "I've been sharing for so long, that sounds really fine."

Del and Maxima strode after them and Glyssa turned to Jace. He was gone. People had separated to give him a large path back to his tent, too.

And she couldn't go after him.

Excitement is over. Lepid sighed. He picked up each paw and his nose wrinkled. *This spell doesn't cover the bottom of my feet. I have nasty can't-feel-pads-well paws.*

"Then you won't be running all over the camp until the morning, will you?" Irritation welled through Glyssa at Jace's refusal to let her help him. She could be discreet.

Lepid whined and gave her big eyes. She huffed and picked him up. "Let's go back to bed."

Her FoxFam curled up as she drafted a simple announcement and appeal for funds for a Healer who'd lost all her belongings in a fire. She'd show it to the Elecampanes, then her friend Tiana, a priestess at GreatCircle Temple, who'd circulate it for her, or lead the effort. And Tiana's sister was a Healer at Primary HealingHall, so it could make the rounds there, too.

That, at least, was satisfying.

But she ached for Jace's emotional hurt and Glyssa thought the camp staff now felt a fear they hadn't before. The explosions seemed all too personal.

$\mathcal{T}$*he next morning . . . the next two mornings, the sullen talk around* camp was that no one wanted to go down into the ship due to the curse. Jace *ached* to do so, but had no illusions that he'd have any partners or backup. The stormy weather had invaded the crew, fear overtaking even greed.

And the person spreading the rumors besmirching his name and smearing the whole project, hung solidly with the rest.

The Elecampanes had tried to casually question the staff, but the community and the owners were always in a delicate balance. The workers needed the gilt—but they *could* hire out somewhere else if they left, and they might not come back. And the Elecampanes needed hands, now and in the future. Not to mention that none of the Elecampanes were well trained in investigation.

Jace had rarely seen the crew so united.

The Elecampanes were savvy enough to leave the glowering staff alone, focusing more on refining the communications system and using most people as laborers to dig.

All the food sticks that had been recovered from the explosions had been taken to the mess tent and given to Myrtus Stopper who collected them in a large box.

Jace picked up his shovel and trudged to the digging. The calluses that had been under the skin of his palms from past physical labor rose again in ridges. The crew still gave him a wide berth, but he was determined not to hide in the tent with Glyssa and Maxima . . . and Maxima's crush on him was becoming a little too uncomfortable.

The deep blue sky holding the white sun showed no clouds and the day soon heated. Zem had not come with him. Lepid and the hawkcel had gone to Glyssa's tent and Jace missed his Fam.

As sweat dripped into his eyes while he labored with other men and some women on the endless digging project, he only hoped that he was repairing his rep, though he still doubted.

Glyssa was deep in the translation and transcription of Hoku's journal when she received a sharp mental command from Raz T'Elecampane. *Glyssa to the opening of the ship, now!*

She jolted, and from Maxima's jerk of surprise across the table, the girl had heard her father, too.

No time for Glyssa to wonder how a connection had formed with Raz enough for him to speak to her mentally, as she stood up quickly and caught her chair tipping over, looking for Lepid.

He wasn't in his bed, as he'd been just . . . how long ago? Dammit, she'd gotten caught up in work. Zem slept atop a chair.

She spurted a word back to Raz, *Coming!* and headed out of the pavilion at a run, followed by Maxima.

People smiled as she ran through the camp, no doubt thinking, as she did, that Lepid had stirred up trouble. Again.

Arriving at the hole in the ground with the girder sticking out, she saw Lepid sitting and looking up at Del and Raz Elecampane. Beside him sat Carolinia, Maxima's cat.

Del looked over at them, relief on her face. Raz appeared to be hiding amusement.

"What is your concern?" Glyssa puffed out.

Lepid shifted his intense stare from the couple to fix on Glyssa. Though he sat still, Glyssa felt wild excitement coursing through him, and through their bond.

"Your Fam, and Maxima's"—Raz used a low, resonant voice—"have volunteered to explore the ship."

I am small and agile and FAST, Lepid broadcast mentally, added a yip. Keeping from hopping to his paws and dancing around was killing him.

I am smaller than he, equally agile, and smarter. Carolinia the FamCat lifted a paw and licked it. She sent a private telepathic warning to Lepid telling him to *stay calm* that Glyssa caught the edge of, though the mental stream was in interesting images with bright-colored emotional tones that she'd never have imagined.

"The ship is very dangerous," Glyssa said, a little weakly.

"And very dark," Del warned. "A darker place than either of you have ever been."

Lepid sat up straight. *I have been in housefluff and mocyn warrens. They are dark and narrow.*

Glyssa found her own surprised expression mirrored in Del's. Glyssa shrugged. "Ah, maybe at D'Ash's adoption office?"

Carolinia gave Lepid a cold stare. *No wonder they wanted you out of T'Ash Residence.*

I can make a spell light with Flair! Lepid proudly demonstrated a weak spellglobe.

The cat followed suit with a very bright spell light. Carolinia lifted her head. *I repeat, I am smart. I am older than the fox, more experienced.*

"What do you think, Maxima?" asked Raz gently.

The girl's face had crumpled into fear, but Glyssa thought she saw pride in her eyes. "I don't know. I should think on this." Her parents shared a look, as if both of them were the kind who made quick decisions.

"Glyssa?" Del asked.

"No!" someone shouted. "The first *things* to really explore the ship should not be *animals*. They should not be able to see the wonders, maybe pick up a treasure or two, before humans!"

Everyone turned to see Andic Sanicle pushing through the crowd, his face angry. "This expedition is for *people*, not animals. They don't get paid."

Carolinia stared at him, claws extended from her lifted paw. *I am compensated.*

"You've got it all wrong, Andic," Trago yelled. "Let the animals go in first, take all the dangerous chances . . . losing them isn't as bad as losing people."

Glyssa gasped, heard Maxima, too. She whirled toward the man. "How dare you think—"

"Maxima," Raz said in a father-tone.

The girl quieted, but glowered at Trago.

"Familiar Companions are loved and valued members of Families," Raz said. "We do not risk their lives more readily than humans."

"That's right," Glyssa said.

"We thought to attach viz recordspheres to our courageous Fams."

The crowd hummed in approval. Del turned to Glyssa. "And I have a question for you, GrandMistrys Licorice. Can you translocate Lepid to you if he gets in trouble?"

Anxiety riffed through Glyssa. She caught her breath. "I am good with translocation of objects," she said. "But Lepid and I have not practiced translocating him, bringing him to me when I need to."

"We all know that. He gets in trouble all the time when you're not around," someone said. The camp laughed.

So that afternoon she and Lepid practiced teleportation and translocation along with Maxima and Carolinia.

After the practice she believed he was too tired to get into too much trouble and allowed him to visit Jace and Zem for the evening while she worked.

Tried to craft the story. The field report was going fine.

She'd finished transcribing all of Hoku's journal from the time he was on the ship, had helped with the founding of the town they'd hoped to live in, and the tragic disappearance of *Lugh's Spear.* She knew the events well, but that was all. She wanted to write it from Hoku's point of view.

After a futile septhour, she flung the writestick aside. Why did she think she could get into a man's head? She couldn't even understand Jace, and she had a bond with *him.* She had definitely misread him from the beginning.

She stared at her pitiful sentences and gulped, then her mouth dried. This story was *terrible.* She would fail her friend. She would fail her field study.

She was doomed.

Sixteen

❦

*Z*em *huddled on his perch, not looking good even in the predawn light.*
Jace strode to him, picked him up. *What's wrong?*

*I am very hungry, FamMan. I must eat often . . . and I haven't
been. I am . . . failing.*

Guilt, fear, roared through Jace. "I'll think of something. Lepid
hasn't been helping."

He does some, but he is young and easily distracted.

"We're heading to the mess tent, now. Myrtus Stopper
will already be preparing for the first breakfast shift. And I'll talk
to him about allowing you in by yourself. Can you allow him to
feed you?"

*A dry cackle. I . . . will . . . try. I do not like him . . . much. He
has . . . stuff . . . on his hands and . . . wants . . . to pet . . . me.
Bad . . . for . . . feathers. But I . . . do . . . not . . . think I can . . .
get . . . to . . . that place . . . alone.*

They were outside Jace's tent now, in the cool morning, moving
along a path to the main road that would hold six across. Jace
walked rapidly, kept his stride smooth.

Maxima's cat appeared and sat in the middle of the path and Jace
jerked to a halt.

Greetyou, Bayrum, the little cat said mentally. Her mouth was full of mouse, not that she was one to verbalize much.

Impatient, but not willing to be discourteous, Jace said, "Greetyou, Carolinia."

Greetyou, BirdFam Zem, Carolinia said, eyes wide with curiosity.

Greetyou, CatFam, Zem said.

I heard you, Zem, Carolinia said. *I was playing with this mouse, but you can have him. He is nice and fat from grains in the stable.* She opened her mouth and the mouse dropped. It lay there for a second, then rolled to its feet.

Zem dove from Jace's shoulder, click, snick, *snap!* He crunched and swallowed the mouse. *Good. I thank you, Carolinia*, Zem said, tilting a bit on the ground due to his injured wing.

Jace checked his own hands for any contaminants that might harm his companion, then picked Zem up, cradled him in his arm. "Thank you, Carolinia."

You are both welcome. She blinked at Jace. *You will continue to sneak me clucker in the mess tent. And egg, now. And cheese, too. I particularly like cheese.*

It wasn't a question. Nothing came free from a cat. "I will," Jace said. "And you will . . ."

I will help feed Zem. She turned and walked away, tail high and waving. *That FamFox is mostly useless. I am a good huntress. I can bring you five bits of food a day, as well as go down into the ship once each day. I am a very efficient Cat.* She looked over her shoulder. *And for my food—I do not stay in the camp. I hunt in the FOREST and by the lake. I am a Fam trusted in the wilderness and not old and lazy like Shunuk fox.*

"You're wonderful, Carolinia," Jace said automatically.

Yes, I am, she said before she turned away.

It will be good to have more live food, Zem said.

Jace sighed, stroked his Fam's head with his forefinger. "I am sorry I'm not providing as well as I should be for you."

You are a big human and cannot hunt like cats or foxes or hawkcels.

"That's right. There must be something I can do to provide you with food. At least newly dead prey."

I would like on your shoulder.

Jace complied.

He continued to mull over the problem as he strode to the dining tent. There he set Zem on a perch and fed him raw ground fur-rabeast bites the cook had ready for them.

Jace spoke with Myrtus about allowing Zem in by himself; most Fams were not permitted to be in the mess tent alone. He told the cook Zem's concern about Myrtus's hands, which surprised the man and he studied his fingers, shook his head. "Gotta admit, I get grease on them, or food, or use lotion. *Cleanse!*" Myrtus ordered. The air around his hands wavered, a tangy scent rose around them. Zem cheeped and lifted his wings and Jace steadied his BirdFam.

After a few seconds, Myrtus held out his hands, glanced up at Zem. "Are my hands clean enough to pet you?"

Let me sense, Zem said. *I will not bite.*

Myrtus lifted his hands. Zem ducked his head. *They are good.*

"Great!" Myrtus stroked him for a minute before Zem said, *That is enough. Jace is my FamMan.*

Myrtus scowled.

*G*et up! *Time to get up. See the sun rise.* Lepid's claws easily pierced the thin sheet.

"Uhng." She didn't often watch the sun rise. Maybe in the late days of winter when the days were so short and she had the first shift at the PublicLibrary, before WorkBell. Then she rose in the dark. She'd never been a fan of early mornings.

Come on! Lepid hopped close to her head and licked her cheek. Wet, rough tongue. Sorta nice. Fox breath with the smell of blood, eeeww!

She rolled and her Fam jumped off her to the bedsponge, spring-ing around. "Don't you go with Jace and Zem in the mornings to get food for the hawkcel?"

Lepid stilled. *I want to be with YOU this morning. Lots of fat skirls in the forest yesterday. I caught enough for him and me.* Lepid's gaze slid away. *He is not eating much and I have found good caches for my remaining bits.* He opened his mouth and his tongue lolled. *Hunting is so much more fun than getting food from a no-time on a plate.*

Glyssa's stomach dipped. Life in the wild for sure. Well, this is what she'd wanted. She swept off her nightshirt and put it away and dressed as Lepid zoomed around the pavilion. "All right, let's go see the sunrise."

It is bee-yu-tee-ful. Another sidelong glance. *Best seen from a special hill outside camp.* Glyssa tensed. "Outside camp?" She'd had a mental picture of Jace showing her the beauties of the wilderness, not a young fox, and hadn't ventured out on her own. "Is it safe?"

Yes, most of the big, mean animals are asleep.

She wondered about the "most," but leaned down and petted Lepid. His fur was soft under her palm, his body wiry and ready to run. "Sure. Show me the sunrise."

Yet when she reached the edge of the camp, and the spellshield against larger animals that the Elecampanes and the staff had erected and tended with monthly rituals, she hesitated. She'd never been in uninhabited countryside. She'd lived in the city most of her life, had visited some of the libraries in other towns and cities safely enclosed in a glider along established roads. Her Family had an estate in the south outside Gael City, but that area, too, had long been settled.

Swallowing, she pushed through the barrier, hurried until she caught up with Lepid, who'd paused in his running to look over his shoulder.

Isn't it beautiful? Isn't it nice? Isn't it FUN? He shot off along the side of the dark and towering trees. As Glyssa stumbled after him and her eyes adjusted to the deeper dark outside of camp, she saw that they moved along a path beaten from grass into dirt by many feet. That reassured her and she let out the breath trapped in her chest.

The sky lightened, a few of the most distant stars being lost as the small white sun of Celta approached a horizon Glyssa couldn't see.

Hurry! Lepid urged mentally, loping up a small incline that was more a rise than a hill.

Her breath coming fast . . . she needed to make this run every day and get into better shape . . . Glyssa shivered in the cool air. She should have brought a thin sweater, but she hadn't anticipated that the warm summer mornings had welcomed a trace of autumn.

As soon as she reached the top and turned to face east, she caught her breath enough to murmur "Weathershield," and warmth pressed around her again.

She stared at the tops-of-trees-and-low-hills horizon, the wisps of high clouds taking on red and edged with gold. Brilliant stars still burned and shafts of sunlight lanced through the forest around her as the sun rose. Beautiful. She only wished Jace was here to share it with her. Missed him though he was no longer thousands of kilometers away.

A mocyn! Lepid yipped and took off after the small fluffy-tailed, long-eared animal that Glyssa only saw as a brown blur. And she was alone in the wilderness.

All by herself. Suddenly she was aware of the freshening breeze that rattled leaves on the trees, a susurration that she hadn't paid attention to before. Other sounds came, animal sounds, a huge thrashing from the path she'd trod.

Alone without a weapon. Her mind scrambled to recall the self-defense all children were taught in grovestudy, a few moves Camellia had taught her more recently. She did recall her teacher saying *use any spell you know that might repel an attacker.*

Before she could think of one, something roared and grabbed her from behind!

She whirled, *whirled! Whirlwind spell!* She snapped the Flair Word and the fast-cleansing-and-clothing spell pushed her attacker away.

Sanicle stared at her goggle-eyed as her clothes whipped from her and they and she were cleaned and they wrapped around her again, her hair was yanked and tugged into fancy braids, Flair enhanced her eyes and cheeks, colored her lips. Other than wearing her work clothes, she was ready for a noble ball.

That's what her personal whirlwind spell did. If she'd been in the pavilion with other clothes near, her very best would be on her now.

Now she had the time and space to teleport away from him to a place she knew well, if she'd been in the city. Or if she could visualize her pavilion, the light, the furniture placement. Or she could summon another spell to send him flying down the hill—one to steady wobbly bookcases. Or she could run, if she thought she could beat him to camp. Which she didn't.

She did nothing but watch the man double over with laughter at her expense.

What? shouted Lepid in her mind from the forest. She felt him streaking toward her.

Sanicle straightened, grinning, and wiped his eyes on his shirt sleeve. He was dressed in sturdy work clothes, not like a man who faced unknown dangers in the wilderness. He carried no weapon.

She was ready for a damn ball.

"Well done, GrandMistrys," he hooted. He didn't mean it. He thought surprising her was funny, her reaction funnier still. She wanted to slap him.

"I'm sorry I overreacted," she said, not meaning her words, either.

"My fault," he said cheerfully, looking as if he still enjoyed her original distress and her reaction. "I couldn't resist, you looked so citified here on the hill in the dawn. Just . . . unique. Everyone comes here."

Glyssa shrugged. "I am not sure how long it will take for my city appearance to transmogrify into something more like the rest of the staff."

His lips twitched, he ducked his head. "Um-hmm."

Lepid bounded up the last few paces of the hill. *What is wrong?*

Glyssa stretched her lips in an unamused smile. "GentleSir

Sanicle"—and that form of speech was a misnomer—"gave me a slight scare."

That is not good. Lepid nudged her leg with his nose, leaving a smear on her clean trous. She actually liked that, wouldn't look so prissy when she returned to camp. From here, she saw plenty of people stirring. She rubbed Lepid's head.

Her fox focused his glare on Sanicle. *You made me lose my mocyn with your stupid human noise!* Lepid accused.

Sanicle frowned as if he barely heard the Fam. Lepid snapped his teeth.

Don't bite him! Glyssa ordered.

Lepid gave the man a disgusted look. *I am going back to camp to the breakfast tent. My mouth was set for more food.* With a whisk of his tail, Lepid shot sure-footedly down the hill.

"What'd he say?" asked Sanicle, but not as if he cared.

"He was chasing a mocyn who got away."

"Oh, too bad. Let's head back to the camp." Sanicle smiled. Was that smile supposed to be charming? Had he had a lot of success using it on women?

Glyssa nodded. Her quiet moment was broken, and as cowardly as it was, she didn't want to be out of the camp alone. "Of course," she said.

She looked for the path, but it curled around the bottom of the ridge. She supposed people and animals went up the hill as they pleased, to one end or another of the rise . . . or the middle where she and Sanicle stood. Halfway down the hill, her feet slipped on dewy grass. Sanicle caught her before she fell on her derriere, steadied her and tucked her arm inside of his.

"Let me take your arm," he said, without letting go.

*J*ace watched *Lepid race into the tent, tongue lolling, skidding to a stop* before Myrtus, where he wiggled. *You can pet me, wonderful cook!*

"Huh." But Myrtus bent down and rubbed the fox. Lepid yipped in pleasure, rolled over to his back, exposing his white belly, and the cook continued to pet him, grinning. When he was done, he looked at Zem, ordered "Cleanse," again for his hands, then held them out to the BirdFam again. "Foxes are nice," Myrtus said, nudging a still lying, all paws in the air, Lepid with his foot, "but hawkcels are majestic, unusual Fams."

Zem bent his head. *Thank you, Myrtus.* His eyes gleamed and he looked healthier. A small breath like a burp came from the bird. *I am done now and would like a nap in our tent.*

Lepid sat up, offered his paw. *I would like the rest of his furrabeast bites!*

The plate didn't hold many, but Jace gave it to Myrtus, who flicked each at the fox and laughed when he caught them in his mouth.

"All gone," Myrtus said. "And I know your FamWoman feeds you well, Lepid, and that you hunt. You don't want to get fat."

I am a young and growing fox, Lepid said, his expression still hopeful.

"Enough of you, take yourself out of my mess tent." Myrtus waved him away, but his tone was cheerful.

"Hmm," Jace said. "Just a minute, Lepid." Jace bent down and stroked the fox, found his collar. "Maybe you could transport Zem here to eat when he gets hungry and I am working." Pray to the Lady and Lord that Jace would get back down into the ship, or doing something more with his hands.

"Let's try an experiment." Jace held his arm out for Zem, when the hawkcel climbed onto it, he lowered his Fam to Lepid's back. Showed the bird Lepid's collar that he could curve his claws over.

Very quietly, gliding more than walking, Lepid went to the door of the tent and through it. There weren't very many people in the mess hall, but those who were there, clapped at the trick.

Jace caught up with the two Fams just outside the door.

Want up! Zem fluffed his feathers. *I do not like being so low to the ground. Bad.*

Lepid yipped. *It is fine! I can slink and run through low holes and hide under bushes!*

Bad, Zem repeated.

"That won't work, then." Jace picked his Fam up and put Zem on his shoulder, and got a wave of satisfaction from his companion through their link.

I am a bad stridebeast, Lepid said, but he sat and his eyes showed amusement. *I will hunt and get more food for you, Zem.*

That sounded good, as did the cat Carolinia's offer, but Jace wouldn't forget again that he should be the main source of food for his Fam until Zem could hunt for himself.

Jace considered. "I could translocate you." He wasn't great at that, or teleporting, and it took a lot of energy, but he could do it. Better start practicing more, in any event.

Why would anyone want to teleport when they could fly? Zem asked.

"Good point, but you can't fly just yet," Jace said. "And I think I could teleport us farther than you could fly."

Running is BEST, Lepid said, and took off.

*G*lyssa *fumed when Sanicle took her arm, but didn't protest. She was* such a coward, fearing the wilderness so close to the camp.

"So, did you like the sunrise?" Sanicle asked.

"Beautiful."

"It is, and that's a good spot to see it. Almost as nice as the lake that's close. I'll have to take you there sometime. Pretty blue. Bluer than the Great Platte Ocean next to Druida. Though not as blue as the Deep Blue Sea." He glanced down at her and gave her another practiced smile. His teeth were white and even. "The Elecampanes usually give us all a couple of weeks off at the end of the season and Del runs a trip to the Deep Blue Sea. You should go."

"That sounds nice," Glyssa said. She frowned. "How soon do you think the season will end?" She hadn't been here that long, wasn't nearly ready to leave. Though her field trip report and the transcription of Hoku's journal consisted of many pages, her story

remained pitiful. She pursed her lips in irritation at herself. She
didn't know what to do to fix that.

"When will the season end? Depends on when the steady rains
come." He glanced around at the trees, the sky. "We might have
almost two more months . . . or not. I don't think the Elecampanes
will leave this year until winter really sets in, there's too much
going on."

"You're assigned to Squad One, people going down into the
ship," Glyssa said.

"Yeah." This time his smile came and went. No one had gone
down into the ship since the explosions except a daily run by Lepid
and Carolinia that brought back images of the first section of the
corridor.

Del D'Elecampane had begun a map showing every item, box,
sack, and odd belonging in the outer room and hallway.

"When will you be descending into *Lugh's Spear* again?" May as
well push and prod. She didn't care what *he* thought of her.

"I dunno." He masked his expression, shook his head. "Bad luck
stalks us."

Glyssa snorted. "Human pranks."

He shrugged and picked up pace. The camp came in sight and
she thought of pulling away but some animal roared in the forest.
She flinched and matched Sanicle's stride. No, she didn't want to be
alone outside the encampment, even if it was within view. She'd take
this lovely adventure in small steps.

"What's that?" Her voice sounded curious, not nervous, good!

Sanicle tilted his head. "Wild bissert porcine, I'd imagine." He
licked his lips. "Good eating. The smarter ones have already left the
area. I'll let Del D'Elecampane and some of the other folks who like
to hunt know."

"Ah."

"The bissert is smaller than the average farm porcine." Sanicle
cocked a brow at her. "Only dangerous if you're alone and citified."

Glyssa couldn't relax with his teasing, mostly because she didn't like his touch, but didn't want to offend him right here and now. She tried to say lightly, "You didn't see my follow-up spell." Damn, she sounded prissy.

"I'm sure you had one." His smile said otherwise. She didn't disabuse him of that notion, and finally they reached the camp.

They walked through the spellshield and into tent town. The first person they saw was Funa Twinevine glaring at them.

Seventeen

<u>*H*</u>*ere she is, Zem! Here she is, Jace! Lepid said as he trotted up to her.*

Zem clicked his beak. *Greetyou, Glyssa.*

"Greetyou, Zem. Greetyou, Jace. Andic, thank you for your company back," she said.

Sanicle bowed and made to kiss her hand. She drew it away before he could do so and he straightened with a flushed face. His mouth turned petulant.

She bobbed him a curtsey and his eyes widened as if not many women had given him one. A self-satisfied expression formed on his face.

"We're late to the first breakfast sitting. The waffles are probably all gone," Funa said curtly. She turned on her heel and walked with rolling hips toward the mess tent. Sanicle's gaze went straight to her backside and he followed, caught up with her and slid an arm around her waist.

Glyssa squatted and let Lepid lick her cheek, rubbing him with both hands. Now his breath smelled more like human food. "Did you eat, then?" she asked.

I got some furrabeast! Jace was with me! Lepid caroled in her mind. She glanced up at Jace.

"That's right," he said.

Clearing her throat—how good he looked, even scowling—she said, "Sanicle said he heard bissert porcine in the forest. Will you go hunt it?"

Jace stroked Zem, scratched him on the neck. "No. I don't need to." He paused. "Though I could if my belly were empty. You look nice."

She simply closed her eyes when her face and neck went fiery, inhaled a breath and fought the embarrassment. When she opened her lashes, Jace still studied her. She rose. "Sanicle frightened me. All I could think of was a whirlwind dress spell."

One side of his mouth quirked. "Whirlwind dress spell." Then his brows came down. "That strips you, doesn't it? Cleans you and your clothes. The guy saw you naked."

Glyssa stood stoically. "Yes." She shrugged. "But if we'd been in a Druida City bathhouse—"

"Personal privacy is more prized here in camp," Jace said. "Because we have less of it." Then his eyes unfocused and his smile returned. "Though a lot of folk don't mind nudity much."

Glyssa thought he meant women. She shrugged.

"You seemed friendly enough with Sanicle," Jace pressed.

"I'm not accustomed to being outside in uninhabited territory alone," she said. Her gaze met his, though she didn't tell him how much she'd wanted to see the natural beauties outside the camp with him.

The bell rang for the second seating of breakfast. "I'm hungry," Glyssa said, surprised to find it was true. "I'll see you later."

Jace nodded. "Yes. Time to have Zem checked out." He walked away and she refused to follow him with her gaze. Instead she strode to her own tent.

Zem needs a lot of food, Lepid said.

Eating like a bird . . . yes, they ate all the time, didn't they?

I will have to hunt more. I would like to go with D'Elecampane to hunt the bissert. Do you think she will let me go to hunt the bissert?

"I think if her own FoxFam is hunting, you should be allowed, too," Glyssa said.

Lepid's tail drooped. *I do not want to ask that Shunuk fox. Will you ask D'Elecampane for me? That will make up for you walking with Sanicle and scaring off my mocyn.*

So Glyssa went past her pavilion and informed all three of the Elecampanes of Sanicle's theory and requested Lepid be allowed on the hunt. Raz said he'd watch out for her fox, and Lepid stayed near the man as the Family discussed the matter.

When she got to her tent, she collapsed in the chair, sinking into the too-soft cushion, began to undo her tight braids, and used her fingers to comb out her hair.

Was she really so naive that scaring her had been irresistible, like Sanicle said? Probably. And she *still* was stiff backed enough not to like the game he had played.

The incident had already soured her morning, and the feelings that had welled inside her that moment on the rise fleetly sped from the grasp of her mind. She only knew there'd been a peace and a wonder . . . and . . . and maybe a love for the wilderness that called to something inside her that had never been touched before.

Or that she'd only found in Jace's arms, years ago.

She liked this place and soon every day would bring a new discovery.

But now relations with five people, including her own self, were smudged. Sanicle thought she was a snob because she'd been stiff with him after his joke. The woman he slept with, Funa Twinevine, saw her as a rival. Lepid was unhappy because Sanicle had interrupted his time together with Glyssa, showed her more of the wilderness. Though that was not Glyssa's fault.

Jace . . . had Jace's feelings been hurt when he saw her hand on Sanicle's arm, or only Jace's pride?

*T*he Healer Symphyta confirmed that Zem needed more weight, and sent Healing through him, but Jace knew it wasn't enough.

And as he walked back down the main thoroughfare, and approached Glyssa's tent, he knew what he had to do. The solution to their problem had teased the back of his mind, but he hadn't wanted to admit it. Hadn't wanted to think he'd have to ask a favor from the woman whose help had made him angry before.

But if anyone in camp had multiple no-time storage units, food or otherwise, it would be Glyssa Licorice who'd been outfitted by GreatLord Laev T'Hawthorn, with no expense spared.

A no-time storage unit for Zem's recently dead, not cold, maybe blood-yet-pulsing prey, would be a good answer for everything. Especially if Zem could access the unit himself.

He angled toward Glyssa's tent.

We are going to see FamWoman? asked Zem, clicking his beak in a manner that Jace sensed was approval.

"Yes. I think she can help us."

Of course. Zem shifted. From the corner of his eye, Jace could see the bird preening.

The Elecampanes left her pavilion, nodding to him and went next door to their own tent. Jace got the idea they were communicating telepathically.

He stopped outside Glyssa's open door. Narrowing his eyes, he could see a strong spellshield, probably more than the one keeping insects out.

That the camp was less secure than it had been, that he thought less of the people he worked with—someone had tainted *all* their reps—dimmed his spirit a little.

"Greetyou, Glyssa Licorice," he called.

We are here! said Lepid, as enthusiastic a greeting as if the fox hadn't just seen them.

Glyssa moved from the side of the tent to the door, interest in her eyes, her brows lifted. "Greetyou."

She didn't automatically move aside to welcome them in. That irked Jace, but he had to admit he deserved it.

Greetyou, Glyssa, Zem said, angling his body a little so the one

shaft of sunlight streaming through the clouds hit a beautiful outstretched wing.

"You're very beautiful today, Zem," Glyssa said. So she'd understood Zem's posturing, too.

So are you.

She smiled and her face plumped and softened and she *was* beautiful. More beautiful than she'd been after the whirlwind spell.

"Come on in." She whisked the spellshield aside with a gesture,
and Jace walked through . . . and too close to her, because her fragrance wrapped around him and lust speared straight to his cock.
He had to use a spell to diminish his reaction, and that was a damn
shame.

"I've got a special perch for you, Zem," she said with another
graceful gesture to a battered, wooden runged chair that Jace had
seen before in someone else's tent. No doubt she'd purchased the
thing for Zem. Tenderness stirred in Jace, not just sexual attraction.
Danger!

"Thank you," Jace said.

Thank you, Zem said.

And I can sit on the seat when you sit on the top rung! Lepid
said, hopping onto the woven seat that contained a jagged hole he
didn't seem to mind.

"Zem is a top rung kind of bird. Top-of-the-pyramid," Glyssa
said. "Can I get you caff or tea?"

The caff in the camp ranged from person to person, but in the
dining tent Jace had just come from, it was great. Tea he didn't get
often and he knew Glyssa carried a selection provided by her friend,
the mixer of tea. He'd taste something new. "Tea's fine." He settled
Zem on the top of the chair, then glanced outside at the morning
and the dark clouds gathering. When he looked back, she'd moved
to the no-time food storage unit in the corner of the sitting room,
the largish one he'd seen in her duffle when he'd helped her set up
her pavilion.

She brought out steaming, fragrant tea in a nice cobalt blue pottery mug, nothing too delicate for a man's hand, and a platter of flatsweets that also appeared to be warm. A cocoa chip flatsweet looked melty.

He sat in the chair she indicated, a nice plump cushion under his ass, so different than the other chairs in camp.

Their fingers did not brush when she handed him the mug, offered the plate of flatsweets. He'd hurt her. He steeled himself against guilt, he had enough of that with Zem. And she'd irritated—hurt, something—him first by insinuating he couldn't take care of his own problems. By wanting more from him than he wanted to give.

Scared him with the upsurge of deep feelings he'd felt when he'd first seen her. Rushed to his defense, claiming a link with him that was all too true but one he'd wanted to deny, to himself as well as others. So he was immature. He never claimed to be a good man. He had his own honor, yes, but he didn't consider himself kind or good. Well, better than his mother, but he had her blood in him.

Glyssa would equate honoring your word with good.

Lepid was whining for flatsweets again. She sent him a frown, then chose one with a raisin instead of a cocoa chip and broke it apart and gave a piece to her Fam.

Jace took the cocoa chip flatsweet. She did, too, though the drink she chose was caff. She put the plate on the study table, sat across from him in another plush chair.

They ate a couple of minutes without speaking, the only sound in the tent was Lepid's crunching. She remained quiet well. Didn't fidget as he wanted to do, though he couldn't say the silence was uncomfortable—yet. He could still smell her, the whole pavilion reflected the scents of Glyssa, her natural body fragrance and the herbal lotions or whatever she used that pleased and suited her.

But the more the quiet pressed around him, the more he thought of the other intimate time they spent in each other's company not talking much. He loved the way she whimpered in her passion. He swallowed wrong and coughed, leaning forward.

She leapt from her chair, placed a hand on his back and muttered, "Clear!" and flatsweet crumbs vanished from his airway. The heat from her hand, the shape of her fingers he could feel through his shirt, reminded him all too well of how those hands stroked him, aroused him, brought him pleasure—both in dreams and all-too-long-ago reality.

Sitting up, he forced her to move away, and gulped down a slug of tea that tasted of mint and plants harvested beneath a hot sun, releasing dark flavor. "Thanks," he said.

"You're welcome." She grabbed her own caff with a hand shaky enough that she spilled a few drops on the carpet. She didn't seem to notice.

More crunching sounds came as she bit into her own flatsweet, though she didn't look as if she was tasting it. Appeared like she was taking a short trip to the past, too.

That gave him an ego boost. Enough that he didn't choke again when he said, "I've come to ask for a favor."

Her eyes went dark brown with wariness. "What?"

He grimaced. "I'm having a hard time keeping Zem fed. I can't catch his prey for him, and he is having real trouble eating long-dead meat like furrabeast bites the cook stores."

"Oh."

"I think Zem—we—would do better if we had a no-time to store the prey Lepid and Carolinia kil—hunt for him."

"Carolinia?"

"We made a deal."

"Ah."

Though he wanted to savor it more, he finished his tea, set the mug on the floor and leaned forward again, *willing* her to feel his need—his need for help with his Fam, nothing more. He was lying to himself, but now was not the time to consider that. "How many no-times do you have?"

"Three."

"Three!" The exclamation—almost accusatory—escaped before he could stop it.

She flushed. Beautifully, accenting her few freckles. Her spine stiffened and she sipped her cup of caff, staring at him with eyes cooler than her cheeks. When she lowered her mug, she said, "I did not pack all the no-times."

"Laev T'Hawthorn," Jace said.

"That's right. There is a very small personal vault no-time for valuable items. Secondly, unbeknownst to me, he took a Public-Library book, papyrus, and document archival storage unit and had it fitted with a cutting-edge spellshield and no-time spell for records and vizes." She waved to the new food and drink no-time in the corner of the tent. "And there is that."

"I see." Well, he only saw the food one. The others must be in her bedroom.

Glyssa stood. "You may have the food no-time. It would be the best for your purposes, anyway. It has an antigrav spell on it so we can move it to your tent." It would take up a good deal of space in his tent.

"You would like to set it so that Zem can open it, yes?" She moved over to Zem, who raised his head and blinked out of a nap.

"Yes," Jace said.

"And you, too, of course."

"Yes."

Glyssa nodded briskly, walked over to the unit and gestured to him. "Come and I'll key it for you."

He stood, then joined her.

She swayed as if she'd step away, but she didn't. Her turn to clear her throat. "I'll key it to your Flair." Taking his hand—had hers always been so soft and smooth? He nearly shuddered at her touch. Her first real touch since they'd parted all those years ago. He'd left her and the teeming Druida City and the best sex he'd ever had. A kernel of a notion—that he'd been a fool—lodged in the depths of his mind.

She put his hand on the ident plate, said, "Jace Bayrum, authorized by Glyssa Licorice."

Light flashed and Jace's hand warmed and tingled as the unit's spellshields accepted him.

Look, look what Zem and I can do! Lepid chortled.

Glyssa withdrew her hand, *did* take a pace away from Jace, and looked at their Fams.

Lepid stood on the seat of the chair. Zem transferred himself to the FamFox's back, curled his right foot around Lepid's collar. With a fluid movement that didn't dislodge Zem, Lepid slid to the floor, glided toward them with a big foxy grin. *We can go together!* Lepid said.

I can ride the fox, Zem added drily.

"Wonderful!" Glyssa clapped. "What clever Fams!"

"Yes," Jace said. He lifted his Fam from Lepid to the top of the no-time. "We'll key the machine to him, and it has capabilities for Fam use?"

"Of course," Glyssa said.

"Of course," Jace repeated with less enthusiasm.

She grinned. "Laev doesn't buy anything less than the best. It can get irritating sometimes."

"Not anything I've ever had to deal with," Jace said gruffly.

Her smile faded and she nodded.

Jace concentrated on getting Zem situated on the ident plate. "Zem, HawkcelFam, authorized by Jace—" he stopped. "This won't hurt him, will it? BirdFams aren't common."

Glyssa hesitated. "I could send a mental query to Laev . . . wait, I have the instructions."

"Of course you do." Jace smiled at her.

She flashed a smile back that warmed him. They were negotiating this situation pretty damn well, not treading too much on tender feelings, not irritating each other—okay, that had been his problem, not hers, so he'd work on it. Probably.

She hurried into the inner room of the tent—would he ever see her bedroom? Did he want to? Yes, but without strings attached, and Glyssa seemed to be made up of sticky threads that led to intimate links and connections.

He heard a low chant of couplets . . . her archival cabinet, no doubt, better secured than the food no-time, though he'd bet it was older and less expensive.

A minute later she came back, with a sheet of papyrus in her hand, her mouth turned down. "I have the specs for the no-time unit, and it states the power-energy-whatever that it sends during authorization, but I really don't know how much that is, what it means." She shook the papyrus as if it would answer her question.

Naturally, Glyssa wouldn't pay attention to the amount of Flair needed to access the units, or the amount it used to interact with people—or Fams. She probably never had to consider Flair limitations in her life.

"Give it to me," he said. He was good with his hands, and machines. He studied the amount, looked at Zem. The bird was Flaired, was an intelligent being. Probably could handle the Flair-energy voltage.

Meeting his Fam's eyes, Jace said, "Let's try something first, all right?"

Yes, FamMan. I love you, FamMan.

"I love you, too, Zem." Carefully Jace lifted the bird from the no-time, set him on the cushy arm of a chair. Spreading his feet, Jace gathered the exact amount of the Flair-energy charge that the no-time papyrus instructions indicated. "On three I will touch your—"

Zem lifted and stretched out a claw. Jace nodded.

This is SO interesting. Lepid hopped around. *Zem will be able to open the food no-time!* He cast a sad-eyed look at Glyssa. *I was not allowed to open the food no-time.*

"I don't trust you not to gorge," Glyssa said, picking up the young fox. Which was good, because the animal was distracting . . . but her words soothed Jace, as if she *could* have keyed the unit to Lepid but chose not to. Zem definitely had the same or more Flair than the FoxFam.

More confident, Jace smiled at Zem. The bird hunched less, feeling the assurance Jace sent through their bond.

Again Jace *felt* the strength of the Flair he'd gathered. It was right. He touched Zem's claw and released it.

Zem's beak clicked once. *Tingles!*

Jace let out a breath. A couple of minutes later, Zem was authorized for the no-time and set on the floor to tap his beak against the
sensitive spot that swung the door and various trays open for him.

Lepid had been told to sit on Zem's perch chair and not get down.
That didn't stop his whole body from wriggling.

"We can change the bottom compartment to be the largest,"
Glyssa said. "So it can hold . . . whatever it needs to hold for Zem,
and be easily accessible."

Jace just stared at the stuffed no-time, the indicator of all the
food and drink. Food for every meal. Food for snacks. Hot and cold
drinks. Hot and cold food. Food for *ritual* meals. "It still reads full,"
he said. There were furrabeast steaks stacked in there. His mouth
watered. He turned his gaze to Glyssa and she pinkened again.

"You've been here a little over an eightday and haven't eaten
anything."

"I've put out flatsweets and drinks!"

He just stared.

She crossed her arms. "All right. We're savers, the Licorices. We
save. Just in case."

He shook his head.

So she flung open her arms, reddened more. "Eat, eat it all! I
don't care. Eat whatever you want." But an odd expression passed
over her face. "Eat it all," she repeated more firmly.

He was tempted, but he knew he wouldn't be eating much in his
tent. The odor of furrabeast steak coming from his place might
cause a riot from his neighbors.

"Better that everyone in camp thinks this thing is empty." He
rapped his knuckles on the no-time. It sounded full.

She blinked, nodded. Oh, yeah, she was smart, she'd already figured out the ramifications. Moving toward him, she gestured him
aside so she could rearrange the inside storage.

"I guess there's no way for you to put some of this in your other
no-times."

Stopping, she sent him an appalled glance. "Put *food* in my document no-time!"

"Guess not."

"Barbarian," she muttered.

He laughed. His stomach grumbled.

Lots of things smell really good! Lepid said.

It took her only a few minutes to reorder the food and change the menu readout. Then they all left her pavilion and paraded with the floating thing through the camp, Lepid broadcasting answers to any questions. When they reached Jace's tent, Glyssa remained outside as he moved stuff around and fit the no-time in.

"Thank you again," Jace said.

Carolinia and I will hunt now, Lepid said.

The FamCat separated herself from the shadows. *I can do that, for some special food from your new no-time.*

"Done," Jace said.

At that moment the announcement bell rang.

Eighteen

$\mathscr{W}$hen they all gathered, the Elecampanes stood as a couple, as always, and Raz Cherry T'Elecampane remained stern, more usual since the "cursed" rumors started. Before then he'd been extremely easy with the staff.

Jace realized now that he wasn't the only one hurt by Raz's cool demeanor. The man had charisma. People wanted to please him and his reserve made the encampment even less cheerful these last few days, especially with the cloudy and rainy weather.

"I have news," Raz said abruptly, addressing the quiet crowd—most of the crew—who'd gathered. He stood easily, legs spread, chin up, in a command pose no one would mistake. "The airship coming next week will be significantly larger than the recent transports. We are bringing in ten guards and another Healer. Del and I will be paying the guards a straight salary."

Which meant that the guards would be loyal to the Elecampanes. And no one, except maybe Glyssa, had enough gilt to suborn the guards.

Raz glanced at Symphyta, who stood on the other side of Glyssa and next to him.

"The pool for Symphyta has been successful and she'll be getting new equipment. We will be subsidizing all three Healers, though, of course, each of them can choose their charges for members of this community."

Jace figured that Trago wouldn't do any Fam Healing at all. He didn't know about the new Healer . . .

"Male or female Healer?" Symphyta called.

A smile flashed across Raz Elecampane's face and Jace instinctively relaxed and smiled himself. Raz dipped his head in Symphyta's direction. "Male."

"Goody." She grinned back.

Trago snarled, stalked away. No doubt he'd undercut Symphyta's prices. Not good, and not good for morale.

"Trago, I would prefer you stay until we are finished," Del D'Elecampane called.

The man stiffened, turned back, and stood with an angry expression, arms crossed.

Raz resumed. "Symphyta, your new tent is for two, but we don't expect you to share unless you wish. It's *your* tent."

"Yay!"

"And we are replacing Funa's." He inclined his head to Funa . . . who'd been sleeping in several tents.

"Also arriving will be two noble sisters."

The slight murmur that had arisen among the crew stopped as everyone focused their attention on Raz when he said, "With regard to the curse."

He swept a cool gaze over them all. "Chlora and Musca Comosum. Musca will test the breathable quality of the air inside *Lugh's Spear.* Chlora can scan the ship for diseases." Raz's expression set into a cool mask. "GrandMistrys Glyssa Licorice has offered to house them in her tent during the time we anticipate the ladies being here. We ask those of you who stay to welcome them."

Those of you who stay!

Del stepped forward. "You all know the offer we made when you signed on for this venture. Those of you who have their return trip paid for can leave. Those of you who have earned enough pay to return to Druida can also leave."

Jace calculated that that might be a quarter of the camp.

Raz continued, "The airship going back to Druida can accommodate twenty-five people. Those with return credit will be served first. After that, we will fill the seats from a list. Contact Maxima immediately after this gathering." He waved at Maxima, who held a clipboard.

Silence seethed among the crew, everyone considering their options. People had stiffened with pride and offense that they would be considered cowardly enough to leave . . . or relaxed with relief that they could shake the camp dust off their boots and go back to Druida as soon as possible.

Jace had straightened.

So had Glyssa. That had him raising his brows, even as her own lowered . . . in self-examination?

I am not ready to leave my nest, Zem said from Jace's shoulder.

Jace wondered where his bird had a nest. Jace reached up and stroked his Fam, told him equally privately, *We will discuss this some time later.*

A pause, then Zem said, *I will not leave my FamMan.*

Love welled within Jace. *I will not let you pine for your home.* Some of the people leaving would be those who were homesick—for the city or for the ocean.

Del kept her hand in her HeartMate's and cleared her throat. "Raz and I have not decided whether to keep the encampment open for the winter yet. If we do *not*, we will hire an airship as we have before, to return us all to Druida City before the new year in nearly two months. If we *do* decide to winter over, we anticipate buying component buildings for the camp—dormitories and common buildings. We would like your input on this decision."

More quiet and Jace felt the Elecampanes' gaze on him as they scrutinized the crew. Raz said, "We are also ready to open this venture to shares. We have contracts ready in our pavilion. Those of you who want to invest, please see us after this announcement. When access to *Lugh's Spear* is opened again, we will be offering more shares in the venture in lieu of the bonus upon finding artifacts."

In unison, the Elecampanes said, "Each of you consider carefully what you wish to do."

Raz gestured around, toward the landing field, the communications tent, the rest of the camp. "Stay now or go. Determine whether you might wish to stay here in the winter and perhaps, found a permanent community here."

Glyssa's wasn't the only gasp.

". . . decide to invest in this project and our vision, or not," Raz finished.

When he ended, Del D'Elecampane waited a moment, then said, "That's all."

People stood still, then noise erupted.

Without really looking at him, as people clumped together and buzzed with news, Glyssa said, "About the Comosum ladies—"

That was the least of the news Jace's brain was zipping around.

She said, "They are bringing something for you. I have been in communication with Gwydion Ash, the animal and Fam Healer. He has been very intrigued with Zem."

More annoyance lit inside Jace. He turned and stared at Glyssa's slightly dipped carroty head and nearly equally red cheeks. "For an extensive report on Zem, he has provided some meals—" she coughed and winced—"newly killed rodents of several kinds, and, uh, smaller birds—for Zem. The Comosums are bringing them in a special no-time."

On Jace's shoulder Zem puffed his feathers and snicked his beak in satisfaction. He leaned down and tugged a strand of Glyssa's hair from her braid. *Thank you, FamWoman.*

Now Glyssa met Jace's eyes. "I love Zem, too. I am allowed to show that love."

Yes, yes, yes! Lepid bounced around them both. *Good food for Zem. I love Zem, too.*

"Provided meals?" Jace kept his tone even.

"In a no-time." Glyssa pursed her lips. "We will switch out the no-times. The one the Ashes are sending is specifically calibrated and designed for Fams."

"Why didn't you tell me this a septhour ago?"

She glanced around, people had separated into clumps. "Zem needs a good solution to his food problem *now*. And I like you in my tent."

"And you like me asking for help."

"Also true."

Her chin came up, her eyes deepened into darker brown. "The ladies Comosums are . . . haughty. They will expect exceptional food. My friend, Camellia Darjeeling D'Hawthorn is sending me a food chest with temporary no-time spells. And the cost of *that* is because *she* loves *me*."

And me! Lepid said.

Glyssa's face softened. "Yes." She smiled slyly. "You are still welcome to eat whatever you like." With a chuckle, she said, "And fast."

"I could give a couple of meals to Myrtus Stopper for being kind to Zem," Jace said.

She nodded. "That would be good."

"And Symphyta."

Glyssa's mouth tightened, could she be a little jealous? "That would be very kind of you. She likes sweets, so maybe the desserts especially. If you want to keep some of the food from the contents, you're welcome to do that, too."

He didn't have anywhere to put it.

"Right."

"You won't be leaving?" she said, then frowned as if she hadn't meant to ask.

"I have the pay, from working with you and Maxima"—and from the damned digging, though that was the minimum—"to return. I'm not going," he answered roughly. "But the Elecampanes were right before. This smear on my name could follow me wherever I go. I'll be investing." If he had enough gilt.

He looked at the cowards and the bored and the stups who'd

gathered around the owners, taking them up on the return trip. So many other exciting options right here!

Across from them, Funa stamped her foot and appeared a little sulky, then perked up when Symphyta teasingly bumped her with a grin. "Guards, new blood. New men."

"Oh, yes," Funa hissed.

*T*hat *evening after dinner, Jace and Carolinia fed Zem and Jace stocked* the new no-time with very warm kills. The cat ate some of the good human food and then had taken herself off with a high and waving tail. Zem himself appeared better already since the cat and a competitive Lepid had made sure he was fed throughout the day and brought food for his no-time.

Lepid scratched at the dirt outside Jace's door. The FamFox's ears flattened to his head. *FamWoman is sad.*

Now that he mentioned it, Jace realized some of the depression that pervaded him came through the bond from Glyssa.

Lepid fox lay down on the ground, and put his forepaws over his muzzle. *Water is leaking from her eyes.*

Jace winced. His shoulders twitched.

Come help! Lepid rose slowly to his feet, walked toward Jace with an ingratiating expression and licked his hand. *Help!*

Jace actually shifted from foot to foot, one of the first things anyone taking self-defense or fighter training was told not to do, and he could usually control that. Not this time. "What makes you think I'd know what to do?"

Plleaaasssee. Lepid sounded pitiful. *We helped you and Zem.*

The FoxFam was good with laying on the guilt. *I'm sure Zem's and your problems are worse than Glyssa's.* Lepid let one ear stand up and rotate. *I am well, Glyssa is well. She is just sad.*

Nothing Jace liked more than jollying up a crying woman.

You can help, I'm sure!

That's because the fox was too young to know any better, Jace figured. He didn't think the young fox had the patience to pester him until Jace caved. But the Fam was right, Glyssa had gone out of her way to help him.

Not as if Jace would be welcomed around the campfire, anyway. He rubbed his chest. "All right."

I will stay here, Zem said, eyes already closed.

Lepid ran ahead. Jace plodded after. When he got to Glyssa's pavilion, he couldn't see a thing, privacy spells shielded the windows and door. He paused.

Jace is here. He will help you! He will help us! Lepid said along the bond that the fox and Jace shared with Glyssa. No choice, the fox had committed him. Jace knocked on the door. It took Glyssa a moment to answer—maybe she was cleaning up her tears? Maybe she was considering whatever problem she had and deciding Jace *couldn't* help?

He became aware of the soft dark, the chirping of insects, the singing of night birds. Tonight the sky was clear with the galaxies that painted the Celtan sky bright and close, the twinmoons brilliant. Maybe there wasn't a better place to be.

Glyssa opened the door, a figure in a thin summer robe with the light behind her outlining her body. He caught her fragrance and he knew he was in trouble.

Here he is! I brought him! I am a HERO and he will be a HERO, too!

She looked at Jace with an expression as doubtful as he felt.

Clearing his throat, he said, "What's the problem?" He'd meant to be brusque but his mouth had gentled the words, pushed more after them. "How can I help?"

With a frown, she shook her head. "I don't know if you can." She stepped aside and let him in, gestured to the desk with Hoku's journals spread out, sheets of papyrus and a writestick. Messy as he hadn't expected her to be. Almost looked as if she couldn't accomplish something.

Stupid idea.

"I don't recall. Do you know the terms of my fieldwork? What I must accomplish to advance in my career?" she asked.

"No."

"Oh. I didn't discuss them with you as well as Maxima?"

"No."

She scrubbed at her puffy face. He didn't comment. With a sigh and drooping shoulders she walked over to one of the chairs at the far end of the sitting room, pointedly ignoring the desk.

"I have to record what's going on in camp, and transcribe Hoku's journals . . ." Glyssa was reluctant to tell Jace her failings.

He can HELP! Lepid pressed, then went over to Zem's chair and hopped up on it, tongue hanging out, encouraging.

"Looks like you might have a problem," Jace said, took the few steps to the desk and stared at her and the mess of papyrus and writestick. "Huh. Thought you were expert in everything."

Too tired to snap at him, she said, "No." If she let it, panic would eat at her that she might fail, fail her fieldwork, and remain a Second-Level Librarian.

He rolled the writestick and smiled angelically. "Whatcha doing?"

"Writing a paper."

His brows wiggled. "*Writing,* huh?"

"All right, trying to write."

Tilting his head, he whisked a sheet of papyrus from the table, read, and winced. Glyssa sat in stiff mortification.

Jace grabbed a legged chair with his ankle, dragged it over, and dropped into it. "This doesn't read like a scholarly paper to me, GrandMistrys Librarian."

And more tears came and everything poured out, Camellia and her need to have her ancestor vindicated, wanting Glyssa to write a popular piece instead of a restrained research monograph. Glyssa's review with her Family, how she felt set up for failure.

He *listened.* More, he patted her back . . . and that simple touch of affection sank into her, warming her all the way to her heart. Yes, he was her HeartMate, and his touch helped.

"Just tell the story," he said. Leaning back, he closed his eyes and folded his hands over his flat stomach, stretched out his feet and began . . .

The blood pulsed hot and fast through him again. He lived. He'd survived, and he was on his way to a new home and future. Even with his eyes shut in the cryonics tube, Netra Sunaya Hoku sensed the thrust of the starship through endless starry space . . .

Glyssa stared. "Where did you learn to do that?"

He shrugged. "When you're in the wilds around campfires with folk, most don't carry vizes or recording disks. We tell stories."

She could feel her eyes round. "Saved! I'm saved!" Hopping up she hugged him hard, noted he stiffened and withdrew, too happy to care that he hadn't wanted her touch.

"Will you help me? I'll give you the recording of the transcription of his journals. You can tell the story, and I can write it." She glanced at his surprised face. "I'll be deeply, deeply grateful. And, of course, I will give you credit as the author."

"Of course you would." His brows lowered as if in consideration. He shifted, shook his head. "I don't know how to write, either." His hands flexed, then he shook his head. "I don't think I want people thinking I wrote stuff. I don't want the credit."

Lepid whined.

Jace said, "But I'll help you. Show me what you've got."

She handed him the first pages of the transcription of Hoku's journals to read and he moved to a more comfortable chair.

She went to her desk and wrote down the first lines he'd reeled off.

When he looked up again, she read them back. "Sound good?"

He shrugged. "I guess."

"You don't think he'd be lonely? He signed on alone, none of his family came with him, whatever family he had."

"Why would he be lonely? It's an adventure! A damn fine adventure and away from those fliggers on Earth who wanted to kill people with psi . . . Flair." Jace's eyes gleamed.

Glyssa tilted her head. She read Hoku as a quiet, precise, serious sort of man, especially after the deaths he felt responsible for. But giving him a little of Jace's joie de vivre . . . why not? . . . especially in the beginning. Who's to say he didn't have that quality? Her own writing didn't completely reflect her, either.

"As for family," Jace said. "Plenty of time for that later. Right now he's concentrating on being a starship pilot." He smiled and his expression looked distant again.

"Yes," she said. One last time she read Jace's opening aloud. "It *is* good." She aimed her writestick at him. "Tell the story."

He did and she wrote it down. Then she sighed. "I can't pass this off as my own work for the FirstLevel PublicLibrarians."

He sent her an unbelieving stare, narrowed his eyes. "You said that earlier and you believe that."

Offended and sitting up straight, she said, "Of course I do. Besides, your style isn't mine. Everyone would know that."

He shook his head, then rubbed his temples with his hand. "All right. Then tell the story yourself. You've got a mouth on you," he said. "I'm thinking you'd feel better if you recorded the story."

Her spine stiffened more. "I've tried and tried and I can't. You can help me." She wouldn't mention Zem.

She didn't have to. "You saved Zem's life." Jace nodded. "I like telling stories. I'll do it." He rolled a shoulder. "You tell your folks or not, as you please, and your friends, but nobody else needs to know I did this."

After nibbling her lower lip, she said, "Maybe I can convince my Family to accept this, even though it isn't solely my work. I know Camellia and Laev will." She pushed the dark threat of her Family's disapproval at her failure away. "We can do this." She hoped.

He came to her that night in her lucid dreams, setting a hand on her shoulder and awaking her. She glanced up, saw him dressed only in a loincloth. She, of course, had her long sleep tunic on, old and soft.

"Glyssa," he said.

Nineteen

❤

"Glyssa," he repeated.

At least he knew who she was in dreams now.

He reached over and took a handful of her hair, fisted his fingers around it as if savoring the texture of the springy stuff.

"Your hair feels like no other's."

Since even in dreams grimaces weren't romantic, she fixed a pleasant expression on her face. Her smile curved naturally as she noted his sex stirring. Old nightrobe or not, she tossed the sheet away and stood before him, thinking she could smell the spicy musk of him as if this was no dream.

He looked down at her, his smile spreading as he touched one of her tight nipples beneath the sagging cloth. He took a step back to scan her and her nightwear. She'd always come to him in the sexiest clothes that she thought would arouse him.

"Interesting," he said.

She would *not* blush in her own dream—all right, their shared dream.

Now he cupped her breasts, his big hands covering her modest gifts. She shifted as her lower body began to ache for completion. She wanted sex. She wanted loving, too, but she'd settle for fiery sex.

She wanted him.

"Are you sure you want to lay—play with me?" she asked softly. "You've been angry with me."

He shrugged. "That doesn't seem important now."

Letting her vulnerability show, she said, "I don't want you to regret this."

Another shrug. "Too much talking."

All right, then. He'd been stroking her breasts. Her turn. She reached out and laid her hand on his shaft.

Jace jerked, probably because she'd never done that before. Giving him one long stroke, she stepped back and whipped off her sleepwear.

He liked her in clothing, seemed even interested in her regular night tunic. She preferred naked herself, but there might be something in this idea of arousing one's partner while he was dressed. He wasn't wearing much, but she was pleased to work with what she had.

Unable to stop her grin, she came in close, very close, until their bodies touched, her hips pressed tightly to him, her breasts flattened against his chest. She slid her arms around his neck, found his skin slightly damp. Even better.

He set his hands on her hips, didn't go for squeezing her derriere. That would change soon. She took his mouth, running her tongue over his mouth and when he opened his lips, she plunged her tongue in to taste him. *Nothing* was like the taste of her man. She sucked his tongue, tangled her own with his, thrust and withdrew as she slowly rubbed her body against his, feeling his sex stiffen, enlarge. His hands moved to her bottom and she broke the kiss, took a pace back.

His pupils were dilated, lips redder from their kiss, his fingers flexed. Again she glided forward, reached for his cock behind his loincloth, stroked hard, down, then up, then down and cupped his balls.

Jace picked her up and threw her on her bedsponge, whipped off his loincloth and pounced.

Her body was ready, needy. She arched up, waiting for his first lunge, and his face set, his eyes wild, he thrust into her.

The race to the shattering ecstasy was on.

No. He stopped. No!

Her nails dug into the back of his shoulders. "Move!"

"Not . . . yet." His gaze was steady now. "Slow. Love being in you. Here. Best. Slow, slow, slow," he chanted softly, propping himself on his elbows and withdrawing incrementally.

She grit her teeth, closed her eyes, experiencing all the incredible sensations of her man moving inside her.

He pulled nearly out, and she whimpered at the loss, her desire ratcheted up.

Then he thrust hard, going deep, she cried out.

He halted and she panted. So delicious, this filling! This connection. She wrapped arms and legs around him, tried to pull his torso closer for a kiss, no go. Tried to arch so he would move. Nothing.

"Open your eyes. Look at me. I don't want you thinking about anyone but me. About Andic."

She followed his demand, lifted her eyelashes. Jace was blurry. "Andic who?" she slurred.

He laughed and sensations rippled through her. They groaned together. He took a couple of short breaths, the cords of his neck showed strain. "Too good. Dammit. Too damn good." Lowering himself, he kissed her, her forehead, her cheeks, her lips.

"Jace!" she cried when his mouth left her own. "I need you."

"Glyssa," he groaned and then he was moving in her like she wanted. Her mind vanished and she clawed at him, moaned, whimpered, demanded. Only craving existed. Only the shattering was necessary.

Her lover would give her that, and she would empty him.

Her HeartMate.

And then she reached the cliff of rapture and held him close and jumped off it and soared and glittering fireworks exploded around her, through her.

His body tensed against her. She felt the rumble of his release, his moan leaving his chest on a long breath, and his weight settled against her.

She recovered quickly, too quickly, as was usual in this dream-time. In reality, her body would be languorous for long minutes. She said nothing, wanting to prolong the time together, wanting him to stay.

Wanting him to walk—run!—from his tent to hers so they could make love in more than dreams. Eyelids cracked, she looked at his face. Satisfied. Soon he would leave like usual, just vanish, sliding deeper into sleep or waking in his tent.

Her breath sighed from her as she closed her eyes again, looking internally for their bond. Huge and pulsing red, changing to orange as passion subsided, soon to return to the standard yellow. She searched her mind for the golden HeartBond, the connection that would forever tie them together. Nowhere.

Like always, it didn't appear in dreams. Now she quietly bit her lip in heartache, and held her arms loose around his back and shoulders, not trying to trap him here, with her, in sex or in a relationship.

He grunted, said hoarsely, "By the Lord and Lady, that was good."

"Yes." She held her breath. He didn't leave. He was *communicating* after sex. She stroked his back, long sweeps.

"Always good with you, Glyssa." He kissed her, a soft touch of lips, then he was gone.

Jace's eyes popped open, adjusted fast to the filtered twinmoonslight and brilliant starlight sifting through the vents in his tent. He smelled of sex. Naturally. Glancing over to Zem, he saw the hawkcel hunched away from him on his perch, and enveloped in a blue white Flair aura. The sight interested, embarrassed, and reassured him all at once. His Fam had the energy to use his Flair and encase himself in—Jace studied the field—a soundproof bubble.

He cringed, rose from the bedsponge, took off the sheets and dumped them in the cleanser along with his loincloth. They'd be pristine by morning.

He waved a hand to freshen the sponge, and suffered through a thorough scrubbing himself. Not so quick as a whirlwind cleansing and dressing spell. The thought made him smile. Andic might have seen Glyssa nude, but Jace knew how she looked in the throes of passion.

And what passion! He shook out his limbs, still energized from the dream sex. The cleaning spells were easy now, taking minimal Flair, he did them so often and knew them so well. He wrapped on another loincloth.

Zem, you want some food? Jace eyed the no-time. He could do with some fancy tasting vittles. Maybe even eat some holiday food, though no ritual time was near. The new twinmoons had passed, he wasn't quite sure when first-quarters or half-moons was, and Mabon, the autumnal equinox, was two weeks away.

But he felt good, and surely the everyday should be celebrated . . . or just get the food in your belly when you could, before the no-time got taken away or the food disappeared for any other reason.

Click-click-click-click of claws, Zem slowly turned around on his perch. His eyes gleamed in the night. He sniffed.

Jace frowned, stamped his foot on the floor tarp and said a Flair spell that took a little more energy out of him, but sent the fragrance of herbs—thyme, sage, manly type stuff—through the area. He didn't mind the smell of sex, but now he had a picky roommate.

Zem lifted his head, opened and closed his beak. *Thank you, FamMan, smells nice.*

Jace nodded.

I think you should add some bayrum scent to that mixture.

"Maybe," Jace said.

I would like some food, thank you, Zem said.

Jace took the pace to the no-time and opened it, examined Zem's menu. "You have skirl, mouse, and portions of rat and mocyn."

Zem snapped his beak and replied with greed, *All instants after death.*

"Yeah." That depressed Jace's appetite a bit.

I will have the skirl. The fox did not mangle it as much.

"Okay."

I feel like eating guts.

"Great."

Zem glided down to the top of the no-time, beyond his plate, tilted his head with gleaming anticipatory eye.

"Right." It would be cowardly to put on a glove to handle the thing. Jace drew in an unobtrusive breath, opened Zem's drawer, and pulled out the bloody skirl. He set it on the plate and pretended not to notice the ripping and gurgling sounds as he looked at his own menu. He decided to go with a spinach, cheese, and egg pastry pocket, yanked it from the no-time still steaming and tossed it around to cool it.

Zem's slurping stopped. *You should have a plate and fork to save your fingers.*

"Yeah, yeah."

A few minutes later, they'd eaten and he put the now-cool remains of the skirl back into Zem's drawer.

The pastry had been excellent. He'd had three. He subsided onto the newly made bedsponge, didn't get under the top sheet. Too hot and humid for that. Stacking his hands behind his head, he breathed deeply of the air that no longer held just day heat and night coolness, but the slightest hint of autumn scent.

Zem flew out of the tent to do his business, then back in and to his stand. Jace thought he looked healthier, chipper, even.

Glyssa was most kind to give us the no-time, Zem said, grooming his feathers and not looking at Jace.

"Yes."

You should be nice to her. Zem hesitated delicately. *She gives you pleasure.*

Jace's whole body twitched. He'd been trying not to think of that and keep from getting hard. Too late now.

*T*he next morning, Glyssa participated in the short ritual for good hunting and blessing the animal to be found and used for food. Then Del,

Raz, and Maxima Elecampane and their Fams went out on the bissert hunt along with Sanicle and some others—and Lepid. When they returned with the dead thing, Glyssa took one look and stayed away from the butchering and rendering . . . or whatever.

In this particular instance, she liked being citified. Hunting and killing animals for food would only happen if she were starving.

That afternoon Del and Raz surprised the staff again by stating that they would accept volunteers to go down into *Lugh's Spear*, if any wished. Every person—being—since Lepid had surged forward—would be fitted with a live viz recording that would send video back to someone monitoring the expedition in the communications tent.

Jace and Sanicle volunteered, and though Sanicle looked askance at Jace, he said nothing.

Lepid had reported that gossip about Jace had turned favorable since he'd humbled himself to ask Glyssa for help in saving Zem. People might be reconsidering recent events and believe he was the easy-going guy they'd always known and not some villain hiding behind a smiling mask.

So, once more, the hole to the breach in the starship was opened and a team of four men and one FamFox went down.

Glyssa watched the live feed with Maxima, pulse racing at her first real glimpse of the place. So very dark! Just snips and slices of a view.

Then the team was back up with another crate and a sack that some colonist had left in the corridor—it was littered with personal sacks and boxes—Maxima left to check out and record what was in the sack. And Glyssa spoke with Camellia and Tiana by scry in the communication tent about the fiction project.

The conversation went well, despite her previous dread. It was great to see her friends and hear their laughter. When Glyssa thought about missing them, it was more than she could bear. They'd gotten together at least once every week, usually more often.

But she knew they could "see" some of the images she had through their bond with her . . . and Camellia had her HeartMate and her businesses to run and probably wouldn't come here, not even for a visit . . . not this year.

Tiana was focused on working her way up the ladder of priest-esses, determined to wipe away the smear on her Family's name by attaining the highest rank in the highest Temple, Lady of Round-Circle Temple in Druida City. Tiana wouldn't be visiting, either.

Glyssa sucked in her breath. Of course the lives of her friends wouldn't stay static. And hadn't *she* been the one to leave? She could have stayed in Druida City, done her "field" study and research there. And let Jace go, frittering away their lives. No, that had been no option.

Her friends loved her. Didn't feel abandoned by her leaving, following her own path. She sensed curiosity from them, a trace of envy of her, but they'd always shared the bad and tough emotions with the good.

They'd laughed when she'd told them she'd failed at creative writing, hummed in pleasure when she said her HeartMate was helping her, since he was a natural storyteller.

Camellia gave her "official" approval of the partnership—anything for a good, popular book.

They finally all had to say good-bye and cut the transmission.

The glow of good camaraderie enhanced the deliciousness of a bissert ham steak at dinner.

Jace worked with her a little bit, reveling in the fact that he was allowed in the back of the ship. She recorded his observations, and they did another chapter on the book about Hoku. Zem had accompanied him and looked very well.

Then Jace and Zem went out to bask in renewed popularity and take their place by the fire.

Jace had actually asked her to come and sit next to him, and how she'd wanted to! But bitter as it was, she knew her duty. She had to tell her Family about the change of plans with regard to the book.

Her Family would *not* approve of her failure. A Licorice should be able to turn her or his hand to anything and succeed.

She had to do it. So she walked back to the communications tent, scanned the schedule and, doing the time change arithmetic in her head, chose the closest time, in three-quarters of a half septhour.

To wait, she crossed to a nearby bench that looked out on the forest and sent a mental call to her Family. *FirstLevel Librarians of Celta, from SecondLevel Librarian Glyssa Licorice.*

Her sister contacted her first. *FirstLevel Librarian Enata Licorice here.* The thought seemed to echo as if in an open space or room—the image Glyssa always got when waiting to speak with more than one of her Family.

She nerved herself as her mother stated, *Here, Rhiza D'Licorice,* then her father's warm mental joined them, *Here, Fasic Almond T'Licorice.*

I request a viz communication with you in half a septhour for a formal update of my fieldwork.

Surprise fireworks showed in their thoughts.

/

Twenty

*W*e will have to go to the Ship! her mother grumbled. *That's the only terminal for the new viz tech. You did not give us much time!*

Wonderful! her father enthused.

I suppose I can do that, her sister said.

Yes, Glyssa was overwhelmed by love at their response. *May I expect to see and hear you, then?* Not that she really wanted to see and hear them, well, except her father, and even he would be disappointed with her, shake his head. She *hated* the expression of disappointment on his face.

We will be there, her mother confirmed. *We are leaving now by glider since we don't know either* Nuada's Sword *or* Landing Park Teleportation Pad *well enough to 'port there.* She dropped out of the conversation.

Her sister said nothing as she left, either.

Greetyou, dear daughter, her father said, even as Glyssa *felt* him exploring the surface images of the camp and everything in her mind. She "heard" him sigh. *Wish I could go there . . .*

How is your own project proceeding?

I was allowed to continue your former HouseHeart project. Another, larger sigh. *The Families who have HouseHearts—mostly the FirstFamilies, the descendants of the colonists who paid for the ships and crew to make the journey—are very wary and slow to grant my request to see them. They will NOT let me record the inner sanctums. For the couple that I have had success in entering, I have had to take a mind Healer with me so she could immediately wipe the knowledge of the location and how to access the House-Heart as soon as I left the chamber.*

Glyssa felt the weighing of his considerations, and he continued with a little lighter tone, *Perhaps I will report the intransigence of the Residences and the Families and recommend that we shelve the project for the time being.*

Not quite saying that he had failed, and it wouldn't be held against him, like it would her, because the issue was out of his control.

Just as stringing words into images and stories was out of Glyssa's control, but the Family wouldn't understand that. It would be a rationalization and an excuse. The Licorices had low tolerances for those.

I think I will be able to convince the other FirstLevel Librarians that this project should be set aside in a couple of months. His mind voice went upbeat. *Then maybe I could join you, or at least visit!*

Having her father watch as she wooed her HeartMate. How fun. *I am not sure how long the Elecampanes will keep the excavation going this year.* She frowned, understood her father felt that. *I hadn't planned on staying during the winter, and the owners haven't continued the project during the winter months.* And Jace was recalcitrant to her wooing, barely accepted friendship, though he liked their dream lovemaking just fine.

Time to move on him in the flesh . . . and she hid those thoughts deep from her father.

She said, *But the project hasn't progressed to breaching the full ship and exploring it, either. They MUST have some sort of permanent team here, for security, if nothing else.*

Her father's default thinking sound, a low and simple melody, rumbled through Glyssa's mind. Yes, she missed him, too!

I love you, Glyssa, he responded to her stab of homesickness for him.

I love you, too, Father.

We will see if I can come there. Longing infused his tone, more for the excitement and adventure than to simply see her.

But he didn't know, now, that she would have to report failure. She kept that dread from infusing her mind, too. *I'll talk to you shortly,* she said.

Merry meet, he offered.

And merry part, she replied.

And merry meet again!

She closed the telepathic link between them and rose from the bench and stepped into the evening-shadowed paths between the tents, dread slithering through her as she walked until it was time to scry her Family.

She'd been right. It did not go well. The legitimacy of her whole project was called into question. Her mother beat questions upon her as to *why* she was determined to stay since the *Lugh's Spear* venture was in jeopardy. Glyssa edged around the truth of wanting to be with her HeartMate.

Her sister picked and picked and picked.

The excavation was not proceeding in an orderly manner.

The project had such problems that workers were leaving.

The venture might be shut down, and what was Glyssa doing with all her time when the project was stalled?

Glyssa could not handle the work of popular fiction by herself.

And the last point that had Glyssa's mother frowning in worry—dangerous explosions had occurred.

Finally, the FirstLevel Librarians ordered her to present herself back in Druida City for another formal hearing within an eightday to defend her field study.

And, yes, when her father lingered to softly sign off, disappointment limned his features.

Glyssa held back tears until she'd crept to the edge of the gathering by the fire, then let them come. Lepid sprang over to her and curled on her lap, licking her face, but he didn't make her smile.

Her career hung by a thread over a terrible cliff. But if she left now, she might never see Jace again. Her stomach tightened.

*J*ace *wrapped up his story—went for a shortened version—when a deep* cloud of depression infused him. It didn't take more than an instant and the bolting of Lepid from dancing around the fire to understand Glyssa hurt. The ache radiated to him through their bond in throbbing waves. He realized their bond had grown just from being in the same place at the same time, and maybe even, contrarily, because he'd put effort in avoiding her during the time he'd been angry with her for wanting more than he wanted to give.

Yeah, he could tighten the bond to a thread again, but why would he when the idea of comforting her in person stirred him up? Murmuring his good nights to his companions as they applauded, he rose, then headed to the back of the circle and some of the tall bushes where he felt Glyssa.

Zem, who'd been sitting on his shoulder, soared to the top of a tent pole. *There is a nice scent to the fire and the wind and even the people tonight. I will stay for a while. My wing is almost Healed, and I feel very good.*

I'm glad, Jace said. He figured the scent from the people Zem liked was the relief of the cowards who actually believed in the curse stuff and were ready to leave on the airship back to Druida City when the shuttle came in four days. Or for those who waited for the noble ladies to tell them whether the ship was safe or not. Or thought having guards might solve all their problems. Who knew? Maybe it would. All he really knew was that the "bad luck" thing had divided the camp.

And here was Glyssa. Even in the twinmoonslight he could see the silver paths of drying tears on her face.

Hello, FamMan! Lepid hopped to his feet. *You will stay with FamWoman? I want to check my caches for a nibble or two.* Without waiting for a response, Lepid zipped off.

The glow of Glyssa's hair, the fragrance of her, seeing her vulnerable and feeling their open bond fired his blood. He couldn't ignore the attraction between them anymore. And in this night of starshine and moonslight, he didn't want to. Holding out his hand, he said, "What's wrong?"

She just shook her head. "I don't want to talk about it now."

He hesitated. He could push, but that was her way, not his . . . and the night and the woman moved him. If he couldn't comfort her with words, he could do so with actions.

Share with her. "Come on, I'll walk you to your pavilion."

Her breath caught, and he felt her gentle touch on their bond which pulsed with desire. Pretty color darkened her cheeks and he wanted to see the pink of them, the fire of her hair, drive himself to a hotter bonfire than the one he'd just left.

"Come, Glyssa," his own voice was darker, richer, than the tones he'd used in his storytelling.

She took his hand and he pulled her up, then went further and slid his arm around her waist. This close he could smell more of her natural scent and his heart picked up beat and his sex thickened. No walking away tonight. Not even if she was his doom.

Soon they were in her tent, in her bedroom, a bedsponge more than a meter thick, with a soft top, nice linens, a couple of fluffy pillows. Vaguely noticed as background to Glyssa.

She whispered a Word and a dim yellow spellglobe appeared, brightening and turning her hair to copper. Yes, pink still showed on her cheeks, but her darker lips beckoned and he turned and drew her even closer.

His hands plunged into her hair to touch it, finally, after so many years. Fool, he! And he pressed his lips to hers and they were soft and her mouth opened and his tongue tasted her once more.

Perfect. So perfect he groaned . . . too perfect to walk away from, and fear gibbered from the back of his mind and he kicked the negative emotion *out*. And missed her stripping his tunic down from his shoulders and away so her hands against his chest surprised him and he had to groan again.

Heated lust surged so high, so fast, it exploded all thought. He yanked at her clothes and they fell away under his hands and he should step back and look at her, her hair that about seared his eyes, so untamed out of its coil and her shining brown eyes, but her skin was smooth under his palms.

And she smelled of desire, too, and her tongue dueled with his. Yesss! This was his Glyssa, his lover who he'd never forgotten and he had his hands on her and her clothes fell away.

She said another Word and his clothes and even his boots were gone and he needed her. He'd be destroyed if he wasn't burning in her heat, exploding into fiery fragments in the next instant.

So he lifted her and tossed her on the bed. Her legs opened and he saw completion. He flung himself on her. Thrust inside. Better than anything, ever. Sweet. Hot.

No way to make it last, pleasure so pure. Everything pouring into his senses. The dampness of Glyssa's skin, the cut of her nails on his back. Glyssa!

One more lunge and ecstasy poured through him. Glyssa keened and her arms and legs squeezed him and they held each other tight.

When his brain began working, he noted they'd moved to lie on their sides, facing each other. And though Glyssa appeared happy and relaxed, he thought he could still see faint traces of tears.

"What made you cry, sweet Glyssa?"

She snorted, chuckled. "I'm not that sweet."

But she obviously had a tender heart for some things. "Maybe not, but I don't think you're the type to cry easily or often."

After a sniff and a long sigh, her gaze slid away from his. "The FirstLevel Librarians of Druida are not pleased that I can't write a good story."

Jace blinked. "It's a skill, like anything else. I can't tell you how many bad or pointless or long-drawn-out stories I've listened to at campfires."

"You're a natural."

He smiled. "You think?"

"Maybe it's your Flair."

His shoulder hunched automatically. "I don't have great Flair."

"You had Passages, though."

"Yeah, but nothing obviously manifested."

"Storytelling?"

"That doesn't feel right."

She chuckled, rolled toward him, and he got a good hold on her so she couldn't wiggle away from the next questions he was planning to ask.

"If storytelling doesn't feel right as your main Flair, that skill probably isn't it," she said.

"Told you." He stroked her cheek. "What happened to make you cry? Can't be that stick-up-ass librarians don't understand you."

As he'd expected, she stiffened. But unexpectedly, she didn't try to draw away, though her lashes lowered so he couldn't see her eyes. She took a couple of long breaths, and not looking at him, said, "The FirstLevel Librarians of Celta are my mother, father, and sister."

He winced. "Ouch."

"Yes."

"The Family expects technical expertise in a variety of areas, such as creative writing."

"Huh. How are their stories?"

Her eyelashes fluttered and she leaned back to meet his gaze. Such a lovely woman, a vivid woman with red hair and deep brown eyes and freckles that got more color when she flushed.

"I don't know."

"Something to keep in mind. But I sense that wasn't all that bothered you." And he did. Their bond seethed with rough emotions regarding her Family.

Glyssa pushed him a little, moved to lie with her head on his shoulder, her hand stroking his chest—he'd wait a little before sliding it lower. It occurred to him that they'd never talked about serious matters in dreams or during their quick affair. They had more of a bond than sex, now.

"They—the FirstLevel Librarians, in their official capacity—have ordered me to return for an interim hearing on my fieldwork."

A jolt to his heart. His breath stopped. His arms pulled her over his body as if trying to bind her closer still so they could not be separated. And his fear of intimacy was back screaming and questioning what he was doing. But his body, and, right now, his emotions, wanted her and would not listen to stupid fears.

He wished for a drink to whet his suddenly dry mouth. "What does that mean, exactly?"

"It means they are doubting that my field study work is acceptable."

"Because you can't write a story!"

"That was one of the provisions, and it was for Camellia, but she is fine with you helping me with it. My Family isn't."

"Family," he said bitterly. His had never supported him much, just the opposite, especially his mother.

"They love me, they do. In their own way."

Jace had always thought the same of his father, but in the end, didn't know.

"It's just that my mother suspects much of anything outside of cities and towns and is so very proud of the Family being FirstLevel Librarians. Nothing is better than that, anywhere, ever."

He sifted his fingers through Glyssa's soft and bouncy hair, and as a lock tickled his palm his whole body shuddered. Why had he waited so long to do this? Pure stupidity.

"Will you go?"

"Of course."

"Of course?" he pressed.

"It's what I've been working for all my life. I'll go, and I'll have my daily reports on the excavation, whatever documents the Elecampanes will give me, my notes as their expedition recorder, the transcription of Hoku's journals, and as much of the story as we can get done."

"Bury them in papyrus?" That sounded good.

"Show them I haven't been frittering away my time."

He snorted. "No one could say that of you."

"Yes, they could, but they won't."

He didn't like this idea. "When will you go?"

"It's the weekend and the airship won't come until Mor. That transport will be a big one and some of the crew will be abandoning the camp. The shuttle might be full so I can't return."

"I hope the shuttle isn't full of people who want to leave," Jace said.

"If they don't want to be here, will be a burden, they should go," Glyssa said.

And she was back, the woman with definite opinions. She moved atop him, shifting upward to look down on him and lower her lips to his. Just before they touched, she smiled that smile he'd never seen on her face except during moments of sex. "I suppose you wouldn't consider coming with me." He flinched at the idea, but any objection vanished as she nibbled on his lower lip, feathered her tongue over it.

"Just a little jaunt, a break, to keep me company." Her breath teased his mouth with an anticipatory kiss.

He managed to grasp one single thought as he put his hands on her hips, began to slide her down where she belonged. "You'll be coming back to the camp?"

"Yes."

"Even if they"—someone, who? Glyssa felt so good, moved so *right*—"don't want you to come back?" He almost forgot how important the question was.

"Absolutely. This is *my* project." And as she lifted and lowered, he almost thought she meant him.

Four times. *They'd made love four times and now Jace slept in her bed.* Finally! Glyssa smiled in the night. She'd heard Lepid patter through the door and into the sitting room, give a little grunt, a mental, *Night, night, FamWoman*, and collapse into his bed, with snores following in a couple of breaths.

Even better, she'd heard the soft whir of feathers as Zem flew through her spellshield and into the outer room and onto his perch. Sounded like a fully Healed and well predator to her.

She thought she'd taken the right approach in asking Jace to come with her to Druida. Not that she had planned it that way, she'd acted from instinct.

But this sex had certainly cleared her mind with regard to what was important in her life and should remain a priority. Her needs and fulfillment. *Hers*, not her Family's. She could not—should not, she amended—live life to please them and their wants and needs.

They weren't so hidebound or of such social status that they would demand that of her, ultimately. She didn't have to marry to keep the Family in funds, or for any other practical reason. She wasn't even the heir to the Licorices. That was her sister, Enata.

Daughter? Her father's quiet tones came into her head. She did a quick calculation. Even accounting for the time change, he was up late.

It's midnight, there? she asked.

She heard his grunt, sensed he was relaxing in one of his shabby overstuffed chairs in his personal library. They all had personal libraries in their Residence.

Her father replied, *One of the FirstFamilies let me visit their HouseHeart with the proviso that it had to be late at night during the heir's hours. Can't name the Family, of course,* he grumbled. *FirstFamily designated anonymously as FFA2 in my report.*

Was the HouseHeart lovely?

Gorgeous. I got to remember the chamber. They only insisted I have my recollection how and where to enter removed.

Jace snuffled beside her and she smiled. Soon her father would go up to his HeartMate, and now she knew firsthand how sleeping next to her own felt.

But that is not what I wanted to speak to you about, Fasic Almond T'Licorice said.

Yes, Father? Since apprehension tickled her spine, she put her hand in Jace's. His fingers curled around hers, but he didn't wake.

Twenty-one

There is an underlying reason you wished to make the excavation at Lugh's Spear *your fieldwork,* her father said with the sureness of knowing his daughter and having spent time thinking about the whole issue.

Glyssa hesitated. If she told him the reason, he would tell his HeartMate, Glyssa's mother, and her mother would tell Glyssa's sister. No privacy. And then work and Family would slop around together in a mess.

Perhaps I should state another conclusion, her father said. *You will not give up this project, will you? Even if it costs your career?*

One huge breath in, released in increments. *No.*

What would be so important that you would forfeit your career, might have already taken steps away from becoming a FirstLevel Librarian?

You are doing fine with your deductions, she said. She wanted to tell him, but with Jace's arm moving around her shoulders, drawing her to him, she would not say why. If she didn't, her father, no matter how much he guessed, how much he sensed, couldn't state with conviction to the rest of the Family that he was certain why Glyssa had acted the way she had.

She thought her father rose from his seat and poured himself some liquor, then settled again. She could feel his mind turning over facts as he plucked a little at the bond between her and him.

Your HeartMate, he said. *You have found your HeartMate! He is there!*

I will neither confirm nor deny, she said, but she was smiling at the joy she felt from her father.

Wonderful news, and completely understandable that you would take steps to claim him. But that will not appease your mother. She fears for you there. She tracked down some terrible rumors today.

I will be there within the time period to defend my fieldwork, Glyssa said.

Your banker informed us that you have invested heavily in the venture.

Glyssa flinched, rolled and scooted so she was against Jace's body.

You are considering staying there . . . or spending the summers there and the winters here, aren't you?

Yes. It is wonderful here, this project—and her man—*is fascinating and has so much potential to change our view of our world. I'll see you soon, I love you, Dad,* Glyssa said.

I love you, too. And I'll be talking to Camellia tomorrow—later today. *Good night, dear girl, blessed be.*

Blessed be, she sent back to him, and they both pinched off the telepathic mindtalk link. A good thing because she scooted back to spoon with Jace and found his body hardening.

Through the osmosis of camp gossip, by morning everyone knew that Glyssa was returning for a short time to "consult" with people in Druida. Maybe her GrandHouse Family, maybe her *FirstFamily* friends. Her popularity increased, and so did Jace's own.

Everyone also knew he'd spent the night with her. The fact that her rep reflected well on his irritated him a little, but he accepted it as the boon it was.

The staff—and the owners—had gotten to know Glyssa. And though she rubbed some people the wrong way, everyone believed in her honesty and honor. And, like everything else, gossip had gone around that the Elecampanes had checked her out and found her background pristine.

The Elecampanes treated him much like before the whole "thief and bad luck" incident. They might also have finally listened to their daughter Maxima when she said he was a good man. The tension that had stiffened his sinews, settled into his nerves, eased.

He'd volunteered to work over the weekend and was back to exploring and documenting the interior of *Lugh's Spear* with the rest of the volunteer team . . . proceeding through the long corridor that the breach opened into. Earning top gilt. The pay for digging was a whole lot less than exploring the ship, and those who wanted to leave on the next transport had to put in backbreaking time.

Speaking of luck, it had certainly been with *Lugh's Spear*. Raz Cherry T'Elecampane had made a stirring speech detailing that. The ground had given way underneath the starship, enough that it had plunged down, but it *hadn't* broken. *Lugh's Spear* lay as it had landed, just sunk fifty meters straight down until it rested on bedrock.

It was as if there had been a perfect storm of circumstances conspiring to preserve the ship. The breach they'd come through had been the break that had occurred during the landing, the rest of the structure had held, and the corridor was clear of rubble . . . as were the rooms they began to investigate, one by one.

Zem didn't like the inside of *Lugh's Spear* and made no attempt to enter. Jace couldn't blame him because once outside the immediate hole, the area had to be lit with spell lights. They *were* underground, and constrained by the structure of the ship, and the hallway was as wide as any of the individual rooms they'd found.

Doors were both open and closed and they found more items just left in the hurry to depart, all jumbled together.

The corridor they worked in held larger quarters, for the officers, as noted on the blueprints. Inside the rooms, items—possessions—had been tossed around, but only the delicate had broken, and those could be easily reconstructed to show what they had been. And some of the furnishings, even in these "high status" people's quarters, were pitifully shabby. Enough to make the heart . . . and the eyes, sting.

Such courageous people.

Jace was working with Andic Sanicle vizing all on a recordsphere before touching anything in the latest room—one shared by a married couple—when Zem contacted Jace telepathically.

You have a scry from Druida City.

He just stopped. He knew no one there. *I am working!*

The Raz says to come up and take the scry.

Jace cursed.

"What is it?" asked Sanicle.

"Scry for me. Ordered up," Jace grumbled.

Sanicle grinned. Now he'd be the one doing most of the work, would get most of the cut. And if he was the thief and slipped a few objects on his person . . . Jace ground his teeth, jerked a nod at the man. "I'll be right back."

He ran lightly down the corridor, ducked under the wall that still slanted, and walked up the girder. As soon as he was on top, Raz T'Elecampane nodded at him and gestured another man down. "Go ahead and join Sanicle, continue with the work."

Jace felt his face freeze into a mask to hide his anger.

"I promise you'll get a cut," Raz said.

But it wouldn't be the same amount, for sure. Jace jerked a nod. "Right. Who's scrying me?"

Raz's eyes gleamed. "T'Licorice."

Jace grimaced. "I'll be right back."

Raz lifted a brow. "Take your time."

Jace jogged to the communications hut, noticing the avid eyes of Funa who hung around it, and inside if she could manage that, more often than not. He suspected she was the one who'd told everyone about Glyssa's calls.

"You can leave now," he said as he took the stool in front of the scry panel.

She sneered at him, flounced her plump ass as she ducked through the opening of the tent. "You're welcome," her voice drifted back. "I was just keeping the connection open for you!"

Jace swiveled to return the stare of the man looking out from the screen. At first glance, he didn't look much like Glyssa with his sandy hair and washed-out blue eyes. But the shape of those eyes, and the intensity of the gaze, he had passed down to his daughter, along with freckles.

"I am Fasic Almond T'Licorice," the guy said.

"I'm Jace Bayrum," Jace responded.

More silence.

"I am sure that you have heard that my daughter will be returning to Druida City to"—the man's gaze focused behind Jace toward the tent flap. Yeah, no doubt Funa was straining to eavesdrop—"to brief us on her discoveries there and the project."

"I heard," Jace said. And obviously the man had heard his daughter was sleeping with Jace.

"I would be pleased to invite you to visit us with Glyssa."

Embarrassed heat fired up Jace's neck. "No."

The guy's nose pinched. "We are a hospitable Family, you'd have your own suite."

Didn't want him in Glyssa's rooms.

"And we'd respect your privacy."

"I'm sorry," Jace lied. "But I can't get away now." He ducked his head. "Thank you for the invitation."

T'Licorice's gaze drilled him. "I'm sorry you can't accept. If you change your mind, please scry . . . *viz* me. Blessed be."

"Blessed be."

Thankfully the panel went dark.

But Jace didn't head out, seemed stuck to the wooden seat of the stool. How the hell had T'Licorice learned . . . well, the man was far from stupid. Glyssa and Camellia D'Hawthorn had been friends for years, which meant Camellia was on easy terms with Glyssa's Family. Jace was sure Glyssa had reached out to her good friends for support.

He wasn't sure what her friends might say to Glyssa's Family, but was sure they'd be on her side. In any event, Glyssa's friends might have mentioned his name. That's all a quick man would need to figure out the rest.

He didn't like knowing his affair with Glyssa was being talked about way back in Druida City. Lord and Lady knew what would be said of him, how he'd be judged, since he didn't want to go along with her and be judged in person.

There came a shout, and just outside the tent, Funa exclaimed, "What, Andic? You're done? All right, I'll shower with you." She laughed and her steps ran away.

Jace's ass came unstuck from the stool and he followed. He'd missed the rest of the time down in the ship.

Too much thinking wasn't good for a guy. Maybe he should back off from Glyssa. Maybe he should, but he didn't think he could.

And the next two nights, despite himself, he spent rolling around with Glyssa on her bedsponge.

*O*n *Mor, the first business day of the week, a huge airship descended* lightly onto the landing field. Two women walked off the ship, obviously mother and daughter, and wearing Holly green. They stood at the bottom of the airship ramp, examined most of the staff who'd come to see the newcomers, then gestured to those behind them. Thirteen more guards descended, all Hollys, both genders. The Elecampanes had hired the best guards in the business and they didn't come cheap.

A ripple of comment went through the watching crowd and some clumps of people faded back into the larger encampment.

In quality, the security of the camp had just increased exponentially.

Jace got the idea that the casualness and lightheartedness, maybe the whole sense of community, had decreased by that amount, too.

Glyssa sniffed beside him with some meaning he didn't understand.

"What?" he asked.

She slid him a glance. "I sense you're blaming the Elecampanes and the Hollys for a situation someone *else*, someone who dislikes *you* has caused."

She had a point.

He could read her pretty well, too. "Think they'll fall for your tea and flatsweets?"

"I'm sure most nobles appreciate good food and those who fight and burn up Flair and energy truly do."

"Huh," he said.

"They should be able to find out who the villain is."

Lepid shot to the front of the crowd. *Welcome, welcome, new guards.* He darted in and sniffed the older woman's boots, danced back as she glared.

I do not know you, but you smell like Tinne's The Green Knight Fencing and Fighting Salon, and HollyHeir Holm, and T'Holly!

Though most of the staff were smiling and even a couple of the guards, the women's stern expressions did not crack.

Raz, Del, and Maxima Elecampane strolled forward and Raz raised his voice slightly, "Glyssa?"

Glyssa straightened beside Jace, pulling on a manner he hadn't seen before. Noblewoman manner to greet others of a noble Family. Though these Hollys weren't part of the core FirstFamily members, they obviously had spent some time with them.

On a small and whispered sigh, Glyssa said, "Be right back."

She joined the Elecampanes in bowing and curtseying to the Holly guards. "Lepid, to me," Glyssa said and her Fam ran to stand beside her, uncaring that he'd ruined the serious and proper introduction the Elecampanes had planned.

Still a young fox, Zem commented from Jace's shoulder. Jace stroked his bird. "Nothing changes that but time."

Some never outgrow immaturity.

The last people down the ramp were two noblewomen dressed in the highest of Druida City fashion, with long tunics—heavily embroidered in patterns that Jace would never copy for his leatherwork, too fussy—that had the equally long, rectangular pocket sleeves. They wore extremely bloused trous, gathered at their ankles.

Raz broke away from Del and the Hollys to give each of them an elaborate bow. The Comosums, who would test the atmosphere of *Lugh's Spear* for bad air and disease.

Jace knew right then that things had taken a turn for the worse, and his hunch was confirmed a septhour later when the two were led to the hole.

He'd never seen such a fuss as when the Comosums realized they had to descend into a *hole*, either by actually walking down a girder for *three whole stories* or being lowered by harness. Their protestations were only cut short by Raz T'Elecampane silkily reminding them they'd been paid and if they wanted to cancel their contract, they could . . . and pay the penalty and the airship fare to and from the camp. And the more they fretted, the longer the whole thing would take.

The women layered themselves in great Flair spellshields and were lowered by harness, but refused to carry viz recordingspheres or cameras.

They went into *Lugh's Spear,* their shrill voices rising behind them, and stayed down what Jace figured was the shortest amount of time they could get away with and not be called lazy slackers or cowards, less than a half septhour.

When they returned topside, they both looked pasty with fear and announced the ship was *NOT SAFE AT ALL!!!*

Raz T'Elecampane dealt with them with extreme and deadly courtesy, wishing an oral report of their findings, and gently reminding them that he would expect a lengthy report within the eightday, and then led them back to Glyssa's pavilion for tea and goodies.

Jace shared a look with Sanicle, who rolled his eyes and shrugged. "They were terrible."

Looking around at the crowd who'd gathered for amusement or the confirmation of their fears, Jace said, "This just made it easier for people to complain and leave."

"Yup, that's right," Sanicle said, looking as wistfully as Jace back down into the hole. "The Elecampanes will probably close this up again, have us all digging or studying the few items we *were* allowed to bring up."

"Maybe we're tapering off for this year, but I'll bet my next paycheck that Raz and Del will have other experts out first thing in the spring," Jace said.

Sanicle snorted. "No bet there." He cast a sideways glance at Jace. "But you could take that little break with your lover in Druida, if you like."

Jace's gut squeezed and he said the same thing he did every time the subject came up. "No." He was torn. He wanted the sex, to stay with Glyssa, and Druida City might be fun. But not with her Family and the Hawthorns and every other person he'd have to meet.

But his insides got a real workout as he strolled toward the Elecampanes' and Glyssa's tents and heard more carrying on by the ladies Comosums.

They wanted to leave immediately, but even they were smart enough to see the airship that had brought them had already departed while they were throwing their fits. Flatly refusing to remain a week, they used the communications tent to arrange for another airship to come and pick them up late morning the next day, the soonest possible time for the fastest airship. And they positively preened with lifted snobby noses that Glyssa Licorice was supposed to accompany them back.

Glyssa's jaw had flexed, her brows lowered and she'd tromped off to the communications tent herself.

Jace kept an eye out for her as she returned and noted her high color and very stiff spine and knew things had not gone well for her.

And suddenly the import of the whole thing struck him. She was leaving in the morning. He'd really have to decide what to do.

Twenty-two

That evening, as Jace ambled while Zem and Carolinia and Lepid hunted—banned from Glyssa's tent since the two snotty noble-women were there—he noticed an odd glow at one corner of the Elecampanes' tent, a golden glow. One he hadn't seen earlier. In fact, one that he hadn't noted the day before. The more he stared at it, the more he felt a small tug toward it. He strolled near until shock rooted him and his pulse pounded in realization.

This corner of the Elecampanes' tent was where they kept a spellshielded storage no-time for the crew's valuables. Most of his pay stayed there until it was banked.

His pay wasn't glowing. It was that other thing.

That other one valuable item he carried around always, nearly for-gotten in the small, heavily shielded pouch. His HeartGift, imbued with the energy of his Third Passage that could still glow to his and his HeartMate's sight. Especially if the HeartMates were in the vicinity.

He couldn't deny it anymore. Glyssa Licorice was his HeartMate. Queasiness washed through his gut. Sex was fine, but he didn't want anything more. Didn't want to be tied down. Made to follow other people's rules, forced to fit into someone else's life. Other peoples' expectations.

Most of all he didn't want to be linked to someone who could break him, as his mother had broken his father. Or someone *he* might break, if ever he gave in to his mother's influence and bad blood inside him.

Glyssa was leaving tomorrow. He could let her go without speaking of this, of the heavy fear that had thudded through his mind at the discovery and rippled all the way through his body.

If he really wanted to be a coward, he didn't have to see her again. No, that wouldn't work. She would no doubt hunt him down. Hadn't she already done that?

Pulse throbbing hard and hurtful in his temples, his eyes already dilated with shock, he swiveled his head to her pavilion. She had a safe no-time. If she'd brought the HeartGift she'd made for him, and she had great Flair so she would have done that during her Second Passage, and maybe even connected with him in her Third, and didn't he recall the previous incredible sex dreams he'd had, yes, he did, and he was babbling in his own mind.

No glow in her tent where she kept the secure no-time. He rocked back on his heels. She didn't have the HeartGift she made him with her?

Before he could figure out what that meant, Zem swooped down to land on his shoulder. The hawkcel's breath was warm and smelled blood laden, but he moved like the king of the sky.

We were invited to the city with FamWoman? he asked.

"Yes."

But we are staying here.

Reluctantly, Jace asked—as he'd forgotten to ask before—*Did you want to go to the city?*

Zem tugged at a piece of Jace's hair, not hard enough to hurt. *You are my FamMan, I will go with you, but seeing a city once might be interesting. You will not stay here during the winter?*

"No."

Then I will go with you to wherever you go. But first I will show you my nest. It is very well constructed.

"Yeah, that would be good." Jace understood his Fam, had

bonded greatly with the hawkcel, and yeah, it had changed him, but he'd welcomed that change into his life.

He didn't welcome being a HeartMate.

"Jace! Jace, wait up!" Maxima Elecampane joined him. She smiled up at him brilliantly. "I haven't seen you very often to talk with you lately, and my parents and Glyssa and those gluttonous noblewomen are eating courses and courses of *food,* gorging on a *feast* tonight." She wrinkled her nose. "Rather have been at the mess tent, looking at the new Holly guards."

"Uh—"

"Let's walk," Maxima said.

Soon they were at the edge of camp and headed toward the outline of the stubby wing of the ship. Farther than Jace had anticipated going. "I'd rather stay in camp," he said and turned to stroll between the tents and the spellshield surrounding the encampment. In this area, the personal tents faced the opposite direction.

"I am *so glad* your reputation has been restored," Maxima said. "I told my parents over and over that you couldn't be the thief. The Hollys will find the culprit!"

He looked down and though he kept a steady pace, his insides stilled when he saw what could only be called her dewy gaze. "I believe in you. I will *always* believe in you." Her chin lifted, and she gripped his hand. "I understand how you feel."

He sincerely doubted a pampered teenaged girl had any idea of his worries, the foremost of which was a sexual need for a woman his body wanted and his heart feared. Not to mention the simple fact that he had very little gilt, and no gilt meant no damn options.

No. She couldn't possibly understand him, and irritation at her rose.

"I will always be loyal to you." Another hand squeeze and he jolted as his brain caught up to his emotions signaling alarm . . . and horror. The girl definitely had a crush on him!

Dammit. He'd hoped to avoid this situation. He walked a little faster, back toward the main tents.

He had to handle this smoothly and right. And worse was the

fact that her father, the actor, was the smoothest man Jace had ever known and Maxima would definitely expect all the other men in her life to be equally sensitive. Urgh.

Touchy, touchy subject. They'd reached a common area and he stopped. His turn to squeeze her fingers, then take a long step from her as he drew Zem down from his shoulder to cradle him, keeping his hands busy and the Fam between them. "I thank you for that, GrandMistrys Elecampane." He stroked Zem's head with a forefinger. The bird chirred in contentment.

Maxima frowned, a little confused. He didn't often call her by her title. More fool he for forgetting how high above him she was, with clear descent from one of the colonists on her father's side, and a noble name on her mother's, along with great wealth.

Even Glyssa was closer to Jace in rank than Maxima, if he'd been foolish enough to think of her in any sort of terms other than a sister. He suppressed a shudder. He had no doubt that her father would make him disappear in the wilderness if he hurt Maxima—if her mother didn't do that first.

Zem turned his head toward Maxima, lifted his wings a little and snicked his beak. *Pretty girl!*

Maxima smiled and Jace laughed, too, even as he calculated how to handle this. "You are a pretty girl . . . Maxima." He ducked his head a little and tried for a shy smile, hoping he was a smidgeon of the actor her father was, and that she wouldn't see through him. "You know, I don't have any family, and it's nice to hear that you believe in me . . . like a younger sister would."

She bridled, stepped back, hurt and confusion on her face.

He couldn't be brutal, but he had to be clear, so he went on as if he hadn't noticed her shock. "I always wanted a younger sister, and though most folk in the camp are friendly, you're special, almost a mascot. Everyone likes you, and I'm honored that you let me be your friend."

Maxima gasped then hurried into speech, plunged forward to close the distance between them. "Jace . . . that's not what . . . Jace, I lo—"

"Maxima, there you are!" Raz Cherry T'Elecampane's mellow tones rolled easily over his daughter's stammer.

Keeping his Fam in his arms so no girl could throw herself into them, Jace let out a sigh of relief. He'd never been happier in his life to see an employer. He angled his body toward the man whose stride looked casual but was very fast. Again he ducked his head, inclined his torso. "GrandLord T'Elecampane, good evening to you."

The man's quick but intense stare took in the situation. In fact, Jace sensed Raz had come to protect his daughter from Jace. He sent a narrowed gaze to the actor.

Raz eased. "Greetyou, Bayrum. Dear Daughter, we missed you at the table." Cheer lilted in his tone.

Zem squawked, demanding attention. Excellent BirdFam. *Greetyou!*

Raz came near to stroke the bird. "Greetyou, Zem." He met Jace's eyes, his own calm. Maybe he wouldn't misinterpret the circumstances. Maxima gave a couple of choked sobs in the background, but Jace could only ignore her hurt. To do anything else would either hurt her more or get him killed.

Raz said, "Zem's looking better, and his feathers seem less brittle."

"His wing is as good as new." Jace couldn't bear the stifled sounds any longer. "Would you care to hold Zem, Maxima?" He didn't actually meet her damp eyes, kept a smile on his face.

"Th-thanks, not now, J-Jace."

"Anytime, Maxima," Jace said softly. "I appreciate your help with him, and your friendship."

The girl's face worked, she gulped, and Jace looked hastily away.

"Hey, baby," Raz said. "Your own FamCat is whining for you."

"S-she returned to our pavilion before me. Oh, Papa!"

Raz scooped up his daughter, swung her around to his hunched back. "Been a while since I've given you a ride. Let's head on back. We're having one of your favorite desserts, crème brûlée."

Good for them. Jace thought of the same old stuff the mess tent served or the jerky sticks he kept in his tent. The other no-time had been returned to Glyssa's pavilion. He wouldn't be welcome in Glyssa's tent tomorrow morning, either.

A horrible thought intruded. Would they have *no* time to have sex between now and when she left? He had to get her alone.

"Maxima, your mother and I want to talk to you about a new project we have in mind for you," Raz said, jogging in place as if his daughter was a baby to be distracted and amused by the movement.

"I'll see you tomorrow, T'Elecampane," Jace said, "and Maxima."

Raz nodded. "Tomorrow. And, ah, Bayrum? Unless you want to dig, you can continue working with the plans and our copies of Hoku's journals."

Not great, but better than the hard labor. "Fine. Good night, you two."

Good night! Zem echoed.

"Good night, Bayrum," Raz said. Maxima waved a limp hand at them.

"You'll be well compensated for the study work," Raz said, jogging away.

So Jace was being rewarded for being an honorable man and not seducing a girl? The thought tightened his stomach. He didn't like to think anyone would believe that of him. His relationship with the older Elecampanes had sure gotten tangled lately.

He set Zem back on his shoulder, watching Raz run with his daughter on his back. Jace thought he heard a giggle from the girl. Good. The sooner she got over her infatuation—hopefully shallow—the better. It was touching that she'd chosen him for her first puppy love, but would continue to be so very difficult and complicated.

Zem sighed. *Danger averted.*

"You're telling me," Jace said. "Women."

Females, Zem huffed.

Jace's thoughts went to the lovely Glyssa. His body ached in anticipation of a drought of sex.

Zem tilted his head and caught Jace's eye. *Glyssa will have new food, too.*

Yeah, her friends—one of whom was a damn good cook—would have sent . . .

"Treats."

Treats, Zem and he said together.

Still, as Jace walked into the camp and encountered a sleepy Funa, who standing in the opening of her new tent gave him a sexy look that lingered on his body, then glanced back at the tent in invitation, he felt he had a target on his back that females were aiming arrows of emotion at.

But when Glyssa slipped into his tent during the darkest part of the night, he welcomed her, body, mind, and heart. Yeah, she was very, very dangerous.

Luckily, he saw no HeartBond that rumor said showed up during sex—at least when he could think again after the great orgasm.

She left just before dawn while he pretended to be asleep, still conflicted about so much. Her being his HeartMate.

Not wanting to go to the city with her. Knowing he'd miss the sex. Not wanting a future with her. Really.

Lepid the FoxFam bit his big toe.

Jace jerked up. "What!"

The Elecampanes summoned FamWoman to their pavilion. You go, too!

Examining the dent in his toe, Jace said, "Why?"

Because she wants you with her.

"But I don't—"

Lepid snapped his teeth. *You should do things she wants, sometimes. That is only fair and kind and loving.*

"I don't love her," Jace said. Didn't want to love her, be bound closely to her.

Zem snorted behind Jace, then glided down to his Fam no-time, pecked at it and it opened. Lepid joined the bird, and a silent shadow padded into the tent, Carolinia. Zem opened one of his drawers, snapped up a mouse that Jace thought he still saw twitch, and crunched it. Then the Fam laid out a portion of skirl for Carolinia and some mocyn for Lepid.

Zem said, *I am giving these pieces of food to my friends because it is kind.*

Zem and Carolinia and I will all have treats I just got before we go, Lepid sent Jace mentally as if to emphasize the sentiment.

Jace grunted, said a quick scrub spell, and pulled on his clothes. "Better to travel alone. You can always count on yourself, and nobody else."

Carolinia lifted bloody whiskers and hissed at him. *Apologize to Zem!* she insisted.

But it was too late, Zem had lit on Jace's shoulder, nipped his ear, then taken off to outside the tent without another word.

Slamming the no-time door shut, Jace stalked from his tent and toward the Elecampanes. Always better not to count on other people—beings. His mother had taken what he'd had and walked away . . . leaving him to suffer through Passage alone, find his way in the world without a silver sliver to his name. The last woman Jace had traveled with had made off with his tent and most of his supplies, abandoning him in the wilderness.

A jerk blew up someone else's tent and everyone turned against you.

Not Zem. Zem had never let him down, wouldn't. Neither had Glyssa, and she was his HeartMate.

No, he didn't want to think of that. But he plodded to the Elecampanes' tent all the same, only noting that the Holly guards seemed animated and everywhere.

Yeah, the camp had changed. He planned on staying the same. He liked his life the way it was.

When he appeared at their open door, Raz and Del Elecampane glanced up from their study table as if they'd been expecting him. Glyssa and Maxima sat in camp chairs, sipping drinks.

Raz smiled and gestured. "Come on in." His brows went up and down as he glanced at a timer. "Before those fliggering Comosums wake up and we have to have another exquisitely prepared and delicious, but wretched-company breakfast with them."

"They fliggering lied about the ship," Jace found himself saying as he walked in.

"I don't think so." Del rose and offered him a mug of caff and as the wonderful scent teased his nostrils he salivated and took it. "I think they were so frightened of the whole experience their minds shut down and their Flair didn't work right." She scowled. "Paid them a fliggering fortune."

"We'll get some of the gilt back," Raz soothed.

Del said, "Meanwhile two Fams and several people have been down in the ship fairly often. I'm going to ask our Healers to do a complete health examination of them all."

She shot a look at Jace. "All right with you?"

"Yes, I'll go to the new male Healer."

"Fine."

Raz continued for his wife. "And we'll ask the Comosums to have a complete exam and send us the results. The hole has been open to the camp for some time, and no one is showing any kind of physical problems. I think we're all right."

Del nodded. "Like you said before, we'll get more flexible people out here to do an atmospheric study, maybe even instruments from the other starship, in the spring. We can at least continue digging down the levels near the main entrance." But Del sighed. "Dammit."

Raz offered his hand, sat and pulled his HeartMate into his lap.

"Good morning, Jace," Glyssa said.

"Good morning, Jace," Maxima mumbled.

"We have news that we hadn't quite gotten around to telling Glyssa," Raz said.

Reaching out to ruffle Maxima's hair, Del grinned and said, "As you may or may not know, a late cuz of mine invented the scry pebble. Maxima has the same kind of Flair." She hugged the girl. "And we've arranged that she will work with the starship of *Nuada's Sword* in Druida City to see if we—they—can figure out how scry pebbles can also link with the satellite."

Maxima's eyes rounded and her mouth dropped open. She turned and hugged her mother back. "Really? Really!"

"Yes. We're sending you to stay with the Blackthorns and your cuz, Doolee, who lives with them."

Maxima jumped up and down, joy on her face. "I will work with Dani Eve Elder and *Nuada's Sword* and stay with my cuz!"

"That's right." Raz's smile was indulgent. He nodded toward Glyssa. "We'll be sending Maxima with you on the airship that comes to take the Comosums back to their comfort zone of the noble strata of Druida City."

"Of course I am pleased about that," Glyssa said. She sounded resigned.

"Truly no way to wiggle out of going back home now, eh?" Del said.

Glyssa sent a wry smile at Maxima. "No offense, but I was trying my hardest to drag my feet on that." She slipped a glance to the Elecampanes. "You know you have very loving and supportive parents, right?"

"Yes! Letting me stay with the Blackthorns in Druida and work hard on something my Flair is really suited for!" Maxima enthused.

Sounded to Jace like her crush on him was a thing of the past . . . and the Elecampanes had just slipped their daughter into the highest of the high. The Blackthorns were a FirstFamily. If she developed any new infatuation, it would be with a man more her equal.

"GrandLady, GrandLord," said the Holly in charge of the guards.

"What is it, Cornuta?" Del asked.

The guard stared at Jace and Glyssa.

Raz flipped a hand. "You can trust them."

The Holly just raised a blond eyebrow, nodded, and reported, "The lower cooks in the mess are scrambling. Your chief cook, Myrtus Stopper, disappeared from the camp last night."

Twenty-three

$\mathcal{R}$az seemed stunned.

Well, they all did.

"He had in his possession some artifacts from *Lugh's Spear*?" the chief of the guards asked.

Del scowled. "What?"

"The subsistence sticks," Glyssa said. "He gathered them all."

"The subsistence sticks," Raz repeated.

Del D'Elecampane grimaced. "Nasty, ugly, of little intrinsic value."

"But artifacts from the lost starship, for sure," Raz said grimly. He stood and rubbed his hands over his face, his head. "We were stupid about that."

Glyssa's mouth thinned, and she said in a stilted voice. "All of us were foolish in this matter."

Raz made a wide gesture. "So innocuous. Things none of us liked and every one looked just like the rest. And a man we trusted." Raz colored in anger and what Jace felt himself, embarrassment at being a stup.

"He's been the villain all along!" Maxima said.

Cornuta Holly sent a stare her way. "He certainly planned well.

He stole a stridebeast—the animal has returned by itself unharmed. My people found its track and followed it to a large clearing where it looks as if a small airship recently landed and took off."

"Huh," Del said. She gathered Maxima close and stepped up to Raz and linked her arm around his waist. Family solidarity . . . and affection.

Jace had never known that. Didn't quite believe in it even as he saw it in the Elecampanes.

"Myrtus'd be able to trade a stick or two for a ride," Jace said. "Contact someone in Druida City through the communications system or telepathy or with a letter given to one of the shuttle pilots."

"I liked him," Glyssa murmured.

"We all did," Raz said.

"He didn't actually hurt anyone with those explosions that sent the sticks flying. Some of those sticks were destroyed, but there are plenty still left in the ship. So he wasn't much of a villain," Maxima said, leaning her head on her mother's shoulder. "He was just greedy."

"Sorry to give you the bad news," the Holly said with an expressionless voice. Jace thought that everyone in the tent heard her unspoken message that real security had been lacking at the camp.

"I like how the camp's been run," Jace said.

The guard captain gave him a flat stare and he smiled at her. "You'll like working for the Elecampanes, too, and the . . . uh . . . energy of this place." He hoped that didn't change much.

"Go ahead and follow up, do what you think you need to do," Del told the woman.

The Holly nodded, pivoted, and marched out.

Raz T'Elecampane blew out a breath, turned to Jace. "I want to put you on moving the communications array. We got word yesterday from the Elder Family and *Nuada's Sword* that a different pattern might be more efficient and increase the clarity of transmissions."

"All right," Jace said.

"But I don't think I'll be able to concentrate on that until late morning. See me then." A smile twitched on and off his lips. "After Glyssa and Maxima and those noblewomen leave."

"All right," Jace said, very aware of Glyssa, tense and silent beside him.

At that moment the tinkling of a silver bell came from Glyssa's pavilion. Everyone but Jace flinched.

"That's the noble Comosum sisters now," Del said. "Another interminable meal." Her tones were gloomy.

Glyssa managed a chuckle. "I don't have to attend this one. Only those with titles."

Maxima brightened. "That leaves me out, too. I think I'll walk to the communications tent and see if anyone is using the viz. If not, I want to scry Doolee."

Lepid shot through the door, along with the other fox and two FamCats. *Did you HEAR? Our friend Myrtus is GONE! He left us to bad cooks!*

Glyssa managed a laugh and lowered to accept his licks. "I heard."

"Wait, Maxima and Glyssa," Del said, flinging out her hands. "We're hosting the breakfast. Help us set up. I've got the food in the no-time."

Jace lent a hand, and was impressed at the results. When they were done, the Elecampanes' pavilion sitting room resembled something that he'd expect a nobleman's dining room to look like, with nice chairs and proper linen softleaves, flatwares, and delicious odors rising from covered dishes.

Del grunted. "Well, it's the best we can do. Go on over and escort those ladies here, please, Maxima."

The girl left, and Lepid shot from the tent as if he wanted to avoid any chance of meeting the sisters.

"I think I'll take a last walk around the camp," Glyssa said, "then pack." She sighed. "I was hoping against hope—"

"Sorry to box you into returning, but we trust you with Maxima, not those Comosums or even a Cherry pilot," Del said.

Glyssa nodded.

"You do have a significant interest in this venture," Raz said smoothly. "I have no doubt you'll be back." A slight pause. "We will need a historian, if *you* need options."

"Thank you," Glyssa choked.

Jace found himself taking her arm. "Let's walk and talk." He didn't know what he'd say. Something.

And the light of the HeartGift he'd made Glyssa that was stuck in the safe glowed so brightly he didn't know how anyone—including her—managed not to see it.

"I want to show you one of my favorite places," he said.

And her smile for him glowed, too.

"Zem has his nest there." Probably had observed Jace before they'd met. Jace took her hand and they walked, talking about nothing in particular for several kilometers, to a lake where Zem and Lepid already hunted and played. He gestured to a solid log where he liked to sit.

She didn't speak or break the quiet, and words popped from his mouth. "You're my HeartMate," Jace said.

She gave him a long, cool stare. "Yes."

"You came here because of me."

"One of my reasons. As well as the project of *Lugh's Spear* itself." Her head turned back toward the lake. She'd gone tense beside him, but continued to look straight ahead.

He glanced at her hand that he'd held as they'd walked. She'd been rubbing the rough texture of the bark absentmindedly, but now her fingers had fisted.

Instinctively he reached out and curled his hands over hers. She didn't relax, didn't turn her hand over to clasp his, or intertwine fingers in the easy affection they'd been showing to each other.

And he knew with wonder, that pushy in many other things, she would not push here and now.

He said, "You didn't give me your HeartGift. You could have offered it to me and I would have accepted it and you could have claimed me as your HeartMate and I would have had to go with you."

She lifted and dropped a shoulder. "That's the logical course of events with regard to a HeartGift." Finally she turned her head and showed him a very serious face, so pale that her freckles stood out against her skin, brown eyes wide. She shook her head. "That would be forcing you into a situation you didn't choose. I couldn't do that. That would be wrong."

"You didn't even bring your HeartGift for me." He'd have sensed it if it had been in the camp.

"No."

For an instant his mind spun, whirling and flipping the situation. *He'd* discovered she was his HeartMate. He'd gone after *her*, and with his HeartGift.

He didn't think that he'd've refrained from offering it to her. Imagined triumph surged into him when she'd accepted it and he claimed her. A flush had come to his skin, and he was both pleased that she hadn't forced the issue and irritated at the fact that he might have.

She believed in rules, in strict standards of honesty. He liked to bend rules and . . . fudged on honesty now and again.

He nudged her with his shoulder. She was so stiff she toppled and he grabbed her and settled her close to him.

"Thank you." Equally stiff words from Glyssa at her primmest.

"Yeah, you'd think claiming me with your HeartGift would be wrong, since I've made it clear I don't care for anyone else but me deciding my fate. And I'm just not ready for this. At all. Don't know when I will be. Sex is enough." He touched her cheek—she wasn't looking at him again, but staring at the blue, blue lake. "But I think part of what kept you from offering me your HeartGift was also your pride. You didn't want a man you had to constrain."

She sniffed.

This time he touched her cheek with his lips, brushing a kiss. "And even if it was your pride, I thank you for not putting me in such a situation."

She relaxed a little into him, leaning against his side. He liked that more than he'd liked any woman leaning against him, and now he knew why. Fate. Destiny.

"Not ready," he repeated. "I've been on my own for a long time. Just thought you should know."

She said, "As if I couldn't deduce that?" But her tone lost an edge.

"We have excellent sex. We have great affection for each other. Sometimes we even make love instead of having sex."

To his horror he heard tears in her voice.

"Yes," he responded quickly to stem any soggy reaction, though he didn't want to admit that. He stood and drew her up and kissed her, tangled his tongue with hers, luxuriated in her taste. Her city librarian taste that he would lose in a while. He'd miss her. Didn't know how he'd manage nights without her, his body quickened so fast and fierce when he was with her.

She broke the kiss and stepped away, looking the most beautiful she ever was, after a lusty kiss. But those brown eyes of hers were steady. "You won't come with me?"

He hesitated.

"You don't want anything more from our relationship than sex?"

He winced. That sounded bad, when all he wanted was to go slow . . . really slow. But he swallowed and let the truth out. "I wasn't even sure of that to begin with. We're just getting to know each other outside of bed. This is a small community. I was concerned about gossip if we hopped right into bed together."

"Concerned you might not get to have sex with others if you have a real relationship with me." Her tone held bitterness.

But he couldn't deny it, not even now, didn't know that he wanted to. That had been his life, and he'd always treated his short-term lovers well. Better than some of them had treated him. He still shuddered at being left in the wilderness with a stridebeast and barely enough provisions to get him to the next town.

That woman was long gone, his mother and her betrayal more than a decade past. This was Glyssa. He turned his head to look at her, squashed his irritation. He *did* care for her. Facts and feelings got mixed up. "We never spoke about exclusivity."

She flinched, turned pale.

He reached out with both hands toward hers that were clamped together, then dropped his.

Quietly he went on, "And I haven't been with anyone else in camp since you got here. You know that." After a short exhalation,

strangled words came from him. "I haven't wanted to be with anyone else." He turned on the log to face her fully. Dipped his head so
he could meet her downcast eyes. "The truth is, Glyssa, that I haven't
ever had any long-term relationships. Not in all of my life. I'm sorry
if I'm hurting you." Since he didn't think she wanted to be touched,
he rubbed the heel of his hand against his chest. "I gotta go slow,
and showing up in Druida City and meeting all your Family and
friends isn't slow." They'd judge him, people so different than he,
people who'd spent their lives in the same place and a completely
different social status. They'd definitely have expectations of him,
his behavior, his intentions, that he might never figure out.

Again he fumbled to put feelings into words. "And you're not just
a few nights' lover, Glyssa . . . I never forgot you. You're a forever
kind of person, Glyssa, and the HeartBond is a forever bond. I'm not
used to forever kinds of people or HeartBonds and I'm not ready."

Her brown eyes drilled him as she kept her gaze matched with his.
"I don't think this is too much to ask. I want you to come with me."

And that shot him back into the past. His mother's demands had
always started, "I want you . . ." She'd never asked what his father
or he wanted. And that last time, she'd demanded "You must!" How
often did "I want you . . ." escalate into "You must . . . !"? He didn't
know, had tried hard to avoid finding out.

Glyssa wasn't his mother, either, but her words echoed in his
head and reminded him of all the bad times, dark thoughts clouded
his mind, blackened his emotions. He shook his head but couldn't
dispel them. "I'm sorry. I won't fit in. I can't be what your Family
will expect me to be."

Now she flushed. "They won't expect anything—"

"Won't they? Didn't they call you back to judge *you*? You bring
me and they'll judge me, too, think I'm not good enough for you. I'm
not wealthy, I'm not noble." He stood and offered his hand. "This is
your career you're defending. You'd have to defend me, too." She
would, she'd stand up for him and might even earn more demerits or
whatever from her friends and Family and that would hurt her.
Hurt, because of him.

"You're my HeartMate!"

He slanted her a look. "I can barely think of that . . . that concept." He slapped his chest. "And I sure don't know what it means here."

She rose, too, but didn't clasp her fingers in his, met his eyes again. "You're more important to me than my career."

"I don't even have a career," he said bluntly. "I have jobs. One in particular right now." He had little to offer her.

"You bought shares."

"That doesn't mean I'll stay, that any of us here who bought shares will stay. I know your career is important to you." He sucked in a breath. "And I know you . . . want . . . me there with you. But that doesn't feel like the right decision for me now . . . and I'm not sure it's a good one for you, either."

Her mouth set. "You don't know my Family."

He heard what she didn't say. "And I don't know you well, either. I understand that. And I understand that we might know each other better if I go with you to Druida City. But it seems to me we'd be under a lot of pressure."

She stared at him, repeated, "You don't know my Family."

Irritation flashed. "I know families can trap you!" He jerked a gesture at her. "Look, they have your whole future in their hands, a career you love and you have to follow their rules. They put pressure on you. They manipulate you. They use you to fulfill their own wants. Just like my mother used me." Nausea welled as he recalled how his mother had used him, drained him, and hadn't cared whether he'd lived or died. Had used his father to the death and discarded him.

She shook her head. "My Family *loves* me!"

"Love is a lie." His mother had told his father often enough that she loved him, even told Jace all through his childhood when he'd wanted to please her as much as his father did. Family relationships were hard to overcome, and most didn't look healthy to him. Not that he would know healthy.

"No, love is not a lie." She swallowed, then yelled to their Fams. "We're going now, come on!"

Zem was decorating his nest, and Lepid began running back. Later, Jace didn't watch as she and the fox left in the airship.

As soon as the small ramp descended, Glyssa saw her friends and two tough-looking men, one older and the other in his twenties. She held back Maxima from running until Camellia called, "It's all right, it's FirstFamily GrandLord T'Blackthorn and his cuz, Draeg Betony Blackthorn."

Glyssa let go of the girl's arm and Maxima raced toward the older man and jumped into his arms. T'Blackthorn gave Glyssa a nod, then his face broke into a grin and he tossed the girl up in the air as if she was three instead of a teen, and Maxima giggled like that, too.

Then Glyssa was swamped by her friends Camellia D'Hawthorn and Tiana Mugwort and they all talked at once and cried. Lepid bolted from his basket and yipped and circled them, jumping to lick a hand or some fingers.

The Comosums walked right by them to an elegant Family glider.

Glyssa took a deep breath. The air in Druida City smelled different than the plains and forest of the excavation site with a hint of Jace spice when he was near.

During the glider trip to the workday-empty D'Licorice Residence and their long gabfest in Glyssa's suite, she detailed every little thing about Jace to her friends. They shared a glance, but said nothing about her HeartMate. Then they quizzed her about the events at the camp and the looks of *Lugh's Spear,* and her studies, ate goodies from Glyssa's sitting room no-time, and laughed and cried some more and shared a tiny three-person ritual of welcome homecoming and gratitude for a safe journey.

Glyssa promised to have dinner with Camellia and her Heart-Mate Laev the next evening, but Tiana said she couldn't make it. As Glyssa walked her friends to the main teleportation pad in the common Family library, both she and Camellia nagged at Tiana for putting in too many hours at the Temple.

Then her friends were gone and the quiet of the shabby house enveloped her, even as her ears rang with the last of their laughter.

Greetyou, Residence, Glyssa said. She'd said it as they'd walked in, but absently.

Greetyou, Glyssa, SecondLevel Librarian, it replied austerely.

She winced. The Residence wasn't overly formal in furnishings—bordered on the old and comfortable—though the Family had plenty of gilt. But it reflected its owners and Glyssa had been drilled on courtesy. "I am pleased to be home, Residence." Even as she said that, she wondered if it were true.

I am pleased to have you back—its tones unbent. *It was quite interesting hearing about the excavation of* Lugh's Spear *and the encampment.*

Of course it had listened, and now it knew everything about how she felt about Jace, and that he was her HeartMate. But it had heard all of the individual Family members' secrets and rarely told anyone, unless it spoke to her mother, who was discreet as the house.

D'Licorice and T'Licorice already knew your HeartMate was Jace Bayrum.

Glyssa hadn't thought her father would lose much time winnowing that bit of information out and telling her mother.

I believe their feelings were hurt that you didn't confide in them. Another wince. She'd been pretty closemouthed within these walls, too, didn't think the Residence had known. "I'm sorry, and I'm sorry if I hurt your feelings. My emotions seemed too huge to talk about, and too chaotic to frame in good words."

You are forgiven.

"Thank you."

The Residence said, *However, we have found very little information about this Jace Bayrum. We only have some data on the jobs that he took for the merchant guild, and notations about his work at the excavation. We have viewed all the copies of the vizes from that venture.*

So they knew what he looked like. "I am exhausted, Residence. Traveling such a distance shouldn't be so wearying, but it is."

Go rest now.

"Thank you, Residence." Impulsively she stroked the molding around her bedroom door. "I love you, Residence."

I love you, too, Glyssa. Take a nap."

When she stepped into her bedroom, she noted the Flair glow in her personal safe. The HeartGift she'd made for Jace. She sank onto the bedsponge and stared, recalling the sweaty time of Passage at seventeen. She'd taken a huge piece of Flaired papyrus—two meters square—and folded a large piece of origami for her HeartMate.

In the shape of a hawkcel in flight.

She'd been right not to take the delicate HeartGift to the site. The size of it—seventy-five centimeters—would have dominated any room of her pavilion, especially since a HeartGift always needed to be spellshielded against the lust it engendered.

And she'd have been tempted to give the piece to Jace. Especially after he had a hawkcel Fam. Smiling, she wondered what Zem would make of the thing. She hadn't tinted it, the origami remained the original beige of the papyrus, but she could . . .

No, not now.

Lady and Lord, it wouldn't have fit well in Jace's tent.

Her reunion with her parents wasn't as easy or joyful as with her friends or the Residence, much more constrained. Nobody mentioned Jace.

She ached for him, more than sex, just for his tender stroking after they'd made love, their spooning together.

Loneliness ate at her, and anger. The wretched man wasn't ready. After . . . well, a couple of weeks. She'd thought she was good at patience. She was wrong.

*F*or Jace, that night without Glyssa, missing her, was hideous. And even as his mind ran and ran all the excuses, explanations he'd given her—and they still sounded pretty good—he literally *hurt* at the distance between them.

It wasn't only sex. There was a . . . comfort about her that he missed. Comfort. He wouldn't call it anything more that might frighten him, bind him.

Comfort was precious enough. More than he'd ever gotten from his family, except for a rough rub of his head from his father now and then. More than he'd even wanted from any other lover.

Grimly, Jace filled the next day with work. The starship, *Nuada's Sword,* and the Elder Family had included several patterns for the communications arrays. Since Raz and Del had grimly closed off the hole to *Lugh's Spear,* it was either digging or moving strange-looking metal things around. Just one design took all of the rest of the day that Glyssa and Lepid left.

Jace supposed he should have been grateful he'd been assigned to the moving team, but he'd awakened grumpy from no sex and no Glyssa in his—or him in her—bed.

Zem preened in the sunlight atop one of the tallest metal tree poles. He helped ensure the pattern was correct. Jace was rolling the muscle strain out of his shoulders when Raz T'Elecampane ambled up to him, a suspicious smile on his face and his thumbs tucked into his belt.

It occurred to Jace that the man had just come from the communications tent. Despite the work, the scry panel continued to function, if not at optimum efficiency.

"What is it?" Jace questioned. "Or should I ask *who?*" Not Glyssa. He knew she'd arrived safely, and he'd tapped into their link to understand she'd talked a lot to her friends, some to her Family, but mostly slept. Near the end of his day, she'd sent a mental *Sweet dreams* his way, but nothing else.

Raz's smile turned sharp. "First Family GreatLord Laev T'Hawthorn."

Twenty-four

Raz T'Elecampane continued, "I told T'Hawthorn I was taking you away from well-paid work. He's going to compensate you." Tucking his hands in his trous pockets, the actor rocked back and forth, heel to toe. "I quoted him fifty gilt a minute."

Jace's eyes widened. "Incredible."

"He agreed, starting from the moment the call came through."

With a shrug, Jace jogged toward the communications tent. He was on the far end of the field from it.

"I wouldn't run if I were you," Raz called, voice full of amusement.

Jace didn't stop, but thought of what he knew about Laev T'Hawthorn. FirstFamily GreatLord. Exceedingly wealthy. Generations and generations of wealth. Laev's FatherSire had been the Captain of All the Councils of Celta, the most important man in the world. More than once.

Jace frowned . . . wasn't there some sort of hint of a curse? Or was that the Holly Family? And the Hawthorns and Hollys had feuded a generation ago, hadn't they?

He didn't know much of the man's background. But T'Hawthorn was the HeartMate of one of Glyssa's good friends.

Camellia had married Laev earlier this year. Glyssa approved of the marriage—the HeartMate marriage—and liked the guy. He'd funded her trip here.

With strings.

Like all the FirstFamilies, strings they set in place tended to be sticky.

But Jace was helping Glyssa fulfill her obligation to her friend and the FirstFamily GreatLord—writing a fictional account of Captain Hoku based on his journals. Jace could take pride in that.

He slowed to a walk, slapped dust from his shirt and trous, straightened his cuffs. Of course he would never be the same status as Laev T'Hawthorn, but he had nothing to be ashamed about in his life. He'd lived it as well as he could have, done what he wanted, just like any man should.

On a big sucked-in breath, he waved the spellshield and door of the canvas tent aside and stepped in to see the screen set up on a small table Glyssa had donated. He had no time to check out the other instruments in the tent because his gaze was riveted to the man in the frame who radiated power even from thousands of kilometers away.

"GentleSir Jace Bayrum?" asked Laev T'Hawthorn, his violet gaze fixed on Jace.

"That's me." Jace refused to let his hand shake as he drew out the stool. He'd never seen such clothing, so obviously made of expensive materials and in a fashion that flattered the man. Tailored.

"Laev T'Hawthorn here," the GreatLord said.

Despite himself, Jace dipped his head. "So I was told. How can I help you, GreatLord T'Hawthorn?" More courteous than asking what the guy wanted.

The man's smile flashed even, brilliant teeth. "Odd you should ask that."

Jace had said the wrong thing. He was in trouble now. Maybe the man wanted him to do something at the site, but he figured the lord was interested in something else. "You want me to come to Druida City."

"And you're very astute. Yes, I do. Glyssa is unhappy that you remained there."

"How do you—" Then Jace recalled that Glyssa "spoke" with her friends telepathically. Distance didn't matter to such mental connections.

"The bonds of love." T'Hawthorn actually looked a little sympathetic. "Glyssa is unhappy and my HeartMate wished me to speak with you, see if I could persuade you to change your mind."

Jace stiffened, and though it hurt him to say it, he continued, "I won't be bought."

A small nod. "I understand. But I'm not offering to pay you to come, though I would take care of all expenses." Now the man paused. "And offer to house you here, in my Residence."

Surprise squeezed the breath from Jace and dizzying visions flashed before his eyes. *Him* staying in an intelligent Residence! With a FirstFamily GreatLord.

The adventure of *that*. Once in a lifetime, if ever. And he still felt the pain of being far from Glyssa. He sure hadn't anticipated that would happen.

"I see that you like the idea?" T'Hawthorn pressed. "You would have the use of one of our new gliders to visit the Licorices."

The bubble of the dream popped. Of course this was all to facilitate Jace meeting Glyssa's uptight and upright Family.

"What's the deal?" His own tone wasn't nearly as smooth as the lord's.

Another smile. Not as sharklike as Jace had expected.

"We—Camellia and I and our friend Tiana Mugwort—get the opportunity to grill you. Specifically on your relationship with Glyssa and, in general, on the excavation, the Elecampanes, and the project."

"Yeah?"

"You'll come? My HeartMate wants this and I like to give her what she wants."

Jace grunted.

"We're still newly wed." The GreatLord's expression softened.

"And I like Glyssa, too. I'm sure I can make it worth your while. I have many projects in my hands."

Now Jace felt like he'd taken a sock to the chest. "I told you I wouldn't be bought," he growled. "Glyssa doesn't need a man to be bought for her—"

"Indeed she doesn't," T'Hawthorn said.

"And I've always made my gilt honestly."

The entrepreneur's smile was charming. "I truly would like to get a take on the *Lugh's Spear* excavation venture."

"I'm loyal to the Elecampanes, and I have a share in it," Jace said.

T'Hawthorn's smile broadened. "Nothing wrong with just talking." He tapped his fingers together then spread his hands wide. "Just think, see Druida City as you have never seen it before"—a pause—"as you may never see it again."

Was that a threat? The guy's eyes still looked mild, nearly guileless. Jace decided the words hadn't been intended as a threat. A lot of people at the expedition were looking at settling near *Lugh's Spear*, especially those with shares.

"I have a BirdFam," Jace said. Even as he mentioned Zem, the hawkcel glided through a crack in the flap to perch on his shoulder.

Laev T'Hawthorn's eyes widened and he whistled. *"Beautiful Fam."*

Tell him thank you, Zem said.

Jace relayed the sentiment.

"Perhaps . . . Zem . . . would be amenable to being paid for information on the area?"

I am not a greedy, dealing cat, Zem said.

With a smile, Jace told T'Hawthorn Zem's words.

The GreatLord laughed, then grew serious. "I want you here, Jace Bayrum and Zem the FamBird. Tell me how I can make that happen." His expression went beyond serious to sad. "Glyssa misses you." He coughed and for the first time his eyes shifted from Jace. "My HeartMate and I had a very rough wooing. If I can make it easier on Glyssa . . ."

Jace stood and the stool tipped over behind him. "I'll come . . . we'll come." He grimaced. "Try not to manipulate me too much."

T'Hawthorn's brows rose, he inclined his head. "I'm sure we'll come to a meeting of minds. Ah, the airship is on its way and will be there this evening. The pilot is one who shuttles there and back quite often. He can bring you back tomorrow."

Jace set his teeth, then had to unlock his jaw before saying, "Pretty sure of me."

But the guy was shaking his head. "Not at all." He smiled. "Sure of Glyssa and HeartMate lo—, sex."

Jace turned. "Later."

"I'll deposit a thousand in your account pursuant to the deal I made with Raz D'Elecampane to converse with you."

More gilt than Jace'd seen in a long time, but he didn't answer. He had no doubt the man knew which bank held his pitiful savings.

Jace awoke before dawn and, with Zem on his shoulder, walked toward the landing area carrying a small duffle. Inside were gifts for each of Glyssa's two friends. Since the pilot had stayed up late, Jace was surprised to see the man checking his vehicle. He waved and grunted a greeting at them, stuffing some food into his mouth as he did a last walk around the airship.

When the sun rose, they were off. The trip passed fast and interestingly as he and the pilot talked a lot about flying, the excavation, airships, starships, and Raz Cherry Elecampane, who the pilot knew from Raz's childhood around the Cherry Airship business.

Zem was fascinated with the trip—how much he could see, and how much he couldn't, just clouds and the blazing white of the sun, set high and tiny in the deep blue sky.

Jace had convinced himself that he was doing the right thing in making this trip, especially since he literally ached due to the last two days and nights without Glyssa. As he'd told her, he had absolutely no yearning for any other woman, which scared him, too. He was *not* thinking about that word, that term, they'd sort of discussed, the one with the permanent bond.

But when Jace hopped down from the door of the sleek, fast airship, he didn't see Glyssa waiting to meet him and his excitement dimmed.

An elegant, richly dressed man stepped from a nearby building and walked toward him and Zem. Jace recognized T'Hawthorn. The man strode toward him and nodded a greeting, not offering Jace an arm to clasp. Maybe he thought Jace wasn't pleased to have been manipulated into coming, or maybe he had excruciatingly proper manners, or maybe he was snobbish, or maybe he didn't like Jace. The world of rich nobles of high status was far different than the world Jace occupied. He wouldn't fit in and he couldn't guess the man's motives.

"Merry meet," said T'Hawthorn.

And, yeah, that ritual greeting wasn't something Jace often had occasion to say. "Merry meet." Again his gaze swept the landing area.

"Glyssa isn't here. She is working hard in the library refining her report and the chapters of the novel she and you are writing, so she can present them to the panel of FirstLevel Librarians before the Field Trip Report Hearing tomorrow afternoon."

That didn't sound so good.

"And I scheduled this trip so that I might be able to talk to you first, before Glyssa, before her Family, and especially before Glyssa's friends, my HeartMate Camellia and the priestess Tiana Mugwort, met you."

"Um-hmm," Jace said. For all his intensity and his rich clothes, T'Hawthorn wasn't quite as tall as Jace himself and that surprised him a little.

T'Hawthorn looked up at Zem on Jace's shoulder. "Like I said before, a very beautiful bird. Quite colorful." He inclined his head to Zem. "Merrily meet, Zem."

The man sure knew a lot about Jace, more than he felt comfortable with a stranger knowing, and just *how much* did he know? What had Glyssa told her best friends? Women she was closer to than Jace had ever been to anyone. What had she told GreatLord T'Hawthorn?

Jace was blind in this and didn't like it.

Greetyou, GreatLord T'Hawthorn, Zem said, with exactly the same amount of mental Flair that he would use with Glyssa.

I am pleased to meet you, the GreatLord responded easily. With a tilt of his head, T'Hawthorn indicated an area where gliders were parked and began moving in that direction. Jace kept up and his mouth nearly watered as he saw a gleaming purple two-seated sport glider that had probably cost more than all the gilt he'd ever made in his life. "Nice."

T'Hawthorn grinned as he patted the rounded front. "Yeah, my new toy. Not that I drive much."

Jace's mind just froze at the thought that the GreatLord had so expensive a vehicle just sitting around that he didn't use often.

The lord lifted his door, slid in, then pressed a button that had the passenger side door lifting, too. Soft cushions covered in prime leather from something other than tough furrabeast cradled Jace's ass.

T'Hawthorn thinned the windows and the top to nothing, then set off along the road toward the more populated portion of the city.

Jace had never ridden in a personal glider before, not even an old and lumbering Family glider as was mostly seen on the roads.

"Better enjoy this," the lord said. "I don't think you'll like where we're going."

That wiped the smile off Jace's face. Did T'Hawthorn Residence have a dungeon?

"Glyssa does know that I'm coming." He'd checked their bond more often than he'd expected. Too bad they hadn't had any really good sex dreams.

Throwing his head back and laughing made T'Hawthorn look almost approachable. When he finished, he gave Jace a quick glance, then set his gaze back on the not-very-busy road. "I am familiar with my wife's schedule. You know my HeartMate owns and operates three teahouses, restaurants?" Pride lilted in the lord's voice.

"Yes," Jace said, though he wasn't sure. He'd known about two, hadn't he? Had Glyssa said something about a third that he hadn't paid attention to? Probably. Which had him brooding about how much *he* should know about her friends and Family and Laev T'Hawthorn that he'd missed. His own damn fault, then, that he didn't know Laev as well as Laev might know him.

"We are going to the newest, recently opened just before Glyssa left for the excavation. My wife is not there today, so I'll be able to take a look at the place, judge the business and tea and food during our lunch, and we can talk in peace."

"Oh." That sounded like an entrepreneur, combining several goals into one trip.

A flash of white teeth from the GreatLord. "It's called the Ladies' Tearoom, specifically aimed at women. I expect to feel a little odd, so you might, too."

"Great," Jace said. The lord laughed again.

Jace repeated the word as they walked into a medium-sized room filled with round tables covered in pastel cloths with napkins folded in the shapes of flowers and delicate silverware and china on each table.

Every woman in the place turned to stare at them. The lord just smiled at them and stood casually, and Jace felt like he'd just emerged from a dirty mancave.

Druida City was a different world, all right.

Druida City of the nobles was hugely different.

And the Druida City of the Ladies' Tearoom was something he'd never imagined, where he didn't really want to be.

Twenty-five

I do not like this place. It is too fussy. I want OUT! Zem said.

T'Hawthorn coughed.

Reluctantly, Jace opened the door. *I will miss you,* he said privately to Zem. *Please stay close.*

There is a strip of park with a fountain across the street. Bath time! Zem sounded thrilled. With only a flip of a wing as good-bye, he soared away.

Dammit, Jace could have used his Fam's advice. He closed the door and turned back to the room as they were led to a table. The place reminded him of his mother and how sweet she seemed on the outside and to other people, and how rotten she was to him when no one was watching. He wondered what she'd told the townfolk when she'd returned to the home containing the *things* she loved more than her husband and child, after she'd left them for dead. Didn't matter. He'd started thinking about that time more often a decade ago, and didn't like it.

"We were all having a very good time until you two gorgeous men walked in," said a waitress, stopping at the table. "Now everyone is preening and watching you." The newcomer laughed. "The manager won't have to tell Camellia that you were here, she'll hear as soon as a guest here scries her, and if that doesn't happen, the gossip will hit her by tomorrow."

The GreatLord set down the menu, rested his arms on the table, and steepled his fingers. "Tomorrow will be fine. In a half septhour, not so much. I have business."

"Uh-huh," said the waitress. "What can I get you?"

Jace glanced down at the menu, printed in very fancy script that he had trouble reading.

"I will have dark roast caff," T'Hawthorn said. "I noticed that at the bottom of the menu you offered 'a full Celtan tea for those who want a larger meal.' That's me."

"Excellent, and you, sir?" The waitress turned to Jace.

"I'll have that meal, too." He thought about drink. Caff was the standard of the day in the camp, most bad, some good, if you knew the right person. He'd had some good tea with Glyssa, didn't remember the name of it, but Camellia Darjeeling D'Hawthorn had provided it. He grinned at the waitress, handed the server his menu. "I'll have the Darjeeling."

She smiled back and T'Hawthorn narrowed his eyes. "Clever."

"I can be," Jace said.

"Have a good business discussion, my lords," said the waitress. "Take any physical disagreements to The Green Knight Fencing and Fighting Salon. The ladies might be delighted to see a fight—or might not—but, I assure you, Camellia would be displeased."

Jace sat stunned at being addressed a lord.

After the two women left—and he noticed that the next party that came in was seated on the opposite side of the room—he finally shook his mind from a trance. "I'm not a lord."

T'Hawthorn shrugged. "I'm sure she feels it's better to err on the side of courtesy and respect. And though I don't think T'Blackthorn or his sons or cuzes, especially Draeg, would step in here for any amount of gilt, you are dressed much like the trackers when they are working."

"Oh." Jace frowned. "I thought T'Blackthorn . . . that the Blackthorns . . ." Jace stopped since T'Hawthorn's face went still. The Blackthorns *did* have a curse, sterility or something.

"Straif and Mitchella have adopted. They also consider the young Betony men, Straif's cuz's sons, as his own."

"I don't know too much about Druida City or the FirstFamilies, haven't ever associated with nobles."

"Until now." The GreatLord leaned back in his chair, floral patterned like everything else from the walls to the rug.

The waitress appeared with two floral china pots, one long and slender, the other short and round, the standard teapot.

"You're really going to drink that?" the GreatLord asked.

Since Jace had figured out that the man was here to warn him off, or about hurting Glyssa, he just grinned. "I've had plenty of bad caff and bad tea and bad drink in the wilds and in the camp. Some of it I've made myself. This is going to be a pure pleasure."

"Ah," T'Hawthorn said, again studying Jace. "Who do you know in Druida City?"

Jace thought that was T'Hawthorn's idea of light conversation, since it didn't sound patronizing or snobbish. "No one except Glyssa." Then he thought about it. "I suppose some people in the Merchants' Guild, merchants or guards, might be here."

"My cuz Cratag T'Marigold is associated with the Merchants' Guild," T'Hawthorn said.

The legendary Cratag Maytree T'Marigold. "Never met him," Jace said. The waitress walked toward them pushing two anti-grav trays loaded with food.

Wonderful smells teased Jace's nose—there was a cold vegetable and clucker salad showing sprinkles of fresh herbs and thick slices of three kinds of cheese next to equally thick bread, butter, a bowl with a leaf salad, and fruit. His mouth watered.

When the waitress set the plates on the large table, Jace saw that his food differed from T'Hawthorn's, and actually looked better. The lord had a hearty soup that Jace thought might be too hot, sausage rolls, and a couple of hard-boiled eggs. Well displayed, naturally, but not nearly as delicious looking as his own fare.

"What's with this?" T'Hawthorn demanded, staring at Jace's clucker salad.

He stuck a fork in it, tasted. "Really great!"

The waitress smiled smugly. "Naturally we suit the food to the beverage. You got dark roast caff. *He* got Darjeeling tea."

"Oh." The lord's look was grumpy.

"You can have some of my grapes," Jace offered, just to rub it in.

"Thanks."

"Enjoy." Even with just one word, Jace heard her suppressed laughter. She swished away.

"Excellent food. Your wife create this menu?" Jace asked T'Hawthorn.

"My *HeartMate*, yes."

Jace's stomach squeezed a little at the word, his taste buds soured a bit, and he freshened them with tea. "I like this tea. I'm not sure Glyssa had any."

"Probably since she drank it a lot growing up with Camellia, and for many years since . . . from the lesser varieties to the rare," the lord said.

"I understand," Jace said.

"I believe you do. You're sharper, more clever than I reckoned."

Since that sounded like an irritated but sincere compliment, Jace said, "Thank you."

T'Hawthorn glanced at the room. The noise level that had quieted when they'd walked in, then risen as they'd been gossiped about, had settled to regular levels. It was still odd to Jace that he only heard women's voices in the background.

The lord cleared his throat. "I want to talk to you honestly about Glyssa. And I want to make sure we are clear between us about her."

T'Hawthorn *couldn't* be romantically interested in Glyssa, he had a HeartMate, yet Jace's hackles rose. "In what way do you want to warn me off her?" Jace bit into a chunk of creamy, nutty-tasting cheese.

Wincing, T'Hawthorn shook his head, used his knife and fork to cut into the sausage roll. "I've come to know her and value her."

Jace concentrated on eating. "You've been married, what, three months?" Hadn't Glyssa mentioned that while he *was* paying attention?

"Like many, I have visited the PublicLibrary, know the Licorices . . . and knew Glyssa before Camellia and I wed."

"I thought you FirstFamilies had ResidenceLibraries that knew everything and shared info back and forth with the PublicLibrary." Jace wasn't sure why he was poking at T'Hawthorn, just that he felt irritated enough to do it—or wanted to distract the man from the original topic.

"As I said, I value Glyssa. Your relationship is your business—"

"That's right."

"But," he hesitated, "speaking as one who . . . had troubles with his own HeartMate, I want to let you know that she has friends who will not be pleased if you treat her ill."

Jace met the man's purple gaze. "I hear you. And one of the first things I noticed about her when she showed up at camp was that she had high-powered friends. That huge duffle she had sort of broadcast the fact. The pavilion is luxurious."

T'Hawthorn's eyes gleamed. "I chose the best for her."

"Everyone in the camp was impressed," Jace said politely. "I helped her put up the pavilion myself, very nice."

"Yes." The man stabbed at a piece of hard-boiled egg with his fork and when he glanced up at Jace his gaze was sharper than the knife. "Don't think you can be casual with Glyssa's feelings, or treat her like some . . ."

"Low-class Commoner?" Jace said, edgy himself, then squashed a couple of juicy grapes between his teeth, sweet flavor spurted nicely.

T'Hawthorn sat poker straight. "I do *not* often consider the class of a person."

No "considering" needed, that was probably innate in a First-

Families lord. Jace said nothing, broke off a bit of cheese and popped it in his mouth.

"I planned on saying," T'Hawthorn said with great dignity, also something Jace thought was innate to him, "do not treat Glyssa like she's"—the lord glanced around, no women were near—"a casual lay."

Jace's neck burned. "You've made that mistake."

"Yes." The lord stabbed another piece of egg.

Jace thought about that, didn't believe it, figured it was a story he might hear later if he and the GreatLord ever got friendly.

Rearranging his expression into a pleasant one, T'Hawthorn said, "Tell me how that miniature furniture worked."

"Not quite the quality of this place." Jace gestured around.

"Ah, well, it's a new technique." The lord grinned with a sparkle in his eyes. "Nothing better I like than seeing how new techniques work."

They ate the rest of their meal with a discussion of some of T'Hawthorn's entrepreneurial projects, then the man began to casually probe Jace for information about the excavation of *Lugh's Spear.*

The door opened and an energy came into the room that caught Jace's attention as much as the woman did. She was tall and willowy, with a pretty face and dark brown hair. Something about her stance, her manner as she scanned the room with a satisfied smile, tipped him off. Camellia Darjeeling D'Hawthorn.

T'Hawthorn, who had his back to the door, stiffened.

In a few strides she was there and sitting with them. Her smile broadened as she saw the remains of their meals. She stared at Jace's cup and her nostrils widened, then she turned to him and smiled. "Jace Bayrum, in the flesh."

He raised his brows. "That's right."

She offered her hand. He stood so he could bend over it and kiss her fingers, desperately murmuring a Word to clean his breath. "I'm pleased to meet you, GreatLady D'Hawthorn, I know Glyssa treasures your friendship."

The lady withdrew her fingers. "As I treasure her," D'Hawthorn said. Jace sat again.

She pulled up a chair and sat, too. "And, Laev, did you think to warn GentleSir Bayrum about hurting Glyssa without telling me?" she asked.

"A gentleman's understanding," Jace murmured, thinking it might get the GreatLord in more trouble. T'Hawthorn glowered at him.

"Uh-huh." D'Hawthorn translocated a pretty china teacup in a pale green and poured the last of the tea from Jace's pot into it, sipped and stared at Jace with serious eyes. When she put down her cup, she said, "I'm not a gentleman, and I'm not as noble and honorable as Laev here, and I know what it's like to be poor and scrabble to keep body and soul together, like you. Not all nobles are rich, you know."

He'd probably known that, if he'd given it some thought.

"*My* bottom line here with regard to your . . . relationship with Glyssa, is that if you hurt her, I'll hurt you." She nodded to the teapot. "Despite your excellent taste in tea. Understood?"

"Oh, yeah," he said, then leaned forward and gave her a flirtatious smile. "But you drank the last cup of my tea, and I wanted it."

She laughed and more gazes fixed on their table. The waitress hurried over with another pot, no doubt summoned mentally by D'Hawthorn and replaced the old pot with a new one. D'Hawthorn poured more tea into his cup and hers. "I like you. May I call you Jace?" she said.

He wasn't used to people asking. "Sure."

"And you can call me Camellia."

"You can call me Laev," T'Hawthorn said.

Like hell. That man didn't mean it.

Camellia glanced at her husband. "Are you done here?"

"Who scried you?"

She grinned. "One of my regular customers came from here to Darjeeling's HouseHeart to 'buy some tea' she couldn't get here."

"Nonsense," Laev said. "You stock all your teas in all your shops and you don't run out."

Camellia's smile softened, and she reached out and touched one of her husband's steepled hands. "That is true. How well you know me, HeartMate."

For the first time since they'd met, Jace saw Laev T'Hawthorn transform into a casual man instead of a powerful lord. He linked fingers with his wife, kissed her lips. When they'd parted, T'Hawthorn nodded at Jace. "I have invited him to stay with us."

"No." Camellia D'Hawthorn was definite, but her eyes were kind. "He has to stay with Glyssa and the Licorices." A smile hovered around her mouth. "They are a little . . . intense, but good people. You just have to get to know them." She blinked. "They always treated me well, no matter how tough times were for me."

The pressure in Jace's chest didn't ease much at that, but hair on the back of his neck that had risen at the thought of spending time with Glyssa's Family lowered a bit.

"All right," he said, lying. Naturally he didn't have much of a choice in this unless he dug up a place to stay himself, a hostel or something. His words came out more sourly than he'd wanted. He stood, took his wallet from his trous and set out the amount of the bill and a good tip.

Camellia stood, took Jace's gilt and held it out to him. "My place, my treat. I'm taking care of this."

When he moved to take the papyrus notes, she plucked the wallet out of his other hand, studied it, and nodded. "Very nice. You have talent."

"Let me see." T'Hawthorn stood, too.

But because his wallet was an early, uninspired piece of leatherwork, Jace stuck it and the gilt back into his pocket fast. "Thank you." He gave her a half bow.

She glanced at her timer. "I'm behind schedule." She kissed her husband. "Later." She looked at Jace. "We'll expect you and Glyssa midmorning tomorrow to talk about the novel. Of course there will be food." Then she aimed her gaze at her husband. "Where do you go now?"

"*Nuada's Sword*," T'Hawthorn said.

The starship!

Twenty-six

When Laev took Jace and Zem to _Nuada's Sword,_ Zem remained outside in Landing Park.

The one sentient starship wanted to hear every last detail that Jace could remember of its fellow ship, an older ship, _Lugh's Spear_—the size of the corridors, the amount of dust in the air, the smell. What components comprised the smell that it could correlate to atmosphere.

Jace spilled everything he knew about inside the ship, commented on the blueprints and the vizes from the expedition, the pics, and the maps drawn up by Del Elecampane. He had an attentive audience in the Ship and Captain Ruis and Dani Eve Elder.

Finally T'Hawthorn put an end to the interrogation, and they walked out into the evening air. Air that wasn't like _Nuada's Sword,_ or _Lugh's Spear_, and nothing like the camp. Druida City was next to the Great Platte Ocean, and the sea air, with a touch of salt, dried on his lips.

"Jace!" Glyssa called and ran across Landing Park toward him. She looked good, better than anything he'd seen since they'd walked back from the lake. Outrageous the need he felt for her, how his heart thumped when her body met his and his lips took hers and they tasted each other, cradled each other.

Everything else faded until a continued fake coughing brought him back. Yeah, his mind had been totally gone while he was in a strange place, unaware of his surroundings. Not good.

But he couldn't bear to release his hold on her, even if he only cherished her fingers in his own.

"Can I stop coughing now?" asked Captain Ruis Elder.

"Of course," Glyssa said.

"Laev T'Hawthorn is taking you home by glider." The man gestured and Jace peeled his gaze from Glyssa to see another glider, also purple, also streamlined, but able to carry four.

The GreatLord leaned against it, grinning.

Envy and something more like fear moved inside Jace. That man could crush him, make him disappear, do all sorts of things to him and no one would say a thing. No one might ever know. How did people live in the shadow of such power?

Glyssa sighed. "EveningBell has rung. My Family will be awaiting us."

D'Licorice Residence wasn't how Jace had imagined. For one thing, it wasn't in Noble Country where all the oldest Residences were, wasn't even in any other noble neighborhood, but in a small parklike estate near CityCenter. In fact, the Licorices' land connected to the grounds of the PublicLibrary. Within walking and scaling-walls-and-spellshields distance, just beyond a thick bank of pines and other trees.

Though he understood it was an intelligent house, a real Residence, it wasn't large. Not nearly as large as the PublicLibrary itself. Barely three stories, an interesting-looking place, but not palatial or castlelike, like so many nobles preferred.

When he went through the thick wooden door, he found himself in a small entryway, no grandhall, and the furnishings weren't something his own mother would have thought of as good. No doubt they were sturdy antiques, and well enough cared for, but they had chips and dings, scratches and the occasional tattered area, worn spots in the rugs.

"So you are Jace Bayrum," said a woman's light voice, and he stiffened and immediately stopped scanning his surroundings to focus on Glyssa's mother.

She wasn't as tall as he, or quite as tall as either of her daughters, but she held herself with pride. Her face was thinner than Glyssa's, with worn lines around her mouth and across her forehead, her hair a dark auburn, her hazel eyes intent.

Jace untwined his arm from Glyssa's. With his best manners, he stepped forward and gave as graceful a bow as he could manage to her. "I am," he said. He didn't drop his eyes.

She nodded briefly, then her eyes flamed with curiosity as Zem flew from his shoulder to the newel post at the end of the wide banister edging the stairway to the upper floors. "A hawkcel, nicely colored."

Thank you, Zem projected at the same time Jace said the phrase.

A quick nod. "I am Rhiza D'Licorice." She gestured to the man standing just behind her right shoulder. "My HeartMate and husband, Fasic Almond T'Licorice, whom you spoke with a few days ago, and my older daughter, LicoriceHeir, Enata."

That daughter, too, had darker hair, greener eyes. Her gaze bored into Jace. He sensed she already disliked him for some reason of her own.

D'Licorice's mouth turned down. "I suppose I shall have to put you in the rooms next to Glyssa." Her lips pressed together a moment, then she said, "Come along." She took off at a good clip up the stairs to the second floor and down the hallway to the right. After a glance at the others, who remained expressionless, he followed the GrandLady. "The suite does *not* have a connecting door to Glyssa's rooms. It is our best guest suite and the colors are blue and cream. The furnishings feature a lot of lace. I trust your fascinating Fam will not tear the lace."

He didn't know whether she was being sarcastic or not.

Zem, who rode once more on Jace's shoulder, replied, *I do not have a nest here that I would like to decorate with lace.*

For a moment the woman stopped, though she didn't turn around, and shivered. "You nest in the *wilderness*."

Jace found himself soothing her. "There's been a camp near

Lugh's Spear for a couple of years now. The land is cleared, and there will soon be a town."

"I hope not," she murmured, then headed down the hall, threw open a doorway on the left, facing toward the back of the House, with a view of the PublicLibrary in the distance. *This* was more like he'd imagined. Gleaming curves of expensive and polished furniture. Delicate lace and silkeen wall coverings in a watery blue, trim of a cream tint with an edging of gold. Lace accents everywhere. "Please," the woman said stiffly, not meeting his eyes, "be at home." She looked at her wrist timer. "Dinner is in three-quarters of a septhour." She paused. "The waterfall in this suite is one of the best in the Residence."

"Thank you for your hospitality," he murmured, again doing the half-bow thing.

Her glance grazed him, didn't stay. "You are quite welcome," she said, and he knew she lied.

"I'll be down in half a septhour."

She nodded and left, closing the door behind her. Jace set his duffle on the thick, pastel Chinju rug.

The lace is very pretty, Zem said. *It WOULD look good in a nest.*

Jace closed his eyes, went to the nearest wing chair and sank down into its soft depths, leaned his head back.

"Welcome to D'Licorice Residence," said a low and mellow, yet austere, voice.

Jace was too tired to flinch. He didn't open his eyes. "Thank you, Residence." He wet his lips. "I'd like to sit here for ten minutes. Could you notify me when that amount of time has elapsed so I can use the waterfall room and get ready for dinner?" Not that he had any appropriate clothes.

"Certainly," said the House. "Glyssa is obtaining a couple of perches for Zem. One for here, and one for her sitting room."

"Sounds good," Jace said. He could hear the slight whir of Zem as his Fam flew through the rooms, but still didn't open his lashes. The whole day had twanged at his nerves, and this last bit . . . on his way to this suite, he'd passed Glyssa's. And through the very walls of her rooms, he could see the glow of the HeartGift she'd made for him. He hadn't brought his own. Hadn't wanted to give it to her in an impulsive moment he couldn't take back.

But the radiance of the thing shook him.

When the Residence gave him the time, he opened his eyes and saw a room his mother would be ecstatic to be in. One she'd have done anything to live in.

Jace got up and paced to the waterfall room, stripped off his clothes and stood under the huge, rushing water, soaping himself with nice-smelling, foamy stuff.

He came from the massive greed of his mother, a woman who'd pick, pick, pick at a person until she got what she desired. He came from a man loving a woman and working himself to death to give her what she wanted. And Jace never forgot that.

He always kept his relationships light, always surface, never deep so they roused anything he couldn't control.

So he was selfish himself, wouldn't let himself be manipulated by a woman for what she wanted that wasn't good for him, too.

No, he didn't want to think about any HeartGifts, way out of his league. The whole day, far from his comfort zone . . . the Ladies' Tearoom, for fliggering fligger's sake.

He snorted, tossed wet hair from his eyes, and managed to scrape up some equilibrium.

Until dinner.

D'Licorice herded them all into a dining room, where food in covered dishes already awaited. Everyone took their seat at the table that would hold eight and passed around the food. Jace got the idea that D'Licorice alone chose the menu.

Glyssa's father introduced a general topic of conversation that rapidly escalated to something Jace didn't understand, but was of interest to the four Family members.

He ate steadily, and listened, and looked at the quality of the things around him. His mother would have loved them, too.

"Eat your greens, Jace," D'Licorice said.

He *hated* bitter greens.

"I noticed that Glyssa needed more greens when she got home. She wasn't getting the best nutrition at that camp," D'Licorice said.

Jace ate the greens.

"And you must tell me," the woman plowed on. "Since you're working with Glyssa on this fiction project. Are your story stylings rooted in good research and fact?"

Jace was sure that Glyssa would have assured her Family, all of them staring at him intently with judging FirstLevel Librarian eyes, that everything they'd written was minutely researched.

He swallowed a mouthful of nasty greens that dressing couldn't make palatable and said, "Of course. Glyssa is a very good historian for the project, recorded everything right for the Elecampanes, and transcribed Hoku's journal well."

Glyssa's sister snorted.

D'Licorice frowned. "How could you judge? You have no formal train—"

"Enough, Rhiza." Glyssa's father smiled at Jace, then stood, went to a cabinet in the corner that turned out to be a disguised no-time, and pulled out a plate of raw spinach, placed it on the table. He served himself, Glyssa, and raised a brow at Jace.

"Thank you." Jace held out his plate.

"Those aren't nearly as nutritional as bitter—"

"We know," Fasic T'Licorice said. "You're the botanist, but we all know. But it tastes better."

"Humph."

Eventually dinner ended. While the Family proceeded slowly to the sitting room for more conversation, Jace retired to his rooms on an errand. He asked and received instructions from the Residence on how to send the small gifts he'd selected to Glyssa's friends. A cache teleporter was built into the fancy desk. He rubbed the back of his neck, wishing he'd included gifts for the Licorices, too . . . but he'd expected to stay at T'Hawthorn's. Should have chosen gifts for the Licorices anyway.

A knock came at his door and he opened it to Glyssa's father.

Fasic T'Licorice gave Jace a direct stare. "Come into my personal library, why don't you, son?" the man asked.

Twenty-seven

*J*ace *knew T'Licorice's offer was more of an order, but kept his posture* easy as he followed the man downstairs. "How many libraries are there in the Residence?"

Laugh lines crinkled around the lord's eyes as he smiled. "There's the main library, the hereditary GrandLord or Lady's . . ."

"That would be your wife's," Jace said. This man had married into the Licorice Family and become the Lord that way, just as Raz Cherry had wed Del D'Elecampane to become T'Elecampane.

"That's right," GrandLord T'Licorice said mildly, but his smile had vanished. He gestured to an old but expensive-looking fur-rabeast leather chair in gleaming deep red. "I sense you're very wary of my wife."

"She's a very good manager."

As he sat in another chair angled toward Jace's, T'Licorice hooted, grinned again. "That she is. Some people don't know how to handle those types."

Jace said nothing. If there'd been a way to handle his mother, neither his father nor he had learned it.

Glyssa's father studied him in silence, and the truth was, Jace didn't feel uncomfortable with the man, or the quiet. The guy had his own strength, his own confidence, and Jace bet that people would look at the couple and see—as he had before this moment—a very opinionated woman and a man who seemed to let her set the terms of their marriage. Perhaps a woman smarter than her husband, definitely sharper in manner—as his own had been.

Those conclusions didn't feel right to him now.

"My HeartMate is a strong-minded woman, a forceful woman. She's *the* PublicLibrarian of Celta, and that's an honor and a position that carries some weight here in Druida City, even all of Celta. Something that she is always aware of. Our daughter, Enata, will be the next GrandLady D'Licorice in her time, something she's been trained for and is always aware of, too."

"I understand."

"Do you? I come from a noble GraceHouse myself, one with a small but fairly loving Family." He shrugged. "The Licorices are as you see us—me, my HeartMate, our two daughters. Rhiza is a lot less . . . formal . . . than she was when we met. I take pride in that." He glanced around the room. "And the Residence is beautiful and healthy."

"Yes." Something they could agree on.

"It's always interesting to know one's in-laws' backgrounds. For instance, Rhiza's father died quite early in her life and her home life, and this Residence, deteriorated." A hard note entered Fasic T'Licorice's voice. Jace raised his brows.

"Neglect bothers me, as it does Rhiza. HeartMates usually hold common views. She and I have worked hard to restore the Residence."

Jace didn't know what to say, so made a show of studying the library, really a nice and welcoming place for a guy, then murmured, "Good job."

"My darling Rhiza didn't have much of an example on how a strong woman should lead and behave when she was growing up. Her mother is a kind but selfish woman, very vague, constantly misplacing things, and, as I said before, this Residence wasn't kept up in the manner that it should have been."

"So Glyssa's mother reacted to her own mother," Jace said, as he continued to react to his own.

"That's right," T'Licorice said. "And I believe we have done much better with our daughters. I am very proud of Enata and Glyssa."

"Where's Glyssa's MotherDam now?" Jace asked.

"She is living quite happily in Toono Town, the artists' colony. Rhiza's father was the hereditary Licorice."

"Oh."

"The PublicLibrary was lucky to have a couple of FirstLevel and SecondLevel Librarians to keep faith with the people of Druida City and Celta during my HeartMate's minority, but she tested for her FirstLevel Librarianship as soon as she became an adult at seventeen, and was confirmed by the testing board then, of course."

"Of course."

"I deeply admire Rhiza's dedication. And she's my HeartMate. I love her, though I can see her faults when she tries too hard to be perfect."

"Uh-huh." So much revelation made Jace uneasy.

"Enata doesn't have a HeartMate and that hurts her. You wouldn't know about that," Fasic ended softly.

Jace flushed but didn't answer.

"Now, speaking of in-laws' backgrounds . . ." the man prompted.

"I don't think—"

"Whether or not you intend to marry into this Family—and I am quite sure my daughter will win you over despite my wife and any other problems that lay between you—I *do* want to know more about you."

"Who my family is?" Jace asked with more bitterness in his tone than he'd anticipated.

T'Licorice blinked. "Not that so much as how they might have affected you . . . for instance, why you might react more negatively toward my wife than many."

Jace remained silent.

"Or I could hire Garrett Primross to check into your background. He would probably speak with the Elecampanes first."

"And you know I've been having trouble at the camp."

T'Licorice shrugged a shoulder. "I know you're an honorable man. The Lady and Lord wouldn't give my daughter a HeartMate who didn't share that trait. Whatever happened or happens at the encampment will not affect my opinion of you."

"I have no Family."

Sighing, T'Licorice said, "That is an all too unfortunate occurrence here on our beloved world." He reached out, offered his arm like one man to another of his own rank. "Think about this, Jace Bayrum with no living relatives. You *can* have a Family. A Family who will admire and respect you. A Family of name and status that will stand by you. Always."

Jace took his arm, got the clasp over with as soon as possible. "Sounds too good to be true."

"You don't trust easily, do you? Well, we can work on that." T'Licorice smiled as if liking a challenge. "What you might not see is that my wife is fully aware that her brusque manner can make people wary of her, but behind that shell of professional and personal competence, she is tender and easily hurt."

"Ah." Jace fought not to squirm. "I do not care to be ordered around."

Another smile flashed from the lord. "Who does? Just stand your ground." He winked. "Or slide out of her request, or ignore it. All three options will work. Perhaps."

"Uh-huh. I think you'd find it easier than I."

"Because she loves me. And despite what you might have surmised or thought, she loves our daughters very much. She's like all parents."

"Most parents," Jace replied before he thought. The quiet conversation, the man's easy manner had reduced his guard.

"Ah."

Again quiet graced the room. Fasic simply looked at him with compassion in his eyes. "Your mother?"

Jace hesitated, but the serenity of the man drew words from him. "She killed my father. Drained him of energy and Flair to save her life and walked away from us."

T'Licorice's eyes fired, his face set in lines that promised retribution. He leaned forward. "Where is this female?"

"Dead."

"But not before she sorely hurt you." The man scanned Jace. "I understand trusting will be difficult."

The door simply opened and Glyssa stood there. "Mama wants to speak with you," she said to her father. All three of them knew it was a lie.

Jace said, "If you'll excuse me, I am weary." He stood, letting his tiredness show, though he was close to lying also. He'd gotten his second wind.

Fasic rose and stared at him. "If you insist."

Glyssa took her father's arm. "*I* do."

Inclining his head to Jace, Fasic said, "Sometimes it's best not to push, to let the bird come to your hand." His full smile was endearing. "And I hope your BirdFam is enjoying himself."

"I'm sure he is. I left a window open," Jace said. "He can come and go as he pleases."

"And I hope you feel you can do the same," Fasic said. Glyssa smiled at Jace, and he felt the warmth of it heat all the blood in his veins, before she took her father away to another Family gathering Jace didn't need to attend. Thank the Lady and Lord.

"What do you wish to do, young man?" asked the Residence, voice coming from a speaker Jace couldn't see. House was probably riddled with them.

Jace jumped, cleared his throat. "Call me Jace."

"Do you wish to explore my halls and rooms? Go to the Public-Library through the tunnel? Wander our grounds? Leave the estate for sociability with other humans?"

"Do you have a workroom for physical tasks?" he asked.

"To use your creative Flair?" The Residence sounded approving. "Yes."

"I will give you instructions to the basement workroom."

A few minutes later, Jace entered that chamber. The workroom had walls of small cubes stuffed with materials and tools, neatly organized and clean . . . but idle. He *felt* his spirit expand. No one in the Residence used this room, had used this room since . . .

"The former T'Licorice made books," the Residence said, turning on bespelled lights along the long walls. "My current Family uses their own suites for their creative Flair, but T'Licorice liked this space."

"It's great," Jace said, and it held very few echoes or vibrations of the Licorices. "I am a leatherworker."

Lights flashed over a table against one of the short walls. "Leathers and tools for such work are here." The Residence's voice warmed. "The former T'Licorice, Red Rhiz, occasionally used leather to bind his books, though he preferred cloth."

Jace crossed to the table, found the finest tools. He swallowed. "I use gold gilding."

"I know. I have often seen the wallet of yours that Glyssa has."

Jace blinked. He didn't recall her mentioning such a thing.

The Residence said, "We have plenty of gilding for you." A small wooden drawer protruded holding a stack of fine gold sheets. Jace stared, gently took one and laid it on the table. His head swam. No, he wasn't used to the offhand wealth these people commanded *at all*. Wetting his lips, he asked, "Do you know what kind of wallets and pursenals the Licorices prefer?"

"Rhiza and Enata like long, thin envelope pursenals. Glyssa always carries your wallet, and Fasic likes a trifold."

"Thank you. I'll make such for them." Something to do with his days rather than exploring Druida. "And you, Residence? Would you like a gilded leather panel somewhere?"

A creak came as if in surprise, then a hum. "You could make a rectangular panel fifty by seventy-five centimeters in a dark maroon with gilding for me."

"Sounds good. We can talk about what kind of pattern you prefer later," Jace said absently as he reached for a piece of leather that was red, nearly black, that should suit D'Licorice.

Sometime later, he heard the door open, and even later after that, the Residence dimmed the lights. "You should retire now."

Jace nodded. He hadn't quite come to a stopping place, but stupid to argue with an intelligent House. Stretching the kinks from his muscles, he turned to see Glyssa sitting in a bar chair, watching him. She blushed. "Your work is beautiful."

"Thank you."

She slipped from the chair, came and took his hand. "Come, let's go to bed."

His work was forgotten, he put nothing away, just walked fast with her out the door.

And made sure that he had sex with her slowly, tenderly, thoroughly.

Jace had thought he'd gained his balance. Until it was time for the midmorning appointment at the Hawthorns.

As soon as they exited from the glider, the Fams took off to hunt on a FirstFamily estate. For some reason they thought the game would be richer here, though Glyssa had told them she didn't think the Hawthorn mice and skirls were fatter than anywhere else in Druida.

Camellia D'Hawthorn opened the door with a warm smile.

"I brought the unfinished manuscript of Netra Sunaya Hoku's story for you to listen to," Glyssa said.

"Listen to?" Camellia asked. "Now? Yay!" She gestured them in and Jace entered the castlelike residence. The grandhall showed two stories of wooden paneling.

"With goodies," Glyssa said firmly. As if food and a more casual manner might make Jace less nervous. Didn't work.

"That's right, goodies," Laev said smoothly. He picked up Camellia's fingers and kissed them as he led them to a hallway off the entrance. "I have been told by a cook that eating food at the right time is important."

Camellia grinned. "Yes, you're—and I'm—right about that, though I don't cook much here." She rolled her shoulders. "I usually get enough of that at the teashops."

"Which are doing well?" Glyssa asked.

"Extremely well," Laev said with a smug smile.

Jace couldn't help himself. He kept craning his head at the luxury surrounding him, the antiques, even the rich smells . . . and his breathing came faster and shallower. He strove to follow the easy conversation.

"The novelty of me, the owner of the tearooms, becoming a FirstFamily GreatLady hasn't worn off yet," Camellia grumbled.

"I think it has," Laev contradicted.

"But there aren't many places where Commoners might catch a glimpse of a FirstFamily GreatLady on a daily basis," Glyssa said.

"I've told my staff that I have no influence with my husband in what he might care to invest in, if people approach them to talk to me," Camellia said.

Laev bent in laughter and his HeartMate cuffed him.

"Great emotions also affect the taste buds. Stop laughing," Glyssa said.

A housekeeper appeared and opened the door to the small sitting room facing the back gardens that led to the ocean. "The goodies are ready."

The sun cast black shadows of midmorning, dappling bushes still heavy with summer flowers, and the perfectly cut lawn of a green that epitomized lush abundant growth.

Glyssa took Jace's hand and drew him to the twoseat and sat next to him. They all nibbled on small cakes and had caff and tea.

Finally, she dug into her bag and pulled out the manuscript pages that she'd recopied earlier.

Jace sat stiffly beside her, waiting in dread. She bumped him with her shoulder. *You will be fine.*

The Hawthorns leaned together on a sprawling sofa, Camellia encircled by Laev's arm, against his chest, her bright gaze and easy smile fixed on Jace.

He made sure his fingers didn't tremble when he took the pages. "It would be better if Raz Elecampane read these." He could swear his voice was a whole tone higher.

Camellia D'Hawthorn's stare narrowed and her mouth set. She made to sit up straighter, but her husband kept her close against him.

Both formidable people, but T'Hawthorn was in charge of that relationship, Jace thought, and wondered how he managed the feat. It wasn't just because of his status and wealth.

"I don't want Raz Elecampane to orate this. I want you, Jace Bayrum. You wrote it, right?" Camellia asked.

"Glyssa—"

"No, you wrote it!" Camellia insisted.

"No." He was firm. "I told the story—"

"And I transcribed it. We revised it together." Glyssa's mouth drooped. "I don't have the storytelling or writing ability."

"You can't cook as well as I do, either," Camellia said. "Nor multiply silver slivers into vast piles of gilt like Laev. We all have our abilities. Jace, is your primary Flair storytelling?"

"No," Jace said.

"Maybe," Glyssa said at the same time.

"I don't have any large primary Flair," Jace said. He was beginning to sweat, now wanted to do nothing more than read the damn words and get it over with. This dragging the event out was torture.

"I'm not sure of that," Glyssa said in a thoughtful tone that caught his attention. "I've seen your leather-crafting work. It's exquisite."

Heat flowed up Jace's neck to his face. Man, he hoped he wasn't turning red! Ruddy. He'd look ruddy, right?

"If your wonderful leatherworking is your creative Flair, your primary Flair should be equally strong and lovely," Camellia said.

Laev frowned. "I haven't seen his leatherworking." He drilled Jace. "Why is that?"

"Maybe because it's none of your business?" Glyssa put in.

Before Jace's eyes, the coin purse he'd given to Camellia appeared in her lap. Since she wore a midnight blue gown, the white-dyed leather with the fancy gold tracing showed up just fine.

Exclaiming, Laev touched the tiny pursenal before Camellia snatched it away. "*My* gift," she gloated.

"You didn't bring me a present?" Laev asked, though he didn't turn his penetrating gaze Jace's way. The GreatLord still stared at the coin purse.

"He brought my good friends gifts," Glyssa said.

"Tiana got something, too, and I didn't?" Laev held out his palm to his HeartMate, obviously asking to see the small work. This whole thing jittered Jace's nerves.

"You have to be a friend more than a few weeks to be counted as a good friend," Glyssa said, teasing.

But Laev just waved that aside as he gently rubbed the leather with his thumb, studied the golden pattern of flourishes that Jace had made. Laev opened and closed the coin purse, and when he shot Jace a look, it held irritation. "The metal for the closure is far inferior to your work."

Jace's flush had just begun to settle down when those words brought it back. The clasp was the best he could afford at the time, as usual. He sure wasn't going to say that.

Finally Laev glanced at him again. "I'll commission you to replace—"

"No!" Camellia said, grabbing the leatherwork away from him and holding it to her breasts. "It's mine and I want it as it was originally made."

Laev's eyes gleamed. He rubbed his hands, looked at Jace. "Perhaps if you and I were to deal—"

"No," Glyssa and Camellia said together. Glyssa continued, "Laev, you can't go into business with all of your friends."

"Why not?" He grinned wickedly. "They should want to go into business with me, I'm the best. What do you say, Bayrum? I could give your work to T'Ash or offer it at the Enlii Art Gallery." He nodded to Camellia. "You might want to take it to the Enlii and see what Apple says about a show."

Your mouth is open, Glyssa said through their private bond.

Jace shut it.

One of the glass panels along the wall out toward the lush gardens opened and a cat strolled in. *You said you got a gift! I heard you.* She bounded across the room and hopped onto the couch next to Camellia, pawed the coin purse from Camellia's grasp and sniffed loudly.

It is like the present I found at the Salvage Ball and gave to Glyssa, the creature said, and Jace heard her perfectly.

The cat scanned the room, opened her mouth and curled her tongue in that way cats had of using their extra sense, then hopped down from the sofa and trotted over to Jace, sniffed at his boots. He wasn't sure he liked that. Zem never did that. She jumped up and stretched, putting her claws in the fabric of the twoseat to anchor her as she got close to Jace, sniffed again, and revved a purr.

"Take your claws out of the furniture, Mica," Glyssa snapped.

He smells very good, too good for you. Mica gave him a wide smile. *You will make a present for me?*

"Friends of mine for only a few weeks don't receive gifts from Jace," Glyssa repeated.

Mica butted her head against his shoulder. *He smells of bird, too. FamBird. I met your FamBird, Zem. He is a very interesting Fam.*

Camellia sighed. "I'll commission a piece—"

"Jace has a lot of things going," Glyssa said. "He's bought a few shares in the excavation of *Lugh's Spear* and he's helping me with—"

"We haven't heard from Bayrum," Laev said. "Want to deal?"

"I'll consider it," Jace said, just to stop all this.

The cat crawled onto his thighs and licked under his chin. He winced.

"Come here, Mica," Camellia said. "Come and sit and think about what you might want Jace to make you."

With a tiny nip at his chin, the cat left him for her FamWoman and Jace was real glad he had a bird.

The three Hawthorns settled in and Laev nodded at the papyrus sheets Jace held. "And if the story is as good as your leatherwork, we can talk to a playwright or Raz—"

"No. Absolutely not. The story is *mine*, too. My ancestor's life. I will decide how to handle it." Camellia leaned back and crossed her arms until her cat pawed to be petted, then her expression relaxed.

And it was time. Jace began to read.

Twenty-eight

Jace cleared his throat one last time and read. He paused for breath after the opening.

"Oh, oh, oh," Camellia's voice sounded like mournful coos. Tears ran down her face and her husband pulled her close and her Fam purred louder.

"We already know it ends happily," Glyssa said in a soothing tone.

Camellia gave a watery sniff and looked at Jace. "I think I'd rather stop for now, until Tiana can join us."

He put the papyrus down with relief, but another big feeling moved in his chest . . . he'd made a GreatLady cry with his words, his storytelling! Incredible.

"You have another gift," Laev said to him.

"Just modified the man's journals," Jace said. Glyssa picked up the papyrus and took them to Camellia, set them beside her.

"I doubt that," Laev said. He stood and picked up Camellia who held the cat and papyrus and nodded to Jace. "You're a man of many gifts."

Jace stood, too. Glyssa slid her arm around his waist. "We'll teleport home," she said.

"To the Licorices," Jace said.

Lepid zoomed through the open door bringing with him the coolness of the ocean breeze. *Zem and I want to stay here for a while,* he announced. His feet pattered as he jiggled a dance, leaving damp spots on the carpet. *We can play in the ocean! It is not like the Sea that Zem knows. WE CAN FISH!*

Everyone laughed. Glyssa flapped her hands and said, "Go!"

He came over and rubbed against Glyssa and then Jace. *MY FamWoman. My FamMan.* He lifted his nose and fluffed his tail at the cat.

Foxes, the cat sighed.

I caught you and your mate a rat, cat.

The cat's ears perked.

Brazos is eating most of it, Lepid said, barked a laugh, and ran out into the day and to the GreatLord's estate. The cat followed. Jace quashed a thought that he would have liked to see the place.

Good day, FamMan, I will be back in a couple of hours, Zem said mentally.

Where are you?

In a large oak just outside the door. The hunting has been unusual and good. There is excellent prey in the tide pools I want more of.

That's fine, Jace replied. He was walking arm in arm with Glyssa. She hugged the Hawthorn couple, Camellia still in Laev's arms, then stepped aside.

He decided to bend down and kiss Camellia on the cheek. After all, she was one of Glyssa's best friends, and more importantly, she loved his gift and his story. "Thank you for praising my work."

She reached up and patted his chest. "It deserves it."

Jace bumped his fist against Laev's shoulder. "Later."

Showing teeth whiter and more perfect than Jace had ever seen, Laev said, "Yes."

"He means that, you know," Camellia said. "He'll hunt you down."

Jace winked. "I think I can handle him."

Camellia chuckled and rubbed her head against her husband. "They all do. But even Glyssa got entangled."

"I'll watch out for traps," Jace said.

"You'll never see them coming," Laev said, nodded at him. "Merry meet."

"And merry part," Jace said, the response coming automatically now. He'd never said the phrase so much in his entire life as in the last couple of days.

Laev lifted a brow. "And we'll definitely meet merrily for both our profit again." He turned and walked up the stairs with his wife.

After a sigh, Glyssa said, "They look so good together. I'm glad they found each other and worked through their problems." She tugged on Jace's arm, so he followed her down a wide corridor.

"They had problems?"

"Doesn't everyone?"

He didn't think she wanted an answer, which was good because he wasn't going to address that topic. She opened the door to a small room with a tall, opaque window, closed the door, and flipped the teleportation indicator that would show the pad—the whole room!—was in use. "A whole room set aside for teleportation," he said.

"One on every floor," Glyssa said. "Like in the PublicLibrary. But unlike the library, most visitors here *can* teleport. There's a marked-off area in most of the rooms here, too."

"Huh," Jace said, stepping up onto the pad and opening his arms. He could provide Flair for Glyssa if she needed it to teleport them, which she didn't. Otherwise she'd be doing all the work, 'porting them. "Where are we landing?" he asked.

"My bedroom." She paused. "I hope you will stay."

"Sure." Energy ran through her, too, and he finally said what they'd been ignoring. "We can spend time together before your hearing. And Camellia approved of the novel, so your Family shouldn't be able to use that against you—us."

"Probably not." Glyssa sounded doubtful.

"*Camellia* is the judge of the quality of the story, not the First-Level Librarians, and I think she's happy with what we've got so far."

"Yes."

"I know something that will ease those nerves." He grinned, and she leaned back against him and his body hardened. She snuggled her ass around his cock and the blood drained from his head.

"Glad we're going to your bedroom," he said hoarsely.

She said, "You're right. The reading, as short as it was, went well. I'm sure Camellia will say so for my progress report hearing."

Before he could say anything else they were in her bedroom, a couple of minutes later naked and rolling on her bedsponge.

He was having a difficult time getting enough of the woman. But he wouldn't stay in the city with her.

Still, in two septhours he sat on a hard wooden bench in the corridor behind the door marked "PublicLibrary Administrators Only." Across from him was the door the Licorices had gone through, Glyssa lagging two steps behind for a quick hug and kiss.

"You can do it!" he said, though he didn't know whether she'd be successful in defending her fieldwork or not. He sat on the bench and waited, completely out of his element.

Inside the room, Glyssa blessed her bespelled formal tunic and trous that wicked away sweat as she gave her progress report and answered questions about her studies and work at *Lugh's Spear*.

Her mother, mouth down with lines bracketing her lips, examined every detail—still not happy at all with the project, with Glyssa being outside of the PublicLibrary and Druida City.

Her father watched her with a shuttered gaze. She had no clue whether he'd vote approval of her report and continued support of her work or not. She did decide that how her father voted would be partially due to Jace. And she had no idea what her father *thought* of Jace.

Enata simply scowled and drew sketches—no doubt unflattering ones of Glyssa—with her writestick.

"You continued to work with Maxima Elecampane and Jace Bayrum on the blueprints of *Lugh's Spear* in your third day at the excavation," D'Licorice said.

Lady and Lord help her. They'd only gotten to the third day. Maybe she could move it along, jump along the timeline a bit.

"Yes. And I began my work on the novel for D'Hawthorn. Later, I heard GentleSir Bayrum's storytelling at the bonfire and within a week we were working together." She smiled as she lilted Jace's name, couldn't help it.

Despite everything, she'd achieved one goal. Yes, she desperately wanted to become a FirstLevel Librarian, and it would leave a hole in her, destroy her notion of the future if she didn't . . . but Jace remained more important.

So did the sheer discovery of *Lugh's Spear*.

Her sister snapped up straight. "With the current information we have regarding the SecondLevel Librarian's field project and paper, we can determine whether they are acceptable and can be continued or whether they are unacceptable. Further, we can promote or demote her instead of wasting any more time on this issue now or in the future. So, I call the question of the SecondLevel Librarian being approved to become FirstLevel. And if she fails, that she be remanded to the Gael City Library immediately."

Glyssa gasped. Why would her sister do this to her?

Her parents appeared surprised. Her mother recovered faster and wiped expression from her face, turning impassive.

Her father looked appalled. "Enata," her father snapped, then shut his mouth, but his brows went down over his eyes.

Enata flushed and lifted her chin. "It's an acceptable action." She coughed. "I have doubts about SecondLevel Librarian Licorice being at the excavation of *Lugh's Spear*, about the importance—uh, her recording of that project, since nothing much seems to be occurring. As for her transcription of Captain Hoku's journals, she has help with that."

"I have help with *telling Captain Hoku's story*, creatively." Glyssa lost her temper. "I thought writing such a story would be easy for me. It's not. It's not one of my talents, is that what you want to hear?"

"SecondLevel Librarian!" Her mother's voice was frigid.

Glyssa pulled the old shell of professionalism around her. Too small and tight, it hurt. It *hurt* being the person she'd been before the camp, before Jace. She stood straight and stiff. Her eyes burned and she shifted so her whole body faced her sister.

Who looked defiant and scared and . . . miserable? Glyssa hadn't checked on her bond with her sister lately—it tended to be prickly. Her sister was unhappy and blaming her unhappiness on Glyssa. Why? Glyssa searched her face. She couldn't tell. All she could feel was that discontent. Her own irritation died, though it wouldn't have a month before. She'd have fought and fought her sister hard, lined up arguments. Her mind would have scrambled for defense, words cool and logical would have emerged from her brain, issued from her mouth. Her brain would have lined up options . . .

Instead, with the experience of the additional close bonds of Lepid and Jace, she did what she'd do with them—her young Fox-Fam and her touchy HeartMate. She opened her bond with Enata wide and sent love. Just complete acceptance and love. The situation would work out some way or another in the future, Glyssa didn't have to handle that now. She only had to love her sister.

Enata's eyes rounded and her mouth opened in surprise.

"The question of promoting SecondLevel Librarian Glyssa Licorice to FirstLevel has been called," their mother said. "The vote must be unanimous."

"I believe this vote is untimely and untoward," their father said. He stared at Enata. "But I vote that SecondLevel Librarian Glyssa Licorice be promoted to FirstLevel Librarian." There was a rare note of challenge and warning in his voice that Glyssa had heard only a few times and that had her standing straighter still. Her father supported her.

The silence from her mother stretched longer than Glyssa anticipated, giving her time to become nervous as she yet looked at her sister, continued to send the woman love, mixed with a little wish for forgiveness if Glyssa had hurt her feelings somehow. Glyssa didn't look at her parents, thought there might be a private, mental discussion between them.

"Ah." Her mother began, paused a few seconds, then spoke. "With regard to the promotion of Glyssa Licorice from SecondLevel Librarian to FirstLevel Librarian, I state her work is acceptable by . . . our . . . standards and affirm her promotion," D'Licorice said.

Now Glyssa's feet unstuck and she turned to see her frowning mother. Glyssa could barely hear over the pounding of her heartbeat in her ears.

"I . . . I . . . vote for Glyssa to become FirstLevel, too," Enata said. There was a clunk as her heavy empty water glass tipped over when she pushed back her chair and rose from the table. She rushed from the room.

Glyssa goggled.

D'Licorice's gavel hit. "SecondLevel Librarian Glyssa Licorice has been considered and raised to FirstLevel. The board has spoken and it is done." Another bang of the gavel. "Congratulations."

This was supposed to have been a progress report hearing. Now she was a FirstLevel Librarian! Wonderful!

But how would this change her life, and her relationship with Jace?

Twenty-nine

*T*he door slammed open, and Jace, legs stretched out and staring at the window at the far end of the hallway, came to his feet. But the running woman wasn't Glyssa, but her sister. He held out his hand to her. "Can I help?" dropped from his mouth before he could stop it.

"*You!*" she spat at him, then hurried down the hall. "No, no, no!"

He carefully set the book he'd been looking at aside. The meeting had to be over. And if Glyssa's older sister looked like that, his lady must have won the skirmish.

D'Licorice and T'Licorice exited next, his arm around her waist, very unprofessionally. "We will deal with our children, Rhiza."

"But she wants to return to the wilderness . . ." D'Licorice nearly wailed. "Why can't Glyssa be happy here? And what was Enata *thinking?*"

T'Licorice nodded at Jace. "Bayrum will take care of Glyssa."

"Maybe now she's a FirstLevel PublicLibrarian, she'll stay?" whispered D'Licorice, not glancing at Jace.

"No, dear," T'Licorice's voice was soft. They turned down the hallway, too, in the same direction Enata had gone.

Jace took three paces to the door and opened it. Glyssa was

leaning against a big wooden table, looking dazed. She held out her arms to Jace and he gathered her into his arms. Her voice was muffled as she spoke. "Enata exploded the whole meeting. She forced everyone to decide whether I was ready to be a FirstLevel Librarian or not."

His heart jumped in his chest. "Are you staying here?"

She blinked. "No." Inhaled. "No!" Then she tilted up her head and gave him an amazing kiss.

A quiet hum and a vibration rubbed against Jace's thigh, making him flinch. Glyssa's expression went blank for a minute, then she said, "My scry pebble." She frowned, snapped in disapproval, "Who would be scrying me when they know I would be in a meeting?" She fished in her sleeve and pulled out the pretty marble, sighed. "Laev T'Hawthorn. He's leaving a message." She slid her thumb over the pebble and a full-sized Laev holo jumped into the room.

". . . and I have news of the cook, Myrtus Stopper." He winked at Glyssa. "Greetyou, FirstLevel Librarian!"

"You know already?" she asked.

"Your surprise leaked to Camellia and Tiana. Camellia told me." He nearly smirked. "Camellia is baking a cake, I think."

"Oh."

"News about Myrtus Stopper?" Jace asked.

"Yes, I'm going to visit a business acquaintance and thought Glyssa . . . or you, would like to come?"

"How do you know of Myrtus Stopper?"

Laev raised his brows. "The Elecampanes asked Straif T'Blackthorn to track him, but when Straif found the money trail, he called me in to—ah—deal with a low-level entrepreneur." Laev smiled. "Because I am competent with finances." Then his expression turned serious. "Every one of us in the FirstFamilies takes the theft and sale of colonial artifacts seriously." Laev's eyes gleamed. "Want to come? This could be fun."

Glyssa shook her head. "I need to talk to my sister. She's hurting emotionally."

Both Jace and Laev flinched. "Good luck," Laev said heartily.

"I could join you, Laev," Jace said.

"Excellent. I'll send a hired glider for you. It will be outside the PublicLibrary shortly. Later." He signed off.

"You're sure you don't want to come?" Jace asked.

"Something's wrong with my sister," Glyssa said. "I need to help her."

"She hasn't been kind to you," Jace said. Remembered what T'Licorice revealed to him, and as much as he didn't want to bring up the subject, said, "She doesn't have a HeartMate?"

"No. Not this lifeti—Oh!" Glyssa's frown deepened. "Our bond . . . yes, that *is* it. She's envious." Glyssa kissed his jaw, moved in to hold him again, and then dropped her arms. "You go find out about Myrtus." She turned away.

"What's down that hall?" Jace asked.

"The teleportation room."

"Oh."

Glyssa kissed him again and smiled. "My parents are taking a little break, then will return here. My sister is off for the rest of the day. I'll see you in a while."

"Yes."

And she was striding down the corridor. Jace thought about teleportation. Flinched again at the memory of his father's death. The amount of time he was thinking about that lately . . . maybe he'd develop some sort of callus over the pain. Instead of denying the pain, he accepted it and moved on with his thought.

After his Second Passage, he'd done a little teleporting. But the skill was mostly related to light, knowing the light of the place you were 'porting to, and he didn't stay very long in one spot. Might be interesting to study the guest suite and try a couple of times.

Glyssa opened a door, waved back at him, then went through it and he headed out of the library.

*T*he meeting with Laev T'Hawthorn's contact was short and boring, but better than being with Glyssa and her sister.

Jace enjoyed the glider trip through Druida, recognized the area where they were meeting—a lower class neighborhood—if not the man.

Who turned out to be a guy who dealt in stolen goods and black-market artifacts. He'd genially admitted to selling a lot of subsistence sticks as genuine *Lugh's Spear* objects, which they were, since Jace studied the one he had left and confirmed it.

The man appeared pained at Laev's veiled threats, but refused to give up his client list, stoutly stating that he expected an honorable FirstFamily Lord such as Laev wouldn't punish him just for doing his job—and well. Hinted himself that he might be helpful in the future . . . if he wasn't arrested for theft. After all, *he* hadn't known the sticks were stolen when he'd sold them.

One extremely important fact Jace and T'Hawthorn did learn, and that was Myrtus had insisted to the fence that he hadn't been the one who'd set the explosion. He'd just taken advantage of having all the subsistence sticks. The temptation had been too much for him. The low-level entrepreneur had stated virtuously that he wouldn't have dealt with a man who'd hurt anyone.

As for Myrtus Stopper, he had acquired a fortune, bought some gems, and set out to the south with a merchant caravan. Lucky man.

Then Laev had consulted with T'Blackthorn and the Elecampanes regarding the thefts and they agreed the issue was a camp matter and that the Holly guards would investigate. The first small box stolen had not turned up.

Jace accompanied Laev to his home and one of T'Hawthorn Residence's workshops. He didn't *quite* make a deal with Laev to handle his leather goods. Despite everything, he didn't want to make a business of practicing a private joy.

Laev had shrugged, then scried to set Jace up with trial memberships at various clubs, a social one or two, and The Green Knight Fencing and Fighting Salon.

Then Jace and the Fams—Zem, who'd flown in, and Lepid, who'd teleported there—got to tour the castle Residence and the seaside estate of a FirstFamily GreatLord.

*   *   *

Glyssa mulled over her words and made some hot cocoa with white mousse to take up to her sister.

She knocked on Enata's door, stood as her sister checked mentally who was there, heard the refusal in Enata's mind before she voiced it.

"I have hot cocoa, with white mousse and cocoa sprinkles just as you like!" Glyssa called.

Curiosity flowed from Enata through their bond and she opened the door to her sitting room, which appeared to have been recently redecorated.

"Nice," she said.

Enata shrugged. "It had been more than a decade since I'd changed my rooms."

Glyssa nodded.

"Where did you get the cocoa? It's not accessible from any of the regular no-times until after Halloween and Samhain, the new year."

"I took it from the ritual no-time."

Enata's eyes bugged a little.

"That's not a good look for you," Glyssa admonished, handed her sister the drink, pushed open the door, and went to a new wing chair of deep teal furrabeast leather. "I've learned that enjoying the moment is important. The hot cocoa drink option in the ritual no-time was completely full. So we should use some."

"Not like it will go bad," Enata said, then, "What do you want?"

Glyssa lifted her brows and Enata rolled her eyes and sighed. "Sorry for the rudeness," she said, sounding anything but.

"I have a plan."

"Of course you do." Enata settled in a comfortchair that conformed to her shape, excellent for reading or watching vizes.

Sipping a little of her own cocoa, Glyssa said, "I think we should buy an appointment for you with the matchmaker, Saille T'Willow."

Enata gasped. "Such expense."

"You're worth it. And you're the only one without a HeartMate this generation," Glyssa tried for matter-of-fact. "You deserve that from the rest of us."

A mixture of feelings crossed Enata's face. She swallowed. "You think?"

"Yes, I do, and I can make a good case to our parents."

"The expense!"

"Gilt is not as important as happiness," Glyssa said. "We all know that."

"Ye-es."

"And it isn't as if the return won't be worth it. The GreatLord will find you a husband, a partner, a helpmeet." Stupid of Glyssa to think that so far her own HeartMate wasn't quite at those points. "You'll be happier, your work will show that. We aren't meant to live alone."

The small silence was only punctuated by tiny sipping noises. "You believe that," Enata said.

"Yes, I do."

"It's easier to believe, I think, if you have a HeartMate."

"Perhaps. And I think we need to put it in the Family charter held by the Licorice ResidenceLibrary that all individuals without Heart-Mates will be allowed an appointment with the T'Willow or D'Willow matchmaker, if they so choose."

Enata was shaking her head. "It costs a lot."

"Stop harping on that!" Glyssa said. "What is gilt for except to make us happy?"

"To further our research? To ensure the Family never is poor."

Glyssa waved the comment aside. "I insist. T'Willow has a ninety-eight percentile success rate with matching people."

"You insist?"

"Yes. And if necessary I will pay for your appointment myself!" Not that she really could without selling something.

More wide-eyed surprise from her sister. Glyssa leaned forward. "Just think, some man out there for whom you are perfect is as alone and as lonely as you."

Enata smiled, looking years younger. "It's . . . intriguing. By the way, there's quite a lot of alcohol in this drink."

"Yes, there is."

"I think you should take some to Mother and Father," Enata said. She set the tall mug on a coaster on the table and had her fat comfortchair tilting back, the panel for leg support unfolding, then lifting. "I would like to see T'Willow. T'Willow! For a husband for me!" She giggled. "How exciting."

"Yes."

"I do love you, you know, Glyssa."

"I know. I love you, too."

"Even when you're being a flitch," Enata said.

"Yes," Glyssa answered. "I love you even when you're being a flitch."

Convincing her parents was a little tougher for Glyssa but not as difficult as she expected. Enata's behavior that afternoon that had resulted in Glyssa being elevated to FirstLevel Librarian before she was quite ready for the honor had been a revelation for all of them.

Her mother and father had consulted the ResidenceLibrary for figures regarding appointments with matchmakers for Licorices without HeartMates and had come up with equally revealing numbers. Only one or two single Licorices had asked for appointments, and they had been given them, and mates found. Most unwed Licorices shriveled into bitter people—the Residence's words.

That had shaken all three of them, too.

"We certainly have the gilt to provide Enata with this boon," Glyssa's father said.

"True," D'Licorice said, frowning. "But I am sure that T'Willow is booked."

"We've done a few favors for him and his," T'Licorice said.

"We will call him tomorrow," Glyssa's mother said.

"Meanwhile, why don't you and I retire to the HouseHeart to consider this matter more deeply?" her father suggested.

Her mother smiled. "That sounds wonderful. We'll see you tomorrow, Glyssa."

"Yes, Mother." Glyssa hugged her mother tightly and kissed her cheek. "We're doing the right thing."

"I think so, too," said Glyssa's father, embracing her. "Good idea, Glyssa."

"Thank you."

"Later," he said, then he whistled as he and her mother walked hand in hand to the tiny, secret elevator room that would take them to the HouseHeart.

Glyssa was left alone by herself in the mainspace. She hoped Jace was having a good time by himself, but for her own self, she wasn't enjoying her solitude. She was lonely.

Then he and Lepid and Zem arrived and she prepared them the evening meal and they worked as they had in the camp. Later she and Jace satisfied each other, both on her bedsponge and the one in the guest suite.

Now that she was a FirstLevel Librarian and her fieldwork approved, Jace wanted to return immediately to camp.

She wasn't quite ready. *She* wanted more time with her friends, to see a new exhibit at an art gallery. Glyssa wished just to enjoy the solitude of home, the comfort of her rooms.

When she lay awake after sex, stupid tears dribbled from her eyes. No, she and Jace weren't nearly as close as her sister believed.

*E*nata's appointment with Saille was in four days. The man had been booked, but had made time. Glyssa hadn't been able to finesse the reason why they were being given preferential treatment from her parents.

And after the morning appointment came the afternoon wedding between Enata and her true love. Apparently, T'Willow had already known of a man who'd take one look at Enata and fall in love with her—Barton Clover. Barton was the security head for that extended clan and the Clover Family saw no reason for one of their own to wait for his happiness. Thus the quick wedding that had the Licorices reeling.

Thirty

Jace wanted to be anywhere but at the marriage ritual. The Clover Family ily was huge, and their joy at the wedding filled the great Temple.

The whole vast circle of people seemed to be nothing but couples, from young teens who were engaged, to oldsters who'd obviously spent most of their lives together. Well, there were the children, too, interspersed between the couples. More children than he'd ever seen at one time, including when he was one growing up in the village.

And Fams, too. Zem had been given permission to fly free. The other Fams, including more foxes than Jace expected, were confined to the edge of a quadrant.

Being linked together in the circle wasn't like the large circles at camp. More of these people had greater than average Flair: the high priest and priestess; GrandLord Walker Clover and his wife who belonged to the FirstFamilies, as well as Laev T'Hawthorn. Camellia D'Hawthorn and Tiana Mugwort, who led the ritual, came from lower noble Families. There were also more noble Families than he'd ever seen gathered together, let alone been a part of.

Power throbbed through him in waves as he stood between Glyssa and her mother, nearly awed at the Flair cycling around the circle.

The whole atmosphere made him envious of the close bonds of the Families—the Licorices as well as the Clovers—and wary at how each person seemed to have a press of expectations on him or her to do certain things, fit into a Family slot.

Glyssa's future had blown open, troubling Jace. Barton Clover was the head of security for that Family and had to live at Clover Compound. He wanted Enata with him. Maybe even wanted Glyssa's sister to forego her heritage as D'Licorice and living in D'Licorice Residence.

Glyssa could actually become D'Licorice. He saw that her Family and the Clovers would accept her, and how she herself could grow into that status. That would be good for her. But not for him, and he was beginning to accept that she would be in his future. In fact, he couldn't imagine a future without her.

Enata, the bride, spoke a little piece, thanking her Family, saying she loved them, including her new brother, her sister's HeartMate.

Jace cringed. No, still not ready for that word. The ritual ended on a huge surge of joy that dizzied him and he shouted and could almost see the love aura around Barton and Enata. The circle was opened and he was finally outside of the circuit of Flair and more confused in his life.

Especially when folk treated him and Glyssa as a married couple.

She left his side for a few minutes and it was a relief until some Clover woman started asking about *their* marriage ritual and he choked on flatsweet crumbs.

Glyssa handed him a tube of alcoholic punch, made their excuses, and took him away from the main Temple area, through the circular corridor to a small room.

He blinked as he looked around. It was sort of like Glyssa, but different in a couple of basic aspects. A holo painting of the three friends was on the wall. All of them holding each other.

"Tiana Mugwort's office?" he guessed.

"Yes," Glyssa said. Thankfully she didn't sit in the chair behind the small desk, or make him lie down on the chaise lounge. Instead she took his hand and sat on the lounge, upright, of course, and tugged on his hand so he'd join her. He sat next to her, his thigh touching hers.

She closed her eyes and a long sigh compressed her chest and he focused on her pretty breasts.

"What an event!" she said. "So many people!"

"Ah, nice."

She laughed and her eyelids opened and she smiled. "I thought you'd be in your element."

"Not really," Jace said. "Hard to connect with so many strangers at one time, especially when they aren't strangers to each other."

"Yes."

Silence fell between them, like it hadn't since they'd come to Druida, like it hadn't since they'd had that walk to the lake. And suddenly he missed the camp and the forest and the lake so much it was like a physical blow.

Glyssa studied his face with more of the compassion of a friend than the tenderness of a lover.

"They're saying you could become D'Licorice in the future, if you wanted," he said.

She shrugged.

"Do you want that?"

"I haven't given it much thought," she said. And though he was sure she told the truth, he figured she'd already come to a decision.

He took her hands, and stared into her lovely brown eyes flecked with green, and couldn't find words.

More quiet between them and it hummed with questions Jace couldn't nail down.

"What do you want, Jace?" she asked.

And his thoughts sorted out and he could let them out of his mouth. "I want to return to the camp." He sucked in air. "Druida is interesting." His lips twitched up. "Especially as seen with Laev T'Hawthorn, and experiencing it as almost a noble."

He shook his head. "But I don't want to live here. I don't even want to live on this coast."

"You love the camp."

"I love that area," he corrected.

Her brows arched and her fingers went limp in his. Her voice dropped to a whisper. "Is that all you want?"

He squeezed her hands, his own voice came out rougher than he liked. "You're pushing me to say what I want?"

"Yes."

"And you're pushing me to stay here?"

"I asked you first." Her hands twisted in his.

"I want you to come back to the camp with me."

She stopped trying to pull away and her smile bloomed. "All right." She took a choppy breath. "But things have changed between us here, and I want that change to be seen by the camp."

Her body might be vibrating, trembling, but he froze. "In what way?"

"We will be a couple. *I* want us to be seen as a couple. Not just convenient sex partners."

Simple relief. He squeezed her hands again. "Agreed. We're a couple."

"You can stay with me, or we can use your tent now and then, but we *are* a couple."

"Yes. The regular shuttle leaves day after tomorrow, on Midweek. I'm finished with my gifts for your Family and left them in the mainspace." He smiled. "Though I don't anticipate Enata seeing hers for a while."

"We can go on Midweek," she said.

His turn to close his eyes. "Thank you." Then, "Your Family will miss you."

"And I'll miss them, and my friends even more. But my fieldwork isn't done, nor is our story."

More staring at each other. "My Family has accepted you," she said.

He wasn't sure and grunted. After a minute, he said, "They don't seem to be bad." They'd been nice to him since the hearing.

Her lips quirked. "No, they aren't. Sometimes they aren't easy to live with, but they aren't bad people. We follow our own paths and standards, as do you."

Standing, he drew her up. "Right. Now let's go break the news we're leaving Midweek. Easier in public with a big crowd."

"I suppose so."

A week *passed in the camp and Glyssa's relationship with Jace took on* a certain pattern and rhythm. Jace slept and made love with her in her bedroom, the Fams slept in the sitting room or roamed outside. But her HeartMate kept his own tent. Both of them showered and ate with everyone else. They'd moved the furniture around to feel more comfortable and so they could work together on the journals and the story. They celebrated Mabon, the autumnal equinox, in the camp with the crew as a couple.

And with their news about Myrtus Stopper, how he'd profited from all the work that everyone did, Jace was welcomed back into the campfire ranks and the smudge on his reputation disappeared.

Neither she and Jace nor the Elecampanes shared the information that Myrtus had claimed not to have stolen the original box or set the explosions.

When Jace wasn't working with Glyssa, he was with those digging, with Flair and shovels and the two earthmovers, down toward where everyone believed the main entrance to be.

The Elecampanes had announced that no one who'd been in *Lugh's Spear* showed any harm and they didn't want to break up the camp for the winter yet. They'd do more research on the atmosphere in the spring, including getting opinions other than the Comosums'. Since no one had liked the ladies, the staff was willing to accept their findings as "mistaken."

Everyone who'd wanted to leave the project was gone—and some folk had even reconsidered and bought shares.

Little by little Glyssa's relationship with Jace expanded and deepened, with small revelations and vulnerabilities on both their sides. Progress, but not as quick as she wanted.

One night that held more than a hint of autumn chill, as they headed toward her tent, Glyssa felt a tickle on her mind from Camellia in Druida City, and gently pushed it away.

Because Jace's breath was tickling Glyssa, too, as he nuzzled her neck. "Gotta have you, now." His words were guttural and he took her hand and put it over his groin.

Her own core melted as she felt the strong length and thickness of him, the heat of him that had her breathing in pants.

She stroked him, her mind clouding until she only wanted him inside her, thrusting, riding her. Or . . . "And I want you, too. Me on top," she whispered. "So I can tease us both."

Only she could hear his rumbling groan, and it sent more liquid fire coursing through her.

They pushed through the spellshield, the door to the tent.

"Clothes off!" Jace ordered and she was naked and holding him, stroking him, and his body trembled with need before her.

Her breasts went heavy, her nipples ultra sensitized. Her anticipation of him, of their loving, making her damp.

Jace picked her up, and she had to let go or hurt him. He held her high with arms corded with muscle, the moonslight filtering in to accent the power of him, sinew, muscle, masculinity.

"Can't wait." He turned, sat in a wingback chair, slipped her onto his sex, her legs wide over the arms of the chair.

Totally delicious.

They simply sat for a moment, her enjoying the pressure of him inside her. As she angled her body for more control, their whimpers of need soughed out together. She grabbed his shoulders, lifted, hovered when he was barely inside her. Tiny movements, tiny thrusts, in and out. His hands on her hips encouraging, not forcing.

"Glyssa, Glyssa! Lady and Lord, every time is better! What you do to me!"

Then he forced her down, hard, and she screamed at the pleasure.

"Only you," he said.

She liked hearing those new words, felt the sex bond overwhelm, thought she saw the glitter of the golden HeartBond, didn't care.

Only desire, yearning, delight mattered. Only the sharing of the climax.

"Glyssa, lover," he moaned as he came.

She leaned against him, her damp body moving against his, one, two—and pure ecstasy flung her into the stars, with him, holding him.

His arms clamped around hers.

He teleported with her to the bed, arms and legs tangling, lips seeking each other's, still joined, but ready to conquer bliss once more.

A knock came at the pavilion door.

Jace's hands tightened on her, so nice! She snuggled closer, ran her fingers along his side to his hip.

"It's the Elecampanes," called Raz, projecting his voice and completely breaking the after-sex-and-before-the-next-round moment.

Jace dropped his arms, rolled. "You take the first waterfall."

Her lips tightened. "No, you go ahead, I'll summon a cleansing spell."

His eyes hooded . . . that she had more Flair than he? She still didn't quite believe it. She *sensed* strong magic from him. She wished she'd suggested that he be tested by T'Ash and his Flair-determining stones when they'd been in Druida.

"Glyssa? Jace?" Raz called, knocking again.

Del murmured something. "No," Raz said. "We need to discuss this now."

Glyssa whisked a cleansing spell around her that sent wildflower fragrance throughout the tent, listened as Jace grumbled about the tiny shower. Pulling on underwear and a long tunic, she muttered a Word and the field that looked like a door thinned.

Thirty-one

R*az Cherry Elecampane strode in like an autocratic king. Glyssa* sighed. He was followed by his HeartMate who nearly slouched her way into the tent, the ultimate in casualness.

Glyssa gestured to the chairs, flushing a little as she saw the one she and Jace had made love on out of alignment. Thankfully, the tent-cleaning spell had cleansed it, too.

Del took a different chair, stretching her legs out and crossing her ankles. She winked at Jace when he came in. He strode over to "their" chair and sat, grinned at Glyssa, and patted his lap. She flushed deeper.

Raz stood staring at her coolly. "I had thought you'd have told us of any plans by T'Hawthorn?"

"What?"

"I received a communication today from Laev T'Hawthorn. He informed me that at least thirty people are coming to the camp. Most of them wish to check out the countryside and found a town. T'Hawthorn will study this camp, too, since so far we've been successful in keeping him and other FirstFamilies from investing and meddling in our project. After the tour of the site, they want to move on to look at the landscape around the Deep Blue Sea."

"Neither he nor Camellia said a word to me about this a week ago." Walking over to Jace, she sat on the arm of the chair, put her hand on his shoulder. "Did they mention this to you?"

"No. But from what I've seen, Laev T'Hawthorn moves fast," Jace said.

Glyssa nodded. "That's right. From the moment I announced I wanted to do my fieldwork here, it was just two days before I arrived."

The Elecampanes focused their stares on her, then Raz relaxed, went over to Del's chair and lifted her from the seat, settled in himself with her on his lap.

"T'Hawthorn stated that there will be other investors in the party with whom he is not associated, as well as a group of cross-folk looking to found another town of their own. Outsiders are moving faster, so we have to move up our plans, too. But they find they will get nowhere without our help—at least if we go along right now and don't force them to mount an alternative expedition to this area." Raz smiled. "Which is why I'm inclined to help, so we can control events better." He finally relaxed, saying, "They're coming in the newest, most luxurious passenger airship of Cherry Shipping and Transport." He linked his fingers and stretched out his arms. "And I get to fly it to the Deep Blue Sea!"

Del snorted. "You should let the pilot do that."

"But she doesn't know the area," Raz said smugly.

Del chuckled and shook her head, but her own smile showed amusement at her HeartMate. A small twinge went through Glyssa. The couple was HeartBound, their connection so deep that should one die, the other would follow in a year.

Their hands linked and Raz absently kissed Del's capable, scarred fingers.

Looking directly at Glyssa and Jace, Del said, "The Cartographers' Guild is sending a man along to update some of my charts. There are a few people who want to travel overland to the Deep Blue Sea with him and me, if you want to come along, Glyssa . . . and Jace."

"I'd love to! How long does it take by stridebeast? Do we have enough mounts?"

"About three very long days."

Glyssa winced, she wasn't a good rider.

"And we should have enough stridebeasts if some of the people here want to rent theirs out to the interested parties."

"Sounds good." Glyssa angled her body to Jace. "Do you think you'd like to come?"

He tensed a little. The couple opposite him watched with weighing gazes. She was tired of repressing herself so she wouldn't ruffle his issues. She was in his life. She was his *HeartMate*. He should learn to deal with it.

"Jace, you haven't been to the Deep Blue Sea lately," Del said.

"I'll decide later," Jace said. He didn't touch Glyssa.

Urgh! The man was maddening. Every time she thought they were getting closer, he took a step away. And *that* was tiresome.

"The transport will be arriving in three days," said Raz. "We'll let the visitors look around for a day, maybe two, then leave for the Deep Blue Sea." Raz winked at his HeartMate. "I and my lot who fly in the airship will be at the Deep Blue Sea in a couple of septhours. The small group going with you, Del, will be latecomers. By the time you show up, I'll have investors thinking that a village by the Sea might be an interesting prospect, and the cross-folk ready to settle down, too."

"I'm sure. But they'll start out small," Del said, as if she and Raz had talked about this before.

"We'll be larger, and they'll rely on us." He smiled wolfishly. "I like that idea."

He set Del on her feet and stood. "We've decided that we want at least one permanent building up in camp *before* our guests arrive. We'll be harvesting some lumber and building a common gathering place." He frowned. "Not circular, but octagonal. We believe that spending the energy, physical and Flair, is worth the effort."

"We already have plans, of that building and the whole future community, drawn up by the famed architect, Antenn Blackthorn-Moss," Del said.

Glyssa was impressed.

As he had weeks before, Raz focused his attention on Glyssa. "We will be asking for volunteers from our investors and our shareholders to help with the construction. Are you in?"

She loved the camp, but go deep into the forest? Well, she'd be with others. "Of course."

Raz stared at Jace. "And you?"

"Yes. I can give you more muscle than Flair." His smile was lopsided.

"Done." Raz nodded in satisfaction.

"Good doing business with you," Del said.

Raz chuckled and bowed elegantly to them. "Thank you for relieving our minds with regard to your communications with Laev T'Hawthorn."

"You're welcome."

The HeartMates left and a quiet humming with questions filled the tent. Lepid trotted into the tent. *I heard, FamWoman. I heard, FamMan! We are BUILDING THE TOWN, and having an adventure first!*

"Sounds like," Jace said.

Glyssa's Fam had relaxed him while she hadn't been able to.

*T*he next day Raz T'Elecampane handed out the assignments and Glyssa got one to "find a tree or trees for the door, dead, please." The GrandLord handed her Flaired markers to set by the wood that could be tracked, examined, then hauled away by physical means instead of Flair.

She'd started out with Jace and Zem and Lepid. Jace was looking for strong, tall trees for the trusses and the weight-bearing poles of the building.

I know of a good place where many trees fell recently, excellent for building, Zem broadcast to them. He glided to a nearby tree. *So this will go fast and be easy. Follow me, Jace!*

Lepid chortled and hopped up and down. *We will be heroes!*

Yes, Zem replied and took off. Jace and Lepid followed him. Glyssa hesitated.

There was a grove of old growth and large trees to the south, Glyssa. Zem banked in that direction.

There! The huge tree appeared newly downed, with dirt still clinging to roots and leaves crisping dry in the summer heat. Satisfied, she grinned, using the last marker she had. This would be perfect for most of the door planks. Then she continued to search for fallen trees ready to be harvested and having no wildlife living in them and no rot.

One small glen led to another as she scanned over the waist-high brush, and pushed through to find another perfect log for the door.

She stopped, petrified, lost in a tangle of green. She hadn't watched where she was going. A rill of panic slithered through her, leaving a film of cold sweat in its wake. She'd never been by herself in the wilderness before. Where there were kilometers and kilometers of forest, unexpected lakes.

Unexpected beasts.

Her. Mind. Froze. She turned in place. Weird sounds thundered in her ears, birdcalls she didn't know. Rustlings, were they really trees or something else?

She didn't know where she was. She didn't know what to do. She was *not in control.* She *hated* this.

Thirty-two

*S*top *and breathe and think.* She was still uncomfortable, but able to handle her fear. Pressing her lips together, she decided she would not cry out to Jace or even Lepid. She should be able to handle this herself.

But looking up, she only saw diffuse light through the tall trees, not a trace of the sun to tell her what direction it was. Narrowing her eyes, she noted some disturbed bushes. Surely she'd come through there. She took a step toward them, then they burst open as Lepid jumped into the small copse.

Relief whooshed through her, making her light-headed enough that she let her weakened knees fold and sat on the downed tree. She wouldn't have to depend on herself to find the camp.

We are heroes! We found lots and lots of good trees! Enough for the WHOLE building!

Lepid hopped on the log and pranced up and down it. When he butted her side with his head, she stroked him with a shaking hand he didn't notice.

A niggle of cowardice settled into her. She didn't know how long she'd have been lost, and hadn't known how to return to the camp, solely by her own means. She had to depend on others.

She'd begun to love the wilderness, but had avoided it, and avoided survival training if she got lost. She could have used that training a few minutes before, she'd put it off too long. Now events seemed to cram her days even more full and she didn't know when she'd get to that learning. She should have instituted a plan for training the moment she'd arrived at the camp.

This tree is very nice, too, said Lepid, sniffing it. *I looked at the others you marked. Very nice.*

"You can be a hero with me, too."

Yes! He licked her face. *Time to go back to camp and have clucker for lunch.* He darted back through the bushes. *I only ate one or two little mice.*

"Wait for me, please." At least her voice didn't quaver.

Lepid zoomed back in, barked three times, then pranced his way through the forest. The hair on her nape rose as she realized he wasn't going back the same way she had come. She had faith in her Fam, especially since he hadn't seemed to understand that she'd been lost and fearful.

The camp was a bustle of activity, with a cheerfulness that she hadn't seen since the first days she'd arrived. Jace's face creased in laugh lines as he ate, entertaining people with the story of the amount of salvageable timber he'd found, and adding Zem's dry comments.

Everyone else had seemed to have had good luck, too, and this new project to build a community center was ahead of schedule.

All through the day, Glyssa remained busy, and stayed fairly close to her HeartMate, and definitely in sight of someone at all times. By the time she showered and loved with Jace in the tiny cubby in her pavilion, then fell into bed, she'd almost forgotten about the scary experience . . .

*G*lyssa and Del stood watching their men help build the community center. Though he was older, Raz was in just as fine shape as Jace, though the actor moved with more deliberation—because of his profession or age or status, Glyssa didn't know. It did seem to her that he was extremely aware of his body. An attractive man who sparked nothing in her except for a wish of friendship with an interesting person.

Jace, now, simply seeing how he moved, somewhat careless of his body, accepting his strength and skills without thinking, heated her blood. Zem sat on a post, watching, and Lepid darted in and out, "supervising."

"Hmmm," Del hummed approvingly as the two worked shirtless together to raise a pole.

Glyssa sighed. "Yes, beautiful men." Then she caught the slide of Del's gaze to her, a tint of red gracing the tan of the cartographer's cheeks. "You know," Del said, "even as HeartMates our courtship wasn't easy."

"What? I mean, I beg your pardon? You are so well suited. You're HeartMates!" And so were she and Jace, and that sure wasn't going as well as she'd wanted or expected.

Del rolled a shoulder, fixed her gaze on the men. "I'm a cartographer, I wasn't ready to give up my career of exploring and mapping the world. Raz was an up-and-coming actor in Druida City, he lived for the stage, the audience, applause."

Glyssa blinked, considering that. "But you worked it out."

"Not before some heartbreak, and we both had to change."

Jutting her chin, Glyssa said, "I'm willing to change."

Del hesitated, then simply shrugged. The men gave a shout of satisfaction as they set the last pole.

Glyssa linked her fingers and stretched. "Time for the crossbeams and the fancy trusses." She shook her head. "This building is not minimalist."

"No," Del said in satisfaction. "It has a few good features and doesn't appear like a crude frontier hall. The proportions are good, so is the octagonal shape, and the design. Antenn Blackthorn-Moss did a fine job with the plans."

Unlike the blueprints of *Lugh's Spear*, Glyssa hadn't seen the town plans. "Maybe you could show the rest of us?"

"We did, after Antenn finished them. He came out earlier this year," Del said. "We had a meeting with everyone who thought they might buy into the town."

"I haven't seen the design," Glyssa pointed out.

"Oh, sorry." Del flashed a smile as Raz shouted, "All Flaired workers please report to the Community Hall building."

"Maybe later," Del said, moving toward the structure.

Glyssa frowned but headed over to the raw frame, held out her hands to join with Raz and Del and a few others. "Shouldn't we be doing a ritual for this? Wouldn't that be easier?"

"No time," Del grunted. "We'll be putting out more effort than if we were in a circle, but let's face it, the community hasn't really come together enough for everyone to trust everyone else with as much of a connection as a work ritual demands."

"Oh. I thought—"

"Enough talk," Del said. "Let's get this done if we want a complete building by the end of the day."

"Right," Raz said, adding a smile for Glyssa.

Nodding, Glyssa inhaled deeply and prepared to help with her Flair, sending strength and energy to the others. As she concentrated on the building and the images the others held in *their* minds, she used her own Flair and sent them what she believed was the most efficient way to organize the materials and build the structure. She sensed Raz's and Del's surprised thoughts, then approval.

Then they began, and that was the last deep breath she had for the rest of the day until the evening turned into night and she slumped with the others on the polished wooden floor beneath her.

Pretty! We did good! Lepid twitched the tip of his tail. He, too, had funneled energy into the effort and was exhausted. The first time Glyssa had seen him that way.

Only those who'd finished the interior paneling were still inside— eight of them, all completely spent. Jace wasn't one of their number.

A knock came on the door.

"Who's there?" whispered Raz, sitting, back braced against the wall. Both he and Del leaned on each other.

"It's Jace and Zem," Glyssa croaked. "They can't hear you. Can I tell them and the others who've subscribed to the community to come in?"

"Might as well." Raz's formerly strong gestures had devolved to limp fingers lifted toward the large door.

"Beautiful building," Del said. "But too much effort today. Mistake to have done it."

"I don't think so," Raz said. "Makes a statement. Will impress both our staff—those who are wavering about investing in the town—and the outsiders who come in tomorrow. We could get more funding for the town because of it."

"Uh-huh," Del sighed as she fell asleep.

Come in, Glyssa projected to Jace. *All those who've bought shares in the town can come in.* She scooted back across the glossy floor to the wall.

Jace flung open the large door, stepped in and stopped, tucking his thumbs into his belt. "Wow. Looks great."

The floor was a darker shade than the honey-colored wood inside and out. Four of the eight walls held a window, square and multipaned and hideously expensive, in terms of making them permanent, with the Flair they'd had available. The ceiling angled up to a point with rafters that Zem immediately flew to. When Jace had opened the door, all the spell lamps set in intricate cages flickered on. *Those* were only funded for the eightday week.

As people filed in, exclaiming with surprise and delight, Raz nudged Del awake and helped her stand. Glyssa braced her feet against the floor and began to shove herself up. Jace hurried over and drew her into his arms, let her lean against him. He chuckled.

"What?" she asked.

"You smell like Glyssa."

She grimaced, but he nuzzled her. "Must have used a lot of Flair if you sweated."

Sighing, she said, "Yes."

"It's a wonderful place," he said but didn't take his eyes off her and she warmed. They were a couple, and accepted as a couple, but that didn't quite satisfy anymore.

Let's eat! Lepid got to his paws.

*O*nce again a huge transport set down in the ever-increasing-in-size landing field. This one was less battered, smoother, sleeker; no doubt it had incredible opulence inside.

Pursuant to recent custom, most of the crew, save the guards, gathered to watch it. The hatch opened and a small platform extruded from the airship. The first passengers appeared in the doorway, several nobles whom Glyssa didn't recognize but thought belonged to the Grace class. All had dressed more for impressing each other than the dirt of the encampment.

They made room for Camellia D'Hawthorn, carrying a large basket, a grin on her face. A man behind her, dressed in the red of Cherry Shipping and Transport, gestured and a large shelf extruded from the airship in front of the door. Camellia stepped upon it and the ramp descended slowly to the ground.

Glyssa ran to her friend. Camellia set down her basket and opened her arms and they hugged and rocked.

"I'm so glad you're here!" Glyssa said.

"Is anything wrong?" Camellia asked.

"No. I don't know. But I wanted you to see the encampment *so* badly." Glyssa's future was here, wasn't it?

"And we're glad to be here and view the venture," Laev T'Hawthorn said as he strolled up to them.

After a last hug of Camellia, Glyssa frowned at Laev. "You didn't say anything about founding a town in this area a week and a half ago."

Laev smiled, twitched his fingers at a duffle that was half the size as the one he'd bought for her and it rose, began to follow them as they walked. He slung an arm around Glyssa's shoulders, linked hands with his HeartMate. "It was something I was kicking around in the back of my mind. Talked a little about it with my journey-woman, Jasmine Ash—she's very excited about such a project. But I hadn't firmed up any plans until Vinni T'Vine visited me at the beginning of the week."

"Vinni T'Vine," Glyssa said. She hadn't often met *the* prophet of Celta.

With a lift of his brows, Laev added, "Yes. He convinced me it would be a good thing to establish a town out here. He was even so helpful as to point out where . . . a spot by the Deep Blue Sea."

"Oh."

Laev glanced at the Elecampanes' pavilion where Del and Raz stood, waiting for them. "I contacted the Elecampanes. They are not too pleased." Laev's teeth flashed. "But they agreed to work with me to show advisors and prospective settlers the land." His smile faded as he looked over to the huge outline of *Lugh's Spear* wistfully. "They've been adamant in not allowing FirstFamily investors in the excavation of *Lugh's Spear.*"

"They want to keep control, nothing wrong with that," Camellia said. "Just like I won't let you buy into my teahouses."

"Advisors?" Glyssa asked.

Nodding toward some of the stragglers disembarking from the airship transport, Laev said, "We have representatives from T'Vine, T'Reed, T'Blackthorn, and D'SilverFir of the FirstFamilies. Antenn Blackthorn-Moss sent a journeywoman from his architectural firm. The Clover Family sent an advisor, as did a consortium of other noble investors. The cross-folk religious group provided a priest, though I think the cross-folk want to establish one of their own towns in the same general area . . . or perhaps in the opposite direction, by Fish Story Lake." He shrugged, but Glyssa believed he knew to the last silver sliver the amount of gilt each investor had in mind to apply to founding a new community, as well as all their motivations. She looked back and saw a few of the camp watching her and her friends including Andic and Funa and Trago.

"They will be staying tonight in the airship berth comfortchairs, but I brought some tents so we can experience every moment of the camp," Laev said.

"Absolutely," said Camellia.

At the back of the airship a door opened and a ramp angled down. A man—the cartographer—dressed in leathers much like Del's, led a few stridebeasts from the vehicle.

"That should be all of them," Laev said, his gaze skimming over the people decanted from the airship. He gestured for Glyssa and Camellia to head toward the tent town.

She and her friends reached the Elecampanes, and Laev swept the couple a deep bow, smiling what Glyssa considered to be his least calculating and most charming smile. She wondered if he'd forgotten just how good an observer and actor Raz Cherry was.

"Thank you for allowing us to see the excavation, and to stay here tonight," Laev said.

"You're welcome." Raz was just as gracious. He looked over at the transport and raised his brows. "I'm glad to get my hands on the controls of that airship."

"If you want to refresh yourself after the trip—" Del Elecampane began.

"No need," Camellia interrupted. "The airship contains all the luxuries." She'd put her basket down, opened it and took out only a slightly smaller basket, offering it to Del. "I know that we are imposing, and we thank you for your hospitality. Please take these food-stuffs as a gift."

"From your tearooms?" Raz asked as Del took the basket.

"No, I cooked them this morning." Camellia smiled. She dipped her hands into her long-sleeved pockets and drew out a large enve-lope. From that, she pulled out huge flatsweets that wafted delicious smells as she offered them to Raz and Del, Glyssa and Jace.

"Thank you," Raz mumbled around a bite. "Wonderful."

Del bit into hers, closed her eyes. "Wonderful," she echoed. "So fresh."

Camellia said, "I'll be going along with you, Del, on our stridebeast excursion to the Deep Blue Sea. I've packed enough food for us all for the trip there."

Chuckling, Del said, "Good thing we have a limited amount of stridebeasts, otherwise the whole camp would ride with us just for the food." She looked at Laev. "You have quite an asset in your HeartMate."

Laev flung his arm around Camellia. "Don't I know it."

Raz said, "We've cleared an area for your pavilion." He glanced at Laev. "I anticipated that you would bring a pavilion."

"Three," Laev said. He waved toward the airship. "One is quite large and will remain in the airship until we arrive at the Deep Blue Sea. Designed especially for me. For us." He sent a look to Jace. "There's a secondary bedroom for Glyssa . . . and you, if you care to come along."

"Sounds fine," Jace said. Then he began to eat his flatsweet, which seemed to take both hands.

Laev shot him a considering glance, but went on with his spiel. "We also brought two smaller ones for travel. One for Camellia and one for Glyssa and Jace. I'll stay in Camellia's tonight." He stepped toward a shallow rectangular area on the far side of Glyssa's pavilion, set between the main pathway and a row of bushes—she'd sent him the dimensions earlier.

From an end pocket on the duffle, he pulled out four sticks. She didn't see any transparent gauze like what made up her pavilion. With quick steps he set up the stakes, then waved his hand. The onlookers "oohed" as purple-tinted, transparent, Flaired walls sprang up . . . in two stories, one cantilevered out over the bushes. Before the walls of the "tent" turned solid, Glyssa saw a solid-looking wooden staircase up to a sleeping loft, the floor of which included a bedsponge.

More gasps sounded and the crowd grew. Laev took a bow, grinned at Glyssa, and whirled his wife in his arms to applause.

Then someone huffed, "Thank you, GrandLady D'Elecampane, GrandLord T'Elecampane, for welcoming us to your encampment.

Since time is so short and we leave for the Deep Blue Sea tomorrow morning, can we be shown the excavation of *Lugh's Spear*?" The woman wore the colors of T'Reed's household and had the thin features of the banking Family.

Del D'Elecampane shoved the last of her flatsweet into her mouth, chomped down and nodded, then wiped her mouth with a softleaf she plucked from her trous pocket. "We are pleased to show you our endeavors." She raised a hand and the head Holly guard strode from between the Elecampanes' and Glyssa's pavilions.

"Cornuta, Laev T'Hawthorn—"

But Laev stepped forward and offered his arm to clasp and the Holly guard did, too. "We know each other," the guard said. "I worked at The Green Knight Fencing and Fighting Salon for some years."

"Ah," Raz said. "Cornuta will show you around."

Laev put a sad expression on. "Not you or the lovely D'Elecampane?"

"He's afraid he'll spill more about our project plans and the excavation than we want you to know," Del said.

With a smile, Laev shook his head. "I don't think so."

Del made pushing motions with her hands. "Go on the tour. You'll see the hole we found where *Lugh's Spear* broke open when it landed—"

"My poor ancestor, those deaths hurt him so." Camellia twisted her hands.

D'Elecampane snorted. "The Captain was too sensitive, then. The deaths were those who didn't follow the proper landing procedures. Weren't where they were supposed to be. I've read enough of Hoku's journal and Raz's ancestress' diary to know that.

"Anyway, we've covered the hole and access is forbidden, got that?"

"Yes," Laev and Camellia said together.

"You can follow the pegged outline of the ship to the excavation where we believe one of the main entrances lies. Both areas are now guarded, and that's about all there is to see of our main project. You're welcome to look around the camp, enter our new Community

Hall and eat with us in the mess. Personal tents of our staff are off-limits, though we'll make the sitting room of our pavilion available to you, Laev and Camellia. Any of the others will have to ask for permission."

"Of course my pavilion is your pavilion," said Glyssa. She laughed. "Especially since you bought it."

"Sounds like a plan," Laev said, glancing over at Jace. "You want to come along, Jace, and tell me about the camp and the land around here . . . and the new town?"

Jace shrugged. "Sure. Zem wants a good flight."

"Glyssa?" asked Camellia.

"I have to work, and to continue to prepare for the trip tomorrow," Glyssa said, and Jace knew that, but he preferred not to stay with her. That hurt.

Feeling a little stiff, Glyssa waved to her friends, then headed back into her pavilion and moved some of the furniture around to accommodate Laev and Camellia if they wanted to spend the evening talking with her in her tent.

With a little difficulty, she buried herself in her work, struggled through some of Hoku's more technical entries about the status of the ship after landing, and while the colonists set up their own camp. She made one-sentence notes about events that she and Jace could spin into the story.

At dinner in the mess tent, Camellia studied the gray-tinged noodles on her fork before she took a bite. "Interesting."

"Not really," Glyssa said. "Too bad Myrtus Stopper was a villain, he *was* a good cook."

Jace rose from the table with an absent wave at Glyssa. "Zem calls. He wants some help with his nest. Later."

"I'd like to see that," Laev said.

I can show you! Lepid put in, and the two men and the fox left the tent.

Camellia frowned after them. "We need to talk."

Thirty-three

Glyssa and Camellia sat in the best chairs in Glyssa's pavilion, the basket at their feet.

"You're staying here," Camellia said quietly.

"Ye-es."

"What's the problem?" Camellia's tone remained soft.

She could tell her friend anything. But she grimaced and looked down at her hands. "I'm afraid of the wilderness."

Camellia snorted. "Sounds wise to me."

Glyssa met her friend's eyes. "I haven't gotten the nerve to go out of the shelter of the camp by myself. Not even to a nearby hill."

"Hmm." Camellia passed her a flatsweet.

They ate instead of talked.

Then Camellia nodded. "If you're going to stay, you should overcome that fear."

Glyssa frowned. "Yes."

Tilting her head, Camellia said, "And Jace hasn't discovered this about you, yet? After four and a half weeks?"

"No."

"I watched you quite a bit today," Camellia said. "I'm sorry, but

I think he takes you for granted. That he doesn't give you the respect you deserve. Glyssa, you aren't getting what you need from him. You have to tell him that."

"I'm hesitant to."

"I understand."

"He's not accustomed to listening to anyone but himself."

"And because of circumstances, he's gotten to do that most of his life. But not if he wants to be part of a couple. He has to change, Glyssa, want more for the both of you."

"Yes." Glyssa sighed, then took a long, long breath. "Two birds with one stone. I'll ask him to meet me to watch the twinmoons rise at the top of the hill. I'll go by myself."

"In the dark?"

"It's not that far, and there really aren't any dangerous animals out there so close to the camp." She was pretty sure. "We can talk then, and I'll tell him I have this problem, too."

"All right," Camellia said. This time when she reached into her basket, she pulled out a sphere and handed it to Glyssa. "Not much background on Jace, but you might want to take a look. Laev and your father hunted for it, of course. But I think this might ease matters between you."

Yes, that got her interested. But she could look at it later.

Kissing her friend on the cheek, she said, "They'll be finished building the bonfire shortly, I'll take you there. You'll like it, snuggling with Laev."

"Yes, I always like that. And that new Community Hall of yours is wonderful, very impressive."

"Just the reaction the Elecampanes expected. We're very proud of it." Glyssa changed into heavier clothing and led her friend to the bonfire where Laev and Jace and Raz T'Elecampane were talking, with a couple of other people listening.

Glyssa slipped her arm in Jace's. "A moment, please." She smiled at the rest.

"Sure," Jace said.

She walked with him to an open area on the other side of the bonfire. Glancing toward the edge of the camp, from here all she could see was big trees. Scary trees that could hide anything.

"Jace," she said, her love for him making her lilt it.

He bent down and brushed her lips with his own, then said, "You're serious. Yes?"

She swallowed, gestured in the direction of the hill, kept her eyes on his. The whoosh of the bonfire catching sounded, along with a cheer, and more light let her see the gray of his eyes. "I'd like to meet you atop View Hill to watch the twinmoons rise." She paused for four heartbeats. "It's very important to me."

"Sure." He looked at the sky. "That will be in about twenty minutes?"

"Yes." Just short enough that she wouldn't have to wait and lose courage, long enough that even walking slowly, she'd get there in good time.

Again he kissed her. "See you there."

She sighed. "Yes." She made herself turn from him and walk away. Knew from the lack of heat in their bond that he didn't watch her.

Yes, they were a couple, but she wasn't quite satisfied with that. Camellia was right. Time for a frank conversation and to ask for what she needed, to know exactly where they stood. What he saw in the future for them so she could make solid plans.

Summoning all her courage, she walked out of camp with only a weathershield around her. Next year she'd bring a blazer—and over the winter she'd learn to use it. Learn wilderness survival skills, too. A small spell glow helped her watch her step, and as she walked, the noise of the camp diminished and the small light pollution from humans vanished.

She was left alone in the wilderness under a galaxy-laden sky bright with stars. Anxiety quieted inside her, allowing room for awe at the beauty.

The night scents were different from those she'd smelled that one morning when she'd gone out with Lepid at dawn. She walked steadily and reached the top of the hill with more acceptance of the wilderness, and more faith in herself.

In the distance, the edge of the auras of the twinmoons showed above the horizon.

Jace lingered by the bonfire, talking to a couple of the noble advisors who wanted to quiz him on the building and the prospective town. Minutes ticked off in his mind, but he was flattered enough to wait for the last second so he could run to the hill.

He nodded a good evening to them, and turned to lope away, when the Clover guy caught his arm.

"Jace Bayrum? My cuz Walker told me to talk to you. About Myrtus Stopper."

"Myrtus?" Jace asked.

The Clover whispered. "We have more contacts with the Merchants' Guild than the FirstFamilies. We think we have a lead on him, the real amount he got for those artifacts, and some of the people he sold them to."

Intrigued, Jace faded to a deep shadow to talk.

At first Glyssa just enjoyed the beauty of the night, looking out at various directions from the top of the rise. The wind from the south brought humidity from the Deep Blue Sea—at least that's what she told herself. And she imagined she could smell more water, freshwater, in the air of the northwest and Fish Story Lake.

Blinking hard, she could see the faint outline that delineated the shape of *Lugh's Spear*. Then she turned east again and jolted. The rims of the twinmoons were definitely over the horizon. With a whirl back to the camp, she strained to see movement. Nothing.

Through her bond with Lepid, she found him playing with the camp Fams—no Fams had come on the ship—in the forest. Zem dozed in Jace's tent.

And Jace . . . she would *not* check her link with him, nudge him.

Tears rose, trickled. She was being oversensitive, shouldn't think anything about his failure to show.

But she'd made a point to tell him this was very important to her. And it was. Her first foray outside of the camp completely alone. She'd wanted to show herself—and him—her courage.

When was the last time she'd asked him to do something for her, something that was very important to her?

Never.

Well, of *course* he'd been there for her during the hearing on her fieldwork.

She should definitely not be hurt by this.

But she was. Deeply. If he had asked her for something, that would have been *the* priority for her, no matter what.

And she wasn't a priority for him.

Not enough of a priority for him, as his HeartMate, that he would instinctively think of her first, as she would him.

She was so very tired of bending to make this relationship work—without actually knowing what he thought of her.

So a lot of her hurt was because she'd not been herself, had been afraid she'd lose him. Instead it felt like even as she was growing in one direction, she was intentionally cramping herself in another, and she'd lost a part of herself for doing that.

She wept all the way back to camp and asleep.

*D*ammit! *He'd gotten sidetracked, distracted. And Glyssa had made* a point of asking him to meet her, something she didn't often do. Guilt crept through Jace and he ran from the camp. He didn't see her silhouetted on the hill, but jogged up it anyway. The twinmoons weren't high in the sky but they'd definitely risen. Hell. He returned to the camp and her tent, saw her already abed, no doubt resting for their trip tomorrow.

There'd be plenty of time to make up this lapse in romance on his part when he walked with Glyssa along the shores of the Deep Blue Sea.

He slipped into bed with her and when she reached for him, loved her tenderly.

*Y*ou *are wrong!* *L*epid *said.*

He was sitting on her chest before she got out of bed. Jace was already gone . . . and Glyssa had decided what to do.

It was going to hurt, a lot.

And obviously Lepid had discovered her plan through their bond.

She stared into her Fam's eyes and replied. "I am not wrong. I can't go on loving Jace and not getting what I need."

Lepid snorted, looked away. *I don't mean that. But I love my FamMan.*

She did, too. But the man had never said anything about loving her. That was the problem. Maybe he couldn't change or compromise. But she wouldn't let that circle forever in her mind again, she had to confront him, and today was the day. She'd had it all planned.

You are thinking that we will return with Camellia and Laev to the Druida City! That is wrong, us going back to Druida City. We belong here.

Glyssa sat up, held Lepid as he started to tumble backward. He wasn't a small fox anymore, and she wondered how she'd missed that, too.

"We don't have to go . . . well, maybe for this winter, since I'm not sure how the pavilion would handle cold and I don't think there will be any more permanent buildings. No doubt the Elecampanes will go back to their home in Verde Valley. I thought Raz mentioned a winter theater season."

Lepid's ears flickered. *We could go see them?*

"Yes, and not in a glider. Teleporting to Verde Valley from D'Licorice Residence is exhausting, but I can do it," she admitted proudly. She was the only one of her Family who could—though they shared their Flair and energy with her so she could 'port them all.

Where is FamMan staying?

The question made her breath catch in her throat, pitched a bit of acid in her stomach. She had to harden her nerves. Wasn't she tired of going on like this, not having his love and support? Having no words from him? Watching her step with him, not being pushy. Not being herself.

How could she live with a man and not be herself?

Was she asking him to change? She didn't know, especially since *she* had changed.

Lepid nipped her. She'd been silent too long. "I don't know where he stays during the winter." She *wouldn't* think that he'd stayed with a woman these last years. That was past and done and none of her business . . . unless he returned to the lady.

And if she broke up with him, and he did stay with a woman, that would be none of her business, either. HeartMate or no.

Misery transformed to jealousy mutated to anger. *She* had changed. Because of her career, yes. Because of being at camp, of course. Because of interacting with him, her lover, her HeartMate, indubitably.

Just how much had *he* changed? How much had he tried?

WHERE WILL FAMMAN STAY? Lepid demanded.

"Not at D'Licorice Residence. If he doesn't stay with the Elecampanes at Verde Valley, Jace could come to Druida City. He made friends there."

Lepid nodded. *So did Zem.*

Glyssa managed a chuckle with a clenched jaw. "So did Zem."

*J*ace checked on his bond with Glyssa, he found her angry and very tense.

He should have apologized last night with words instead of actions.

I'd like to talk to you privately, she sent him mentally.

Uh-oh.

The camp was full of activity, everywhere. On the landing field with the visitors there and preparing the airship to take off in a while. Near the stables where Del D'Elecampane lined up the stride-beasts for the trip. At the mess tent where folk ate.

Swarming people everywhere. And he didn't think it was wise to suggest the hill where he'd failed to meet her the night before.

What about the far side of Lugh's Spear? *That little dip in the land behind the wing?*

Fine, I'm leaving now.

Jace decided it would be better if he reached there first. As far as he could recall, there were a couple of boulders they could perch on.

May as well grit his teeth and let her steam at him. Though, dammit, there'd be little time for makeup sex.

He was sitting on a flat-topped rock big enough for two when she came striding up. Neither Lepid nor Zem was around. Zem had felt the turmoil of Jace's mind and said he wanted to stock his no-time. Lepid was with the Hawthorns for some reason that also probably involved food.

Jace's gaze was attracted to her head and her wonderfully wild hair that she hadn't tucked up into a tight braid or bun or coronet like she usually did, and which he disliked.

Narrowing his eyes, he saw that it *was* confined a little by a spell.

She stopped a meter from him, hands on hips. The tunic she wore had the square pocket sleeves, that nearly brushed the ground.

Drawing in a big breath, she just stared at him for a full minute, her eyes hurt, and that squeezed something painfully in his chest. "I'm sorry I got distracted last night, and that you're hurt. I don't like hurting you," he said. "Come sit and talk."

She hunched a shoulder. "I've been thinking and thinking about this. Right now you have everything your way. You get sex. You get good food. You get loving from me."

"I give sex and . . . and loving," he said.

She jerked a nod. "And affection. But I want more and you won't give me that. I want a HeartMate marriage."

He stood. "I told you, I'm not ready."

Nodding, she said, "You're frightened."

"What!"

"Frightened of being in a Family again, that you'd have to change your ways to accomodate others. Selfish."

That stung.

"Just selfish." She sighed. "You've lived on your own for so long."

"I've scraped by for so long."

But she was shaking her head. "And I admired you for your adventurous streak, for following the wind."

He didn't like the past tense. Straightening tall, he reached out for her hands, she let him take them, but they were cool and she didn't intertwine her fingers with his. "My life hasn't been as easy as you think."

Her eyes, brown and deep, met his. "I didn't say that your life was easy. I did say that you have grown accustomed to living life on your own terms—and that works when you don't have close Family. You don't have to accommodate them, don't have to please anyone more than yourself."

"I want to please you," he said.

But she was shaking her head. "I don't know that you do. You haven't had a steady lover, either, not to mention a HeartMate."

He flinched.

Her laugh was unamused. "You rarely say it, refer to me as your HeartMate. Call me HeartMate."

Putting on a smile, he squeezed her hands. "Getting used to it."

She nodded solemnly. "But you aren't accustomed to change . . . and maybe it's too late."

"What?"

"You've gotten by on your charm, on your friendships. Is that all you want, Jace? Surface relationships?"

His throat began to dry.

"You've continued to do what you want, and I've allowed you to, because I've done so much what everyone else has wanted for so long. Obeyed all the rules to do what I thought I wanted."

Surprise spurted through him. "You don't want to be D'Licorice?"

She blinked fast. Somehow he felt her slipping away from him.

"I don't know," she said. She glanced around. "I don't think I want to live in Druida City, though. I'm not sure." She pulled her hands away, stared off in the distance, to the tall forest.

"Glyssa, H—lover."

With her sigh he felt the last of her anger dissipate. She tilted her head so she matched his gaze. Her eyes were liquid with tears. When she answered, he heard them in her voice, too.

"You can't say it. You have this scary, adventurous life, following rules that only you wish . . . Situations that change around you, events that might possibly move you one way or another, but you don't truly change much. I think that *I* am more flexible than you, since I've always had to bend to the uncomfortable demands of loving Family and friends." She swallowed. "And I don't know if you can do that. Perhaps it is too late for us."

Yes, her eyes were hurt, nearly despairing. But her words had thrown his mind into a scramble to find defenses. And he couldn't.

Thirty-four

Glyssa continued, "I won't give up my Family, no matter how irritating, or my beloved friends." Her beautiful breasts rose with a deep breath. "I am going on a stridebeast journey to the Deep Blue Sea. You know that will take me three days. I wanted to go as a *Heart-Mate* couple. But I guess that's too scary an idea for you, too. I think you should stay."

"I—no!"

Her gaze had clouded. "I *do* expect a lot from you. More than you seem to be able to give. Stay, Jace. Please move your things from my pavilion into your tent while I'm gone." Another humorless smile flicked on and off her face. "You're the one with charm, the one people relate to better, so I think you should be the one to deal with our changed circumstances in the camp. I won't be sleeping with you again, and I won't have sexy dreams with you, either."

Her face was utterly serious. "I understand that this encampment is too small for the both of us, so I will leave on the next airship shuttle back to Druida City." She bit her lips, met his eyes again. "I'm not sure where I'll be going, but you'll always be able to reach me through my Family and friends."

Turning on her heel, she said, "Blessed be, my HeartMate, Jace."

She walked away and he couldn't seem to see her. Chills chased heat through his body. He felt nauseous.

She was leaving him.

That couldn't be.

He caught up with her in two strides, whipped around to stand in front of her. "Wait. That's not true." He waved his hands. "None of it. I only want to make a . . . enough gilt that we can live together on *my* income."

She shook her head. "You're deluding yourself, Jace, making gilt an excuse. If a fabulous treasure was found on the ship tomorrow that would keep the entire camp for the rest of our lives, you would still not want to live with me as a HeartMate."

His hands were on her shoulders, but he stopped himself from shaking her. "No."

"You *have* gilt, Jace. You never went back to your village after the trip you took with your parents."

That stunned him. She knew about that? Yet . . . no one knew exactly what had happened on that trip. He'd told no one.

"You walked away from your mother and your friends and your community—"

His lips were cold. He should try and tell her about his mother, but his mind was equally cold, frozen in panic so he couldn't *think*. He laughed bitterly. "My mother didn't want me. Wouldn't even have missed me. If she said so in whatever info you got, she lied. As for the rest . . ." His mind couldn't even contemplate returning to the village, meeting his mother again, even after the fevers of Passage had subsided.

Glyssa stared. "I heard your mother wasn't . . . a good person." Glyssa's eyes were still sad and bruised looking. "But one of the things you do also is never look back."

She wet her lips, but didn't need to because now tears were sliding down her face to dampen them.

Jace wasn't sure whether all his guts were twisted inside him or whether with her slicing words, they'd spilled to his feet.

"You never looked back at our wonderful fling, though subconsciously you must have realized eventually, as I did, that our connection during that time was more than casual lovers, we were HeartMates. You never looked back," she repeated.

He opened his mouth but couldn't deny that truth.

"And you never looked back when you left your village. Your father wasn't a smart man, but he was a better man than you believe, I think. He didn't give your mother all of his pay. He had some set aside for you by his employer in an account she didn't know about."

That notion simply skewed his life in a different direction so fast that he barely heard her words.

"One of the merchants you apprenticed with for a while invested that gilt . . . and when your mother died, the merchant liquidated her estate. You have a respectable inheritance, Jace." She reached into one of her sleeve pockets and pulled out a piece of papyrus, handed it to him.

Complete disbelief. He mouthed, "How?"

"*My* father and *my* good friend Laev T'Hawthorn talked together, looked into the matter," Glyssa said.

All right, a little anger to burn away the panic. A good thing. "Checked me out."

"Yes, I am precious to them. I'm sorry you're only precious to me and Zem."

Another emotional blow.

"Good-bye, Jace. I'll make sure to stay out of your way when we return. It will only be for a day or two." Her eyes gushed and she whirled and ran this time.

Ran away from him.

Women didn't do that. He was smooth in his affairs with them.

He stood there, hollowed out, unable to think. Only able to hurt.

His lover, his HeartMate, had run from him.

She'd taken too long with Jace. Worse she'd dawdled on the way back to the encampment. Anyone who glanced at her would know she and Jace had broken up. Resorting to a glamour spell, she ensured her eyes weren't red and face swollen, though tears continued to well and her calm expression must look forced.

People in the camp bustled around. Not a lot of them would stay. Most were packing into the luxury airship for the shortish flight to the Deep Blue Sea. Ten were leaving with Del Elecampane for the overland journey. All of the stridebeasts were lined up, most packed, and most of the riders standing near their animals.

Camellia caught sight of Glyssa, flinched, then distracted Laev who was turning in Glyssa's direction. She hurried into her pavilion, changed into riding gear, finished packing, distractedly moving furniture around, shrinking some of it, dithering over the research materials and her origami supplies.

Her hands would need work, she took a lot of papyrus.

Lepid strolled in, stared at her, locked his legs . . . and hit her with betrayal.

With narrowed eyes, his muzzle set stubbornly, he said, *I don't want to leave the camp.*

Glyssa stared, her throat closed and she had to clear it. "You don't want to visit the Deep Blue Sea?"

Her Fam shook his head. *We can go there lots of times, but the camp won't always be mine!*

"Yours?"

That Shunuk fox and those Elecampane cats are going away. I will be the alpha Fam of the camp. I want to stay with my friends Zem and Jace, too. Lepid's glance slid away from hers.

"You broke up with Jace?" Camellia entered the pavilion. She grimaced. "I think it's the right thing to do and the right time to do it. You'll have the trip to put a little distance between you." Glyssa sighed and shook her head. "But Del sent me to get you. We're leaving now."

"Lepid wants to stay in camp," Glyssa choked out.

Camellia stared down at him. "He is little."

Glyssa decided not to whine that she wanted him with her. So unattractive.

"And my Fam decided to stay home at T'Hawthorn Residence,"

Camellia smiled. "Where it's safe and she can be pampered. So did Laev's."

You see, I will be the primary Fam of the camp! Lepid pranced in place.

Camellia chuckled, then aimed a stern gaze at Glyssa. "Come *on*."

Glyssa looked around at the pavilion and winced. "I'm running late. This place is a mess."

"Maybe Jace will clean it up after he moves his things out," Camellia said.

"Dream on."

"Let's go. It will be better for you on the road. You can put your troubles and Ja—the past behind you."

"D'Hawthorn! Licorice!" Del Elecampane yelled.

Swallowing hard, Glyssa bent and rubbed Lepid, scratched his head. "I wish you'd come with me, and I'll miss you."

He swiped his tongue against her cheeks more than once. *Salty*, he said.

"Yes." She grabbed the full saddlebags she'd packed. "I love you, Lepid."

I love you, too, FamWoman, he said, and trotted out the door beside her, heading in the direction of the ship.

Camellia put her arm around Glyssa's waist. "Let's go. It gets better, I promise you."

Well, Camellia's and Laev's HeartMate romance had been rocky, too, so Glyssa's friend knew what she was talking about.

Pulling a softleaf from her riding tunic pocket, Glyssa dabbed her eyes and blew her nose, said a cleansing word and tucked it away again. She'd be using it some more.

Del D'Elecampane gave her a sharp look, but said nothing as Glyssa mounted the stridebeast and they rode out of camp.

Glyssa had to admit that she didn't pay much attention to the scenery. Camellia let her quietly weep and mutter about Jace and everyone else ignored her, which was fine. Later, no doubt, she'd be embarrassed.

She'd handled herself well with Jace, but with Camellia's

sympathetic ears and soothing murmurs, she broke down. Glyssa would rather have hidden in her pavilion, but being away while Jace moved his property back into his own tent would be best. Not that she thought it would take more than one trip. He hadn't left much of his stuff, of himself, in her pavilion.

To be honest, the scenery they passed through looked a lot like that surrounding the camp—pristine forests with a winding path wide enough for two stridebeasts, rolling land too low to be called hilly, ponds and lakes.

As the septhour wore on, Camellia stayed beside her, talking and making Glyssa think about her answers. Her shoulders relaxed—her whole body relaxed and she moved better with her stridebeast, though neither she nor Camellia were experienced riders. Good thing that they both knew minor Healing spells. They'd need them at the end of the day.

Glyssa's emotions evened out, and she repeated the mantra that all rejected HeartMates must—life was long on Celta and people changed, their minds and their emotions.

But she was done with chasing after Jace.

He would definitely have to come after her in the future.

Help, FamMan, help! The frantic call came from Lepid late in the morning while Jace was embellishing a woman's pursenal in the workroom. He jerked, sliced his thumb with his knife, swore at the thin, hurting cut, but better than ruining the piece.

What? he mind-yelled back, putting down his tools.

Help, FamMan. I am trapped in the ship!

What! You shouldn't even be in the ship! Too late to scold the FamFox, even as fear sourly coated his tongue.

There was a smell! the fox whined, but even his mind-voice quavered. He was scared. *I followed it. Someone trapped me. Locked me in!*

Jace put away his knives with trembling hands, rolled up his work and stowed it in a satchel. *What about the retrieval spell on your collar?*

I outgrew my collar and Trago gave me another without the

spell. *I did not want the spell and I knew he wouldn't make me have it. Nobody noticed.*

Hell! *Can't you teleport to the pavilion or my tent?*

You . . . an . . . FamWoman . . . have . . . been . . . movin . . . stuff . . . arounnn.

Too true. It was emotional pain that slashed him hard and deep, now. He set it aside. *Lepid?*

Fun-ny smell. Sleep-py.

Then Lepid's voice disappeared from Jace's mind. Sucking in a breath, Jace opened himself emotionally to all his bonds . . . winced as he noticed the connection between him and Glyssa might be down to a stream of a few molecules. His link with Zem showed huge, about the thickness of his heart, sizzling light blue like the freedom of the skies.

What is wrong, FamMan? asked Zem.

A villain trapped Lepid in the ship. I think he's unconscious. I'm going to get him. He'd made the decision.

Zem hesitated. Jace sensed the hawkcel perched on a high tree limb, kilometers from the camp.

Do not come, Jace said.

This is dangerous. If they got the fox, they could get you. You must tell the Elecampanes. They are alphas. They will help.

They are gone to the Deep Blue Sea. Like Glyssa. Jace tested his bond with Lepid . . . the fox was still alive, he could tell that . . . and that link was solid and fox-red and as wide as his wrist.

He felt his Fam's hesitation, then Zem said, *I will eat and work a little on my nest, then go back to camp.*

Fine.

Be careful! Zem said.

I will.

Andic Sanicle strolled into the workroom at that moment, nodded to Jace. The man was whistling, seemed too cheerful. Especially since he'd been downright surly to Jace for weeks. Maybe it was the fact that Laev T'Hawthorn called Jace by his first name last night and this morning, but who knew?

Had Sanicle been the one to lure and lock the FamFox in the ship? Whoever had done so must know the ship better than everyone thought . . . still, venturing down the hole the Comosums had condemned while the rest of them dug and dug for the main entrance? How was that possible?

Jace jerked a nod. "Sanicle."

"Bayrum," Sanicle said lazily, stretched languidly. He'd just had sex? Or was pretending that? No question that Sanicle remained for whatever gilt, big score, that could happen. He hadn't bought into the project.

"Later." Jace strolled from the workshop tent, wanted to run, fast, to the ship. But he also didn't intend to tip anyone off that he was after Lepid.

He wasn't sure what kind of security the Hollys had around the hole since most everyone had left the camp. And once the opening was off-limits he hadn't tempted himself by hanging around it.

Someone had been making forays into the ship, Jace just knew it. And now that someone had hurt Lepid.

And might want Jace, himself. He'd have to be careful.

The Elecampanes' whole "going to the Deep Blue Sea" thing could be a ruse, too, to find out who might betray the owners and biggest shareholders. He wasn't privy to their decisions. Glyssa might be. Irritation nearing anger riled him. He hadn't played his cards well for this whole thing. Had let his stupidity get in the way. He could have been as respected as she was . . . and she was. He remained a lowly adventurer.

Somehow that wasn't enough for him anymore. Not that all Glyssa had said to him was true. He tried not to think of all the word darts she'd aimed at his heart that had struck dead-on.

And this particular adventure could end his career. If he was found in the ship, he'd be thought the thief. He'd be proven untrustworthy, no matter the reason. He'd have broken the contract with the Elecampanes he signed, forfeit all his gilt.

His rep would be trashed. No one would hire him on again.

End of his career. Maybe it wasn't much of a career, but he liked the camaraderie of ventures like this, the risk, the excitement. Didn't matter that he had some sort of inheritance, he loved his life.

In his tent, he stowed his knives, murmured a security spellshield. He took a minute to loosen his tight muscles, consider his options. The person in charge of the camp was the head Holly security guard, and she didn't like him. Not that he thought she liked anyone . . . but she got on with Glyssa and the Elecampanes all right.

He didn't think the Holly was a snob so much as she'd decided who was trustworthy and who was not.

Lepid hadn't made that grade, either. Zem had.

Think!

If he told the Holly woman, what would happen?

Nothing. She might not even believe Jace. Lepid had proven he could be anywhere in the camp at anytime. She certainly wouldn't let Jace go down into the ship to find Lepid. Not alone, because he could steal artifacts, and she wouldn't risk someone to go with him. He didn't know her, couldn't anticipate her thought processes like he might others he'd been with for a while.

Would she be in telepathic contact with the Elecampanes? Probably not, but scry pebbles would work. All the Elecampanes carried scry pebbles. Jace had one, somewhere.

Time was dribbling away. The urge to act stampeded across his nerves. Even taking this time to think, instead of blindly acting and trusting to luck, was a change for him.

Due to Glyssa.

Fligger it. *Act!*

He didn't know what he might need, took an all-purpose Flair-imbued tool and slipped it in one of his trous pockets. After a minute's hesitation, he folded two bespelled air masks into another pocket. He didn't believe the snotty Comosums. He thought the air in the ship along the corridors under the girder was fine.

Keeping his connection with Lepid open, trusting in it, he strolled from the tent to a place where he could see the former hole. Stood in the shadow of a group tent.

Thirty-five

Only *weathershields and spellshields and canvas covered the hole* leading down to the inside of *Lugh's Spear*. One male guard, plump and bored, walked back and forth.

The spellshield set to prevent human and animal access was a problem. But Lepid had obviously gotten through it . . . and so had the mystery person. Had the villain set a trap and Lepid fallen into it? Or had the bad guy actually been on scene? Maybe closed a door, several, after Lepid?

Jace knew how the fox had gotten in. Teleportation into the hole beyond the localized spellshield's reach.

If Lepid could do it, Jace could. He forced his mind to quiet and sank into his balance. Jace had been in the hole at the time of the forays of Lepid and the cat, before the arrival of the Comosums. He remembered how the area looked. Held a strong image in his mind of the dimensions, the angles. The light.

It would be darker now, not open to the sun. But he'd lived under canvas and at the camp for a long time now. He could extrapolate.

The fox was still unconscious. Jace had to take a chance.

His *mind*, his *balance* was better. His center core stronger. He was more self-aware—all gifts from Glyssa, too, that would be better for teleporting. He shut her and the pain at the thought of her from his mind.

Taking breaths as he counted down, he muttered, "One, Lepid Fam. Two, Jace Bayrum. Three, to the rescue!"

And lit hard, soles stinging, bending his knees, teeth snapping shut. He'd been too high—a couple of inches. He coughed instinctively, expecting dust to rise around him.

No. The area was suspiciously clean, no footprints. So the lurker was better at teleportation than most? Damn, who knew? Jace wasn't the kind to hide his talents from everyone else. People knew up front that he had the general, minor Flair of most people, that he was a skilled leatherworker . . . and storyteller.

But other people did keep secrets like their true ability with Flair, and it looked like this character had. Who knew what else he or she had concealed? Probably had been pilfering objects all along, hiding them and keeping quiet, ready to sell them and get rich when the camp broke up for the winter.

Jace's eyes adjusted to the dimness. The little space seemed the same as it had the last time he'd been here, rubble gone from underfoot—gone altogether. He angled under the crumpled wall.

"Hey, hey! What are you doing? Get away from there!" The guard's voice sounded too close. Jace froze.

"What are you *doing?*" the guard roared.

Glancing up, Jace saw a boulder plummet through the canvas, ripping a huge and ragged hole. It hit the girder and split into two. Jace jumped backward.

"Why did you do that, you fligger?" yelled the guard. "You come back here!" His voice huffed and diminished as if he ran after the person.

A tingle zipped down Jace's spine. Had he been seen? Was that boulder aimed for him? Was his enemy in the camp? Or in *Lugh's Spear?* Or were there two or more working together, a whole gang?

Returning to the edge of the entry space, he peeked into the area. The tarp flapped in the wind, flickering the weak sunlight from a clouded-over sky. Canvas slapped against the ground, the hole tearing farther.

On the floor, the boulder had broken into several large and jagged pieces, one shard as tall as his knees. The rock must have been thrown with Flair.

Jace grimaced as he looked at the messy entrance, glanced up at the ripped covering. If he came back this way, he'd have to clean it up before he teleported—No. He'd just teleport to his tent.

For now, though, the entry area had changed so much that whoever was outside wouldn't be able to teleport past the spellshield, not to mention what other covering they'd put over the hole. It looked as if the girder had moved a little, too.

But he had to get Lepid, so he turned toward the hallway. A few steps into the wide corridor and the darkness that infused the ship enveloped him and a shudder worked up his spine.

Like most other people, he could summon light-spells. He kept them dim until he was well away from the hole in case the guard was more alert than he thought.

His footsteps echoed as he walked on a floor that had nothing of Celta in it. Another odd-feeling thing—the darkness, the sound of his steps in a huge ship that had been home to Earthans several centuries ago, but had no human in them for so long.

He sniffed cautiously, smelled nothing unusual, but he sure didn't have Lepid's nose. As he trod through the eerily silent ship with deeper-than-night darkness just outside the circle of sun-white light provided by his spellglobes, he could understand the atavistic fear this atmosphere might have had on the two noble Comosums. They were women who moved in high strata where they knew everyone. Women who thought they knew everything there *was* to know about their topic.

But they knew nothing about how their ancestors lived—never had *felt* how the colonists had lived—as alien people.

The Comosums would have been unnerved and prejudiced. He wondered if they'd ever visited the starship in Druida City, *Nuada's Sword*, more than during a couple of grovestudy trips.

Not that he had before he'd gone with Laev.

Glyssa had visited *Nuada's Sword* often. This shouldn't be the time to think of her, either. He *wouldn't*.

He passed through the corridor, and the longer he was in *Lugh's Spear*, the more settled he became. Yes, the Earthans were alien to current Celtans, but they'd had the scope to dream huge. Like he did.

His strong link with Lepid told him the Fam remained unconscious, a concern, but Jace sensed no terrible harm had come to the fox. Yet.

Straining his ears, he listened for any sound, nothing. He walked softly, rolled tension from his shoulders, but couldn't determine whether anyone else lurked in the ship or not. The distance to Lepid was farther than he'd anticipated . . . more than a kilometer. Jace called up the blueprints in his mind, figured that the fox lay near the Captain's Quarters.

An hour before NoonBell while they rode through a wide meadow, a baby's cry split the air. Both Glyssa and Camellia flinched and looked at each other. From the beginning of the line, Del D'Elecampane took a scry pebble from a leather trous pocket.

Three minutes later she rode back to Glyssa and Camellia, her expression tight.

"Jace Bayrum has packed his tent and left the camp."

Shock zinged along Glyssa's nerves. She opened her mouth to deny he'd do such a thing . . . but shut it again. Blinking, she said, "Didn't he arrive by airship?"

Del nodded. "Yes, but he has the skills to travel back to Druida on his own."

Glyssa shook her head. "Over thousands of kilometers? I don't know that he'd do that."

"Or maybe he's on our backtrail?" Camellia added. "Maybe he decided to join us."

Grunting, Del said, "There's also been some problems with the hole down into *Lugh's Spear*. Someone flung a boulder past the weathershields and spellshields and into the entrance. Ruined the canvas."

Glyssa lifted her chin. "I've never seen Jace move heavy objects with Flair. In fact, when I loaned him my no-time for Zem, I was the one who set the anti-grav spell on it. Jace wouldn't vandalize the camp like that."

Del still scowled.

"He's bought into the venture," Glyssa added. "And he signed contracts. He wouldn't violate them."

"Lepid stayed with Jace," Camellia said, smiling at Del's Fox-Fam, Shunuk, who watched them from his seat behind Del.

"That's right," Glyssa said. "Jace wouldn't leave camp for Druida City with Lepid."

"So it's more likely he's coming after us." Camellia beamed.

"I asked him not to," Glyssa mumbled.

Camellia lifted her chin. "Coming after us to apologize."

Glyssa caught her breath at the hope surging through her. Hope destroyed was so very painful, the worst experience in the world.

"Maybe you should contact your Fam," Del said.

Glyssa feared to. Worse scenario was that Lepid had left her, too, preferring the more adventurous Jace.

CELTAROON NEST! Shunuk FoxFam yelled, leapt off Del's stridebeast and headed down the path toward a spot on the right.

"They're poisonous!" Glyssa gasped.

"He'll be fine," Del said. "He loves to kill them. Good skins for boots. But, hell, we can't leave something like that near the path ready to hurt human or animal." She followed fast, mobilizing the small party to stamp out the vermin.

*A*dventure sang in Jace's blood and he jogged lightly down the hall, ignoring open doorways he glimpsed on either side.

He even refrained from the temptation of examining objects along the corridor. Sacks, boxes, other items dropped by the colonists.

Finally he stopped before a huge bronze door. As he studied it, he gulped. Engraved on the door was a list of the Captains of the ship. What a find! He wished he had a recordsphere. He'd definitely acted without too much consideration. But who would have thought the fox would be so deep into the ship?

Legend had it that people had rushed back into the ship when it began to plummet. Thankfully he saw no human skeletons—no skeletons at all. But the ground access doors were stories beneath him. This hallway housed officers, those higher up in the status of the ship.

Jace shifted, trying not to think of the amount of dirt lying atop the ship, or the distance he'd walked from the only open entrance. The hair on his body rose. Once more he stretched all his senses for anything, anyone, any inimical feeling aimed at him. Still nothing.

He reached out, but stopped before he laid his hand on the doors . . . could they be booby-trapped? Maybe, maybe. And anyone with an iota of curiosity would yearn, as he yearned, to see beyond those doors, the most wondrous furnishings of the ship. This cabin might have the most valuable items.

Everything in there would be the property of Camellia Darjeeling D'Hawthorn, with a finder fee going to the discoverer and the Elecampanes. Camellia was Glyssa's friend. The one she laughed with as they rode with Del D'Elecampane toward the Deep Blue Sea.

That had his fingers curling, hands fisting.

A slight whimper came, more heard mentally than with his ears. *Lepid?* he projected.

FamMan. Now a loud whine, *not* behind the great door. A few doors along the hall, deeper into the ship. Dammit, why had Lepid gone so far?

Because the young fox had wanted to be a hero. Wanted to reach the Captain's Quarters, see what treasures it contained, who wouldn't? Then, like many young things, had been distracted by something else, in this case, an intriguing spell.

Shrugging, Jace turned away from the engraved door, tilted his head. *Talk to me, Lepid. I am close.*

You are here? In the SHIP? For ME?

Sure.

Jace *felt* relief panting from the fox.

Thank you, thank you, thank you! WONDERFUL FamMan.
Jace smiled, found the closed door on his right and knocked.
Wild barking came from behind it.

With effort, Jace enlarged his light-spells until they showed long
meters before and behind him . . . and no one else in the corridor.
Several dark squares in each direction showed open doors, but he
noted no movement in them.

FAMMAN!

Now Jace could hear the frantic scratching of claws.

*Calm down. I want to check some doorways first, and this door,
too.* He could already tell it wasn't spellshielded. No Flair to stop
him from going in.

Unlike the starship in Druida City, *Nuada's Sword,* Flair worked
fine here.

He powered up his spell lights so the bright brushed metal walls
gleamed and the colonist-abandoned objects on the floor cast hard
shadows. Retracing his steps, he paused outside each open door, sent
another spell light in, and resisted the desire to explore when a gleam
of an artifact or an odd shape teased his curiosity.

Behind his eyes a headache at the amount of Flair he was using
began to build. He turned back, then headed farther down the hall
to check out those doors. Even when one of the usually empty name-
plates announced Umar and Dayo Clague, the former Captain and
his lady, he didn't stop. Narrowing his gaze, he placed the location
on the blueprint in his mind's eye, then turned back to the door that
Lepid yipped behind.

As he returned, he banished his secondary light-spell and let the first
shrink. When he reached the correct door, Jace ran his hands all over it,
from top to bottom, along the recessed panel that would slide aside.

He felt nothing unusual, saw, heard, sensed nothing strange. The
palm control panel came off easily in his hand, showing electronics
and the manual door crank. That moved readily, too, as did the door
sliding open.

Lepid's barks rose to a crescendo when Jace stepped in. He didn't
see the FoxFam in the medium-sized room.

Here, here! In the wall!

In the wall?

He took another step, the door began to close. *Stup!* Sliding his foot into the crack, he stopped it, muscled it back all the way open and looked for something to prop it open . . . just in case. There were no loose items within reach. Testing the inner control panel, he flipped open the outer cover, used the manual crank to test closing and opening the door, set the door lock in the open position. Still . . .

FAMMAN! Lepid shouted telepathically.

"Just a minute!" Jace sat down in the threshold and took off his heavy boots, wrinkled his nose. He really should have gone for the suppress odor spell on these and his liners . . . and he thought that every time he took the damn things off.

FamMan odors, rumbled Lepid, actually sounding cheerful.

Huh, it took all kinds.

Jace put the boots side by side next to the far edge of the threshold, stood up, slipped a little and set his hand against the wall. He walked past the built-in closet on the left and the bed on the right. The small cubicle holding a toilet and a tiny shower was also on the left. Too small for Jace to feel comfortable in.

DOWN HERE! One last, demanding bark.

Lepid was hidden behind a wall panel. All Jace could see were pinholes.

Thank you, FamMan, for the light, Lepid whimpered.

Jace flinched. He hadn't figured that the poor fox had been in the dark. Of course Lepid could see better in the dark than Jace, but all the same it had to be scary. Grimacing with effort, Jace conjured another tiny spell light and threaded it through one of the minuscule openings.

Oh, FamMan, you are so kind. Lepid's tone was such that if he'd been human, he'd be sobbing.

"I'm here," Jace soothed. "Everything's going to be all right."

Panting came from behind the wall.

"So a smell led you here," Jace said.

It was a very interesting smell, Lepid said in a small mental voice.

"Not like the earlier smell that hurt your nose, the chili pepper," Jace said. The perpetrator of these series of crimes knew about animals and odors and effects. Of course, since Jace had gotten a Fam himself, he'd become more aware about birds and animals. He supposed those with Fams would be good suspects . . . though he couldn't imagine hurting a Fam.

He ran his fingers around the outline of the small panel that looked to be for ventilation. The metal didn't feel like Celtan metal, odd, that. He *did* feel a trace of Flair, no doubt some sort of trap.

"So how long have you been exploring the ship?" he asked.

All the time, Lepid whispered. *I thought going into this wall would be fun. It wasn't. It was dark and I got tired and I didn't see any openings to anything else.* He paused for a moment. *There should be openings to other places from the walls, shouldn't there? T'Ash Residence had openings in the walls here and there.* Another small pause as Jace determined the damn panel wouldn't pop off with an application of more Flair.

And the cats in the PublicLibrary got into the walls and laughed at me when I tried to follow. So there are holes and passages in those walls, too.

Jace wondered if the Licorices knew that. Shrugged. Not his problem. Getting Lepid out was. He replied, "I think there should be openings to the walls somewhere. People would have to go in to work on . . . stuff." Pulling the tool from his pocket, Jace pried around the ventilation grate. "But maybe before they landed all the openings were sealed or something. Or after they landed. I think they must have sealed all they could to preserve the ship."

Lepid pawed at the grate again. *Get me out!*

"Did you see who did this? Did you smell him or her?"

Barely probable that the culprit was the cook, Myrtus Stopper. Jace really couldn't see the man coming back to the camp to raid the ship, no matter how valuable the items might be.

Stopper hadn't had to go into the ship to make his score, and though Jace didn't know how much he got for those subsistence bars, it had to be plenty if the amount had impressed Laev T'Hawthorn.

That left the unknown villain who'd stolen the first box. The man or woman Myrtus said had caused the explosions. The Elecampanes hadn't kept Jace or Glyssa informed about that, but the owners would have announced to the whole crew if some other culprit had been caught.

Snapping teeth from Lepid. *NO! I did not see or smell the bad, mean person! I will hunt for the bad one's smells, then I will BITE him.*

"Nope, I think we'll just teleport from here to my tent. We're not staying down here any longer than necessary. We're not supposed to be here."

The fox snorted. *You sound like Glyssa.*

"Look fox, if you got caught in here, they might send you and Glyssa home immediately, and might not let you come back next year. Might cancel her contract and shares."

The Elecampanes wouldn't do that! They LIKE us.

"They could banish the both of you. This venture is more important to the owners than you, or their liking of you and Glyssa. If they sent you home, Glyssa would fail at her jobs. Her Family would be ashamed of her and not let her work in the main PublicLibrary of Celta." The Licorices would be tough minded enough to do that. "Her Family might even throw you both out of the Residence." That might be stretching it, but Jace figured living as a failure with the Licorices would not be pleasant.

A pause as Lepid thought, then he said, *Uh-oh. I like the Public-Library. I like chasing those cats. Not playing there would be bad. I have my own bed in the Residence! And I am the only Fam in the Residence now. I would always be First Fam. Being sent home would be bad.*

"That's right." Jace banged his fist against the panel and it popped off. Lepid shot out, not smelling too good himself. No doubt somewhere in the walls were fox markings and turds.

Oh, oh, oh! I am FREE! Lepid inhaled deeply and nibbled Jace's toes. Jace danced away, laughing, then, stink and all, swept him up.

"What's that sound?" Jace asked.

What sound?

"The ticking. I think it started when I opened your panel."

Thirty-six

I don't know what that ticking is. Lepid nudged Jace's hand close to his nose, slipped his head under it. Jace chuckled, the Fam wanted cuddling, petting. So holding him close, Jace stroked him. Lepid hummed in approval, licked under Jace's chin.

With a jaunty step, Jace headed toward the door.

The ticking stopped. A small explosion came from the door's control panel, fire surged. Flames flashed outside the door, too, before it sprang shut, cutting his boots in two.

Lepid shrieked and leapt from Jace's arms, ran to the closed door and threw himself against it, then subsided, coughing at the smoke in the air.

Jace stood staring at the blackened area where the door control panel had been, his thudding heart nearly drowning out Lepid's barking and the final sizzle of dying circuits.

He inhaled and coughed himself as acrid air scraped his windpipe. He'd never smelled anything like the Earthan tech. But Earthan tech didn't run on psi power, Flair. Most everything on Celta had an element of Flair. Only the Elder Family and *Nuada's Sword*, the starship in Druida City, knew how to work pure Earthan tech.

Forcing himself to calm, he was *not* trapped, he shouted at Lepid's renewed frenzy at the door. "Quiet down."

We are trapped.

"No, we aren't." He had to repeat that just to hear his own words. "No, we are not. I took stock of my tent before I left." Not really, but he could probably bring it up in his mind's eye. He *knew* where the items he moved around lately were, even if Lepid hadn't been able to chance teleporting.

Oh, oh, oh. THANK YOU, FAMMAN. Lepid jumped at him and Jace caught the young fox. Bigger than he'd been when he first arrived, but mentally and emotionally still more like a child than an adult.

"Just let me steady myself." Jace strode over to look at the panel. Nothing but melted black stuff. The crank handle was gone, disintegrated by the explosion or falling into the hole that had opened behind the wall. And there was no sign of the gear or whatever the crank had been attached to.

Looks bad, bad, Lepid said. He wrinkled his nose. *Smells terrible.*

"Yeah." Jace was breathing from his mouth. Turning to the wall opposite the control panel in the corridor, he put his hand against it, yanked it away from the burning heat.

Lepid sighed. *This is not so good. We WILL have to teleport.*

"Yes." Jace squeezed the fox, for his own comfort as well as Lepid's.

He went to the middle of the room, stood and began to calm his body, let his mind drift, squelching thought . . . then quieting, shifted Lepid who'd relaxed in his arms. The fox had faith in him. That was great.

FAMMAN! LEPID! Zem cried.

What? asked Jace, blown out of the beginnings of serenity.

What, Zem? called Lepid. *We are teleporting to FamMan's tent. See you soon.*

Fear struck Jace, jolting through the bond he had with Zem.

NO! screamed the hawkcel, and Jace thought he heard the echo of the real sound from his Fam as he'd wailed into the sky. *Our tent is not there!*

WHAT? yelled Jace mentally.

It is gone, as if you packed everything up and left.

A terrible dread prickled along Jace's skin. He squeezed down his own fear into a small ball, shut it behind a closed door. Breathed for control. *I don't like the sound of that.*

No, Zem said.

No, Lepid said.

I had a spellshield in place. Someone got through it. Jace rolled his shoulders, setting that fact aside to be dealt with later.

Lepid looked up at him with big eyes. *Will we get out of here?*

"Yes," Jace replied through clenched teeth.

I wish I could tell those in charge. None of the guards can hear me, Zem said sadly. *Not even Mistress Cornuta Holly. My bonds with the Elecampanes are not strong enough for them to hear, and their minds are full of busy noise.*

Jace loosened his jaw, made his telepathic tone even. *Zem, I want you to fly to Glyssa's pavilion. I know she was rearranging some furniture this morning.* Because she'd wanted him gone, and she'd left herself.

Teleporting somewhere we don't know is safe is VERY bad. Lepid shivered. *All the Fams told me a man teleported into some furniture and it killed him.*

Jace had heard about that incident a few months ago, too. He continued steadily, *Zem can look at the sitting room.* Jace knew that better than her bedroom, could guess at the light—the most important element in teleporting. *When you are there, you can send us images of the room.*

Send to me, too! Lepid said.

That's what I said, Jace agreed. *Between the three of us, we will put together a good picture.* Good enough, he hoped, but they had little choice.

Very well, FamMan, Zem said.

Pain! Zem's pain.

Someone shot at me with a blazer! Zem cried. Jace sensed him zooming high up into the sky.

Lepid squealed in sympathy. Jace hugged him tight, eased up.

Are you all right? Jace asked Zem, struggling with his own panic at the thought of losing the Fam.

Only some outer feathers singed, but I do not think I can go into camp. Trago wants to kill me.

Trago!

Yes. I saw him. I think he has a hate for you. You made his mate leave him. Most males do not like that. A pause. *I would not like that. Nor would you.*

The idea of, say, Andic luring Glyssa away twisted Jace up. Worse than her leaving on her own.

But he hadn't realized Trago had thought of Symphyta as his woman, his mate.

Critical mistake on Jace's part.

And he could have defended himself with the fact that Symphyta had made her own decision, but obviously Trago blamed Jace.

He winced.

What are we going to do? asked Lepid in a small voice.

Can you recall the corridor well enough to teleport beyond it? Share that image with me?

Lepid paused, then shook his head. In fact, his whole body trembled. *I have been down many hallways, most look alike. I can't remember this one, where the boxes and sacks and other things are, how far apart the doors are.*

Or which doors are open or closed, Jace ended for him. He tried to remember each end of the hall, but couldn't recall, either.

Lepid shivered. *I don't want to teleport accidentally down, down, down into the ship.*

Not good, Zem said.

I don't blame you, Jace said.

Then Lepid's ears perked up. *We can go to the entryway, where the ramp is! Yes, we can do that!* His lower jaw opened in a foxy grin and he wiggled in Jace's grasp.

Jace held him tight, mouth flattening as he replied telepathically. *No, we can't. Someone threw a boulder at me and it broke into big pieces in the entryway, moved the ramp a little. The light is strange from the ripped tarp.* Had he been the target, or had changing the parameters of the entryway for teleportation been the goal? Probably both.

Either way he felt like he was lagging far behind Trago—who he'd definitely underestimated.

Oh, no! Lepid said.

Continues to be not good, said Zem.

How are we going to get out? Lepid demanded.

I don't know, Jace said.

I will think on this, Zem said. *I am going fishing in the lake, then back to my nest.*

We all will figure this out, Jace said. He walked over to the bed, sank onto the hard cushion. Lepid hopped down from his lap and began to pace, but the fox didn't seem to be as afraid as he'd been before.

But this time they really were trapped. The spell light Jace had been using faltered and he boosted it, but he wasn't accustomed to holding an ongoing spell throughout the day. Even though the energy wasn't too much, it was enough to drain him if he kept it up for more than a septhour or two. Soon they'd be in the dark.

His fingers slid into his pocket and tightened on the tool with a wisp of hope that it could cut them out of there. "Let's see if this will get us out."

He strode to the door, put his hand against it. No heat now, the fire had died fast. He stared at the large piece of sliding metal, not really sure how it worked. He didn't recall seeing any protruding lock in the side of the door. Maybe it locked at the top or the bottom. With regular doors you could bash at the hinges. And was it just shut, or shut and locked, or even worse, fused to the jamb?

Applying his tool to the tiny crack where it set into the wall, he sent a steady Flair to the cutting edge.

He scratched the surface, no more.

Lepid yipped. *Uh-oh.*

"Yeah, not so good." He would burn himself and the tool out before he dented the door. "Let's look around for something to pry. Break the wall." Probably futile. "Open the door."

Tail wagging, Lepid said, *Fun!*

As the fox shouldered himself into the closet and began to paw around, Jace scrutinized the control panel again. It, too, was cool. Fried stuff, hole opening at the bottom of the wall that he couldn't fit his hand into. *Now* he could feel lingering Flair from the timed explosion.

He checked the wall on the left side of the door, no heat. He banged on the wall and the door, set his hands on the door and tried to slide it open. Nothing.

The area still smelled of unwholesome smoke.

I found a pretty! Lepid said.

Jace abandoned his worthless efforts at the door and folded the accordion door to the small closet completely open. Lepid turned and trotted out, something gold in his mouth. Jace hunkered down. "Let's see."

Lepid dropped it in Jace's palm, wet with drool. The filigree brooch was beautiful, of no design that Jace had ever seen. In the center of the gold was a black stone and on that a white carving of the profile of a woman. "Beautiful," he breathed. Fabulous find. This piece of jewelry could be sold for a huge amount of gilt. T'Ash, the blacksmith and jeweler, would like it, Jace was sure.

And it could start a whole new fashion trend.

Lepid sat, grinning. *We can give it to FamWoman.*

Jace nearly dropped the piece. Bitterness coated his tongue. "This belongs to everyone who signed up to share in the venture. We have to give it to the Elecampanes."

Lepid's ears drooped. *Really?*

"Yes. And FamWoman and I are . . . not together anymore."

With a large sniff and a swish of his tail on the floor, Lepid said, *Just argued.*

Jace's jaw clenched. No, it hadn't been a simple argument. Glyssa had walked away. But he had worse things to think about than that. "A beautiful brooch." He laid it in front of Lepid's paws. "But it won't get us out of here."

Nosing it toward him, Lepid said, *You keep it for FamWoman.* He turned and pawed at a built-in unit containing drawers.

Reluctantly, Jace picked up the brooch and pocketed it. "How many other items have you found?"

Lepid scrabbled faster at the top drawer, didn't look at Jace. *Not many.*

Which meant more than one. "Did you give anything to Glyssa?"

No. I gave a string to Zem for his nest.

Lord and Lady knew what the "string" was. "And the others?"

Nothing much that humans would like. Now the young fox abandoned the drawers, ran and hopped up on the bed, sniffed along the outline of the mattress.

"Where are the other things you took from the ship?" Jace winced at what the scholars who liked to viz everything in its place would say.

Lepid finally looked at him, twitching an ear. *They are cached.*

"With your cached food?" He hoped he didn't sound as appalled as Glyssa might have been.

No, other caches. I think I remember them all.

Great.

Not only had Trago been thieving, but so had the fox. Jace and Glyssa had been accessories to Fam theft.

Jace bent and opened the first drawer, nothing. He pulled out the second.

I took some rags, Lepid confessed, sitting on the bed. *The people took most of their good clothes.*

All of the drawers were empty. Jace glanced at the pegs in the closet that held a couple of forlorn-looking pieces of clothing for someone smaller than himself.

Lepid hopped from the bed and tried to get under the mattress set on another cabinet . . . slightly lower than an average Celtan man's height.

Jace went over to help him. Not many other places large enough
to hold something that would be useful as a good pry bar. Lifting up
the mattress, he saw a couple of small, torn shreds of papyrus. Lepid
whisked them out and Jace let the mattress fall with a thump. Lepid
dropped the scraps of papyrus at Jace's feet. He picked them up, saw
handwritten unfamiliar words, and put those in his pocket with the
jewelry. Who knew, the papyrus might turn out to be more valuable
than the brooch.

The cabinet under the bed was empty, too. A half septhour later
they'd searched the whole room thoroughly and Jace had placed a
few found items atop the dresser cube in the closet—a shirt, some
small tight bent wires that Lepid said smelled like hair, an odd bottle
they'd found in the cleansing cubicle that had dried stuff in it.

Despite all the distractions the fox and the brooch had provided,
the truth settled hard into Jace's bones, coated his arteries. He and
Lepid were trapped in a buried starship and it didn't appear as if
they could get out on their own.

Only Zem and Trago knew where they were, and Trago would
do his best to smear Jace and point people in another direction.

Jace and Lepid could definitely die—either by hunger and thirst,
or by desperately trying to teleport to an unsafe place. All the other
tents in camp . . . all the walkways . . . anywhere he could think
of . . . could have people in them, coming and going. A botched teleportation would be fatal to them all.

Of course they had one last option, but Jace wasn't quite ready
to surrender to that.

"Come sit with me while I think." Jace sat on the bed, patted the
mattress beside him. "I'm going to let the spell light go out now. I
need to save energy."

Lepid shuddered, jumped onto the bed with him. *I had to do
that, too. Before. I am strong enough to make a light now, though.*

Jace petted him. "In a while. Let's settle in." He lifted his legs,
flattened out on the bed. The mattress was no bedsponge, but some
ungiving material . . . and weirdly enough, Jace could now feel the

contours of whoever had slept there ages before. A smaller someone, both in width and length. Maybe female.

Lepid stepped onto Jace's chest, curled up. *It is good we are together.*

The situation would be better if neither of them were there. Skull-shaped terror gibbered in the back of Jace's mind, ready to bite. He kept punching it in the teeth. Didn't stop the cold sweat coating him.

Lepid whimpered. *Glyssa is the only one besides Zem and you that I can talk to well. What about you?*

"Let me check." Slowly he let the spell light trickle away, sighed when the small energy drain stopped. As they lay in the dark, Jace became aware of the scent of the fox . . . of other smells, residue of smoke and fire, those were Earthan. Now that he couldn't see, he felt surrounded by alien stuff. The covering on the mattress was no Celtan cloth. Even the sound of their breathing and their small movements echoed strangely in a room of metal and fake wood and other Earthan materials he had no name for.

He didn't want to die here.

Again he forced that fear away, breathed deeply and concentrated on the links, the emotional bonds, he had with others. The strongest was with Zem. . . . no, he lied to himself. The strongest, if the thinnest, was with Glyssa. Not surprising since he'd had that, even if he hadn't known it, hadn't discovered it, hadn't admitted it, since the second Passage to free his Flair years ago. He'd *had* Passages, *had* made a HeartGift, but his Flair had never obviously manifested. He stopped himself from shifting.

Glyssa had tended the bond at times when he'd been ignorant of it, when he hadn't seen it or felt it. Unlike a few weeks ago, this time he knew the bond would always be there, would always be tangible.

Of course the solution to this whole mess was to call Glyssa. Stupid not to have done that immediately.

Especially since she was riding away from the camp with every second.

But his pride, his very heart had been wounded by her. She'd shaken his world with her words, made him see himself in an unflattering light. Made him doubt his self-identity.

Made him want to change.

Change wasn't bad, but he wouldn't reach for Glyssa first, beg her to take him back. Not if he could get out some other way. Stupid to want to save his pride, or not want to aggravate a hurt to him, to her, but . . .

He scanned his other ties, precious few. No Family, of course. A strong but thin white one to . . . Raz Cherry T'Elecampane. Jace winced. Calling that guy mentally would be worse than speaking to Glyssa if he wanted to keep the fact that he and Lepid had been here in the ship secret. Not much chance of that, but a sliver . . . if he . . . they called Glyssa. If they could hold out until she came. If they could work together to teleport them somewhere safe.

And her arrival back here, maybe the return of the entire band led by Del D'Elecampane, would not go unnoticed, especially by Trago.

Well, he had that unexpected inheritance from his father now that his word was foresworn and he'd broken the contract with the Elecampanes and the other shareholders and forfeited his stake.

His father had loved him, had tried his fumbling best for Jace, and he should respect that. The thing was, just the idea was surprising. His father had been so in love with his mother, so bedazzled by her and under her thumb that Jace hadn't realized he'd loved his son, too.

Now the last trace of smoke, maybe the closeness of a snoozing Lepid's fur and the dust from him, stung Jace's eyes.

And this wasn't the right kind of thinking to get them out of here.

One thing he *did* know, despite the new info on his father, and Jace's unpleasant look at himself, he didn't want to die here. He especially didn't want to die slowly and watch a loved one die with him.

Which meant he should continue checking his bonds. There was a fuzzy, nasty black sort-of thread that reeked of *wrongness*. What was *that*?

Gently, gently he "touched" it. Shock! Stabbing pain. Anger.

Fliggering fligger! shrieked a high voice in his mind. Trago.

Jace lunged in disgust back from the tiny link.

How could that be?

He hates you. All his anger and pain is focused on you, Zem interjected. Easy for his BirdFam to say. He wasn't stuck in the ship, hadn't experienced the link viscerally.

I felt enough, Zem said. *Felt like the blazer shot that singed my feathers.*

Sorry, Zem. Jace considered the tie, didn't think he could get rid of it. Had never heard of anything like this before.

After some deep breathing, he could feel connections again. The shortest to the closest person was to Andic Sanicle. That man would stir up trouble for Jace. No links to Funa or any of the other women he'd slept with in camp. Nothing with Symphyta, though he'd spoken with her every morning when Zem was hurt, and they were friends.

Glyssa would have stronger, deeper bonds than he, even with members of the camp who she'd recently met.

Stop brooding. Act!

The last one he traced was a faint blue link that surprised him. It resonated of male and headed in the direction of Druida and he understood it was Glyssa's father. Not strong enough for him to contact.

I could fly very fast to Glyssa, Zem offered. *Even with a bad wing.*

Thank you, no. Jace rubbed Lepid awake. "We'll, I'll need to contact Glyssa. Lord and Lady knows how far away she is."

Lepid licked Jace's nose. *She will come. She will save us.*

She already had, both of them. Taken on a rambunctious fox kit as her Fam, Jace as her love.

He still couldn't acknowledge the HeartMate thing. That was on him.

"Yes," he said.

Thirty-seven

*T*hey'd stopped for lunch. *Glyssa was given the task of finding dry* wood to keep her from obsessing about Jace. Didn't help her hurting heart, but kept her hands busy. Everyone seemed glad to take the break and that it would be long enough for a fire. The day had clouded over again, the blue sky septhours gone.

She was sitting on a log with Camellia, greedily eating a meat and veggie kebob wrapped in a flour flexbread when Jace said, *Glyssa. I need you.*

Tears welled and she battled them back.

Lepid shouted into her mind. *FamWoman, FamWoman. HELP! We are trapped in the ship!*

Glyssa bit her tongue, hard, nearly dropped her sandwich, squeezed it so hard a piece of onion popped out and lay on the ground.

What? she cried out mentally to her lover and Fam.

Trago is the mean person! He trapped me, and I called FamMan to help and he came and now we are both trapped in a little room in the ship!

Her vision simply went white, the news was so contrary to what she'd thought. Jace and Lepid sure weren't following her to apologize.

"What's wrong?" asked Camellia.

Glyssa realized she'd swayed and her friend had put an arm around her waist to steady her. "Just a minute, Lepid's talking to me. There are problems."

Glyssa, calm, Jace said. *We won't die soon.*

His mordant humor didn't comfort her. *You are all right.*

Hesitation, then, *For now.*

I'm sure calling me was your last resort. Her reply came out snappish with bitterness and fear.

That is true, Jace said.

She'd flung her bond with him wide and could *feel* the horror in the back of his mind. Her insides squeezed. This couldn't be happening!

Unfortunately, it is happening, Jace responded to her thought. She sensed him petting Lepid who sat beside him on . . . a bed? She thought she felt him sigh, could almost see his lips curving in self-deprecating humor. *But I've been thinking a lot about what you said. I would have contacted you soon anyway.*

She shuttered her mind against her snotty answer. She was less good in a potentially fatal crisis than she'd hoped.

"Something's terribly wrong," Camellia whispered.

"Yes." Putting her food beside her on the log, Glyssa stood and moved to where Del was standing, talking to the cartographer.

One glance at Glyssa had Del dismissing the man, sinking into her balance and waiting for bad news. "What's up??

Glyssa couldn't prevent herself from wetting her lips, even so, her voice came out more squeaky than she wanted. "Apparently Lepid followed Trago into *Lugh's Spear.*" She wasn't sure of the details, why hadn't she asked? Too late now, she had to speak as if she knew what she was talking about. She made her voice strong and steady, matched it with a serious, honest expression. "Trago is the villain who's been sneaking around and raiding the ship."

She *felt* general agreement from Lepid and Jace tickle the back of her mind and continued.

"Your fox went down into the ship," Del snapped.

"Yes, and Trago trapped him." Glyssa lifted her chin. "Jace went after him."

Del grimaced, made a chopping gesture. "Let me guess, Trago trapped him, too."

"Yes, then packed up Jace's tent and things and . . . disposed of them." More affirmation from Jace and Lepid.

"Jace's tent had a spellshield. If Trago got through that, he's more powerfully Flaired than we all believed," Del said.

"Strong enough to send a boulder, by Flair, into the girder hole and ruin the canvas and entryway for teleportation so my guys can't get out of the room he trapped them in."

"Sounds logical," Del said. Her expression hardened. "I will scry our guards to arrest Trago, but I will not authorize my people to go down into the ship after Jace and Lepid. I'm sorry, I will not risk anyone."

Fear jolted through Glyssa. She hadn't expected this. She drew in a deep breath. "They're my responsibility, I'll go. I do want your permission to descend into the ship."

Del hesitated.

Glyssa lifted her brows. "If it were Raz and Shunuk down there?"

"Raz and Shunuk—" Del pressed her lips together. Glyssa knew the Elecampanes well, all of them burned with curiosity as much as she, they were just older and wiser and had more to lose than Jace and Lepid.

"I'll give you permission. I'll let everyone know you're coming and to give you help—short of going into the ship . . . at first." Del raised her hand. "We let a lot of people go down there and we're just asking for it to be looted." She exhaled heavily. "More than, apparently, Trago has already. We cannot let the knowledge the ship contains be more contaminated than it has been. *Lugh's Spear* might be able to answer many questions for us regarding our psi powers, our history, that *Nuada's Sword* does not know. You go first. If there are problems, the Hollys and Raz and I will confer as to who else we might send."

Glyssa stood straight. "I understand." She looked at the line of stridebeasts. "I'll go back."

"I won't turn this band around. Raz is expecting us at the Deep Blue Sea and it's important to get these other settlers out of our way. Happy somewhere other than in our venture."

"I'm still returning to the camp." By herself, alone in the wilderness, for septhours. She swallowed her own incipient panic. This had to be done. She'd lectured Jace about facing his shortcomings, time for her to do the same. Only the celtaroon nest had been a threat in all the septhours they'd traveled.

We will be with you, FamWoman! Lepid said.

You've never been on the trip to the Deep Blue Sea, she said to her Fam.

I have. Jace remained calm. *The path is always visible.*

Del was speaking, "I'll contact my HeartMate first, then my guards. Then we'll decide what to do."

"I'm leaving as soon as possible," Glyssa said.

"I'm going with her," Camellia said.

"No." Del looked straight at Camellia. "You are a FirstFamily GreatLady, I dare not take any chances with your health. I forbid it."

"That's strong language," Camellia said, taking Glyssa's hand. "Glyssa's my best friend."

"I will not allow you to leave, D'Hawthorn. If you force me to take measures to keep you here, I promise you, neither you, your husband, nor any of his investors, settlers, whoever is associated with him, will be welcome in this part of the world. None of you will get the aid you will need from us."

Glyssa turned and hugged her friend. "Stay safe with D'Elecampane."

"I'll worry about you."

"I know, but we have a bond. As I do with the Elecampanes. Everyone can advise me." All the voices in her head could drive her mad, too.

"Glyssa is barely able to make this trip on her own," Del said.

"She doesn't know the area. She has no survival skills in traversing or camping in the wilderness."

Glyssa suppressed a wince, stood tall. "You can't talk me out of it."

"So I see. At least you are accustomed to the camp and the area. You know, in general, any dangers."

Glyssa wished Del would stop talking and feeding her imagination. "Yes," she said.

Del examined her from top to toe, sighed. "You don't have any weapons."

"Nothing physical. I assure you I can defend myself with Flair."

"And I have taught her a few self-defense moves," Camellia said. That was true, though from the evidence a while back with Sanicle—the last time she'd needed self-defense—Glyssa hadn't recalled a thing.

"We've only been gone a few septhours." Del waved a casual hand. "The path is well marked. You should be fine. Shunuk will accompany you."

Del's FamFox yowled in protest. Del frowned at him. "You will go with Glyssa. You know the way back to the camp as well as I do." Del slid her gaze to Glyssa. "And Glyssa will pay you with special foods for your gluttonous nature."

The Fam was reasonably thin, but Glyssa had heard that he liked his food.

"I have some particular fox treats that Camellia brought me from Danith D'Ash," Glyssa informed Shunuk. "Fresh treats."

His tongue swiped over his muzzle and he walked stiffly to one of the stridebeasts—not the one she'd been riding.

Del sighed. "You're right, Shunuk. Glyssa should take the steadiest beast, and the one who likes the camp the best. The mare will be happy to head for the stables." Del gestured to a groom. "Transfer Glyssa's light gear to Millie." Del met Glyssa's eyes. "The provisions you have for two and a half more days on the road, we will keep."

"Fine," Glyssa said. "I'll be back in the camp well before dark. You *will* inform your HeartMate of everything?"

"You can be sure of that." Del's mouth twisted. "We'll probably be talking about this all afternoon, and coordinating with the guards back at the camp." With a jerk of the head, she walked away.

Shunuk bounded away from the stridebeast, headed over to the log where Glyssa had been sitting and snarfed up her food. He grinned as he masticated.

Glyssa's stomach gurgled, but she had no appetite. Jace and Lepid were trapped in the ship and she was about to ride alone, except for a FamFox, into the wilderness . . . not to mention that Trago was still at large. Anything could happen. The earth could swallow the ship once more and her HeartMate and Fam could die. A grychomp could get her. She could stumble into a celtaroon nest. She gritted her teeth and stopped a shudder.

"The stridebeast is ready," the groom said.

Camellia wrapped tight arms around Glyssa. "I love you. You can do this. I love you."

Glyssa let herself rest against her friend for a moment, bask in the warmth of love given and returned, in the loyalty, the deep faith they had for each other. "I'll see you in a little while," she said.

"Yes." Camellia squeezed until Glyssa hurt. "As soon as I can talk someone into flying me back to the camp, I'll be there. Blessed be."

"Blessed be."

A large sneeze and a snort. *COME ON*, said Shunuk.

Glyssa reluctantly let go of her friend, dredged up a smile then, but steel sincerity in it. "I'll get to camp, save the guys, and see you later."

"Later," Camellia said with a strange perky smile.

Shunuk nipped Glyssa's ankle. "Hey!" she protested.

He turned and ran toward her new stridebeast, jumped to his pad behind her saddle. Sighing, Glyssa shook out her legs . . . then there was a short line of people from camp to hug that had prickles rising behind her eyes. They all wished her well, gave her blessings, and wore extremely doubtful expressions.

And then Del was there to help her into the saddle. "No problem going back. Nothing to worry about," the explorer said. Her mouth

flattened and her gaze shadowed. "We'll do all we can to help." She
muttered, rubbed the back of her neck. "Any deaths, especially in
the ship, will put an end to this project for generations. Raz pointed
that out to me. Damn *curse* and bad luck nonsense."

"Merry meet," Glyssa said.

Del blinked, smiled. "And merry part."

"And merry meet again." With that last word, she nudged the
stridebeast toward the dirt path between grasses. The mare trudged
unenthusiastically.

BYE FAMWOMAN, I WILL BE CAREFUL. I LOVE YOU,
shouted Shunuk.

Glyssa winced and turned the stridebeast back the way they'd
come a few minutes ago. The mare wuffled, her ears pricked up and
she went faster. Glyssa could swear she got smudged images from the
beast's mind of *food* and *warm stables* and *no stupid big water close.*

As soon as they'd rounded a curve and lost sight of camp, Glyssa
contacted Jace and Lepid. *I am on my way back and making good
time. I'll be there as soon as possible.*

We'll be here, Jace said, still too calmly. He hadn't narrowed
their bond—his only bond with the outside world?—and she *felt*
how the atmosphere pressed upon him, how he controlled the panic
skittering along his nerves. How he petted her Fam, grateful for
the fox.

She swallowed hard.

We are in the dark, Lepid whimpered. *And we are not moving
around and it is cold.*

The temperature in the ship, like most caverns, was steady, but
not nearly as warm as the earth touched by sun. Glyssa bit her lip.

Shunuk and I are coming. The Elecampanes know of your plight.

She felt Jace wince.

Suppose that was necessary.

Snideness would not help the situation. *I prefer to have all the
support that I need. Where's Zem?*

I am here, FamWoman, said the bird's cool voice in her mind. *I
did not descend into the ship.* To him the ship symbolized a deadly

bird, ready to kill, and now he felt both vindicated and fearful. *I am not with my beloved FamMan.*

Jace choked. His fear rose, then settled. *I am glad you are free and in the open.*

FamWoman, Trago shot at me with a blazer, singed some feathers, but I am not much hurt.

Oh, Zem!

Zem said, *Everyone in camp is running around, looking for Trago. He is not to be found.*

Do you know where he is hiding?

I am watching, but I do not see, the bird said.

We are only two, we can go faster than the whole band. Glyssa pushed enthusiasm at Jace and Lepid and Zem.

Two? asked Jace.

Del sent Shunuk with me. Shouldn't he have sensed that, her conversations with others? She scowled, straining to read all the nuances of their bond. Both of her loved ones were tired, and she didn't know what the future might hold, but it was sure to need action on all their parts—energy and Flair. *Maybe you can sleep?* she advised.

The older fox is coming back? Lepid said.

Yes, Glyssa replied.

Oh, Lepid said, but she heard the pout in his tone.

*I*n the ship, Jace yanked out the cover on the bed and rolled under it, holding it up for Lepid.

Old, old smells, the fox grumbled. *Of woman, maybe a trace of man. Not Celtan. Don't like this cover.* He scrabbled at it.

"Get under here," Jace ordered wearily.

With a low growl, Lepid did. *I don't wanna sleep.*

"Nothing else to do," Jace said, except worry, and that was never productive.

Their body heat began to warm them, and the cover was unexpectedly efficient at keeping the warmth in. He was wondering what kind of material it was made of when sleep took him into dim and anxious dreamtime.

*G*lyssa *shifted again on her stridebeast, refusing to be intimidated by* this stretch of path through towering trees. Jace and Lepid weren't the only ones who were sleeping, the FamFox Shunuk snored behind her and she was glad. Shunuk was not as fun to travel with as Lepid. The older FamFox—a spy on her as well as a guide—complained a lot.

Two-thirds of the way back to the camp, it rained and she used the stingiest of weathershields. A feeling deep in her bones told her to conserve her energy and Flair, that she'd need it later.

Finally, with better time than she'd expected, not quite midafternoon, the camp came into sight and the stridebeast loped toward it.

I'm here! Jace heard Glyssa mentally. *I'll be there to get you out shortly!*

Jace had been thinking. *I don't think we have a tool to break open the door. You wouldn't have the strength for a lever.* He nearly shuddered as he thought of his boots sliced in two. *And I'm not sure a blazer-type tool would work on the metal in a . . . in a timely fashion.*

All right.

Just come and we'll figure it out, he said.

All right.

And, Glyssa?

Yes?

Please go to the Elecampanes' pavilion and retrieve my Heart-Gift. He thought he sensed her gasp.

Are you sure?

Yes. I want it . . . it's a powerful object. And now he knew she felt disappointment. He was almost sure he wanted to give it to her, but wouldn't commit to it yet.

I will do that, she said. *The Holly commander is here. I'll be there as soon as possible.*

Lepid wiggled next to Jace and sighed. *FamWoman comes.*

"Yes."

She didn't sound too mad.

"Not yet. She's worried." Hell, *he* was worried, despite telling himself not to be. "I bet when we're all safe, we're going to get a scolding." But Jace smiled. They'd be out soon, all of them together. Lepid's ears drooped against Jace's arm. *I will never get to explore this ship by myself again.*

"That is very true."

Glyssa, Zem whispered in her mind. *She thought he was close, but didn't* turn around to see.

Yes, Zem?

I want to go with you. My FamMan needs me. Hesitation. *And I need my FamMan. I am no longer a part of the hawkcel community here, whether mere birds or potential Fams. I would pine without my FamMan.*

Underground can't be good for you, Zem, Glyssa said, probably more chidingly than she should have.

I want to go. I will fly down and latch on your shoulder once you are on the girder.

Her stomach tightened with nerves. Going down into the ship didn't feel exactly right to her, either, though she thought she'd prefer it to being lost in the woods. She gave in. *A companion will be welcome.*

Thank you.

Glyssa stood at the entrance down to the ship, the break that had occurred during landing, closer than she'd ever been before. The long rust-colored beam angled down a good three stories to the actual opening into the ship. The other levels were sheered blank walls whose thickness couldn't be measured.

Thirty-eight

ou go down first, alone," the Holly woman said. "I have not been authorized to allow anyone else in there with you at this time." Her expression was warrior-stern, but compassion lived in her eyes. Glyssa hadn't expected that. She got the idea that the Holly woman and her compatriots would volunteer to help if they were allowed. Maybe they were curious, too, and Lady and Lord knew they might be more disciplined than the adventurers in the camp.

"Here's an air mask." Cornuta Holly handed it to Glyssa.

The woman had been helpful, greeting Glyssa as she'd reached the site, handing her off the stridebeast, accompanying Glyssa to her pavilion where she picked up a recordsphere and a datasphere that held the volume of Hoku's journal that dealt with the ship.

Holly had even opened the safe in the Elecampanes' tent and allowed Glyssa to take Jace's HeartGift. The spellshielded envelope was about as long and as wide as both of Glyssa's hands and seven centimeters deep. Flat enough that she could tuck it into the outer tunic she donned over her shirt.

Trago still hadn't been found. The guards believed he was hiding in the forest, and couldn't guess whether he would return to the encampment. He'd had help with his revenge against Jace, and no doubt had enough artifacts from *Lugh's Spear* to buy anything he wanted. So he could go to another secret landing field like Myrtus Stopper had and be whisked away to Druida City or Gael City or anywhere else on Celta.

FamWoman, FamWoman, RUN! Zem shrilled in her mind.

Several explosions hit the camp, roaring flames into the sky, concussing sound punched her ears. The guard assigned to the hole swore, didn't move. The others—the Holly commander—ran for the main camp.

Mouth hanging open, Glyssa watched tents collapse, flattening so she could see past the gathering circle. She turned in the direction of her pavilion, gasped. It was gone.

RUN! Zem yelled in her mind again, swooped down to land on her shoulder, pecked at her head. *Trago comes!*

And there the man was, skin tightly pulled over his skull, sweat gleaming on his face, spots under his armpits, along his shirt, desperate looking. He held something in his waving hand, raised his arm as if to throw. He was at the edge of the forest, long meters from her. Surely the projectile couldn't reach her, even with Flair.

DOWN! Zem flew into the hole, skimming along the glider.

Without thought, Glyssa followed, feeling the odd metal under her shoes, heard the rapid thump of her steps. The descent took longer than she'd anticipated, rushing at an angle down three full stories, using Flair to balance herself as she ran down into the gloom. She tripped at the end of the beam and over rocks at the bottom.

Here, here! Zem said. Even before she could see him, she stumbled toward him, hit her head on some sort of metal.

Move right, RUN! He flapped away into darkness. Panting a word she lit a spellglobe and hurried after.

Whoosh, bang! and glass broke behind her and another explosion at her back pushed her down the hallway. She attempted to stay on her feet, but lost her balance, fell and skidded along the floor, and screamed when something hot seared her scalp.

A huge bang reverberated throughout the ship, followed by a roaring, rushing of . . . earth? And Jace just *knew*, that the girder had fallen into the ship, the entrance filled with dirt.

He sent his mind questing to *see* the area beneath the breach in the ship, the hole. To no avail.

It seemed as if the walls of the huge ship pressed on him. He gasped for air, claustrophobia squeezed his mind.

They were trapped. He and Lepid. No easy way out. His heart hammered in his chest. Trapped and dying, slowly dying.

Could they possibly last the days, weeks maybe, until rescue?

He didn't think so.

Grabbing onto all his control, setting his teeth, he beat back fear.

Then he heard Glyssa scream. Close. Here in the ship.

Glyssa! Undisguised panic raged through their link from him to her. *Glyssa!* He didn't have a shred of quiet in his mind to check the link.

FAMWOMAN, Lepid shrieked mentally. His claws dug into Jace's chest. *Zem!*

"*ZEM!*" Jace yelled telepathically and out loud.

I . . . I'm fine, Glyssa sent, though he sensed her coughing.

I, too, am fine, Zem said. *I am down the corridor away from the explosion. I sensed the top of the corridor and FLEW. I have perched upon a large box. I am in the dark.*

Be right with you, Zem, Glyssa called.

Make a spell light! Lepid cried. Jace got the sense that the fox was more disconcerted by the lack of light than he.

I think we must save all our Flair energy, Zem said. Though he sounded calm, Jace knew from his link with his Fam that Zem could barely move from the panic coursing through him.

Lepid was accustomed to being in holes, underground dens. Jace was human and used to living in houses or tents. Zem had neither of those experiences. That he'd decided to come with Glyssa to save Jace humbled him.

I love you very much, Zem, Jace said, sending his Fam great love, composure.

I love you, too, FamMan, Zem said.

I LOVE MY FAMWOMAN! Lepid shouted.

We love each other, Glyssa said. *I am making a tiny, dim light. I am accustomed to threading through the underground storage areas of the PublicLibrary with such a spellglobe.* But Jace sensed her mouth was dry and she swallowed.

He rose from the bed and took hesitant steps toward the door, stopped when his foot nudged against Lepid. Jace couldn't help it, he could no longer stay on the bed. Like a boy waiting for his girl-friend to come, he sat cross-legged before the door.

Glyssa? Jace? This is Raz T'Elecampane. Can you hear me?

I can hear you, Raz, Glyssa replied.

So can I, said Jace.

And I can link in our Fams who are with us, Glyssa said.

Good you can hear. Unfortunately the rest of my news is bad. I have been told by Cornuta Holly that the whole camp has been affected by several explosions, Raz Elecampane told them steadily. *The mess tent, the workshop, our tent. Your nonfood no-time storage units remain, but your pavilion and all the furniture is gone.* He paused. *The land has shifted, the scenery changed. There is no way you can teleport out here to the camp.*

Jace thought Glyssa had stopped her progress down the hallway and leaned against one of the walls, maybe even trembling.

Raz went on, *We don't know where such incendiaries for the explosives came from. We had no such materials in the encamp-ment. The Holly guards believe that one of our recent visitors brought them to Trago. He's working with someone else. No doubt someone wealthier and of higher status who wants to shut down this operation or make it so costly that they can buy in and seize control.*

"Fligger," cursed Jace.

STUPS! whined Lepid.

Raz T'Elecampane's harsh chuckle came through the telepathic link. *We are all considering how to rescue you, and request you stay put for a couple of septhours. None of you are in immediate danger, right?*

No-oo, Glyssa said. But Jace sensed she ran rapidly toward him.

We will be in touch, T'Elecampane said. Jace got the idea that people surrounded the man, pestering him.

Some minutes later he heard Glyssa's footsteps echoing before her. His heart pumped with hope, with need, with the wish to see her again. He closed his eyes tight against the sting.

Lepid hopped off his lap and began to scratch at the door, whining.

"I'm coming!" Glyssa shouted. A tremor went through Jace at hearing her actual voice resound outside the door in the hollow corridor. "Let me record the Captain's Quarter's door, first."

Sniffing, Lepid thumped his butt on Jace's ankle. Both Glyssa's and Lepid's actions made Jace smile. He rubbed his face. She was only a couple of doors away.

Then she was there, right outside the door. He could feel her presence. "There's a control panel for the door to the right of it." The words spurted from his mouth.

"So I see," she said. "I'm increasing the light so I can examine the mechanism. Can you see it?"

"Not a glimmer," Jace said a little too heartily to sound naturally cheerful. He stood.

Snick. Snick. Snick. Zem pecking at the door. *I do not like this metal. I do not like this place.* Then, on the private channel to Jace, the bird said, *Lepid was a young fool to explore this terrible place.*

Thank you for coming, Jace said as more thumps and bangs came from outside.

"I've tried," Glyssa said. "The door crank won't move. I tried applying Flair power to it until I thought I'd break it, then I stopped."

"All right," Jace said. He wanted to yell.

"I checked Hoku's journal for data about the doors. He said they had schedules for some of the colonists to go in and retrieve their possessions and items they thought they might need to establish a town here, but the power was turned off and no one was supposed to be in the ship when the land beneath it gave way and it was lost." She paused. "He didn't know how much power there might be, but extrapolated that there could be some. It might have lasted, if we could find one of the control rooms."

"No," Jace said flatly. Cleared his throat. "Not until it is our last option."

"All right." Another pause. "I don't want to stay out here when you're in there!" Glyssa cried.

Me neither, said Zem.

Jace could actually hear her pacing. Thump, thump, thump-thump.

"We could at least die together," she said.

That had his stomach curling into a tiny ball. "You don't think help is coming? You're an important person."

"Not that important."

"You're best friends with a FirstFamilies Lord and Lady."

"I don't think they can get to us," she said in a small voice. "And I don't know what our air and food and water supplies are."

"Nothing much alive for Zem, that I know of. But you should stay out there. Out there, you can find food and water maybe. In here with us, you're stuck."

They were both stuck.

A few breaths of quiet passed, the only sound a low level whine by Lepid. He shivered in Jace's arms, feeling skinnier than before, even though they'd only missed two meals, max.

"I think if I tried to blow this door open with all my might I would harm you," Glyssa said.

A longer moment of silence, now. "I think you and Lepid should teleport to us," she finally said. "Zem and I can give you a good visual."

Yes! Lepid said. *I'm ready.*

Should Jace go with him or not? He decided not. "Lepid first. He's smaller and has different vision than I do—we won't have to merge our images. I can give him a Flair push, of course."

I do not need a push. I SEE the corridor like FamWoman and Zem. Nice and light, thank you FamWoman!

"You're welcome," Glyssa said.

I am counting down! One, Lepid fox; Two Lepid fox; Three! the FoxFam said it so fast that Jace didn't have a chance to send him energy.

Lepid vanished and excited barking came from outside the door. *Good to see you, FamWoman! Good to see you, Zem!* Jace couldn't hear the slurps of love but sensed them down his bond with Glyssa, which had expanded. For a moment he basked in the emotions he felt from her, the small sensations he received through their bond, the busyness of her mind. Then he narrowed it a bit.

I'm concentrating. Please send me images, he requested telepathically. They poured into him and he had to lean against the closed closet door. Zem's and Lepid's shades of colors were not the same, and not human, perspectives skewed. From Glyssa he got a great idea of the hallway. Lepid was right, she'd lit it nicely and not too bright.

Lepid yipped. *It is easy, FamMan!*

Jace figured if the fox could do it, he could, too. He latched onto the images that reinforced his recollection of the hall in the direction of going deeper into the ship. Yes, that's how those boxes were positioned, and the doors that were opened and closed.

Counting down, he projected. *One, Glyssa dear; two Zem Bird-Fam; THREE!*

A rush of Flair came from the trio outside the door, augmenting his as he fixed the image in his mind and 'ported.

This time he lit well, softly, and saw the tense face of Glyssa, the short flight of Zem heading toward him, before the bright light faded to dim when Glyssa extinguished several of her spellglobes.

She flung herself into his arms and he was glad to hold her, pulled her close, breathing in essence of Glyssa and the small, lingering smells of the world outside the alien ship that he took for granted.

Zem's claws pricked Jace's shoulders as he dug into the leather tunic, the familiar weight pleasing Jace. He felt the brush of Lepid's body as the fox danced around them.

We are out, Out, OUT! the Fam crooned.

"Yes, out of the chamber."

Glyssa looked up at him with a strained expression. "But not out of the ship. We are all still trapped down here." She shivered and Jace rubbed up and down her back.

"We'll work on that," he said.

A few minutes later he stepped over to the door of the quarters where he and Lepid had spent long septhours and studied the mechanism to the side of the door. When he put his hand in the cavity and touched the lever to open the door, he felt the taint of Trago's Flair. He turned the crank, grunted when it stopped and applied pressure. The metal broke off in his hands. Jace shook his head. "No way we could have gotten out by ourselves, or by this method."

"No," Glyssa said. "And I'm not sure we can get out of the ship by ourselves." She hesitated and said in an even smaller voice, "I don't even know if we can survive until someone comes and gets us." She blinked rapidly, stiffened her spine and when she spoke again, her voice was coolly logical. "There were farms, a conservatory—something like the Great Greensward on *Nuada's Sword*—here, wasn't there?" Glyssa asked.

"I paid attention to the blueprints," Jace teased gently. "Yes, about a quarter of the ship was given over to agriculture and growing." He hesitated. "It failed in some way, or wasn't enough to sustain the long voyage the way the colonists had imagined. The *Lugh's Spear* people needed help."

Glyssa nodded. "I remember that from the play, *Heart and Sword*. But maybe since then . . ."

"Four hundred years of darkness, of being underground, it couldn't have survived. Whatever food we find might have lost all nutritional value like the subsistence bars. I'm not sure whether we can reach other levels. We are on the sixteenth level now and the green ag area was one whole side of the third level."

"But those walls held during the landing, didn't they?" she asked, trying to remember without resorting to the recordsphere in her pocket. That knowledge hadn't been a priority of hers.

Lepid barked once. *I have been down one level.*

"Really?" Glyssa and Jace asked together.

Yes, there is a stairway. And down there I found an opening, a tube that smelled of once-growing things. His nose wrinkled and he sneezed. *Very, very bad smells.*

Jace's lips twisted. "Who knows, something *might* have mutated."

Images from horror vizes flickered through Glyssa's mind. She shivered. "Maybe we shouldn't find out."

Not by ourselves, Zem said. He shifted from foot to foot on Jace's shoulder. *I do not like being here.*

"It doesn't look good," Jace said.

I am cold, Zem said.

There is a big bag of clothing not too far down the hallway! Lepid said, sounding chipper now that she was here and they were all together. He trotted down the hall, into the darkness beyond Glyssa's spellglobe.

She followed slowly with Jace. "We are trapped."

"Sounds like."

"You didn't bring any food or water?" she asked.

"No."

Her smile trembled. "I didn't, either. No one told me I should and I didn't consider it."

"Without Trago's actions, we would have been fine." Jace's tone was casual.

"Did you try the water in the ship?" she asked.

"No, but maybe we should." Jace walked over to the nearest open door, checked the doorway, opened the panel for manual operation of the door, and touched the controls. No feel of any Flair.

A scraping sounded behind him, and he saw Glyssa moving a large box into the doorway.

"It's not heavy, but it's metal and constructed well," she said and frowned down on it. "I think it held subsistence bars."

Jace nodded and climbed over the box and into the room. Summoning a dim spell light, he went straight to the cleansing cubicle where a small sink was attached to the wall, and stared at the lever next to the spout.

That does not look like what is in the shower tent, Zem said.

"It doesn't work with Flair. Nothing in this ship works with Flair," Jace said.

Flair makes the world go around, Zem said.

Jace wasn't going to argue or lecture. Using muscle and a steady pressure, he pushed the lever all the way down. Nothing happened, not a creak, not a gurgle.

Glyssa joined him and they both stared at the tiny basin. "No water," she said.

"No," he said and waved for her to leave the room.

She did and he went back into the hallway, moved the box close to its original position.

"We probably wouldn't want to drink water that sat stagnant in pipes for four centuries anyway," she said.

"Not me," he said.

She shivered. "The ship is always this cold?"

"As far as I know. I'd like to see the entryway," Jace said.

Glyssa nodded and they turned back.

He reached out and took her hand, swung their arms, which had her smiling.

"Thank you for coming to save me."

"I couldn't do anything else."

His chest tightened. "Thank you," he said again, unable to find more words.

They reached the place where the ship had broken, and stood staring at the pile of rock and dirt. "Doesn't look like anything we can handle ourselves," Jace said.

Thirty-nine

Raz contacted them again. *We only have two Flaired earth-moving machines, the best on the market, but they can't tunnel so deep in time.*

Before they died of thirst. Two to four days, max. "Figured that," Jace muttered. He held Zem and stroked the bird.

Another mind stream from Raz, *The greatest building machines are stored on* Nuada's Sword, *the starship in Druida City. I don't know if they are in working order or available. However, the people who could run those machines are Captain Ruis Elder and Dani Eve Elder.*

"Nulls," Glyssa said flatly. "They can't get here on an airship, they would interfere with the Flaired flying spells."

"Figured that, too," Jace said.

Raz said delicately, *I am sure you understand the problems in asking for help from Captain Elder and his daughter.*

"Not to mention the Elecampanes still want to keep this project under their control," Jace said, with no bitterness.

Glyssa lifted her brows.

"What? Not the Elecampanes' fault that we got trapped in here," Jace said.

"I think if we perish they will have significant problems," Glyssa said. "People will blame them." Glyssa shrugged. "Too late now."

Jace's grin was swift. "Let's hope not."

Not looking good, Zem grumbled.

Raz's telepathic voice interrupted them. *We will return to the camp. I am only a few septhours away with the airship. Del is . . . she'll be back in a day. We can send images to you, Glyssa, pull you out, then you can help with Jace and the others.*

Jace's face set into impassivity. He said nothing, but his shuttered gaze met hers.

Perhaps that would work, but Glyssa doubted it. If it had been only her, she'd have risked it.

No, Raz, she sent firmly. *You have a load of passengers there at the Deep Blue Sea, don't tell me they all stayed in camp. Didn't the cross-folk head off overland to somewhere else?* From his lack of reply, she was right. *You must stay for them. I am not sure how long we could survive down here. We have no water. We are reluctant to explore the ship and waste our energy.* She took a breath and continued. *You and I are not that close that I would trust our link. Not even if it were Laev and you. I'm sure there is only limited Flair available to you, I will not be the first one out and leave my loved ones.*

She moved close to Jace, hugged him, looked down at Lepid, whose ears had quivered with fear. "We stay together."

I WILL find a way to rescue you, though it beggars me! Laev T'Hawthorn shouted.

Lepid and Zem gasped, obviously hearing the GreatLord. Jace grimaced.

Glyssa bit her lips. How dire their situation was began sinking in. Her joy at finding Jace and Lepid completely gone. She swallowed and met Jace's eyes. Shaking her head, she whispered, "All the greatest Flaired mages in Celta can't save us."

And she was surprised by a tender look and carefree smile. *There is freedom in hopelessness,* his thought that she believed she wasn't supposed to catch.

"I know," Jace said.

The last-ditch idea that had been cycling in the back of her mind jumped forward and off her tongue. "I think we should try to teleport home."

Jace frowned. "Home?"

She sucked in a desperate breath. "Home. To Druida."

His mouth actually dropped open. "What! Thousands of kilometers!"

Lifting her chin, she said, "I can teleport to Verde Valley from my home in Druida City. That's—" She couldn't recall the exact distance, hundreds of kilometers, though. "That's not close."

He appeared stunned.

Yes! Lepid wagged his tail. *Let's do that!*

"Thousands. Of. Kilometers," Jace said, shuddering. He dropped her hands.

She rubbed her arms. "What are our other options? Scavenging through the ship, hoping to find food and water. We'd just end up waiting on others, depending on others."

His gray eyes deepened and his mouth turned down. "There is that." But he turned and paced—not going far, not beyond her spell light. He glanced in the open doors.

I do not like it here, Zem said. *It is too cold all the time. There is no sunlight. There is no wind. There are no trees.*

Lepid took up the negative litany. *There is no food. Not one little mousie or insect. There is no brook to lap at with fresh water.*

"Yeah, yeah," Jace said. His hands were clasped behind his back, his head down as he paced.

He looked fine, but fear crept along each nerve in Glyssa's body, screaming for her to *do something.* She could be patient. She could wait. Truly. If she knew for certain she'd be saved, *they'd* be saved. But she didn't. She only saw slow and painful death or a terrible risk.

Jace turned back, chin lowered. When he raised his head his face was grim and he flipped a gesture at the hallway with lost and forgotten items around them. "We could scavenge here, for sure, but might not find anything useful."

"That's right," she said.

"And we all could last, what, maybe a full eightday?"

Instinctively at the thought of no water, she wet her lips. "Maybe. Maybe longer if we went into Flaired trances." She didn't think Lepid was able to hold a Flaired trance, too young and nervy.

"You really don't believe any mages GreatLord Laev T'Hawthorn recruits to save us any way they could would have a chance?" Jace asked.

"No."

"And we'll get weaker and weaker." He lifted his hand to stroke Zem. "We're about as strong as we'll ever be, right now."

"Yes." Her pulse rushed in her ears, accepting their death. Not only hers, but Jace's and their wonderful animal companions. She might have sacrificed herself for them if it would do any good, but it wouldn't. She wanted to live, her HeartMate to live, her Fam and Jace's Fam to live.

Jace grimaced. "With all the options for teleporting to somewhere in camp gone, we don't have any choice but to risk the long chance."

She nodded. "I agree." She paused for a breath, then said, "I think it would be best if we trie—if we teleported to my bedroom. I know that room very well, was in it every day for many years. The rest of you have been there, too, so you can add your individual images and knowledge of it. That will be a benefit for all of us." She smiled at Zem. "It will include your perch, which you know the best." She actually sounded confident. "I know the light, and all the furnishings. No one should be there. My Family will be at work in the library."

We can do it! Lepid gamboled around the hallway. Glyssa's gaze met Jace's uncommonly serious one. He thought they'd die, too. He glanced up and down the hallway. "Better than staying here, fading away."

"Yes."

"Then let's do it now." Frowning, Jace lifted Zem from his shoulder. "I think Zem should be held closer."

And me, too! Lepid said.

"What about slings?" Glyssa asked.

"Those would work," Jace said.

They rooted around in a couple of bags of the colonists' pitiful belongings before they found some material and fashioned slings that hung against their chests for both Fams. Jace placed Zem carefully in his, tightened it.

Zem asked, *What happens if we don't make it?*

"Another unknown," Glyssa said. She kept her tone light. "We might disintegrate. Throwing all our effort into this, everything we each have, holding nothing back, we'll probably go unconscious. So, ah"—she cleared her throat—"if we, uh, materialize in, say, a mountain in one of the ranges between here or there, we will probably never know. I'm sure it's quick!"

Flying into a mountain often is, Zem said.

Actually, Camellia, who'd been in the next room from a man who'd died teleporting, had told Glyssa his scream had lasted long, agonizing seconds. But he'd been conscious at the time. She didn't think they would be.

"I'm sure it's quick," she repeated.

A couple of minutes later their preparations were done. Glyssa leaned back to stare into Jace's beautiful misty gray eyes. "You never said what your primary Flair is."

His mouth twisted. "I did tell you that I'm not strong enough in psi power to manifest a primary Flair."

"I disagree. You had defined Passages. You made a HeartGift." She gestured to the bespelled envelope. "Your secondary Flair, leather working, is intricate and gorgeous. That indicates a powerful primary Flair."

He scoffed a sound of disagreement.

She tightened her arms around him. "I think I know what your Flair is. It's extremely subtle, but I've deduced it."

"Deduced it, eh?" He smiled.

"Yes." She framed his face with her hands, made sure his entire focus was on her. "It's luck."

"What!"

"You're luckier than a man should be, especially with regard to dangerous, perhaps potentially fatal events."

He blinked in astonishment. "You must be joking."

"No. I'm not. Think of all the hazardous ventures you've been in, all the chances you've taken, and you're still whole and sane, haven't had any major Healings. You've been able to do pretty much as you please all of your life and recently you came into a small inheritance. You're phenomenally lucky, Jace."

"You really believe this."

"I do. And you need to, also. That's what I'm counting on to get us home." She glanced at Lepid. "When we teleport, you must use *all* your Flair, saving nothing. You must believe that Jace's luck will see us through."

I do. I DO! Lepid looked at Jace with liquid eyes. *I KNOW Fam-Man is lucky. We will be ALL RIGHT!*

Zem said, *He is lucky, and we who associate with him are lucky, too.* He hesitated, then added. *I will use all of my Flair in this tele-portation. I will hold nothing back, though it kills me.*

"Right," Glyssa said with only a small wince. He didn't have to have said that last bit. She met the hawkcel's eyes and nodded, then looked back at Jace, *willing* him to accept this theory. It was a good theory. Perhaps even true. She refused to doubt.

"And you must not doubt, either, Jace. Lover. HeartMate. We need your total belief."

His eyes went distant, as if he considered his life. "Maybe you're right."

"I *am* right. You are phenomenally lucky."

"Phenomenally lucky."

" 'Say it three and it will be,' " she said an old children's charm. Anything that would help. "Phenomenally lucky."

"Phenomenally lucky, phenomenally lucky," Jace said, his lips curving in a smile. "I'm phenomenally lucky to have you and Zem and Lepid."

Phenomenally lucky, phenomenally lucky, phenomenally lucky, chanted the Fams.

He picked up the envelope that held his HeartGift and grimaced. "I'll need to remove the spellshield, and when I do—"

"We'll be swamped with sexual energy." A notion wisped through Glyssa's mind. "Wait, wait!"

He tilted his head. "Yeah?"

"Count down before you release the spell." She squeezed her eyes shut, trying to recall a spell she and her friends had practiced in their teenaged years, transmuting energy from emotional turmoil to physical energy. They hadn't done it very often, because it had left them jittery. Still, she and Jace and the Fams would need every iota of energy they could scrape up. She wet her lips, saw Jace focus on her mouth, then meet her eyes with a smile. "I think . . . I think I might be able to snatch that sexual energy and transform it to, um, regular physical and Flair energy, store it in our bodies. There will be, um, increased arousal, but I don't want to waste any of our time or strength on sex."

Jace laughed. "Having sex is not a waste of anything."

Embarrassment painted hot spots on her cheeks. "Maybe not, but our energy would be better spent making sure we can teleport out of here."

He nodded. "All right. One, HeartGift mine; two, Glyssa mine; three, Flair is *ours!*" He dropped the shield. A teenage boy's lust, her HeartMate's young sexuality hit her with intimate need. Her body clenched. Opening her eyes wide she saw the red orange energy, yanked at it, flipped it, recited the four rhyming couplets.

The intense yearning changed shape into bright blue energy, radiating Flair. An unexpected source of power. Inhaling, she halved it, took some into her body, feeling the lightning jolt, blew the rest to Jace and saw it hit him, sink into him, arc his body.

For a couple of minutes they trembled with the aftermath. Her finger shaking, she pointed at the envelope he'd dropped. Zem hopped over and snipped the soft string tie with his beak, pushed the top up and open.

Glyssa gasped at the beauty of the small rounded rectangular pursenal. Deep wine red, the darker color she preferred to licorice red, the gold of simple and elegant curlicues gleamed in a pattern that settled into her as much as the Flair coating it had. The most innately pleasing design to her.

"*Your* pattern, no one else's," Jace said. Stiffly he leaned down and plucked it from the envelope, offered it to her. A gold filigree clasp showed on the front. "My HeartGift for you, to you."

She took it, tears dewing her eyes. "Thank you."

He inclined his head in a dignified nod. She tucked the pursenal in her tunic.

"One last thing to do." She flung all of her bonds wide. *Family and friends. Jace and Zem, Lepid and I are trapped in the ship* Lugh's Spear *with little hope of rescue. We are teleporting to my bedroom on three. If you can help us, give us Flair boosts down our bonds, please do.*

Madness! cried her mother. *No, we must talk—*

Shut up! Her father cut off any more of her mother's protest to Glyssa.

I love you, I will help, Camellia said.

I love you, but WAIT! Tiana Mugwort said. *I can put an emergency circle together here at GreatCircle Temple to help you. We can channel the light of the Lady and Lord. Give me twenty minutes, please!*

The Licorices are leaving for GreatCircle Temple NOW, Glyssa's sister said. *By glider with the emergency alarm running, to save our energy and help my sister and HeartMate.*

Glyssa looked at Jace. He appeared stunned and blinked rapidly. "A GreatCircle Temple ritual to help us."

"You met my friend Tiana, she's a priestess there."

"I'd forgotten." He grimaced, rubbed his hands over his arms. "Twenty more minutes."

I will form a circle here at the Deep Blue Sea, Laev's voice came even more strongly than her close friends, he was so much more powerful in Flair. *Twenty minutes.* As a FirstFamilies GreatLord, he was accustomed to leading rituals for his Family several times a month and at GreatCircle Temple at least once a year. Like Tiana, he could put together a ritual in a hurry. *I have alerted my allies in Druida City. Those who are willing and able to participate at GreatCircle Temple are on their way*

Thank you ALL! We will wait for twenty minutes and I will try to connect to you all, Glyssa said.

Jace looked at her questioningly.

She shrugged. "I don't know if this works. I don't even know if Tiana or Laev knows if this will work, if we can get Flair from them, help from them through emotional bonds."

Stroking her face, he said, "I am phenomenally lucky to have you in my life. Even knowing there are others ready and willing to help us, eases my mind." He led her to a large, soft-looking sack in the corridor. "Let's all cuddle together, get warm, save our strength and energy for the teleportation." Once again she sent out mentally to all she was linked to, *Please let us know when you are ready, our energy is fading keeping ourselves warm and with light.*

She received a shocked exclamation from her mother, grim determination from Laev . . . and settled down against Jace.

With all of them together, her spell light as faint as she could make it and still give comfort, she settled on Jace's lap and Lepid crawled on hers.

"Put the light out," Jace said.

So she did and let herself relax and quieted her mind. Not only light was comforting. Sharing the darkness with the others— tunneling her fingers in Lepid's thick fur to keep her hands warm and reassure him, smelling Jace, her HeartMate, and the forest scent Zem carried on his feathers—all satisfied a deep need within her. And, oh, how she'd rather be lost in the forest than trapped in this ship! But she'd tensed up again and had to ease her muscles. To her surprise, though Jace's vitality was still evident, his muscles, too, were loose.

"This is nice," he said, his voice a little sleepy.

"Yes."

She let thought go, thin to tendrils and just felt, enjoyed the moment, this precious moment.

Sometime later, she received Tiana's thought. *We are ready for you. I will lead the ritual but the high priestess of GreatCircle Temple is here and will help. The high priest could not make it.*

Our circle is ready, Laev added immediately.

Glyssa stirred and sat up straight. "They're ready." Her pulse sprinted faster, her heart picking up beat. Fear. No, *excitement.*

"I heard," Jace said. He sounded completely calm. She peeked at their link. He *was* calm. More than she.

Zem's feathers rustled. *I heard, too. I am ready. It will be good to get out of this metal tube.*

I am ready for another adventure! Lepid sounded energized by his nap. *We will be heroes again.*

"Well, we'll certainly be famous," Glyssa said drily. "One way or another." She wondered if their bodies would be fou—No! No negativity.

She lit a spellglobe. Adjusting her sling for Lepid, she placed him in it. He stretched up and licked her face and she giggled.

Jace smiled back at her, slipping Zem into his own sling.

She faced her man, her lover, her HeartMate and their hands met and fingers entwined.

Still holding his gaze, she said, "I think it's time to go." She leaned in and kissed Jace, cherished the softness of his mouth, his taste. Then Jace embraced both her and Lepid. She looked at Zem in the makeshift sling strapped to Jace. "All right and tight?"

He bobbed his head.

Sucking in a deep breath, she returned her gaze to Jace's. That his face might be the last she ever saw pleased and consoled her.

She squeezed his hands. Kept her stare locked on his. "We do this together."

"Yes."

"And give it our last iota of strength. Everything. All or nothing."

He winked, as if once the decision was made and he was ready to roll the dice, he was more settled in the matter. A thousand doubts plagued her each second.

"All or nothing." He grinned.

All or nothing! piped up Lepid.

All or nothing, said Zem. He closed his eyes.

Glyssa did, too.

For the last time, she opened herself, gasped at what her inner sight showed her. The huge link between her and Jace had enlarged to more than heart-sized and flowed with sensations from all aspects of themselves, physical, mental, emotional, spiritual. They were linked together, and there was the HeartBond, lying in golden coils.

Jace said telepathically, *I thought the HeartBond only showed up during sex.*

Glyssa shrugged. *I don't know that anyone has ever studied that aspect of being HeartMates.* She let her smile show her love, her unconditional trust. *We might check that out together when we get home.*

He nodded, serious now. "I want to HeartBond with you now." His shoulders shifted. "I have the energy from my HeartGift jazzing in me. It was originally sexual, I bet that will help forge a Heart-Bond without sex."

She thought about the whole matter. "HeartBonding would be good, maybe give us all even more of a chance to teleport well."

To survive.

"More," he whispered. "Because it is right that I show you how much I care."

He took the golden loops of the HeartBond and threw them to her, and she let them wrap around herself, bring her close together to him . . . and, yes, there was the fizz of lust, of sexual need. Not to be fulfilled now.

This was not how she'd ever dreamed she'd be connected with her love, her lover, her HeartMate. She swallowed tears.

What was separate in her was no longer. What was hidden in her—and Jace, too—was revealed but the overwhelming memories, feelings, needs, flaws, came too swiftly for her to sort out. Some sort of terrible memory featuring his parents—his father's death, but they dared not think of death. She concentrated on life, on hope.

He groaned and she whimpered.

We are one, Jace said, awe in his voice.

"Ready to teleport to my bedroom in Druida City?" she asked.

Ready! Lepid said, tucking his nose between her arm and her side.

Ready! Zem said, hidden in his sling.

"Ready," Jace said. He began layering the memories he had of her bedroom from his own perspective. Cozy, female, reflecting Glyssa. The wide bedsponge, the elegant and simple carving on the frame. He let her take care of painting the light right. Zem's perch that Gwydion Ash had made, sturdy golden wood that matched no other wood in the room. Wood, beautiful wood, natural Celtan fabrics. He recalled the sight and feel of those, so different from the complete alienness of this ship.

Zem's visualization merged with his, skewing the image a bit, as did Lepid's. Then Glyssa absorbed them all, set them all so Jace could nearly believe he was there. Jace's heart lifted as he fixed *belief* that they would be there, shortly. They had so much going for them. *They would succeed!*

"Counting down," Glyssa said, sounding as serious as always, though there was just the touch of breathiness in her voice. He sent her love, belief, love, acceptance. Love.

They all joined in a small circle of love, of total dedication and belief.

"One, Jace, Zem; two, Lepid; *three, and home!*"

And they weren't in the ship.

No, NO! You MUST die for making her leave me! shrieked a mad wind in Jace's head, Trago. He felt a slight tug, as if a small hook caught in his clothes. He could *not* allow the evil man to hurt his Glyssa. They were all in this together. Diverting a bit of Flair, he *smacked* the man. Heard some long echoing scream. Jerked as he felt the guy die. The visualization vanished.

He scrambled to build the image again, held it hard.

But knew they were in trouble.

Forty

Teleportation usually was instantaneous. But this lasted for long, long seconds. Glyssa's chest squeezed and she couldn't breathe. She struggled to draw air. What of Jace? What of Lepid? She didn't *feel* them, not physically nor emotionally. A scream stuck in her chest *hurt*.

She would die alone. Though they should all be together, they would each die alone.

She might have felt the tiniest *boost* from Laev and Camellia and Tiana. She *did* "see" a great burst of white energy from the direction they were going—Druida. Had the sensation of passing long miles.

No! Stup! Visualize your room! The light as autumn came, the slant of the sun. How it sparkled on the prisms in her window. Her comforter, her bed . . .

And her vision went black, white, yellow.

She crumpled to the ground, tried once more to drag a breath in, couldn't. Struggled to open her lashes. Raw, raw pain against her eyeballs. Jace, matted hair, gray-looking complexion. Lepid limp in her arms. She couldn't see Zem.

Still felt none of them.

Couldn't inhale.

The floor vibrated. She thought she saw bold, eye-searing colors of Flair as women rushed to her.

Then nothing.

*F*ists *pounded on Jace's chest, Flair enveloped him.* "Breathe, damn you!" shouted someone. It hurt, all of him hurt, but with another compression of his chest, he hauled in air.

He opened his eyes, saw a pretty rug on gleaming wood. Memory spun just out of reach.

Someone rolled him to his back and he stared up into wide green eyes set in a fierce face. The woman looked like someone he should know. She stuck her fingers into his dry mouth, opened it, shoved an oxygen bulb between his lips and squeezed.

Incredible air. Wonderful air. His mind cleared a bit. He still didn't know who she was, but he recognized Glyssa's bedroom.

Shouldn't Glyssa be close? Where was she? He *needed* her.

"*Breathe!*" someone shouted to his left. There came a tiny sound, then the stench of foxy piss, definitely not Glyssa.

Glyssa? The little call speared excruciating pain in his head. A tiny moan, also not Glyssa. *Lepid?* Jace slowly formed the Fam's name in his head.

"We're here," said a woman's voice from a distance. "We're taking the Fams immediately." A small woman and a large young man ran in, cast shadows on him but didn't look at him, then darted from the room.

Another thump on Jace's chest, the bulb replaced. He'd caught his breath, hadn't he? Stopped breathing again.

Lepid was here, but where was Glyssa? More fear swept through him. Zem! Zem should have been strapped on his chest.

Why?

He shut his eyes, but shuddered at the darkness behind him. Fear of the dark clawed and snapped and ate at him.

Opening his eyelids he saw the sunlight, blessed light from Bel, felt as if he'd been reborn from an alien and cold dark to this wonderful room. The Healer was wiping him with a warm cloth, taking strange smelling grime from his face.

The ship! *Lugh's Spear.* The terrible risk of teleportation.

He'd made it!

But had the others? *GLYSSA!* he screamed mentally, hurting his own head. He couldn't feel their bond, fumbled for it. Closed his eyes again to find all the bonds he had, saw nothing. Not to Lepid, not to Zem, not to Glyssa.

She could have died. HeartBound people did, and the remaining spouse died within the year. He wouldn't linger if she was gone . . . just let the darkness take him, not fight against death and cycling on the wheel of stars until his next life . . . and no one could guarantee that they'd meet and love again in their next lives. Maybe she'd like someone else better.

Stup! He should have cherished her more, spent more time with her, acknowledged their bond instead of being careless and selfish for so long.

The Healer moved close with another bulb. "Glyssa," he said. She frowned as if she hadn't heard him. Everything took so much effort.

"Glyssa!" he yelled. Her name came out as the barest hoarse whisper.

A mask slipped over the Healer's face, and he knew that was *bad*.

"Glyssa has been transported to Primary HealingHall and is being tended by FirstLevel Healer Lark Holly."

For sure, bad.

"Want . . . there," he said.

Frowning, the Healer bent close to his lips.

"Want. To. Go. To. Her," he said, once again using up all his strength. Lord and Lady knew how long it would take to regain regular energy and Flair, weeks, months, *years*?

"I'm not sure that would be good for either of you."

"HeartMates, HeartBound!"

"Oh!" She looked into the other room. "Can you come help me get GentleSir Bayrum into a glider?" With an anti-grav spell, she raised his body. "We've all decided that teleporting you is not a good idea."

He shuddered, rippling in the air, a very weird sensation. A big tough-looking guy came in. "Remove the spell, I'll carry him."

Jace grimaced.

"I don't think so, Garrett, he's not breathing well on his own. No putting him over your shoulder. I want him flat."

"Zem?" Jace managed before she stuck another bulb in his mouth and watched with narrowed eyes as it went in and out as he breathed.

"Your Fams are with Danith D'Ash and her son."

He should have known that, hadn't he heard them? What was wrong with him? He sucked harder on the bulb.

"You'll be fine," the Healer said.

He wasn't sure of that, and when he bumped against the stairway rail and blackness overcame him again, he screamed into the darkness before it gobbled him.

Jace awoke sometime later, disgusted with himself. He'd never been afraid of the dark. He'd always been excited by going down into *Lugh's Spear.* Granted, the last few septhours trapped there had not been fun. Or even good. But they'd been manageable. Even taking the risk to die fast instead of slow had been okay.

He didn't know when he'd get the nerve to teleport again.

A groan escaped him and he tried to open his eyes. Footsteps bustled up to him and gently wiped his eyelids with a warm softleaf. His eyes must have crusted over, then, and why now? Why not when he awoke the first time? Had he wept, had stuff leaked out of his eyes due to fear? Had he *bled*?

But he pried his lashes open to look around. Still felt like moving a mountain to turn his head. He was in the richest room he'd ever experienced in his life—some sort of tapestry-type curtains of deep green and light blue shimmered. The chairs and counters were of a solid, gleaming dark wood. He lay on an excellent bedsponge and atop him draped a soft cover. But his senses weren't so dull that he didn't know a HealingHall room when he was in one.

Slowly, moving in tiny increments, he straightened his head, turned it toward the right.

And saw Glyssa. He jolted, adrenaline rushed into his body and it managed to jacknife him up.

"Easy," said the Healer, bracing his upper arms with her hands.

"I should know you," he replied. Still sounded terrible, but the words came out at a reasonable pace and loudness.

She smiled, more than just a Healer's smile, something personal for him. "Artemisia Primross, I'm the sister to Tiana Mugwort, one of Glyssa's best friends."

Instead of grunting again, he nodded. The fog was clearing from his mind. Probably meant he didn't have brain damage, always a plus.

Glyssa appeared completely still, her expressive face immobile. On the far side of the bed a pump stood, with large tentacles, pressing her chest evenly. Her lips were barely open. He couldn't tell whether she breathed on her own or not.

"Is she all right? What's wrong with her?" He leaned forward, but his legs weren't working right. Artemisia easily kept him from leaving the examination table.

"Mostly exhaustion, the same as with you and your Fams."

"The Fams, are they all right?"

"I haven't heard from D'Ash."

"Can you scry and ask her?"

Artemisia hesitated, and he got the impression that she didn't want to hear any bad news, either.

"Glyssa is okay?" he pressed.

"I—we— . . . She should live."

His heart pounded. May as well ask. "Will she have brain damage?"

Artemisia pursed her lips. "The preeminent mind-Healer scanned both of you and is optimistic that we Healed enough of the damage that the brain itself will continue to work with the spells that we placed."

Ouch. Didn't sound good.

Artemisia met his eyes. "It doesn't seem as if the ritual we did for you helped much."

"I didn't realize you were there."

She nodded. "I was, many were."

Blowing out a breath, he said, "I didn't feel you, but Glyssa was mostly in charge of the teleportation. She should be able to tell you more about that."

"I understand. Just to let you know, there will be more than one nobleman or noblelady to question you about the whole matter of this extreme teleportation."

Jace managed to lift shaky hands to his head, run them through his hair. His scalp itched as if it was covered in dried sweat.

"When will Glyssa wake up?" he asked. She *would* wake up. He wouldn't let doubt seep into his cracked mind, creep into his fearful heart.

"We're not sure," Artemisia said.

The door opened and the tough guy walked in, this time Jace could put a name to him. "Garrett Primross."

"I scried the Ashes, like you asked," he said, confirming that Jace had been under observation somehow. Was Primary HealingHall an intelligent structure? Not quite, he thought, so it wasn't the building spying on him. One of the walls must be fake, a window covered by an illusion to the occupants.

Voice tight, he asked, "How are our Fams?"

"Much like you two. They both live. The fox is better off than the hawkcel."

"Zem." Jace's heart squeezed. He looked at an immobile Glyssa, raised his voice. "Glyssa, come on, wake up for me, darling."

He stared at Garrett, lifted an arm slowly. "Help get me over there."

The man grimaced and strode over, set his arm around Jace's upper body and Jace's arm around his shoulders.

Praying his feet would work, Jace accepted help down to the floor. He could barely feel the pressure against his soles. His knees were weak.

Garrett said nothing as they shuffled extremely slowly toward Glyssa. Neither did the Healer.

There came an exclamation from someone who opened the door while Jace was on the long trip of five paces, but until the Licorice Family moved into his vision, he had no idea who'd entered.

Fasic T'Licorice came to Jace's other side and offered support, and the inching along went on. Jace was surprised by the two men. Neither pushed him, neither seemed impatient. Not like he would have been. He'd have also wanted to leave the room as soon as possible.

Finally the trio of them reached Glyssa's bedside. Artemisia waved Garrett away, and gave Jace another oxygen bulb. He breathed a while and prayed that his energy and Flair and regular strength would recover, refused to entertain the thought that he'd be dragging himself around the rest of his life. His shortened life, he was sure, if he didn't recuperate.

Artemisia helped him prop himself against the bed so he could stand. Glyssa's father went to the top of the bedsponge. Her mother joined her HeartMate.

"Hey, baby," T'Licorice said, stroking back a bouncy strand of her hair.

An idea wormed its way through Jace's head. He lowered the bulb and cleared his throat. "Sir, Lady, do you have bonds with Glyssa? I can't feel mine." He made sure he didn't sound pitiful.

The older Licorices joined hands, gazed at each other.

"I can feel her, faintly," said her sister, probably at the end of the bed. It took Jace a minute to turn his head, he was using all his energy to stand and hold the oxygen bulb back up to his mouth. Her face showed dried tearstains and raw nostrils. As he watched, she pulled a softleaf from her large, formal sleeve and wiped her nose, then blew it.

"I have a bond with my youngest child," said D'Licorice. "Again, it is faint, but it is there." She blew out a breath. "She lives."

By the time Jace got his head swiveled in their direction, T'Licorice had his lips pressed together, met Jace's stare with torment in his eyes. "I have faith the bond will return as she gets stronger." His sigh was heavy and he shook his head. "I took part in the emergency ritual. With the high priestess there we raised a great deal of Flair. We—I did not feel my daughter tap into that energy for your ordeal."

The man's gaze got bluer as his face paled. "You two—"

"Four," Jace corrected.

T'Licorice dipped his head. "Four. You four did it all on your own. I wouldn't have thought it possible."

"We had to," Jace said. He held out the bulb to Artemisia and his fingers barely shook. Progress? He hoped so. After the Healer took the breath support object, Jace leaned forward and kissed Glyssa on the mouth, swept his tongue over her lips to taste her, let her taste him, thrust the tip of it at her teeth. Her mouth opened and she inhaled audibly.

"Very good!" Artemisia said. The Healer stood by the chest pump, sharp gaze on Glyssa.

Jace straightened, took her limp, warm fingers in his left hand, stroked her cheek with his right hand. "Time to wake up, Glyssa, HeartMate."

Her sister gasped a second before his lover did. The pump automatically stopped and removed itself from the bedsponge, trundling into the corner.

"Open your eyes, HeartMate mine, my Glyssa," Jace said, then added, "People are waiting on you. I'm waiting on you."

Breath sighing out on a long groan, Glyssa did, touched her tongue to her lips. Her mouth formed the word, "Dry."

"She needs water here," Jace said, altered his body so it looked like he leaned insouciantly against her bedsponge, not that he was propped against it.

Artemisia hurried up with a coarsely woven folded softleaf with a corner that looked like it held orange juice. Glyssa's parents propped up her shoulders. Her eyes opened, but her gaze didn't shift. Jace knew what that was all about.

"You're really tired," he said. "I am, too."

Again he read her lips. "Lep-id?"

"The Fams are at the Ashes, being treated like we are."

Her lips showed the tiniest trace of a pout.

"Glad to see you back," her father said gruffly. He bent and kissed her forehead.

"Back," whispered Glyssa.

Jace went weak, swallowed. "Move her over and help me up."

Garret was there and T'Licorice, helping him, while Artemisia and Glyssa's sister shifted her. Her wavery moan wrenched at him, but not enough that he stopped the action he wanted.

Even when he was helped onto his side to look at her, no embarrassment touched him. Only gratitude and triumph that they'd succeeded.

The door opened. "The Fams insisted we return so they can be with their companions," announced the young Gwydion Ash. He settled Zem—Jace could smell his bird—close to Jace's head.

A very thin and scruffy-haired Lepid was placed near Glyssa. Jace wondered if he looked so bad. He supposed so.

"HeartMate," he said, and moved his hand to touch Glyssa. Then he fell asleep.

This time he thought they'd all wake up.

Forty-one

$\mathcal{A}$ week passed and Jace, Glyssa, and the Fams were recovering. The Elecampanes had shown up a few days after Jace's and Glyssa's ordeal and told them what had happened at camp—how they'd found Trago dead at the bottom of a cliff, and how they'd brought in a barracks for the Holly guards for the upcoming winter. They'd already closed the camp.

Raz and Del had brought Glyssa's file no-times and the materials Jace had left in the workshop tent. He'd turned over the brooch to Del D'Elecampane and Lepid and the older fox, Shunuk, had had a session where Lepid had told Shunuk of his various caches that held antiquities.

As for the brooch, Del had consulted with the great jeweler, T'Ash, and the starship *Nuada's Sword* and the piece was called a cameo and probably originated on old Earth, not the ship. A great find. They'd determined that the room Lepid and Jace had been trapped in had belonged to a female lieutenant who had survived the landing and the long trek to Druida City and had founded a Grand-House that had since died out.

The AllCouncils of Celta had voted to establish a museum for the *Lugh's Spear* artifacts, hired Antenn Blackthorn-Moss to design it, and had purchased the cameo for an outrageous sum that put a good amount in each member of the crew's pockets. As Jace had speculated, the cameo had sparked a new fashion craze. Laev T'Hawthorn had been the first to commission one of Camellia from T'Ash.

Glyssa's friends were often in D'Licorice Residence and soon Jace considered them like younger sisters, sometimes annoying, but often just thinking of the Family he'd acquired filled him with warmth. So had meeting with a banker regarding the middling inheritance his father had left.

That afternoon Jace sat with Glyssa on his lap in the main library of D'Licorice Residence, being "debriefed." Both Laev and Camellia Hawthorn were there, along with a bunch of lords and ladies and the Elecampanes.

A large Fam bed was set near the fire and held a small fox curled around a hawkcel, Lepid and Zem.

"Glyssa thinks my Flair manifests as passive luck, especially with regard to near-fatal events," Jace said.

"Luck!" Del D'Elecampane frowned at him.

"Hmm," Laev said, with a gleam in his eye. "Maybe I should take you on as a partner in a couple of my riskier ventures." He turned his purple gaze to Del. "Face it, if any other of your staff had gone down into that ship and died—something we think was masterminded by a Druidan noble working with the late and unlamented Trago, and we *will* find him or her—this project would be considered cursed for generations."

He waved a hand. "There are plenty of other interesting expeditions and explorations and places nearer to Druida City and Gael City to build communities that people would have preferred to go to instead of the excavation of *Lugh's Spear*."

"But Jace went down, and he's HeartBound with Glyssa," Camellia pointed out. "And she is a determined person . . . and Trago could have been a whole lot more efficient with those explosives of his. He didn't really want to kill anyone except Jace, and you had no casualties in camp."

"That's because after the first explosion, everyone scattered into the countryside except the guards," Raz said. He squeezed Del's hand. "Good call on those Hollys. They all survived, too, and I don't think Trago would have cared if one or more had died."

"The bottom line is that the project is still viable, you have a very tight camp community that is motivated to work with you," Laev said.

Del was nodding. "More, we have the basis of a town, and we'll be getting materials for permanent housing sent soon. This will be our last winter here in Druida City and Verde Valley. In the spring we will get back to work on the camp and on the town."

"That will give us plenty of time to plan," Jace said.

"You're definitely coming?" Jace had never seen Del's face light up so, she was usually serious. A warm feeling welled that he'd pleased her. He liked her. That emotions were coming back inside him was something to celebrate, too.

"Yes," Glyssa said. "You'd better plan a PublicLibrary, too. We have plenty of extra volumes in the main one here in Druida to stock a new branch."

Raz's eyes gleamed. "Excellent." Then he studied his fingernails. "How about vizes? Say of plays?"

"We have copies of a complete set of your work," Glyssa assured him.

"That might limit the amount of plays you might want to do for the camp and the town," Del said, the corners of her mouth tucked in, no doubt to suppress a smile.

Raz did an outrageously surprised goggle, then his face folded back into its regular cheerful expression. "I've contacted a couple of playwrights about a story of the excavation of *Lugh's Spear*."

Glyssa's fingers clenched on Jace's shoulder. She looked appalled. "Not including us!"

Raz shrugged. "Perhaps. I told them as much as I knew."

"Absolutely not," Glyssa said, sounding a lot like her mother.

"Let's get back to this luck thing," Del said. "I agree, the guy's been lucky, *he* didn't end up dead over a cliff like Trago."

Jace kept his face easy. He'd told *nobody* what had happened, how he'd slapped at Trago. When Glyssa got better, if she didn't sense it from him, he'd reveal the truth to her, and she'd want to document it in some sort of record, but he didn't want to speak of Trago's death . . . yet.

Glyssa said, "Trago went mad, first. Something in that man snapped."

Zem lifted his beak from his chest. He, of course, knew what had happened as well as Jace. *The man wanted a woman as mate and she spurned him and that man thought my FamMan caused it. Big emotions. Big anger. Big madness.*

"Huh," Del said.

Glyssa rubbed her head against Jace's chest. He liked that. Loved being with her. Couldn't imagine his life without her.

"Without Jace's luck and our HeartBond, the beacon the ritual here in Druida gave us, and the energy of the four of us, we wouldn't be here," Glyssa said in a low voice. He thought she'd cry again and that made him uncomfortable. He squeezed her.

"You HeartBonded without sex?" someone asked.

"Yes."

"And you couldn't tap into any of the Flair we offered during the ritual?" Camellia continued.

"No. You were too far away," Glyssa said.

"Distance shouldn't matter," Laev said.

"All I can tell you is that it did." Glyssa began to sound weary.

Two weeks ago Jace could have stood with her in his arms, swept her out of the chamber and up the stairs to her bedroom. Now he straightened, set her gently on her feet, rose and took her hand. "That's enough. Glyssa recorded all her thoughts regarding our experience as soon as she was coherent. I did my own and they are being intermixed and edited. The Licorice Family will accept requests to listen to the recordspheres, but will not make copies." And the one in the future where he told of his contact with Trago at or near the time of the villain's death would definitely be limited to a very few. Jace inclined his torso as low as he could—not very—before he thought he'd tip over.

They left the room and Glyssa's parents followed them, her mother with Zem and her father carrying Lepid.

At the door he and Glyssa received kisses from the Licorices and admonitions to rest. Not that they'd been doing much of anything else.

Jace smiled at the older people. No trace of the former wariness had outlasted the announcement of their HeartBond.

Rhiza D'Licorice eyed him. "I'll send some lunch up. Sit on the balcony and eat, get some sun." She put Zem on his shoulder.

"Uh-huh," Jace said, opening the door. Lepid walked in, tail lower than usual. He sniffed at his bed, then went out the open balcony door. Jace placed Zem on the perch. They both gave a tiny shudder. They'd both used that object to fix the image for the long teleportation in their minds. Zem dipped his beak in his water and drank.

"I'm so glad you're here and safe, Zem," Glyssa said.

He didn't look up. *I am, too. I love you all. Up on FamMan's shoulder now.*

"Of course." Glyssa lifted the bird to Jace's shoulder then linked fingers with him.

They walked hand in hand through the door of Glyssa's sitting room to the balcony overlooking the estate's tangled gardens. An edging of tall pines separated the D'Licorices' land from the Public-Library that the Family treasured so much.

He dropped her fingers to move Glyssa's chair out from the café table but she ignored it, stretched her arms high as she stepped full into the sun. He felt a very welcome flicker of lust in his groin.

FamMan, I would like to perch on the rail, said Zem. Jace lifted the light bunch of feathers Zem had become. The bird didn't have any broken bones, but like the rest of them he was exhausted, though the bond between Jace and his Fam remained strong, solid and bright blue.

Jace set Zem on the far end of the white tinted wooden rail that held both shade and sun so the Fam could move to another spot if he got too warm or cold.

This city is not too bad, the trees aren't as large as at my home, and the human and animal smells are interesting, Zem said. He lifted his beautiful wings and stretched them in the sun. *It will be good to have warm shelter in the winter.*

"We could get some bad snow," Glyssa said. "I'm not sure how much snow the area around *Lugh's Spear* receives."

Not a lot, Zem said, and began to groom his feathers.

Glyssa leaned against the rail and looked down at the land, then angled her head toward the large structure of the PublicLibrary. When Jace approached, she turned her head and smiled. Her face wasn't as thin as it had been after their ordeal, but still showed smudges under her eyes. She looked fragile. Gesturing to the landscape, she said, "I want to soak up the view this winter. We won't be back to live here ever again."

"Probably not." He picked up one of her hands resting on the rail and kissed it. "HeartMate."

She sighed and her smile widened. "I never get tired of hearing you say that."

FamWoman and FamMan, Lepid added as he curled in the sun.

Glyssa laughed. "Those are good words, too, revealing our connections."

FamMan and FamWoman, Zem said.

"Lovely Fams," Glyssa murmured.

"Great Fams," Jace said at the same time.

He kissed her fingers. "But there's one thing I haven't said yet," he replied, all too aware of those three small words.

Her eyes widened and the atmosphere seemed to rustle with anticipation. She reached out and took his hands in her own. "I love you," she said.

His heart just thumped hard in his chest. She hadn't said those words, either. He'd been too skittish around her for her to trust those words to him. Maybe she'd been too proud to say those words to him when she thought they wouldn't be returned.

He just realized now how much he needed to hear them.

HeartMating and HeartBonding, all that meant love, but the

simple phrase was a whole lot more necessary than he'd thought. In fact, her soft tone echoed through him, finally sank into his bones where they'd always warm him.

"I love you. I will forever," he said.

She slid against him, wrapped her arms around his neck and their tongues played together. He closed his eyes and simply enjoyed her taste, having her in his arms. Again he felt the beginning of desire and welcomed that.

I love you, too, FamWoman and FamMan. I have said that OFTEN. Lepid lifted his muzzle and opened his mouth to smile and let his tongue loll in a grin.

Zem snicked his beak. *I love you both, too.*

When she pulled away, her face was rosy and she was smiling with a spark in her eyes he'd missed. He shook his head.

"What?" she asked. "I'm getting mixed feelings from you."

"You should be getting all my love, HeartMate."

Now she just beamed and leaned against him, slipping her arms down around his waist. She let out a breath. "I love you, HeartMate."

"You know I'm phenomenally lucky."

"Pretty much," she agreed. "Pretty lucky, especially when it counts."

"You said phenomenally lucky in the ship."

"I wanted to get out. Go, team! We all needed to believe to our depths or we wouldn't make it." She leaned back, meeting his eyes, serious once more. "We almost didn't make it."

"Almost."

We knew it would be scary, Lepid said, the tip of his tail giving a twitch. *But we knew we would WIN!*

Zem whuffed a tiny sigh, tilted his head to look at the fox. *The optimism of young ones. We had no choice.* The bird shuddered. *It was terrible in the ship, no open air at all.*

"Sshhh." Jace went over and gave his Fam a soothing stroke, then returned to Glyssa.

"I'd like you to test your Flair with T'Ash and his Testing Stones," she said.

"No." He cleared his throat. "As I was saying, I'm phenomenally lucky."

She smiled up at him.

He put his arms around her and squeezed. "Because I'm a risk taker. But, let me tell you, Glyssa Licorice, FirstLevel Librarian, you are the greatest risk I ever took, with all my heart, all of me."

"Nah," she said. "I was your sure thing."

Shaking his head, he said, "But I didn't believe that. I was always afraid to believe that."

She felt incredibly good in his arms, fit there like no other. "I didn't believe in love or HeartMates . . . in a healthy love."

She didn't loosen her grasp, and he reveled in the closeness, knowing she'd always be there with him, for him.

Smiling up at him, she said, "But you believe now."

"Yes." He stroked her hair. "I can *feel* it now. But I still say you were my greatest risk and I've been phenomenally lucky."

"We've been phenomenally lucky."

He stared into her brown eyes. "And we'll be lucky for the rest of our lives."

"Yes."

Yes, said Lepid and Zem together.

"We'll see through the excavation—a lifetime of work. And we'll be founders of a new town." She patted his chest. "In twenty years, you'll be very respectable."

"I hope not."

She turned away from the view and took his hand. "We have the time and the resources to craft our future and a Family."

"Very true, and will spend all our lives together and loving each other."

"A future of discovery."

They turned away from the view and that past and moved on to the future together, proving their love in bed.